THE REMAINING
ALLEGIANCE

BY D. J. MOLLES

The Remaining
The Remaining
The Remaining: Aftermath
The Remaining: Refugees
The Remaining: Fractured
The Remaining: Allegiance
The Remaining: Book 6 (coming in 2015)

The Remaining short fiction
The Remaining: Trust
The Remaining: Faith

THE REMAINING
ALLEGIANCE

BOOK 5

D. J. MOLLES

www.orbitbooks.net

ORBIT

First published in Great Britain in 2015 by Orbit

3 5 7 9 10 8 6 4 2

Copyright © 2015 by D. J. Molles

Excerpt from *Fortune's Pawn* by Rachel Bach
Copyright © 2013 by Rachel Aaron

The moral right of the author has been asserted.

A CIP catalogue record for this book
is available from the British Library.

ISBN 978-0-356-50341-7

Typeset in Galliard by M Rules
Printed and bound by CPI Group (UK) Ltd, Croydon, CR0 4YY

Papers used by Orbit are from well-managed forests
and other responsible sources.

MIX
Paper from
responsible sources
FSC® C104740

Orbit
An imprint of
Little, Brown Book Group
Carmelite House
50 Victoria Embankment
London EC4Y 0DZ

An Hachette UK Company
www.hachette.co.uk

www.orbitbooks.net

To William Beaner, Matt Montgomery, and Steve Selogy. Three wise men who are a little crazy, but keep me sane.

ONE

LINES

FROST HAD COVERED EVERYTHING. It crunched under Lee's feet as he made his way steadily through the woods. He wore his parka, zipped all the way up and the hood pulled over his head. A shemagh was around his neck, pulled up to cover his mouth. But still the cold air stung him. It got under his clothes and pried at his injuries. It made his damaged ankle joint ache like an old man's and his progress was slow and plodding as he favored these complaining parts.

Lee breathed the air slowly as dawn began to break through the wooded landscape. It smelled of the nothingness of frost. All the other smells – the tree bark, the leaves, the moss – had been frozen in place. The air seemed to freeze his sinuses. Particularly painful to his broken nose. Reset, but still swollen and probably forever crooked. It was the coldest it had been yet. Maybe around 20 degrees, which was not horrible in general, but pretty damn cold for North Carolina.

He stopped at the crest of a rise and stood for a moment. A tall form. Thinner than he'd ever been, so that his clothes and coat hung loose on him. But for all the size he'd lost, he was not weak. Underneath those loose-fitting clothes he was battered and scarred, but possessed a wiry sort of strength that came only from endless abuse.

He knelt down. His knees cracked threateningly when he did so, the stitches in the gunshot wound on his left side screaming at him. His face showed none of this. His dark eyes were as cold as the air around him.

He looked back the way he had come. Over the skeleton trees he could see Camp Ryder rising out of the forest. The walls built up with surprising speed over the course of the last several days – a last-ditch effort to keep the hunters out. Spikes and barbed wire. Like some reverse supermax prison, designed in a third-world country. Designed to keep things out, instead of in.

Lee didn't know how long it would last. They hadn't made contact with the hunters since the assault on Camp Ryder, but the threat of them still hung over everything. Worse than the packs. Worse than the hordes. These ones were smarter, faster, stronger.

He pulled the shemagh down with a gloved hand. Rubbed the beard he had scissored back to a reasonable length the day before. He watched his breath plume out of him and for a brief moment it obscured his view of Camp Ryder and gave him a sense of melancholy that he could not explain. Equal measures of regret and responsibility.

You cannot be what you once were.

The fog of his breath dissipated and he could see Camp Ryder again. Quiet and still in the early morning hours, smoke trails rising from the fires that were keeping people warm. Soon it would be alive again. Soon it would be awake. Because 'first light' was when the people of Camp Ryder would render their judgment on those that had betrayed them, those that had fought for Jerry. The trials had already been held, overseen by a committee of survivors led by Angela. The facts already weighed. The mitigating and the aggravating. Now the only thing left was to dole out the punishment.

A soft crunch of leaves behind him. A warm snout nudged his elbow.

Lee lifted his arm, put it around Deuce. The dog and the man leaned into each other for a brief moment of warmth. The dog still held his one paw up. Not broken, it had been decided, but probably sprained. He seemed to be getting more movement back into it and was able to put more weight on it than he had before. But it had never slowed the dog down. The dog just kept going, doing what he was supposed to do.

'You smell anything?' Lee asked quietly.

The tawny dog looked around, as though he understood the question. His pointed ears always erect and alert. Scanning like a radar dish. His long, lupine nose constantly working at the air. But Deuce stayed quiet. Didn't whine. Didn't growl. There were no infected nearby. At least for now.

'Come on,' Lee said, as he stood up and began walking again. The dog followed his lead.

Lee cradled his rifle in one arm. Or at least the rifle that had *become* his rifle. The one he'd taken from a dead man named Kev after he'd crushed the man's throat with his bare hands. Tore at him like a wild animal. It was strange how different experiences seemed to have different chemical reactions within your brain. Some horrible things only calcified you. Made you harder and more calloused. You did them and you never thought about them again. Other experiences seemed to be caustic, and they broke you down, ate through you, and stung when you least expected them to. And there was never any rhyme or reason to it, it seemed.

Lee had done all manner of things. He had killed men in many different ways. But for some reason, the crushing of Kev's throat stuck with him. Sometimes he could feel the little tiny bits of cartilage in Kev's neck, cracking under his fingers.

Sometimes he heard a noise and it made his heart stop because he thought it sounded so much like the strange, gasping, rasping sound that Kev had made when he ran out of air. A few nights he had dreamt vividly of that moment, and woke up with his heart pounding.

This is how it is now, he told himself. *There is no room for mercy.*

He made his way through the winter forest, following what had become a familiar path. He recognized small things that sat dimly in the morning light. A copse of evergreen shrubs that grew low to the ground. A patch of briars. An outcropping of stone coming out of the hillside as he began to descend the other side.

Every so often he would glance down at Deuce, make sure the dog was still beside him. Check to see how the dog was acting. Deuce just continued to limp along beside the human that he had decided to trust. Forever soldiering on. Just the two of them.

Lee's 'escapes' from Camp Ryder were against the better judgment of Jenny, their resident medical professional. Though she had been quiet and very reserved since everything that had happened during the assault on Camp Ryder, she'd spared no words to scold him about wandering out of the gates when he was supposed to be resting. It was not only dangerous, she said, but also would slow his healing.

After the second disappearing act, Angela joined in.

Lee humored them by forcing a smile and a nod, but he never told either of them that he wouldn't do it again, because he knew that he would have to. Because he had to do what was required, no matter how ugly it was. All the people at Camp Ryder could turn their gazes away from the truth, they could hold on to morals and ethics – they had that luxury.

Lee did not.

But Lee would not take it from them. He would not spoil that dream for them. Because they needed to believe the ideals and laws of the country they still subscribed to. And no matter how much of a dog and pony show that was, Lee knew he couldn't take it away from them.

So he would do what needed to be done.

But he would do it quietly, and they would be none the wiser.

He came to the edge of the forest. He stopped, just outside the trees, Deuce making slow circles around him. Sniffing the ground, then the air. Before him stretched cropland, washed pink and yellow in the morning light. It was all open acres of harvested wheat that had never been tilled or replanted. Weeds had begun to sprout up during the abandoned summer but were now brown and dead as fall turned to winter. Still, the view gave him pause each time he came upon it. The seemingly endless acres of open fields, rolling down into shallow ravines where sometimes fog would huddle.

Not now, though. Now it was too cold.

But Lee could look at those fields, and some small vestige of himself that dared to take uncertain glances at the future would think that one day they would plant those fields again. And he wasn't sure why this part of him insisted on being optimistic, when every other part seemed to have shrugged off optimism in place of cold reality. But he didn't overthink it. He accepted it. And he looked out on the fields and he thought about sprouting grain seed and cornstalks grown taller than a man.

He allowed himself that moment. And then he continued on.

He followed the edge of the woods for a time. Twice Deuce let out a low growl and looked off into the fields. Lee stopped both times and stayed very still, eyes searching in the distance where Deuce was focused. The weeds in the field were tall, and infected could easily hide there if they just crouched down. Lee thought he saw movement in one of the shallow ravines several hundred yards from him, but then Deuce quieted. Lee gave it another minute and then kept walking.

After about a mile along the edge of the woods, he came to a road. What had once been a well-traveled highway, now barely visible under a layer of fallen leaves. The shoulders encroached unevenly, swallowing the edges of the road in soil and brown grasses. And where the fields always gave him hope, this old road gave him a sense of loss. A sense of loneliness. Like he might be the last human being on the face of the planet.

He did not go to the road, but stayed off of it about fifty yards. He found the same spot he had used before, where an old elm tree with drooping branches provided him with a curtain behind which he could watch the road in secret. He sat down slowly in that place, the tree shading him from what little warmth could be gleaned from the rising sun. Deuce sat beside him, quiet and reserved.

By now, at Camp Ryder, Angela would have noticed that Lee had snuck away again. Jenny would be livid that he was putting strain on his injuries. But Angela would mostly just worry about him. And she would have already seen to what needed to be done. Tallied the vote. Rendered the judgment.

By now, he would be walking. The last man to be judged. He would be walking, and he would be thinking about how he was going to survive out here, all by himself.

What was his name?

Kyle, Lee remembered. *Kyle, who was complicit in the murder of Bus and Keith Jenkins. Kyle, who went and got Abby when Jerry had demanded it, knowing full well what Jerry might do to that little girl just to get Angela to talk. Kyle, who acted all distraught and remorseful. Kyle the young kid, who I almost feel bad for.*

Almost.

A great deal of the testimony against Kyle had come from Sam, the rest from Angela. Sam told everyone how he had been playing soccer and went to retrieve the ball when it was kicked out of bounds. How he had stumbled on Kyle and Arnie, at the back of the Camp Ryder building with Keith Jenkins. How Arnie had swung the pipe that brained Mr. Jenkins, but Kyle urged him to finish Mr. Jenkins off. Then Greg had come and threatened Sam and Abby into silence for what he had seen. Sam told all of this in an unwavering voice, reliving a nightmare for the benefit of others and doing it without flinching.

Angela told how she had been taken upstairs into the office to be questioned by Jerry, just before the assault to take Camp Ryder back. It had been obvious that Jerry wanted to use Abby and Sam against Angela, to harm them in order to coerce her into talking. And when he sent for them, Kyle raised no objections, but simply went to get the children, following his orders, never stopping to think.

And maybe Lee did feel bad for him. Maybe the kid named Kyle had gotten in over his head. Maybe he had never meant to do the things that he was forced to do. Maybe even now he regretted every one of those decisions. But did any of that excuse his actions? Did being sorry for what you did make everything all better?

No. What's done is done, and cannot be taken back.

Actions have consequences.

The people of Camp Ryder, the ones that put their votes

into jars – little pieces of paper with *guilty* or *not guilty* written on them – they had decided what those consequences would be, and while Lee spoke quietly to Angela in the back rooms, he sensed the temperature of the group. He knew what they had been through, and knew that they were only trying to hold on to something there. Some semblance of that old world that they so fondly remembered.

So Lee did not argue with their judgments. It was not his place to do so.

His job was not to govern them, but to protect them.

He should have protected them before. He should have handled Jerry when the man had become a problem, before he could sink his teeth into Camp Ryder and split it right down the middle into two warring halves. He should have handled Professor White when he was merely a dissenting voice, before he could arm his group to help Jerry take over Camp Ryder. He should have handled Shumate those many long months ago when Lee had escaped from him in the hospital in Smithfield.

But he had let Shumate get away. And then Shumate had captured him again, quite recently, and forced Lee into a pattern of actions that still disturbed his sleep. He had let Professor White foment rebellion, and he had let Jerry divide the camp, and now the bodies were stacked up to be buried and the space to bury them was running out.

He had tried so hard to be just, to be righteous. To let the dissenters speak. To not pursue the enemy that was fleeing. Sometimes he had felt that he was being too harsh, but apparently he had not been harsh enough. Because every mercy had been used against him. And the people he cared for had paid dearly for those mercies.

Loose ends always come back to bite you in the ass.

He would not make these people pay the price. He would settle their debts for them.

Behind their backs if need be.

It was the only thing he *could* do. He could not give them medicine, or food or water, or arm them against the threats that surrounded them. He had done what he could before his GPS had been stolen, before he had been betrayed by the remnants of his own country. There was no longer a Project Hometown, and so Lee no longer viewed himself as a Coordinator. Everyone still called him 'Captain,' but to Lee, that identity was fading fast.

At the end of the day, when all those things were stripped from Lee, he found that what was left could still be useful. Because what was left was skill and knowledge. The skills to do what was necessary, and the knowledge of why they needed to be done. That was what made him useful to Camp Ryder – even to North Carolina and what little bit of society remained inside of it. Lee could still help them survive. He could still pass on the things that he knew. And he could still fight.

Those were things that could never be taken away from him.

So he waited underneath the barren elm tree, knowing that the low-hanging branches, frosted and reflecting the morning sun, would hide him. His stomach clenched hard to fight the gradual ebbing of his core temperature. And perhaps also to fight the feelings. Not any particular feeling, but just *feelings* in general. Mercy. Pity. Anger. Indignation. None of those were of any use to him at that moment, though they all swam around him.

No. What he needed now was just coldness. Cold like the ground he sat on. Earth that was fertile, but dormant. Saving its energy. Saving it for another time. And just like that earth, he saved all those feelings for another time. When they would mean something. When they could bear fruit in his life. But now, they were only weaknesses.

Just as the sun began to break over the tops of the trees, Lee saw the figure walking. It was a slow, steady pace. The pace of a man with nothing in front of him and nothing behind him. Just an existence of stasis. Walking. Putting the miles down on the road.

Beside Lee, the dog stirred, his ears rotating in the direction where the man walked.

He stayed quiet, though. This was not an infected.

Lee's rifle remained in his lap as he watched the figure approach. He wondered if he should talk to the man, but then wasn't sure what good it would do either of them. Perhaps it was just an attempt to assuage Lee's own vestigial guilt. Maybe he felt like Kyle wasn't as bad as the others.

But he was, wasn't he? Because ignorance was not an absence of guilt. Because following orders didn't make things okay. It was up to the individual to determine when the lines of morality were crossed.

Lines of morality? Lee almost laughed at himself, but the air was too cold and too still for laughter. Lee had the sense that the world would have fractured around him if he had laughed. So he didn't. He just raised his rifle, leaning the foregrip on his knees to support it, and then he squinted through the iron sights. No scope today. Just irons. You had to learn to use your irons before you could use an optic, and using them was like going home.

You put the circle around the post.

You put the post on your target.

You pull the trigger.

Here, Lee hesitated. He stared out across the expanse of

road between him and Kyle, the young man who walked, ignorant of what targeted him through rifle sights. The young man that wandered now, homeless and futureless. Banished from Camp Ryder. Marked with a brand on his wrist, so that if anyone from Camp Ryder ever found him inside the Hub again, they would kill him on the spot.

That was the solution that the people of Camp Ryder had come up with.

But Lee counted on a different solution.

Something much more final.

Lee took a deep breath. Put the top of the post just underneath Kyle's chin. Then he exhaled and he waited for that respiratory pause. That one, long, half second of time where your body was completely still. And when he felt it, when he somehow knew on some primal level, that the bullet that would leave his rifle would hit his target just where he wanted it to . . . then he pulled the trigger.

Kyle stumbled backward, then fell to his knees. Then he scrambled for the side of the road – heading for the woods, Lee thought, but he didn't make it very far. Just barely made it to the overgrown shoulder, in fact, and then he seemed to go limp. Not dead yet, though. Lee could still see his chest rising and falling in great, big, panicked gasps. He could even hear him from across the distance. The feathery sound of someone trying to speak but unable to.

Lee wondered if Kyle knew why this was happening to him.

He stepped out from underneath the old elm tree, and he stood there in the tall grasses and weeds that lined the shoulder of the road. He could see clear across them to Kyle, and he wondered what he should be feeling in that moment. He thought that there were probably hunters that had shot animals and experienced more emotion.

I've got no soul anymore, some part of Lee welled up.

But Lee just shook his head. Stuffed it down. *I'm just tired. Just very tired, is all. It's hard to feel when you're tired.*

He got up and made his way out from under the elm tree. Even in the cold, dense air, he thought he could still smell the others – that tinge of corruption just barely tainting the air. The smell of rot. Various stages of decomposition. None more than a few days old.

He stood there at the edge of the road for a moment, looking around and checking to see that nothing else was watching him, nothing had yet been attracted by the sound of the single gunshot. Still, Deuce seemed a little extra cautious, and hesitated a few steps behind Lee, his tail hanging a little lower than usual.

The dog stared at Kyle's form, still moving, but faintly now.

Lee considered the dog's reaction for a moment. Clicked his tongue. 'C'mon.'

Deuce followed, reluctantly.

By the time they reached Kyle, he had stopped moving. Lee stood over the man, looking down at him. Kyle had died on his back, face up to the sky, mouth open and teeth red, hand over the hole in his chest. For the briefest of moments, as Lee stood there, he thought that Kyle was looking at him, recognizing him, and knowing why Lee had done what he did.

'Because loose ends always come back to bite you in the ass,' Lee mumbled to the emptiness around him. 'Just like Shumate.'

Deuce growled.

Lee stiffened at the sound of it, instinctively shouldering his rifle. He looked first to Deuce, his gaze ricocheting off the dog and then following the canine's intense focus, up the road and into the woods. Lee stooped. Moved his head around and tried to see through the trees and into the woods.

No movement. Yet.

With more urgency now, Lee slung the rifle onto his back and bent down with a gripe and a groan to hook his fingers underneath Kyle's armpits. The underside of the man's body was wet with blood – still warm to the touch. Lee's nose curled, distastefully, and he lifted the dead weight, the stiches in his side suddenly afire.

'Come on, you heavy bastard,' Lee strained under his breath, despite the fact that Kyle was the lightest of the four men he had killed like this. The only four men that had taken up arms against Lee during the assault on Camp Ryder, and lived to be captured, tried by committee, and exiled.

'Had to do it,' Lee continued as he worked his way backward, dragging the body off the road to where it would be hidden in the tall grasses and weeds to the side. The same place as the others. The others that he could smell even stronger, now that he was so close to them. 'Had to do it this way, Kyle. I know you weren't a bad guy, but you weren't innocent, either. I don't like it, but it's just the way things are now. You know?'

What the fuck is wrong with me?

Talking to dead men.

Lee stopped, a little out of breath. He noticed that Deuce refused to step off the road and was prancing and whining now. On the verge of barking. His attention was still affixed down the road. More intent now. Like he was seeing something Lee was not.

Lee looked down the road.

Froze.

Still standing there with his back and hamstrings aching, his finger hooked under dead-Kyle's warm, bloody back. Breath caught in his chest.

Straight down from him, less than thirty yards away, another man stood, staring right back at him. Except it wasn't a man. Not *really*. Not in any way that counted anymore. It stood on two feet, but the way its shoulders were hunched, its head low and feral, naked as a primitive man – Lee knew what it was.

Lee's first instinct was to break for his rifle, still strapped to his back. But something about the stillness of the moment caught him off guard, made him pause, even as his mind scrambled, *Are there more? There's always more. They're flanking me. Cutting me off. This is a hunt. Right now, I am their prey.*

Deuce was barking.

The thing across the way seemed equally transfixed by Lee. Like the two were in a duel, each waiting for the other to make a move. It looked like it was holding on to something, but over the tall grasses, Lee could not tell what it was.

Lee let Kyle's body slump out of his grasp, trying to free his hands to get to his rifle, but Kyle's body fell forward, and the movement could not be hidden. The thing across from him twitched when it saw the movement, and it snarled loudly, but did not make a move toward Lee. Rather, it took a step back. Still clutching whatever it had in its hands.

I know what it has, Lee thought, stomach turning.

The thing hunched low, snatched down to get a better grip on something, its head dipping out of sight. When it came back up, a half second later, it held what was left of a man. A man that had once been fat, but then lost all of that fat from starvation, leaving only a thick flap of loose skin around his belly, which had been opened up and emptied out, like a voluminous leather bag robbed of its contents. The creature had its jaws clamped around the corpse's neck, and it began tugging backward, eyes still focused on Lee as it did so.

It reminded Lee of a leopard, dragging an antelope into a tree.

Somehow his rifle had gotten off his back and into his hands. Like it wanted to be shot. Like it wanted Lee to take this thing down. This terrifying and repulsive thing. But by the time Lee broke eye contact with it and raised his rifle to sight through the irons, all he could see was the bottom half of the corpse – pale gray legs with old boots and tatters of pants still clinging to them – and it slipped into the trees with a muted rustle.

Maybe that was why the hunters hadn't bothered to attack Camp Ryder for the last few days.

They'd been dining on the bodies that Lee left behind.

Following him like seagulls follow a fishing trawler.

Waiting to feast on the aftermath of whatever he left behind.

Lee realized he was shaking badly. Deuce was still on the road, whining and growling and moving around in tight, tense little circles. Lee looked down and saw that Kyle was far enough off the road that he would not be seen by passersby. He would not be seen by anyone from the Camp Ryder Hub. At least not for a while. And probably not before the hunters came and harvested him up.

But there's no more after that, Lee thought. *No more free meals.*

And then where will you go?

He stumbled, pulling his feet out from under Kyle's body. Then he crossed the road at a painful but deliberate jog, looking over his shoulder to make sure he wasn't being followed.

TWO

KILLER

HE SAT IN A CAGE. Some sort of wooden box, constructed mostly of plywood and two-by-fours and built directly onto the back of a flatbed truck. A sort of mobile holding cell. His hands were still bound, though they had been loosened to allow some circulation, and they had been placed in the front. He could feel his face. The rough-hewn features grown even more haggard and severe. The beard growing and itching. The hair wild and unkempt. The features of a wild man.

Sometimes he would shift where he sat. Other times he would notice that he was incredibly hungry. The bullet wound in his arm ached fiercely. He kept smelling it to see if it was becoming infected. He didn't think that it was.

But the physical discomfort did not bother him much. As he sat there in the dark, surrounded by the muted noises of the camp huddled just outside his holding cell, he would occasionally feel a rising sickness in his gut, and panic would follow. It would attack him in a sudden onrush, making his whole body twitch and his heart begin to pound, his breathing becoming ragged and heavy.

Then when the panic subsided, when the feelings of sickness were gone and his stomach no longer threatened to void what little it contained, he would roll over onto his side, facing the wall of the holding cell, cheek pressed to the wooden floor, right at the joint where the shoddy build had left about an inch of space between the wall and the floor – just right there in the corner.

He could press his face down into that corner and he could suck in the cold, unbreathed November air that chilled its way through the crack and crystallized his muddled mind. And when he held his face down as close as it would go, he could see out of the crack with his left eye. He could see the other cages across from him, the ones with the wooden bars so that he could see inside.

He could see their faces.

He bent down there now, first with his eyes closed, just breathing the air, settling himself. It smelled of the plywood and boards that his cage was constructed of – the piney, raw smell of them, but also the tangy odor of the pressure treatments. But once your nose became accustomed to that, you could smell beyond it. You could smell the air outside.

It smelled like autumn. Oaky, with a hint of campfire smoke. Vehicle exhaust. The distinct rank of many, many people living in one place. Better than the overpowering scent of himself and his pinewood box, though.

He opened his eyes.

Gray light, turning yellow.

It was early morning.

The fifth morning, possibly? Maybe just the fourth.

His stomach clenched, aching in the background of his mind, wanting food. He had not eaten since he'd arrived here. Since he'd spoken to the man named Deacon Chalmers. They gave him water on occasion, but not food. They told him that he needed to purify himself. They told him he had to fast for five days. That it would clear his mind and cement his decisions.

Then he would be required to 'prove' himself.

He knew what the proof was.

Sometimes he dreaded it. At other times, he had no strong feelings about it. He'd done worse things, hadn't he? Maybe. He wasn't quite sure, and things weren't coming in clear right now. Sometimes the 'proof' felt like it would be easy to accomplish. After all, it would be a stranger, wouldn't he? He could kill a stranger. He'd already killed a friend.

Across from him, the shapes that occupied the neighboring cage were huddled under blankets, watching the men that passed by, their eyes wary and uncertain. The eyes of the abused – always waiting for the unknown moment when they would be called upon again to experience pain.

LaRouche watched them, intensely, breathlessly. He searched their faces. There was one in particular that he was looking for. The one with the green eyes – he didn't know her name. She was a small thing, and he didn't think she was much more than sixteen or seventeen years old. She was not particularly pretty, but her eyes were sharp. Clear. They reminded LaRouche of who he was. They kept awake some small part of him that was trying to curl up and die.

For some reason that he could not explain, that girl gave him something while he sat in his little cage, starving and thinking and alternately tormenting himself into a panic and soothing himself into a lull. He sought her out when he bent down to this little crack in his cage. Sought out her sanity.

But now he couldn't find her.

He feared perhaps she'd been taken away the previous night, and not yet returned. That was what they did. They took the girls away for the night and returned them in the morning. Sometimes just late at night, though most of the men preferred the female company. Preferred a warm body next to them. Maybe it helped them sleep. Maybe it reminded them of the wives they had lost.

But they were all lost, weren't they?

Every fucking one of them.

LaRouche included.

He searched the faces again, the concern for the girl supplanting his other worries for a brief moment, and the absence of them was almost a relief, even if they were only replaced by another bad thing. Then he began to wonder why he should care about the girl at all.

You've got your own problems, he thought. Though, when he tried to picture them, all he could think of was a man on a cross. A man with his guts ripped open and spilled out on the ground. The proof of his loyalty.

The proof is in the pudding, he thought to himself nonsensically, staring up at the dark ceiling. *What am I doing here? Am I accomplishing anything? Or am I just ... floating along?*

The panic began to rise in his chest again.

He took a deep breath and closed his eyes.

A rattle came from the door of his cage, and by the time he had managed to sit up, swallowing hard against a little flame that licked up from his stomach and into his throat, the door was open and morning light blinded him along with a rush of cold air and smells that had before been muted, but now assaulted him straight on. And with them came the fresh recognition of his own stench – body odor and stale urine.

A man stood in the light. It was barely an hour past dawn and the sun had yet to even fully rise above the trees, but still he found himself squinting and holding up his hands as though to shade his eyes. For a brief moment, he saw himself as the man must have seen him. Pathetic.

The man named Clyde set down a bottle of water. The label was worn away so that only the little patches of white paper still clung to ancient glue. The bottle was scratched and scarred and tinted with dirt, though the water inside looked clean enough.

LaRouche reached for it eagerly. Almost aggressively. As though Clyde might have snatched the bottle away if LaRouche was not quick enough. He guzzled the water, not realizing how dry his lips were until he tried to part them to take the drink. The water was ice cold and it extinguished the flame in his belly, at least for now.

It also awakened his stomach and the hunger hit him like a cramp.

LaRouche lowered the bottle, gasping for air. When he'd taken a few breaths, his voice came out and it sounded like a reasonable facsimile of the voice that he remembered as his own. 'How long are they keeping me in here?'

Clyde had his oily hair pulled back into a short ponytail this time. He pushed his large-frame glasses up his nose with a knuckle and eyed LaRouche. His expression was aloof. Enigmatic. LaRouche had a hard time reading the man. From the few interactions they'd had, LaRouche had found Clyde to be . . . reserved?

No. Something worse than that.

Clyde had done things. Just like LaRouche. And LaRouche knew that his own lack of emotion and words were not from being *reserved*, but rather from a quiet sort of misery. The kind that you could not escape.

Clyde's breath fogged in the air as he spoke. 'You need to

come with me.' He stepped to the side of the doorway and stood, expectantly.

LaRouche regarded the other man for another moment, and his stomach flipping two ways. First, elated, glad for the chance to be out of the cage. Then apprehensive. Wondering what was about to happen. Wondering if this was some other test he had to endure. Another test of his loyalty to the Followers. Of his belief in their mission.

LaRouche slid forward until his feet hung off the edge of the flatbed truck. After sitting and lying down for so long, the feeling of gravity pulling blood into his feet was almost painful. Like if he set his weight on them, they would burst. So he did it slowly, like someone with bare feet might test out ice-cold floors.

When he supported his own weight, his feet stung and his knees creaked. His back ached from being upright for the first time in days. Clyde watched him, taking visual stock of LaRouche for the first time since he'd been captured in the woods along the river, broken and empty.

Like a cracked bucket.

A cracked *pot*.

Wasn't that another phrase for crazy? Cracked pot?

That was a good description for LaRouche. Crazy and empty.

Clyde gestured to LaRouche's arm, where the bandaging looked alternately brown and yellow. 'How's that?'

LaRouche followed Clyde's pointing finger to the wound on his left arm. 'Could use a fresh bandage.'

Clyde nodded, and that was the extent of the conversation about LaRouche's wounds. Now the man that seemed strangely educated and out of place in this world nodded his head in the direction of a cluster of large, canvas tents. 'Go to the one on the right.'

LaRouche began walking. All around them was the sprawl of the Followers camp – one of many, LaRouche had gathered. This one had taken up residency on a small farm. The original constructions stood out like monuments to a forgotten world. The farmhouse. The carport. The barn. The woodshed. A few moldering one-ton rolls of hay backed into a lean-to that might have once been used for livestock sheltering.

But amid all of this old-world stuff was the evidence of what the world had become. Cars and trucks and campers and tents were crammed in, almost touching each other, filling up the space between the farmhouse and the barn, and between the barn and the woodshed. They bustled and buzzed like a hive. Men with rifles moved about their morning business, all wearing white armbands that bore the black circle and cross of the Followers of the Apocalypse. The only empty space seemed to be the spaces left for the campfires. Some of the fires burned in pits lined with stone or cinder block or brick, and others had been lit in fifty-five-gallon drums.

LaRouche looked over his shoulder again. Looking for the girl with the green eyes.

Clyde followed his gaze. 'What are you looking at?'

LaRouche shook his head, then addressed himself to the tent as he approached it. 'Nothing. Just looking.'

Clyde walked abreast of him, rather than behind. He had a rifle, but he didn't point it at LaRouche. It remained slung on his back. When he spoke, his voice took a quiet, musing quality. 'You're not a prisoner, you know.'

LaRouche watched the ground pass under his feet. 'What am I then?'

'Just someone doing what the rest of us had to do.'

LaRouche thought about asking him who he'd had to kill,

but decided to leave it. Clyde seemed particularly irritable this morning. Probably not in the mood to answer questions. And what business of it was LaRouche's, anyway? It would have no effect on what was expected of LaRouche. That seemed to have already been decided.

'How long until I can eat?' he asked instead.

Clyde reached the tent and pulled aside the flap. 'Soon,' he said as he gestured LaRouche in.

LaRouche ducked into the dim interior of the tent. It was spacious, and high enough for him to stand up fully. There was a metal flue that dropped down from the roof, meant for a wood-burning stove, though there was none. It was cold inside. And it was empty, save for a chair, a table, and an unlit gas lamp.

The chair stood conspicuously in the middle of the room. Clyde pointed to it. 'Sit.'

LaRouche did so. The chair was a metal folding one. Ice-cold. No cushion. But it still felt like a relief to sit in a chair, rather than huddle on the ground. After however many days he'd been in the holding cage, the short walk to the tent seemed to have fatigued him. Or maybe it was the dehydration barely staved off. Or the beginning of starvation.

Clyde crossed to the table and busied himself with the lamp. As he worked, he spoke without looking at LaRouche. 'Deacon Chalmers has made it very clear that you are my responsibility,' he said, his voice bearing very little inflection. LaRouche could not interpret how the other man felt about this new responsibility. 'He's also asked that you reveal what information you can for our war parties before we send them out.'

A glow simmered against the tent wall and then grew until it was bright enough to illuminate the tent. It wouldn't be needed for very long – once the sun cleared the trees, it would glow through the heavy canvas fabric. But at least now they could see each other's faces.

LaRouche felt the rise in his heart rate. He avoided Clyde's gaze, and he began to picture the men he had left behind. The men he had abandoned after ... after ... what he had done. But each time he pictured them, he realized they were dead. Lucky, and Joel, and Father Jim. Who was left but a few men that he only knew in passing?

Except Wilson.

He could picture Wilson quite well. He pictured him as he saw him most frequently. In profile, driving the Humvee. The small-statured Air Force Academy cadet that somehow managed to hold it together better than everyone else. The man that always made the good decisions. The only one that had ever been able to talk LaRouche down. The one that understood the seeming psychosis that took over men's minds here at the end of the world, but never had succumbed to it himself.

Wilson, LaRouche thought. *He was a good man.*

Clyde turned to him, then leaned back against the table and crossed his arms. 'I want you to understand something, LaRouche.' Clyde said his name hesitantly, as though he wasn't sure he was saying it right. 'Chalmers made it clear that I was free to hurt you, if necessary. But I've no intention of doing that.'

LaRouche's jaw clenched for a flash. He thought of the girl with the green eyes and for the first time since he'd come here, bound and blindfolded, he thought about getting away. Then the thought died, halfway out the door. It was ridiculous. Where would he go? What would he do? He had made an enemy of the only friends he had left in the world. And now his old enemies were the only people that would take him in.

LaRouche stared at the dirt floor and said nothing.

Clyde made a tired sound. A long pause. Then: 'Why are you here?'

LaRouche thought it was an odd question. 'Because you brought me here.'

Clyde pulled himself off the table and walked over so that he stood in front of LaRouche, looking at him with something akin to disgust. 'Yes, I brought you here. I found you. In the woods. Drunk. Sitting at the base of a tree with a gun in your hand and it seemed to me that you were waiting to die, or thinking of doing it yourself.'

LaRouche didn't respond. It was an accurate assessment, he thought.

'But why do you think you were there?' Clyde asked.

I know why I was there, LaRouche thought. Instead, he said, 'What do you mean?'

'I mean do you believe that it was purely coincidence?'

'I don't know.'

'I think you do,' Clyde said. 'I think you know, just like I knew, the day Deacon Chalmers found me. I think you know, but you're wrestling with it. And the sooner you accept it, the sooner you submit to it, the sooner things will become much easier for you.'

Providence, he means. LaRouche stared straight ahead into nothing. *Destiny.*

Was I destined to be here? Was everything purposefully leading to this?

It was a slippery rationale. It had a dangerous way of soothing the conscience.

'What were you going to ask me?'

Clyde pushed his glasses up onto his nose again. 'Just about the people you came from.'

LaRouche met the other man's gaze. 'You know about them. Or at least Deacon Chalmers does. You had one of our guys. You tortured him. Carved words in his chest. Shot him dead. Nick was his name. I'm sure he told you everything you need to know.'

Clyde sniffed, eyes narrowed. 'I don't know him. Didn't deal with him. I'm sure Deacon Chalmers would know more about it. He generally supervises ... those types of things.'

'Then he'll know about the people that I came from,' LaRouche said with some finality. 'I've got nothing else to add about that.'

'You know that he'll expect you to cooperate.'

'I feel like I have.'

Clyde's eyes narrowed. A man inspecting a chessboard for his best move. He reached into his pocket and withdrew a knife. For a split second, LaRouche thought that the man aimed to use it on him. To extract information. Would it be so different from the man that LaRouche had captured? The man that LaRouche had strung up by a rope and burned with a cigarette lighter? The man he had murdered in cold blood when he knew he would get no more information out of him?

But instead, Clyde put the knife to LaRouche's bindings and he cut through them, freeing his hands. Then he folded the knife again and put it back into his pocket. He straightened and found eye contact with LaRouche.

'You're not a prisoner,' he said simply. 'But if you walked away right now, where would you go? Would you go back to them? The people you're trying to protect. Would they take you back? Would they forgive you for what you did?'

LaRouche stared at his wrists. His free hands. He twisted

them around. Worked the joint. They felt painful and stiff. Then he rested his hands on his legs, palms down, and thought about Clyde's question for a very long time, though he already knew the answer. He knew the answer, but he had yet to voice it. He had yet to speak it into reality.

And he still did not. He simply shook his head.

Clyde put a hand on his shoulder. 'What's past is past,' he said. 'We are your family now.'

THREE

EDEN

HARPER DIDN'T WANT TO RUN.

He forced himself to walk. Stiff. Tense. Eyes wide and his whole body buzzing with sudden and heart-palpitating fear. Down the narrow alley. Red brick walls to either side. No windows. No doors. The ground underneath his feet was paved with red brick as well. Just a big blur of red brick, somewhere in the town of Eden, North Carolina. He kept moving forward, his back to the entrance and the street beyond. His back to the threat.

Don't run, stay calm, don't run ...

Because running would be loud.

The footsteps would pound and echo. His rifle magazines would jostle and clank together. Bad idea. Best to just walk. Slow and steady wins the race. Stay calm and collected. What was that thing Lee always said? Something about slow and fast ... slow was fast ... no ...

Slow is smooth. Smooth is fast.

Yeah, that's it.

Slow is smooth. Smooth is fast.

But then, about halfway down the alley, when the teetering scales of *speed* versus *quiet* equaled out, he broke into a sprint. It was sudden. Surprising to even himself that he could move that fast when only an hour ago he'd been so stiff he could barely pull himself upright after a shitty night's sleep. But he did it, and he did it fast, breath clenched in his belly, one giant cringe from start to finish.

He reached the end of the alley and turned.

A rifle stock almost slammed him in the face.

Julia pulled back at the last minute, glaring at him. 'Don't come runnin' up on me . . .'

'Shh!' Harper hissed.

The irritation fled from her features, replaced by concern. Whispering, she said, 'Are they . . . ?'

Harper nodded. He let his breath out in a slow, shaky exhale. Took in fresh oxygen. Then he looked around the corner that he'd just turned. They were just a few blocks from where the river bisected the city of Eden. The building they were huddled behind was some boutiquey shop – the kind that Annette used to get lost in for hours.

Behind the shop, where Harper and Julia hid, was a natural area long overtaken by weeds, brown and dead with autumn and disrepair. A stone fountain and benches sat overgrown and unused. A fence ran along the border of it. Maybe it had been a backyard at one point. Maybe a neighborhood park. Now it was just camouflage for a man and a woman trying not to be noticed.

Where Harper stood, on the back side of the business, there was a wrought-iron gate. On the street side of the alley, there was a wooden gate. Harper had propped the iron gate open with a loose brick so that it wouldn't creak so noisily when he opened and closed it. The wooden gate on the other side was completely ripped off its hinges. Pieces of it were in the street. Harper wasn't sure how that had happened.

Something had died in the boutique shop, Harper was

pretty sure. And somewhat recently. Just standing next to the place, he could smell it. Not all the time, but when it hit him, it was like a gut-punch.

I knew this was a fucking bad idea ... shitfire!

But it hadn't exactly been *his* idea.

He'd awakened that morning with no intention of creeping into Eden and trying to get a closer look at how many infected had crossed the river and infiltrated the town. But then Charlie Burke, one of the remaining seven of his rapidly dwindling team, had decided today was the day to do some recon.

Harper didn't want to do the recon, but he couldn't stand the thought of more of his people throwing themselves into harm's way. Nor could he let them see how fearful he'd become. So he lied to Charlie and told him that he'd been thinking about doing the same thing. Then he'd packed his things and made for the door.

And then, of course, Julia had insisted on coming along.

So his plan to keep his team out of danger had backfired. Now instead of Charlie being in the shit, it was him and Julia.

Stupid, stupid, stupid.

In the silence of his own thoughts, he could hear something snuffling around at the mouth of the alley. He and Julia stayed frozen on the back side of that boutique, surrounded by lifeless plants, leafless trees, overgrown flowerpots. He wanted to turn and see what Julia was doing, wanted to take the litmus test of her expression, but was afraid to take his eyes off the mouth of the alley.

More snuffling.

Something leaned into view. Picked at a few pieces of debris with a long, lanky arm, then disappeared again.

There's your closer look, you stupid fuck.

You satisfied? Now get back to camp before you get more of your people killed!

Deep breath in. Let it out.

It wasn't that he was so terrified of one infected. But he knew that it took only one screech, one howl, and then the whole damn horde was rushing toward them. And that did terrify him.

He turned to Julia. She stood there, clutching her rifle in front of her chest in a pale, bloodless grip. Her dusty, yellow-brown hair hung in unwashed and unkempt strands around her face. Her features, once soft, were now locked and hard. Blue eyes intense.

'It's okay,' he said quietly. 'We're good. But they've come across.'

Julia swore under her breath.

'Yeah, I know ...'

He was interrupted by the sound of something running down the alley.

Feet slapping. Breath heaving. Growling.

Harper was able to turn just in time to see it shoot out of the alley and slam into Julia. His rifle snapped to his shoulder but he had the presence of mind not to pull the trigger when the thing and Julia were so close. Julia had managed to angle her body and get her rifle between herself and the infected, and they hit the ground in a tangle of limbs, the air coming out of Julia in one sharp syllable of blunt-force pain.

Harper lurched out to grab at the thing, but the second that Julia and the infected hit the ground, she bridged her back and rolled the thing beneath her. He tried to adjust for a better angle, wanting to shout, but conscious of drawing more attention, so he just kept hissing, 'Pin it! Pin it!'

She thrust the rifle downward, the top of the chamber

sliding beneath its gaping jaw and cutting a shriek off into a choking, gasping sound. Its hands were like talons, taking swipes at her. Harper decided to forget about taking the shot. He needed to get in there.

He dove in, adding his weight to Julia's on the thing's throat.

The three beings, fighting to death in a strange sort of silence, punctuated by sharp breaths and the sound of boots scraping the bricks, and bare feet slapping the ground as the creature began to try to spasm its way out of their control.

Harper tried to think of ways to kill it.

Then he decided that they should just choke it to death.

But that could take time ...

Julia's hand shot out and grabbed the brick that Harper had used to prop the gate open. Then she smashed it into the thing's face. Almost instantly, the writhing seemed to stop, though the body still felt rigid beneath them. All the muscles clenched. Except its jaw. That was still snapping, the teeth clacking loudly. Julia hit it again, then raised her arm for another blow. But the last one had caved its temple in. Malformed the face. Thick blood that Harper thought looked more pink than red began to come out of its nose. Blood, and other things. Gray things. Like worms. Coming out of its ears now, too.

Its eyelids were fluttering, but the jaw was clamped shut now.

No other movement besides that.

'Holy fuck,' Julia said breathlessly, dropping the brick.

Harper gasped for air. Looked behind them to make sure no other unwanted guests were on the way. The alley stretched out. Narrow. Dark. Empty. He rolled off the thing, standing up and feeling the beating of his own heart like a loose engine knocking around inside a car. It almost hurt. It *did* hurt.

'Harper?' Julia asked, standing up, still breathing hard. 'You okay?'

'Yeah,' he said thickly. 'I'm good. Let's get the fuck out of here.'

They fled the scene like murderers, though guilt wasn't what drove them. Not anymore. It had never been the case for Harper, but for a while there, Julia had been on the fence. Where exactly is the moral line between killing and murder? When do you get to decide when an insane person needs to die? Does a person ever stop being a person?

Pointless arguments, now. Morals were the luxury of the civilized.

They slipped through the natural area, out the back, and found themselves in the parking lot they had been through earlier. They crouched at the bumper of an abandoned pickup truck that still smelled of gasoline fumes and rusting tools. Both of them looked around, looked to see if anything else might see them. But it was quiet. At least on this street, Eden seemed abandoned.

They hurried through the parking lot and out onto the street. It curved away to the right and to the left it was nothing but some huge warehouse for things unknown. There was a sign on the gate that said weapons were not allowed on the property. Also a sign that detailed the hours for RECEIVING, but no other indication of what the warehouse held. It had a nice fence around it with a barbed wire top. Might have been a good choice for a base of operations, but now it was a little too close to danger.

They made it down the road and around the building, to the bridge over the Dan River. There they could see the

Humvee sitting and waiting for them. Harper couldn't help himself, but he stared into the windshield as he ran toward it, always half-expecting to see a stranger in the driver's seat, or splashes of gore from the driver he'd left.

But as he drew close he saw that it was just Dylan Harmon, one of the few that was still left alive out of Harper's team. Rumor had it that Dylan had been somewhat romantic with Marie back at Camp Ryder, and had volunteered to keep an eye on Marie's sister Julia, or some such nonsense. At first Harper had resented it, but since then he had come to realize that he was not the best at keeping his team alive. Half of them were dead.

Poor choices, perhaps.

Bad leadership, perhaps.

Too many risks taken.

Still, Dylan was a decent guy, Harper supposed. A little red-neckish, but decent.

Harper just wanted his old team back. He wanted Nate and Devon back.

He climbed into the front passenger seat of the rumbling truck, planting his rifle between his legs and then leaning back, taking big gulps of air. He didn't want to close the door just yet – he needed the cold outside air. He wanted to put his hand to his knocking chest, but didn't want to admit to himself how frail that would look. There would be questions about his heart, and that was ridiculous.

He knew he was approaching the proverbial *hill*, but felt like he was still too young for that shit.

'You okay, boss?' Dylan twanged.

Harper forced himself to nod and closed his door. 'Yeah. I think I'm a little dehydrated. That run hit me harder than I thought.' As Harper spoke, he noted how fidgety Dylan seemed. Like he had something else to say and was waiting for his first opportunity to spill it out.

Julia climbed in, closed her door. 'Let's go, Dylan.'

Dylan nodded, cranking the steering wheel. The truck jolted into a tight turn. 'Boss, the radio's been off the chain for the last ten minutes. I think they're here.'

'Nate and Devon?' Harper asked, hopefully.

'Naw,' Dylan said as he righted the truck, now heading out across the bridge to the other side of the river, leaving the small town of Eden behind them. But Dylan was smiling now. 'The Marines, I think.'

Harper had staged his group off Old State Highway 87. Among the clusters of country homes sitting on one or two acres, they'd located what Harper qualified as a mansion. It was tucked back in the woods and surrounded by a fence. Granted, it was only a simple, white cattle fence, and nothing that would keep the infected out if they really wanted to get over it – but it was better than nothing. And the mansion was defensible and just a mile down the road from their objective. It was the best they could do for now.

They rode down the long drive, the sun yellow and bright through the wintering trees. Everything seemed cold and still. Harper might have considered it beautiful at one point. Now he craned his neck to see through the trees, to see if the mansion they'd left behind was still standing, or just a hollowed-out husk. Wasn't sure why he thought this – clearly Dylan had just received radio contact from them.

But it seemed that everything Harper did lately was marred by unexpected consequences. Since Mike had murdered his wife, Torri, and then committed suicide with a bullet to his own brain, Harper had found every decision clouded by an infinite number of possible negative outcomes. The positive outcomes were in there somewhere. Maybe. But it was difficult to find them.

Julia accused him of becoming trigger-shy. But she had her own set of issues to work out.

All Harper wanted to do was blow the fucking bridges along the Smith River that separated east and west Eden. Find a damn base of operations in Eden, where they could mount simple, straightforward, search-and-destroy missions along the bottleneck created between Eden and the Appalachian Mountains. Just like Lee planned. Simple and effective.

It had taken the Marines long enough to get here with what they needed to cut the infected hordes off – a shitload of ordnance and someone that knew how to use it to cut bridges – and they were fast running out of time. But at least they were here now. At least they could stop the flow before too many more infected crossed the bridges from east to west, and they lost the town of Eden forever.

Dylan pulled the Humvee up into the driveway of the 'mansion' where the other vehicles were clustered about. Past their bulks, Harper could see the front door of the big house that they'd taken over, and the wide brick steps leading up to it. Men in desert digital camouflage stood on those steps in full battle gear and Harper thought he'd never seen such a wonderful thing in his life.

Just a bunch of US Marines, there to blow shit up.

Harper found himself smiling. 'Fuck yes,' he murmured under his breath as the Humvee came to a stop. He opened his door and as he stepped out, the door to the big house opened up and two men exited. One was Charlie Burke, the man Harper had left in charge while he went to get his 'closer look.' The other was a tallish man that wore the same uniform as the other Marines, but apparently preferred a well-used eight-point cover to the helmet that several others wore. He stood at the top step for a brief moment, looking at Harper like he was sizing him up, then he descended the stairs with purpose.

Harper ported his rifle, suddenly self-conscious about how he handled it around these men. He walked forward briskly to meet the tall man in the eight-point cover, his hand extended. As the other man drew closer, Harper noted a few things about him. Younger than Harper, but with a certain aggression in his face that silently instructed others to *be quiet and listen*. Not particularly large or well-built – or maybe he had been at one point in time before food became rationed. Was food scarce for the Marines? Harper thought that it might be the case. Just because you had guns and ordnance, didn't mean you had food. The last thing Harper noted was the man's nametag, which read KENSEY, and the three chevrons on his collar.

The two shook hands, and Harper noted that Sergeant Kensey was one of those types that give a handshake every-thing they have – an almost painful squeeze, and a slight twist of the wrist, his hand over Harper's. Harper thought he'd read somewhere that the twisting maneuver was a dominance thing, but frankly, he could give a shit at that moment. There were bigger things to discuss than the pecking order rituals of human males.

Charlie Burke had accompanied the Marine down into the driveway and now he smiled awkwardly as he introduced the two men to each other. 'Harper, this is Sergeant Kensey. Sergeant Kensey, Bill Harper.'

'You the leader here?' Kensey asked, still holding the grip on Harper's hand.

Harper nodded. 'That's me.'

'Good to meet you, Harper.' Kensey's voice was somewhat

flat. Not much of an accent that Harper could detect. He
released the handshake and glanced at the collection of military vehicles. A slight note of suspicion when he said,
'Where'd you guys come across all these trucks?'

'Found 'em,' Harper said shortly, then started walking
briskly toward the big house. 'C'mon. Let's get out of the
cold.' Harper looked to his right and found Kensey following.
Even though Kensey's demeanor was slightly off-putting,
Harper was still relieved to have them there. You couldn't
complain about your backup. He smiled at the sergeant. 'Glad
to have you guys here. You have no idea . . . well, maybe you
do have a pretty good idea . . . but you got here in the nick of
time. Just saw the first few infected crossing the bridges from
the east side of the city to the west side of the city—'

Harper cut himself off as they reached the steps. 'Sorry. Do
you even know what I'm talking about?'

Kensey grinned, showing sharp-looking incisors. 'No fucking clue.'

'Excellent.' Harper shrugged it off, nodded to the other
Marines on the stairs, and received placid, almost impercep-
tible nods back. Harper took the steps, trying to hide how he
favored his stiff left knee. At the top of the stairs, he turned
and pointed north. They couldn't see the city over the tops
of the trees, but Harper spoke as though they could. 'The
town of Eden is in that direction, right across the Dan River.
There's an offshoot of the Dan River called the Smith River,
and it shoots straight up north and cuts the town in half. So
far we've seen large hordes of infected on the east side, but
none had crossed the river to the west side. Until today.'

Kensey nodded slowly, considering. 'Okay. And why is this
a problem?'

Harper looked at the other man, eyes narrowing. How

much did this guy *not* know? 'Well, if we blow all the bridges along the Roanoke River – which is also the Dan River – then any infected trying to get across into North Carolina from Virginia will have to pass through the bottleneck between Eden and the Appalachian Mountains. We want to use Eden as our base of operations to hit them in this bottleneck.'

As Harper explained, Kensey continued to nod, looking out in the direction of Eden. But Harper got the distinct impression that Kensey was only half-listening. Humoring Harper, so to speak. Nodding to be polite.

Harper felt his neck flush. The sense that he was the tee-ball kid trying to talk to the major leaguer about the finer points of increasing a batting average. He cleared his throat uncomfortably. 'Anyway, when we first got here, we saw them inside Eden, but they hadn't yet crossed the Smith River into the western side of town. If we hit the bridges hard and fast, we can cut them off and only have to do a little bit of cleanup afterward.'

'Yeah.' Kensey's breath fogged in the air. 'Hard and fast.'

Harper eyed the other man in the ensuing silence. Then his eyes tracked off the Marine, down the steps into the spacious driveway – the type of driveway where expensive cars would line up for a dinner party. Or whatever the hell rich people did. Harper had earned six figures but never really considered himself rich, and never really lived the lifestyle. Would never have spent the money for a house like this, and refused to buy a car that was more than thirty thousand dollars.

In this driveway there were no fancy cars, just the military vehicles he'd seen for the last few weeks. Humvees. LMTVs. The HEMTT with the wrecker attachment so they could clear a highway that ran between Eden and Camp Ryder. Keep supply lines open, though now, apparently, there were no supplies to be transported.

'Look,' Kensey said slowly. 'Harper . . . whose plan is this?'

Harper hooked his thumb into the strap of his rifle. His smile faltered. 'Sergeant, where're your vehicles?'

'Excuse me?'

'Your vehicles. Your trucks. Whatever you came in.'

Kensey hesitated for a brief moment. 'We walked it in. We were dropped by helicopter about five miles out from here – didn't want the helicopter drawing too much attention to your position.'

'Motherfuck.' Harper looked skyward, then closed his eyes. 'You've got to be kidding me.'

Charlie spoke up, hesitant. 'What's wrong?'

Harper faced Kensey, though he was answering Charlie's question. 'What's wrong is, I may not know a lot about explosives but I damn sure know that these boys couldn't carry the amount of explosives we need to cut five fucking bridges.'

Kensey seemed to be reevaluating Harper. 'Look . . .'

Harper clutched his face in one hand. His voice was muffled when he spoke. 'Please, dear God, tell me the trucks are on their way. Tell me they'll be here by tomorrow.'

Kensey raised his voice. 'Bill . . .'

Harper took his hand off his face and glared at Kensey. 'Don't you call me that.'

Kensey seemed confused. Charlie shifted his weight uncomfortably, caught in the middle.

'Only two people called me that.' Harper spoke deliberately, his voice sharp. 'My wife, and a very good friend. And they're both dead. You call me Harper.'

Kensey's expression became deadpan. 'Okay. *Harper*. Let me explain something to you, *Harper*. We're not here to destroy infrastructure that we might need in the future. You know we don't exactly have construction crews capable of putting that shit back together, right?' Kensey shook his head. 'But that's just my personal thoughts on the matter. Professionally, I'm here on behalf of Colonel Staley. To feel out the situation and determine if we're going to be investing our resources in this . . . plan.'

For the first time in a very long time, Harper was speechless. He balked. His mouth hung partially open and his eyes stayed affixed to the man facing him for a while. His left hand clutching the strap of the rifle on his back. His right hand limp at his side, still but for the movement of his thumb and forefinger drawing rapid circles around each other.

Really?

Really?

After everything else that had happened? After all their losses. After they'd fought to reach this point, but gotten here just a few days too late to mount a full defense. After being told about Colonel Staley and holding to the hope that his Marines were going to ride in on white horses and save their asses.

And now this.

Harper hadn't even realized that Julia had followed them up onto the steps, and apparently she had heard most of what was said, because now she stepped forward, her voice shaking and livid. 'Is this a goddamned joke or something? We were told that we were getting help . . . '

'And you are,' Kensey said simply.

Harper looked past Julia at the four Marines that stood on the wide set of brick stairs with them. They seemed not to really give a shit about the conversation that was happening. They were watching Julia. Smiling and exchanging glances. Maybe they didn't have too many pretty girls where they came from. Or maybe they were just being Marines.

'Think of us as investors,' Kensey continued. 'We need to

get to know you and your operation before we agree to the monumental bill that you're asking us to pay.'

Julia almost shouted. 'Do you have any fucking idea what's out there?'

Harper reached out and touched her arm. She looked back and when they made eye contact he gave her just the slightest shake of his head. He made his face as blank as he could. There were a million things he would have *liked* to say in that moment, but none of them seemed like they would do the job. And some part of his old self, the part that knew about good investments, had to admit that Sergeant Kensey had a point.

Still, he felt misled.

Harper stepped to the door of the big house and opened it. The air inside was noticeably warmer. He held the door open and gestured Julia inside. Then he looked at Kensey. When he spoke, his words were polite, but his tone still bore an edge to it. 'When's the last time you had real coffee, Sergeant?'

There was hesitation. Kensey seemed uncomfortable with the rapid change in conversation. Like it was a trick.

Harper pointed into the house. 'C'mon, Sergeant. We're letting the warm air out.'

Julia stepped through. Followed by Kensey. Then Harper.

He closed the door behind him. The door opened into an enormous living area that would have been impossible to heat without electricity and gas. But there was a large stone fireplace to the right with some chairs clustered around it, and a pile of dismembered wooden furniture to the side. In the fireplace, flames ate through what was left of the coffee table. On the hearth, a large pot was scooted in close to the fire, the sides of it blackening.

Harper went to the hearth. He could feel anger and frustration inside him, like another man under his skin, flailing about, trying to burst out and take control. But outwardly, he was calm. At the hearth, he took his rifle from his back and leaned it against the stone, then he unzipped his parka. The heat from the fire gushed up at him, almost uncomfortable on his cheeks and ears and hands. It smelled of wood smoke and chemicals. Harper was sure there were untold amounts of carcinogens in the treated, polished wood from the coffee table. But what were a few carcinogens in today's world? Just a minor annoyance, really.

'Look,' Kensey said, his tone changed to *placating*. 'Harper ...'

Harper didn't look at him, but he waved the sergeant off. 'No, no. You don't need to say anything else. Your position has been made abundantly clear. We're all very, very clear right now. No need for further explanation.'

Harper sat on the hearth. Kensey stood beside a large chair, facing Harper. Julia was across from the Marine, staring at him balefully. It was getting easier for Harper to maintain his calm now, though it seemed Julia still struggled with it. There was a collection of ceramic mugs near the fireplace, as well as a strainer, a ladle, and an oven mitt – all items they'd looted from the well-appointed kitchen.

Harper put on the oven mitt, then slid the pot away from the fire. He opened the lid and closed his eyes as he breathed in the steam that rose from inside. It was one of the best smells he'd inhaled in his life. After a moment, he set the lid down and gathered three mugs, the strainer, and the ladle to him.

'You know, my grandmother was old-fashioned,' Harper said. 'Grew up without regular coffee machines. Refused to use one when we bought it for her. To the day she died, she made coffee in a damn pot, just like this.' He smiled. 'Best coffee I've ever had.'

One by one, Harper put the strainer over the mugs and

filled them with the ladle, the coffee grounds catching in the fine wire mesh, the cups filling with dark, steaming liquid.

'Found some coffee in the kitchen pantry,' Harper said as he worked, his voice quiet with concentration. 'A whole, unopened package. Not even expired. Good stuff, too. The kind you paid fifteen fucking bucks a pound for in a health food store.' The mugs filled, he handed one to Julia, then one to Kensey, who accepted doubtfully. 'Used to drink that shit so often, I didn't even taste it. It was coffee, for chrissake. Nothing special. Fill up a travel mug, drink it on the way to work, listening to talk radio and getting myself worked up about bullshit politics.' He stared down into his own cup for a moment. 'Who knew I should have just stayed the fuck home and enjoyed my damn coffee?'

Julia seemed to have relaxed enough to take a seat, but if one were capable of taking a seat contemptuously, she accomplished it. She held the mug up high so that it covered most of her face, but her eyes still glared through the steam at Sergeant Kensey.

Kensey stood stiffly.

Harper blew gently over the top of his mug.

The door opened and one of the Marines leaned in. 'Hey, Sergeant. You good?'

Kensey didn't look back at his Marine. He just nodded. 'Yeah. I'm good.'

The Marine retreated, eyeing Harper and Julia with a suspicious glance. Lingering longer on Julia.

Harper took a sip of his coffee. Scarily hot, but good.

Kensey adjusted the brim of his cap. 'All right . . . '

Anger flashed across Harper's face. 'Shitfire! Sergeant, please! Any one of these days, any of us could wind up dead. So we're going to take a few moments of silence and enjoy this fucking coffee. It may not be the last cup of coffee in the world, but it very well could be *my* last. And while I enjoy this coffee, I'm going to think about how to make you understand the urgency of how fucked we are. But I'm going to do it in silence and I would appreciate if you humored me on this.'

Kensey pursed his lips. Keeping an eye on Harper, he took a slow, tiny sip of the coffee. As though to say he would drink the coffee, but he wouldn't be happy about it.

Harper did not return the gaze and let his own fall to the floor, and it stayed far away. His eyebrows twitched together. He took slow, leisurely sips from his coffee. Sitting in the chair across from him, Julia crossed one leg over the other and propped her elbows up on the armrests, her own cup suspended delicately in the air. She kept her eyes on the fire and they glistened some, but Harper could not tell if it was from the dry heat pouring out of the fireplace, or from something else.

Harper's own gut was a clenched ball. Even though he was at rest, his pulse was still pounding in his head, beginning to make it ache. It was urgency that pushed him. Made him uncomfortable. What he'd seen on his little foray into Eden was not in itself something to panic about – just two or three of them wandering around. A few more on the bridge that crossed the Smith River. Scuttling along and searching for food. Alive or dead. Anything that their body could digest.

But where there were a few, there would be more.

When they'd first arrived at Eden, they'd watched the town from a nearby water tower. The infected were all through the eastern side of the town in surprising numbers. Though they were numerous, there were not so many of them that Harper dismissed the possibility that they were 'locals,' so to speak.

But over the following few days, waiting in this house and sending out scouting parties as they held their breath and hoped for help, they'd seen the number swell. Now there was no argument to be made. In a town the size of Eden, even if every single resident had become infected and stuck around, it would still not even come close to what was on the other side of that damn river.

Everything was coming true.

Everything Jacob had told them.

And now they're coming across the river, and I don't know if there is anything I can say to Kensey that is going to stop that from happening.

Harper rubbed his face, his fingers scratching through his beard. He took a big breath and looked up at Kensey. 'Sergeant, has your Marine command taken any steps to recon into Virginia or any other northern state?'

Kensey considered the question for a moment. Like it might be a trick. 'Some.'

Harper waited for him to elaborate.

Somewhat annoyed, he did so: 'Couple of flybys of the capitol, attempting to establish short-range comms with anyone that might be left behind. Same through Richmond, and up and down the coast. Negative results.'

'Pilots ever report seeing anything?'

'Besides shit-tons of infected clogging up the beltway? No. Not that ever reached my ears, anyways.'

Harper nodded, took a gulp of the coffee that burned his mouth and everything on the way down. He stood up from the hearth. Grabbed his rifle, then went to the door, speaking to Kensey over his shoulder. 'Sergeant, why don't you come with me? Maybe I can help you make an informed decision.'

FOUR

THE SHAPE OF THINGS

THE BOTTOM OF THE water tower was a mess of weeds and shrubs that had flourished in the summer without the regular trimming of the utility crews, but now sat brown and dead after the first frosts had crippled them. The grass was matted and laid down, particularly where Harper and his crew had been through it several times, and Harper could see the tracks from his vehicles when they'd been parked there a few days ago. The clearing was a circular swath of open area, about twenty yards wide all around. Inside the circle, it was gravel, surrounded by an eight-foot chain-link fence. Three strands of barbed wire on top.

Harper stood at the wood line closest to the water tower, squatting down and leaning against a tree. His rifle was tucked into his shoulder, but the barrel was low. His eyes scanned the open area and all around the base of the water tower where the thick steel girders and pylons embedded themselves into concrete blocks. They'd had some infected contact near the water tower two days ago, but it had only been a pair of them. One had died and the other one ran off, perhaps to die a slower death at another place.

Right now, though, it seemed clear.

To Harper's right was Julia, glassing the area with the scope on her bolt-action rifle. On Harper's left was Sergeant Kensey, eyeing Julia, though not in the same way as his troops had. More in a manner that said, *Does she actually know how to use that thing?*

Julia had proven herself incredibly accurate with the weapon. Harper himself was no slouch, but he tended to be more capable in close-quarters shooting, when the shots were reactive. The slow, deliberately aimed shot always seemed difficult for him.

Behind them were two more Marines. One was a dark-haired, pimple-faced kid that Harper swore wasn't old enough to be in uniform. The other was a light-skinned black guy with a lanky form. A boonie-hat shadowed his eyes, and a wispy mustache clung to his upper lip. Not exactly steely-eyed killers, Harper thought. But then again, he supposed that Kensey thought the same thing about Julia and himself.

The fact was, neither party knew the other.

Hold judgment until the shit hit the fan. See how things shake out.

Though the two younger Marines had not said more than 'aye, ser'nt' a few times, Harper had taken a glance at their nametags. The white kid with the acne was Reilly. The light-skinned black guy with the floppy hat was Baker. Baker had his back to the group, watching behind them. Reilly was looking off to the side. Their leader, Kensey, was just sitting there trying to see what Harper was looking at.

'We looking for something in particular?' Kensey whispered.

Harper shook his head once. 'Looks clear.'

He stood up with more effort than he would have liked to admit, and stepped out of the trees and into the clearing that surrounded the water tower. They were coming in from the back side of the water tower. A gravel utility road led up to a gate, but it was on the opposite side of the fenced-in section. This was the way they had come and gone for the last four days, and they'd made a wide cut in the fence that they could easily slip through.

Julia held the cut open as Harper eased through, followed by the three Marines. Baker held the cut for Julia and then the whole group stood at the base of the water tower. Harper looked up the large-diameter steel pipes that made the thing's legs. Then at the rusty ladder that led up to the catwalk.

That damn thing again.

Harper looked at Julia. 'I suppose you're coming up with us?'

Before she could answer, Kensey looked up with a clear expression of discomfort. 'We climbing that thing?'

Harper smirked, glad that he wasn't the only one a little uncomfortable with the heights. 'Best vantage point around.' Then he added, 'You'll be okay.'

Kensey gave him a flat expression. 'Thanks.'

'And yes,' Julia said, taking the rusted metal ladder in her hands. 'I'm going up.'

Harper just waved her up the ladder. 'Yeah, I figured. Go.'

She began to climb. The ladder creaked and groaned treacherously, bits and pieces of rust trickling as she put her weight on it. But it held steady. Just some surface rust, Harper reassured himself.

Baker spoke up. 'Sergeant, you want us to climb that thing?'

Kensey slung his rifle. 'No, I want you stay on the ground and keep a lookout.' He shook his head. 'No sense in all three of us dying on this fucking contraption.' He gave Harper another, less-than-pleased expression. 'Live through the fucking collapse and get taken out by a rusty ladder.'

He began to climb.

Harper waited for some headspace, and then started up after them.

He refused to look down. He'd made that mistake last time.

Just keep climbing.

At the catwalk that ringed the water tower, Harper climbed up to find that Julia had already taken her rifle off her back and was scoping north, in the direction of Eden. Kensey stood a few feet back from her, one hand on the rail, the other resting on his rifle.

Harper brushed rust from his hands and straightened his parka over himself.

Julia took the scope away from her eyes and exchanged a knowing look with Harper.

She turned and pushed the rifle into Kensey's chest. He seemed surprised, but his hand came off the rail and accepted the rifle that was being passed to him.

'See for yourself,' Harper said.

Kensey looked at the rifle in his arms. He looked at Julia. He looked at Harper. Finally, he sighed and raised the rifle. He tilted his hat back so he could sight through the scope. He stood there for a long time. The muzzle wavered a little this way, a little that way.

'Okay,' he said. 'I'm seeing buildings. Small city. Couple of infected moving in the streets. Anything else you want me to see?'

Julia leaned close to him. 'East side. Toward the outskirts, hon.'

Harper watched Kensey's eyes jag at Julia, possibly

uncomfortable with how close she had spoken to him, or perhaps simply not wanting her to tell him what to do. Nevertheless, he begrudgingly shifted his viewpoint to the right, overlooking the eastern side of the town.

Harper waited. Watched Kensey's face absorb it.

To the sergeant's credit, he did not react as poorly as Harper had when he'd seen it. But Harper could see the relaxed, humoring attitude suddenly leave him. His body language became stiff. His jaws clenched. Fine lines standing out around his eyes. Not the kind that came from smiling.

Kensey lowered the scope, stared out at Eden with his naked eye.

'That's fucking impossible,' he said.

'No,' Harper said with a shake of his head. The only difference between him and Kensey was that he had been mentally prepared for it. Sure, when he'd seen it, he'd cussed a blue streak, but *mentally*, he'd been ready for it. Because Jacob had told them this was coming. Jacob, the unassuming, bookish man from Virginia, the scientist from the CDC who had researched the progression of the infected, and then crossed hundreds of miles on foot just to bring them this information, he had told them that the hordes from the big cities in the Northeast were coming. And he told them that they would number in the millions.

Kensey shook his head. 'Eden was only a town of ... what? Twenty thousand?'

'Less than that,' Harper said.

'How the fuck?' Kensey swallowed. 'That's gotta be ... '

'A lot more than twenty thousand,' Julia said.

Harper waited for Kensey to look at him. When he finally did, Harper was not pleased. He was not smug. Not self-satisfied. How on earth could you feel that way, facing this situation? Maybe he was relieved. Relieved that Kensey and him were at least somewhat on the same page.

Harper pointed to the ladder. 'We should talk.'

Wilson dangled in midair. Swinging uncomfortably when the wind caught him. He looked beneath him and saw slow-moving water, dark brown, almost black, and cold-looking. Above him, he saw the five steel I-beams that made up the substructure of the bridge that spanned this section of the Roanoke River. This one was just a typical, two-lane bridge, which was a relief.

Where Highway 13/17 crossed over the Roanoke at Williamston, the bridge had been a double – two lanes north, and two lanes south. Total of ten I-beams to cut, plus he had to jump from one section of bridge to another. Between setting the bridge for demolition and dealing with the small horde that was left in Williamston, it had taken every bit of three days. But it had been a success.

The previous day they'd spent traveling to this bridge. Clearing the area and anyone they didn't want nearby – survivors and infected alike. Then they'd made their plans until it was dark, bedded down, and waited until morning.

Now here he was. Dangling underneath a bridge once again. Hoping that the ropes didn't somehow fail and send him plunging into the icy water. The height wasn't so bad. But the water below ...

Wilson wasn't a fan of what he referred to as 'wild water.' Ocean, lake, river ... didn't matter. He disliked them all. There were *things* in wild waters and he wanted no part of them.

A nice, chlorinated pool was the only thing he'd ever had the desire to swim in.

Strange the horrific things he'd become accustomed to over the course of the last several months, and yet the concept of a fish with teeth or a snake in the water still gave him a chill.

'Little more!' he yelled.

Above him, on the bridge, the sound of a diesel engine going into reverse and then he was lowered about five feet and halted again.

'That's good!'

All he had with him was a pistol strapped to his chest and a long pole that had been bent into a hook. After some trial and error at the last bridge, they'd refined their methods to include a few of these jury-rigged items. He used the pole to hook the I-beam that sat on the first cement support and he pulled himself over to it, slowly but surely. He could feel the rope-sling around his waist and legs tightening as he put extra strain on them. Just some knots he hoped would hold.

Come on. Hold together.

Just a little farther.

The rope creaked, shifted, making his heart jump.

Then he put his hands on cold cement and colder steel. He clambered up, quick but careful, breathing a sigh of relief not to be dangling over the water anymore, though he was hardly out of the woods just yet. Plenty of other ways to take a plunge.

With his feet planted firmly on the top of the cement support column, one hand gripping the first I-beam, he used the other hand to place the hooked pole very gently onto the lip of the I-beam. His fingers brushed through old bird shit and God only knew what else. The pole would be secure there – hopefully – until he was done setting charges.

Once the pole was out of his hands, he did the part that he liked least. He undid the knots that tethered him securely to the rope. He had formed a little cradle for himself, one rope going under his buttocks, the other going around his waist. As close to a safety harness as they could manage. And he always felt a sensation of lightheadedness as he watched the rope fall away from him.

You probably can't die from a twenty-foot fall.

Probably.

Unless something in the water gets you.

'I'm good,' he called to the men up top. 'Send it on down.'

The rope that they'd used to tether him zipped up and away in jerks and spasms until it disappeared over the top of the bridge. Wilson waited there on the underbelly, feeling the sweat in his armpits and at the small of his back beginning to cool. The riverbed was a channel for cool wind and it sometimes gusted up against the underside of the bridge with discomfiting force.

After a few cold minutes, Wilson heard a voice shouting down to him. 'On the way!'

It was Dorian's voice. After the loss of Father Jim and LaRouche in a single night, Dorian had stepped up. Done anything that Wilson needed him to do. And Wilson needed guys like that. Because honestly, he was so far out of his depth, he preferred not to even think about it. He was twenty years old with zero experience commanding troops. He'd made it through the very basic first weeks of the Air Force Academy before everything went to shit. And now he was supposed to be leading men? On a mission to blow the bridges along the Roanoke River? A mission that had to be completed in a short time frame? And the consequences for failing were not bad grades or an ass-chewing session with an instructor. No, the consequences here were death. For him, and for everyone he knew.

Best not to think about it.

From over the side of the bridge, a satchel dropped. One of the voluminous green 'seabags.' It was packed with what looked like bricks – a bunch of rectangular lumps. Some blue cordage stuck out the top in briarlike loops. This bag would be the first load of five. One for each I-beam.

Wilson retrieved the pole from its resting spot and used it to pull the bag to him. It was heavy. Maybe sixty pounds. He heaved it up onto the cement pylon with him, very careful not to let the weight set his balance off. He left the rope secured to it, and when he had it firmly on the pylon, he opened the top of the bag.

Loops and loops of blue det-cord on top.

Bricks upon bricks of C4 below.

He knew it was completely stable until detonated – you could throw it, toss it, slam it on the ground, hit it with a hammer, or even shoot it and it wouldn't go off. Still, it was never comfortable to have sixty pounds of high explosive between your legs.

He pulled the det-cord out and got to work. He moved as quickly as he could, but tried to stay meticulous. They only got one shot at each bridge, and each time used an incredible amount of their explosives. Mistakes would lead to half-destroyed bridges that infected would be able to cross, but which would be near impossible to rig with explosives again. And Wilson was far from an expert with explosives. In fact, the extent of his training came from whatever LaRouche could teach him when they had a few minutes of free time.

P is for 'Plenty.'

That was Wilson's big takeaway from the few times LaRouche had taught him anything about explosives. It was better to overestimate how much explosives you needed.

Then you slapped them on both sides of an I-beam, and that would give you a single cut. You needed two cuts. And you had to do it for each I-beam on a bridge. Then some on the underside of the concrete superstructure for good measure.

Then you made a big knot with the det-cord – what LaRouche had called a 'uli knot' – and then you cut into one of the bricks of C4 and embedded the knot of det-cord into the cut. Then you mashed it in with the rest of the C4. Again, you had to do it for each side of each I-beam. Then you connected all the det-cord, like electrical wires, until you had them all running to a single cord, and you would hook that to your detonator.

Then it was 'one, two, three, fire in the hole.'

It had worked for the Highway 13/17 bridge. Wilson just prayed that it hadn't been a fluke.

But still, for all of his caution, he couldn't stop himself from rushing. He knew what was out there. He'd seen them on the opposite banks more than once. And at the last bridge, though he could not see them, in the silence before he had detonated it, he could hear them. A buzzing crowd in the distance. And even now, as he worked, he stopped frequently to listen and to stare out at the opposite banks of the river. To see if anything was moving.

But all he heard was the steady trickling sound of the river moving slowly beneath. And the banks only revealed gray sticks and twigs, jutting every which way, their roots dipping into the black waters. Stillness, save for when the wind blew. Then the shuddering rattle of branches clamoring together, like bones rattling.

Two hours in, he finished prepping the first cut. Now, despite the cold, he was sweating profusely and his shoulders were aching from working overhead. His legs trembling from maintaining his balance so intensely. He'd worked his way over the width of the bridge and from up top dangled a length of det-cord, which he affixed to his series of charges.

The green bag, emptied now for the fifth time, was drawn up and then the rope came back down, this time for Wilson. He got ahold of it with the pole and drew it into his hands, then tied the same knots he'd tied before, forming the harness for himself. Then came the leap of faith.

'All right, take me up!' he shouted, then hung on to the rope.

The sound of the truck revving again, and this time the slack was drawn out. Wilson bent his knees and got low to the pylon, letting the tension draw him off of his perch slowly to reduce the swinging. Then he was hanging in midair again, and the engine grumbled louder and he was being lifted.

Never a sense of relief until he made it over the top and put his feet on solid ground.

Then he took the ropes off of himself, almost a little too eagerly, and let out a big breath.

Dorian was there, smiling, and he gave Wilson a pat on the back. Dark-haired. Olive-complected – Italian, Wilson thought, or maybe Greek. He couldn't recall. Some sort of Mediterranean descent. He had an aloof manner, but he'd warmed to Wilson over the last few days, and with Wilson's two best friends dead and missing, he accepted it without much question. It was nice to have someone to talk to.

'God, I really fucking hate that,' Wilson said under his breath.

Dorian gathered the rope up in his arms, still smirking. 'You look like a cat in water.'

A new voice called out. 'First cut all set up?'

Wilson turned in the direction of the voice, found a blocky-looking man in desert digital camouflage and a tan fleece cap looking down at him from the bed of one of their LMTVs. Behind the man stood stacked crates of explosives, det-cord, and detonators. Some other odds and ends, but mostly just ordnance.

Wilson nodded to the man. 'Primed and ready.'

'You packed each side of the I-beams?' the man asked.

'Yeah.'

'And you got det-cord going to each side? It's all connected?'

'All connected,' Wilson confirmed.

The man in the LMTV swung his legs over the gate and hopped down. After meeting Colonel Staley four days ago, they'd received very little assistance, except for the man that was now standing with them. Lance Corporal Gilmore. Gilmore wasn't a demolitions expert by any means, but he had more experience with the stuff than Wilson did. He didn't do much but offer advice and instruction, but acted more like the liaison between Wilson's crew and Colonel Staley.

More pragmatically put, Gilmore was a way for Staley to keep an eye on them.

Wilson got the distinct feeling that Staley wasn't going to commit much to them until he had a better grasp of the situation, and certainly not until he'd powwowed with Lee, which had yet to happen. On the one hand, Wilson understood Colonel Staley's reticence. On the other hand, it irritated the fuck out of him, because he could have really used some help taking out these bridges in a timely manner.

Now they were getting down to the wire, racing the clock every fucking day and trying to stay ahead of the massive infected hordes on the other side of the river. And it seemed like the Marines were nowhere to be found.

Gilmore blew warm air into his thick, stubby-fingered hands, then rubbed them together. 'How about you? You good? You need to grab some water? Some food?'

Wilson shook his head. 'No, we need to get rolling on the second cut and get the fuck out of here before our friends show up.'

'Which ones?' Gilmore asked with some biting sarcasm. Alluding to the fact that they were deep in territory that was being pushed hard by the Followers. Infected hordes on one side of the river. Violent radicals on the other. Framed in on all sides by enemies.

'Either-or,' Wilson said without humor.

'We're making the second cut close to the far shore, right?' Gilmore asked, already knowing the answer, but wanting to make sure that Wilson was on the same page.

Wilson started to answer, but all he got out was a nod.

The sound of a roaring engine and screeching tires cut off any further conversation.

Wilson, Dorian, and Gilmore all snapped their heads toward the far side of the bridge. Coming off the highway, seeming to vault its way onto the bridge, a green Humvee charged toward them, a hand held out the driver's-side window.

'That's Tim,' Dorian said.

Wilson felt his skin prickle. Electricity tingling in his fingers and toes.

No one wants to see their scout come back, hauling ass like that. It rarely means good news.

The Humvee screeched to a stop just a few yards from Wilson, still coming in so fast by the time it reached them that

Wilson and the other two men took a step back, thinking for a half second that the big green vehicle was just going to bowl them all over.

The engine went out of gear, the tone of it changing to a high idle.

The driver's door swung open and Tim flew out, his long, thin limbs flailing about like a stick-built marionette. One hand gripping his rifle, the other pointed back behind him to the far bank. 'The infected're about five miles out, Wilson! And they're coming in quick!'

FIVE

HEAD GAMES

WILSON TOUCHED HIS HEAD with both hands. He could feel his own icy fingers against his scalp as he pressed them through his hair. His eyes darted for a second and he had to remind himself that five miles was still too far to see in this terrain.

'Shit, shit, shit,' he whispered to himself, his mind gone to calculations. The ones in these massive hordes moved at a steady clip. Not quite a run, but not quite a walk, either. He'd watched them, his stomach turning, from the opposite bank of the river. They would jog forward, then stop and shuffle along for a bit. They went in spurts, bumping into each other, always scanning around and sniffing the air. Always looking for something edible.

They were also spread out across a large swath of land. It forced them to be unable to stick to roads, and these boggy backwoods would slow their progress. Did he have enough time to set the next cut in the bridge, or should they just run right then and there? The average man could walk three miles per hour over varied terrain. Wilson decided to round up to be safe.

'I give them one hour,' Wilson said, a little shakily. He looked to Lance Corporal Gilmore questioningly. 'If you helped me rig the second cut, do you think we could get it done in an hour?'

Gilmore grimaced. 'Fuck, that's cutting it close.'

Wilson felt a little flash of anger that he couldn't quite explain. He wasn't the angry type, but you couldn't just completely ignore the irony of a man who could summon the cure to all your ills with a single direct dial call from his satellite phone, telling you that he wasn't sure you were going to make it.

'You could always make the call,' Wilson said, trying to mask the heat in his words.

Gilmore's lips tightened. 'I'm not the one making the rules here, bud.'

Wilson looked away from Gilmore before his expression became a full-on glare. 'Yeah, I know.' He looked at the ground. Under his feet, thick concrete. Under the concrete, more than a hundred pounds of C4 rigged to blow. You'd think it would be enough to blow one of these fucking bridges, but no. You had to have *two* cuts. One would just mangle shit up. It would make it impassable for vehicles, but people would still be able to get across, and that included the infected.

What if they decide to start swimming? Wilson wondered. *Then this would have all been a damn waste anyways.*

He hadn't seen them swim. Hadn't seen them do much but splash around in knee-deep water and then scramble out, like it scared them. He wasn't sure if they didn't like it, or just weren't sure what to do with it. Maybe they would eventually figure it out. But he hoped they didn't.

Hope. What a joke.

He looked up at Tim. Pointed at his chest, decisively. 'Take one more with you and get down that service road that borders the river on our side. As soon as you get a visual on them, I want you to get their attention.' Wilson took a big breath, exhaled pure anxiety. 'Hit them with the fifty. Keep rolling east. See if you can't convince them to follow you. Or at least slow them down. Can you do that?'

Tim nodded. 'We're runnin' low on fifty-cal ammo.'

Wilson shot another glance in Gilmore's direction. They probably had stockpiles of that shit. 'Fine,' he said to Tim. 'Just do what you can. Try to buy us some time.'

Tim nodded hastily, then ran for the Humvee.

Wilson spoke to Gilmore again. 'So you gonna help me or what?'

Gilmore was already walking to the LMTV with all of the ordnance piled in the back. 'If we're gonna do it, let's do it.'

Lee waited in the woods, facing the back side of Camp Ryder. He was shielded from view by a copse of some evergreen bush that stood as one of the few blots of color in the entire winter-gray landscape. A few other bushes like it ran along the low points and small gullies that came off the hill, created by centuries of rainwater runoff. It provided perfect cover and if he was quiet, his comings and goings went unnoticed.

Well, not unnoticed.

His *absence* was noticed. But when and where he left and returned was a mystery to everyone else, though he was sure that most could make an educated guess.

Do you feel guilty for this? he questioned himself.

I don't know. Should I feel guilty?

Maybe.

In the cover of the bush, he waited with Deuce at his side. The dog was a natural hunter. There was no need to teach the dog how to sneak because it seemed that when they left the confines of safety, the dog was doing it automatically. Now the dog stood next to Lee's crouched form, and he did not move. The dog's head and tail were low, and he was motionless, except for his eyes and the occasional drift of his head as he peered through the foliage. Much like Lee.

Through the small green leaves of the bush, Lee could see the top of the building and the figure that stood there. The moment that Camp Ryder had been taken back into his control, Lee had posted a guard on the roof, where they had a three-sixty view of the entire camp and could alert the rest if anyone was attempting to breach their fence – particularly any infected.

Particularly the hunters.

The guards did a good job, but they were hardly a challenge for someone with Lee's training and experience. They developed their patterns, even when they didn't mean to. And Lee knew this guy. He knew that this guard spent a lot of time facing into the sun. Whether he was just trying to warm his face, or if he thought that hostile forces might use the rising sun as cover, Lee wasn't sure. But the sun was in the opposite direction as Lee, and at any moment Lee knew the guard would turn himself east, putting his back to Lee for a good minute or two.

When the time came, Lee slid quietly forward, though it was not without effort. Being stealthy was a lot easier when your body was not broken. Deuce followed Lee up to the fence. Lee lifted the chain link and Deuce scooted under, but Lee would not fit, so he opened the cut in the fence – the same one that Devon had cut in the chain link during the assault, as an entry point for their team to take back Camp Ryder from Jerry and his men. They had closed it up with heavy-gauge wire to keep the infected out, since fine motor skills seemed close to impossible for them. But a few twists with nimble fingers opened the gash back up.

It took some dexterity to wrangle the wire from the chain link, especially with cold fingers. The cold, stubborn wire made his fingers ache as he twisted the links open. He sucked on his fingertips to warm them, then continued. He opened the bottom of the cut, crouched down to move through it, checked to make sure the guard was still looking away, then secured the wires again.

He remained calm and steady, tried to control his heart rate and respiration. Being caught worried him, though he was sure he could simply repeat the lie that he told when Angela asked him where he went in the mornings. 'For a walk. To be alone for a while.'

'Why do you have to sneak out?'

'Because I don't want to be followed. And knowing you, Angela, you'd send someone to keep an eye on me and make sure I didn't get myself killed.'

Plausible enough, he thought. But somehow he knew that being caught in his comings and goings would deepen any suspicions that people might be harboring about what Lee was doing out beyond the wire. It was best to leave it in the realm of the hypothetical.

If you were doing the right thing then you wouldn't need to hide it from people.

He stood up, started walking. Glanced up at the guard, who was still facing away.

Deuce was trotting out into the open area behind the Camp Ryder building, occasionally looking back to check on Lee's progress. The dog liked the back wall of the building. It was his personal bulletin board for pissings. With no other dogs inside Camp Ryder, Lee imagined it was like talking to yourself. But Deuce didn't seem to mind. He made his way to the wall and lifted his leg to give it a sprinkling. Then he stood and waited for Lee.

Lee hesitated. He was close enough to the building that the guard would not be able to see him unless he leaned over the edge and looked down. But here was a moment of relative safety and privacy and in it he leaned against the frosted cinder-block wall of the building and he closed his eyes for a long moment. If only for a moment, he could let his guard down. And he needed to close his eyes. He could feel the start of the pain, creeping around the back of his head, hiding behind his eyes, and slithering down into his gut.

It would come on strong within the next hour. But he was grateful that at least it had waited this long. There was really no way to get it to leave him. No technique that solved the problem. How do you solve the jangled insides of your head after a bullet has struck your skull? The answer was that you didn't. In the past, you would take heavy doses of pain medication. Now you waited it out. It would go away on its own. Eventually.

A warm presence leaning up against his legs. A curious whine.

Lee let his hand hang down and touched the dog's head. Cold fur on top. Warm hide below. He pulled himself off the wall of the building, opening his eyes and smiling down at the dog. If a dog could grasp the finer concepts of reality, the weak filaments of our thoughts that kept us bound to our moralities, then Deuce would understand why things were the way they were. Deuce would get it.

When Lee looked up from the dog, he found himself looking at Brian Tomlin.

His heart thudded aggressively for a moment, but then revved down.

Tomlin stood at the corner of the building, arms crossed over his chest, and Lee could not tell whether the body language was *stern* or simply *cold*. His expression seemed to be one of concern, instead of confrontation.

'Your head?' Tomlin said quietly.

Lee nodded once.

Tomlin's eyes tracked up and down, as though trying to see if Lee carried with him any evidence of where he'd been. Then his eyes came up and they bored into Lee, all those questions being funneled into one look. Tomlin seemed to be trying to find the right words.

Lee broke the gaze and looked around them. He spoke before Tomlin could. 'Not here.'

'What?'

'We'll talk. But not here.'

'Okay.'

Lee pointed toward the front of the building and began walking. 'Inside. Out of the cold.'

And out of the light, he added silently.

Tomlin fell into step with Lee and Deuce, and they walked to the front of the Camp Ryder building and then inside. Neither spoke. They looked outward, catching eye contact from other people in the camp. Lee searched the faces of the people that they passed, and wondered if they knew the truth. But they either didn't know or didn't care one way or the other. They all gave him a nod, and that funny half smile that people give another person they seem to respect but simultaneously view as unapproachable.

He'd gone in and out of the Camp Ryder building so many times now that the smell seemed more familiar and present in his mind than the smell of his old house. The smell of grease and old fuel, still just faintly clinging to the building despite everything else that had inundated it since it had been used for those purposes – all the cook fires and the shanties that had once been erected in here, and the reek of filthy people sweating in the summer heat.

That was when Lee had first come to this place.

A lot had happened since then.

Many people had died.

Many nightmares had become simple facts. All of them had changed. The world without, and the world within, each always affecting the other. So the world changed, and people adapted, and their adaptation forced more change. This was the laws of thermodynamics, Lee knew. Everything is in a constant state of atrophy. And yet the decay had no bottom, no endpoint. It seemed there was always room for things to worsen. Unless they all died. Unless all the people in the world killed each other, and the few that were left were eaten by the infected. Then what had been an aberration would be the new humankind. Unless, of course, they then simply ate themselves. Ate themselves until there was only one, fat, engorged bastard left. And then he would die. And he would become dirt. And everything else would continue on, sans humanity, and probably, it would be okay.

These types of thoughts tended to crowd Lee's brain just before the onset of his daily nuclear headaches. He wondered if it was something that had been knocked loose, some little gland somewhere in his brain stem that wasn't getting a signal to stop spewing nonsense chemicals into his brain. Or maybe it wasn't physiological at all. Maybe it was all just a state of mind.

Maybe you just need to quit bitching, he told himself, halfheartedly. *You're alive. You're still kicking. Still doing work. What else do you need?*

Soft bed warm shower hot food.

Bullshit. He turned up the stairs toward the office, clomping up them. *Luxuries. You're whinin' and moanin' about fucking luxuries. Life. Air. Enough blood to keep your heart pumping. Water. Calories. That's all you need.*

Tired. That was the parting shot of the weak man slouching inside him, before he succeeded in stuffing it back to the dark place where it belonged. Back to the mental dungeon to be tortured to death. But never quite to death. You could never really get rid of that little creature in you that just wanted to be warm and well fed and comfortable.

Up the stairs, looking around, catching a few glances from people down on the main floor. Tomlin followed, his steps a little quieter, Lee noted, though he couldn't really do much about it. The various injuries he'd accumulated made the stairs a little awkward to ascend with any grace. Maybe nobody else noticed it, but Lee certainly did.

A little frustrating. To be so accustomed to being in control of a well-tuned body, and now to have it breaking on you. He just needed time to rest and heal, but time he did not have, nor was he willing to make it. He considered it an unrealistic expectation in his current position.

At the top of the stairs he found the office door hanging open, and figured he knew what that meant. Deuce edged past him and slipped into the room without even touching the door. Lee pushed his way through and immediately looked to his right. He found exactly who he expected to find, sitting on the desk with arms crossed over her chest.

Angela was not abrasive about it. That simply wasn't her style. But there was a set to her jaw, a tightness in her lips that Lee correctly interpreted as concern. And maybe a bit of anger. There were other things, lying under the surface of that expression that Lee suspected had to do with forcing someone to leave Camp Ryder. Banishing a young man named Kyle.

Deuce had made his way to her. She was one of the few people besides Lee that Deuce was warming up to. He was hesitant around Tomlin, shy around most others, and downright aggressive with a few. But he treated Angela gently and with affection, as though he could sense what was good in her, when it had spoiled in so many other people. Now he went to her and sat, leaning heavily against her leg and looking up with something like adoration.

Angela did not seem to notice. She was clearly preoccupied with other things.

Lee decided to let her speak first, since she clearly had things to say. He nodded to her and then set his rifle up against the wall and waited, his mind already rehearsing what he had decided he would say.

For a walk. To be alone for a while.

'He cried, you know,' Angela started, eyes dropping to her own boots.

Now here was a curveball.

'Kyle,' Angela clarified. 'He tried not to, I could tell. He was trying hard. But he was ... he was pretty torn up, Lee. And when the gates opened up, that's when he started. And I didn't like it one bit. He looked back at me' – her eyes came back up to Lee's – 'at me. At *me*. Like it was all my fucking fault.'

Angela shook her head, brow furrowing. One of her hands freed itself from where it had been lodged against her torso and went to her mouth. She bit the fingernail, making a muted *crick*.

'Dammit.' She withdrew her finger and inspected the nail as she spoke. 'He never said anything, though. Just looked at me, like he was telling me that he was sorry. Like he was begging me to let him stay. Like I had . . . had . . . you know . . . '

'It was the group's decision,' Lee said, evenly.

'He was a kid.'

'He was a man.' Lee shook his head. 'Same as the others.'

Had to die, same as the others.

'I could have used you,' Angela said suddenly.

Lee was blank.

'The group could have used you. There. To make things seem less . . . '

'Cruel?' Lee offered, and immediately regretted the choice of words.

Angela's face fell. 'Yes.'

'I'm sorry.'

She frowned, but it lacked true anger behind it. 'And dammit, Lee, you shouldn't be out in the woods by yourself. Not in your condition.'

'My condition is . . . ' He hesitated to say *fine*.

'Wounded. And not yet recovered.'

Tomlin raised a hand. 'Angela, me and Lee actually just had a very frank conversation about this. I can promise you he won't be taking any more early morning walks from now on. Especially by himself.'

Angela looked at Tomlin. Then back at Lee. 'If you say so.'

Lee nodded. 'I won't. I'm done.'

She walked between the two men, her steps slow, methodic. At the door she stopped, her hand on the frame, and she didn't turn, but just looked over her shoulder, right at Lee, and the look that she gave him was a knowing one, or at least *prying* to know.

'We killed them by forcing them out like that,' she said. 'You know that, don't you?'

'Maybe,' Lee said, and hated how fluidly the lie came out of him. Or the untruth, you might call it. Lying by omission. Not quite lying, but not telling the truth, either. He didn't like it. Didn't like deceiving Angela.

She kept her eye on him for a short time after that, and then she went through the door and was gone. Lee could hear her footfalls on the stairs outside, descending to the main level, growing quieter as they went, and then disappearing as resonant steel turned to dull concrete. Deuce stared at the door for an extra moment, and then grumbled and lowered himself into a lying position.

Tomlin poked his head out the doorway to confirm that she was leaving. Satisfied, Tomlin pulled himself back into the room and closed the door gently behind him.

Lee grabbed the nearest chair and sat down in it with a huff. It was a relief just to take the tension out of his body. The stitches in his side glowed and throbbed. Goddamned ribs. It didn't matter what you did, you couldn't avoid using them. Sitting also seemed to bleed some of the building pressure in his head. He grabbed the bridge of his nose, slowly pressed his fingers into the corners of his eyes.

'Is it done?' Tomlin's voice.

Lee removed his fingers and opened his eyes. The world swam darkly, the edges of his vision mottled and sparkling. He found Tomlin in the darkness and focused until things became normal again. That little bit of abnormal vision was just because he'd pressed his fingers against his eyes. But sometimes his vision would darken, all on its own. And it scared the shit out of him when it happened.

'Yeah,' Lee said. He leaned back in his chair and unzipped the front of his parka and then began working at the layers beneath. 'Done.'

Tomlin leaned against the wall, regarded his friend with a grim smile. 'You didn't have to do it alone.'

'No.' Lee's voice was quiet. 'I didn't. But I think it was better that way.'

'You didn't have to do it at all,' Tomlin continued, rehashing things that had already been said. 'I mean, I could have done it on my own.'

Lee didn't look up. He pulled up the innermost layer of his clothing – a dingy white thermal shirt that was badly in need of a washing or at least an airing out. Underneath that dirty cloth, the skin of his belly was pale, almost white. But hard. Stretched tight over what looked like cables crisscrossed beneath the thin layer of flesh. They twitched and jumped as he twisted and pulled the clothing up to inspect the wound on his side. There the gauze was almost completely bled through.

Busted a stitch, Lee thought. *Dammit.*

He pulled the clothing back in place, then looked at Tomlin. 'You know Deuce wouldn't have gone out there with you.'

Deuce looked up, hearing his name.

'Besides,' Lee finished. 'It was my problem to correct. Not yours.'

Tomlin wiped the corners of his mouth with his thumb and forefinger – a habit that Lee had seen him doing a lot lately. 'You know, Lee, it *is* my problem.' He pointed to the ground at their feet. 'Anything that happens here is my problem, too, Lee. Just as much as it is yours. We're working on this thing together.'

Lee wanted to close his eyes against the pain in his head. Growing now. Sharp with every heartbeat. It was gathering itself around the true culprit – the long, hairless slash that ran from his right temple all the way back behind his ear. No use suturing it closed – it had been exposed for far too long before he'd gotten any medical attention for it. Now he simply had to keep it as clean as possible and stay on a religious round of antibiotics. It was nasty-looking, jagged flesh and scabbing blood.

Lee blew air out of pursed lips, like a leaky valve. 'I need to talk to you about that.'

Tomlin's brow quirked. 'About what?'

'About how we're going to keep this place alive. If we intend to keep this place alive.'

'Okay . . .'

Lee shook his head – carefully, so he didn't aggravate the head wound. 'Gimme an hour, buddy.' He realized his eyes were closed and he didn't really want to open them again. That was okay. It was time to shut it down. Shutter the windows and wait for the storm to pass. 'Just an hour and I'll be good to go. One hour.'

SIX

THE DEACON

CLYDE STEPPED OUT OF the tent. He turned and glanced over his shoulder as the flap fell, and for a momentary glimpse saw the man inside. The rough-looking, broken man that seemed oh-so-familiar to Clyde. A memory of another time. A dark time. He'd worked hard to forget how things had been for him. He had whitewashed the walls of his mind and boarded up the subconscious. There was a part of him that resented LaRouche for stirring those echoes back up.

The convenience store.
Your wife.
Dying.
A box cutter.
Your unborn child.
All the blood on your hands . . .
Just leave it alone.

LaRouche wasn't bound, but he wouldn't leave. Clyde knew he wouldn't leave, because he knew that look. He knew the feeling of hopelessness that went along with it. He knew that for LaRouche, just as it had been for him, this was a period of cataclysm. This was a man watching his old life die in the bloody birth of the new.

Seeing it only reminded Clyde that he had not always been

who he was. And when he thought about that time past, and what had brought him to his new life, the series of events that had taken place in order for him to become the man that he needed to be, he felt something like fear. Fear that there might be some part of that old self still lurking inside him.

The weakness. The inability. The cowardice.

He turned away from the tent.

That's not me. I'm different now. Things have changed. I have changed. I can't go back now. I don't want to go back. I won't ever go back.

He realized he was gripping the strap of his rifle with white knuckles. His palms smarted as his fingernails bore into the skin. He forced himself to relax and he looked to the left, where another man stood, his arm bearing the mark of the Followers – the white band with the black circle and cross displayed prominently on it.

Clyde sniffed the cold air and jerked his head back toward the tent. 'He's not bound,' he said in low tones. 'But I don't think he'll leave. Just make sure.'

The man nodded. 'Will do.'

Clyde walked away, perhaps a little stiffly. Perhaps a little quickly. But the ghosts of his past lifted off him like a fog as he put distance between himself and that tent. Distance between him and things that dredged up old memories.

The camp all around him was tents and trucks. Nothing was permanent. Except for the dilapidated farmhouse that Deacon Chalmers was using. They had been at this encampment for almost three weeks, but they never built. Everything they did was based around movement. They had to be mobile. Except for New Bern. That was where the church was. That was the beating heart of the Followers. That was where Pastor Wiscoe heard the voice of God.

After dodging his way through the collection of tents, he found the main gravel drive. He turned right and followed it to the farmhouse. The one with the rotted, wooden siding. Shingles missing in places. Cobwebs strung in the dark corners of the front porch. Two rocking chairs still sitting there. Everything else in the house had been gutted and tossed out or used for firewood. But Chalmers had not touched those rocking chairs.

Strange.

Even in the morning light, the house seemed dark on the inside. Through the cloudy-looking windows, Clyde could see only the impression of shapes inside. But that was not unusual. Chalmers did not seem to appreciate a well-lit workspace. He preferred more of a den. But that was just a part of who he was, Clyde believed. He was cordial with others, but he brooded.

Clyde knocked. And waited.

He stepped off to the side, just slightly. He couldn't shake the feeling that there was a shotgun leveled at him through the other side of the door, though it made no sense. Or did it? Chalmers was known for some ... mood swings.

Perhaps a dash of paranoia.

The door opened and Chalmers stood there, half-smiling, as though seeing Clyde was a pleasant surprise. As though Clyde were a friendly neighbor, dropping by to exchange small talk. He stood there in the doorway wearing only his pants, his gun belt that held the giant old revolver, and unlaced boots. His torso stood out, wiry and pasty white, with a few dark scars in his side. A mat of graying hair over a barrel chest. But he was not a large man. Just widely built across the shoulders. He did not seem to be affected by the cold.

'Clyde,' Chalmers said, and stepped out of the way, sweeping his arm inward, like an usher. 'Come in.'

Clyde stepped through and Chalmers closed the door behind them. Out of the morning light, it took a moment for Clyde's eyes to adjust to the dimness inside. They were in a tiny foyer. A bedroom off to the right. A living room off to the left. Through the living room, a small kitchen. Everything old and wood-paneled. Peeling wallpaper and the smell of must. Ancient hardwood floors creaked loudly underfoot.

From the kitchen, Clyde could hear the sound of water.

A muted trickle. A slight splash.

'Are you here because of our new man?' Chalmers asked, like he already knew the answer.

Clyde nodded. 'Yes. I did what you told me to do, but . . .'

Chalmers held up a hand and made a face that indicated Clyde should hold his tongue for a bit. Then Chalmers looked through the living room and into the kitchen. Clyde closed his open mouth and followed the other man's gaze, but couldn't see anything. The quiet splashing again, but then it was silent. As though whatever was making the noise suddenly realized it was being listened to.

Chalmers seemed slightly bemused. He stepped into the living room and motioned for Clyde to follow him. Clyde obeyed. They stepped through the musty room. The fireplace had the remnants of burned wood in it, some embers glowing at the bottom, the hearth still giving off heat as they passed by.

They stepped into the kitchen. Clyde stopped in the threshold, not sure whether he should keep going. Chalmers continued in, casually. There was a small dining area and then a counter separating it from the cooking area where the defunct electric stovetop stood dark and piled with ancient pots and pans with white fuzz growing on them. The kitchen smelled sharply of spoiled food, undercut by the pleasant smell of warm water and . . . soap.

The dining area held no table, but instead, the subject of Clyde's uncertainty.

A blue, plastic fifty-gallon drum occupied the center of the small open space where Clyde could imagine family dinners once taking place. The drum was filled with sudsy water, steam still rolling off it. Huddled in the water was a young woman that could have been sixteen or seventeen years old, by Clyde's reckoning. She was naked, her hair hanging in wet sheets around her face. She peered intensely and cautiously from behind the curtain of her own hair. Her eyes tracked Chalmers first as he walked around the opposite side of the counter, not paying her any attention. Then her eyes switched to Clyde and the look of caution became one of recognition.

Clyde looked away from her, very deliberately. He forced himself to keep walking. Hoped that Chalmers hadn't noticed the hesitation, and wasn't quite sure why he suddenly felt so unsettled. It felt like his heart had stopped, but the blood was still rushing. The beating muscle in his chest turned to a mechanical pump, just cycling blood through at a constant, dizzying speed.

He felt flushed.

You're weak! LaRouche is pulling up old memories, and they're making you weak!

Clyde followed Chalmers to the other side of the counter, carefully ignoring the girl in the water, but feeling her gaze still lingering on him. He wouldn't look at her, but the image of those eyes boring into him stuck in his brain.

He thought of two nights ago.

And then perhaps a week before that.

The first time, about a month ago, when she'd first been captured.

'Clyde, would you like some bread?'

Clyde realized he'd been staring lifelessly at Chalmers while his mind clouded with intimate thoughts of the girl sitting in the washtub. Thoughts that warred in the center of him. Some part of his old self raging and telling him he was sick, a pedophile, a rapist. But the other, larger, stronger part of him that believed. Believed that he was doing God's work. Believed that the girl was blessed to receive his seed, blessed to have a chance to bear a new generation of the Lord's Army.

I've done nothing wrong. I have done as God commanded.

'Excuse me?' Clyde asked, carefully.

Chalmers gestured to the counter next to him where there was a wooden cutting board and three oval pieces of what looked like thick, dense, flatbread. They looked slightly blackened on the bottom. Powdery on top. 'Would you like some bread?'

Despite his soured gut, Clyde felt it would be rude if he refused. 'Yes. Please.'

Chalmers smiled like any gracious host. Then he took one of the small, oval loaves and Clyde got the sense from seeing how it did not give under the pressure of Chalmers's grip that the loaf was hard. With two hands, Chalmers broke the loaf in two. It was not as hard as Clyde had thought. Chalmers handed one half to Clyde and kept the other. Clyde held the loaf in his hand, felt the warmth still hiding in it. These had been baked recently.

'You ever hear of hardtack?' Chalmers asked, breaking off a small piece of his loaf and putting it in his mouth. It crunched beneath his teeth.

'No.'

'Hardtack biscuits were a staple of a Confederate soldier's diet during the Civil War. These are fresh baked, but the ones they had were dried so they would keep longer and they were so hard you could break a tooth trying to bite one.' Chalmers smiled. 'Eventually, these will get that hard, too, and then they'll keep for a long time. You have to break them up and cook them with some water to make them edible, but it's a simple and easy way to feed a lot of people. Easy recipe, too. Just two parts flour and one part water and then you bake and dry it out.'

Clyde watched the other man chew noisily for a moment, then realized he was probably expected to do the same. He broke a piece from his loaf with some effort, then put it in his mouth. He didn't want to break a tooth like Chalmers had mentioned, so he approached chewing with care. The bit of hard biscuit in his mouth didn't have an unpleasant flavor, but it was simple. Like saltine crackers.

He chewed and swallowed. Hoped he wouldn't be expected to eat the whole thing right then and there because he was sure it would take longer than he wanted to be in the house with Deacon Chalmers. And the girl. The girl, still sitting there in the drum of water, watching them.

Don't look at her.

'Do you know Nicole?' Chalmers asked casually.

A bit of hardtack seemed caught in Clyde's throat. 'Excuse me?'

Chalmers gestured to the young woman in the water. 'Nicole. Do you know her?'

Clyde finally looked at her.

The conversation now focused on her, she lowered her gaze. Staring at nothing in particular. A false façade of *demur*, with tension like a dry branch underneath. Clyde considered lying, but then thought, *What if he already knows? What if he knows and this is just a test? Maybe he's testing my honesty. And 'a righteous man is honest, even to his own undoing.'*

Chalmers had quoted that scripture many times.

Clyde nodded once. 'Yes. I know her.'

Chalmers smiled. 'Good, good.' He walked around the counter that divided the kitchen and dining area. He stopped in front of the drum, standing close to it. One hand idly scratched at his chest, the other still clutched the hardtack biscuit. Chalmers regarded the girl in the water, as he sucked food from his teeth.

Nicole seemed frozen stiff, even in the steaming water.

'Stand up,' Chalmers said, his voice blank. 'Let me see you.'

She hesitated only momentarily, then stood. Clyde stared at the water running over her pale skin, sheeting off her small breasts. He looked away, shame causing his face to burn. He instead watched Chalmers, who seemed to be inspecting the girl with a critical eye. If he derived any pleasure from the sight of the girl, he did not show it.

He stepped up to her, leaned over, and inhaled deeply. Not as a man smells a woman, but rather how you would sniff to find if something was offensive or not. He took her wrist and raised her arm, this time checking her armpit. Then he looked behind her ears. All the while Nicole simply allowed him. Her face was a practiced lack of anything. When Chalmers let go of her wrist, it simply flopped back down to her side.

Chalmers nodded, ruminating. 'And you cleaned your lady parts?'

'Yes,' Nicole said, her voice as expressionless as her face.

Chalmers smiled again and then turned his attention back to Clyde. 'Cleanliness is close to godliness, so they say.' He walked back over to the counter and set his biscuit down there. 'If I didn't make these poor girls bathe every once in a while, Lord knows what kind of filth they would be living in.' Chalmers's eyes hazed over and his finger rapped twice on the countertop. 'The dirty bastards out there wouldn't see to it, I'm sure of that.'

Chalmers seemed to recover himself. He turned partially, and spoke over his shoulder. 'Nicole, you're done. Please dry off in the bedroom.' He wagged a finger, as an afterthought. 'Remember not to leave the house without me.'

It was an important warning. Because if she were caught outside without an escort, at the very least she would be beaten and dragged back to the cages. But there was always the possibility that she would be shot to death. The holding cages were overcrowded, and young wombs tended to be weaker, and therefore less valuable to them. Besides her age, all women were to be in their designated areas, or they needed to be with a man.

Chalmers waited, staring at the brick of dried flour that sat on the countertop. As he watched it, an ant meandered across the counter, in search of things to take back to its colony. It came to the hardtack and seemed to consider it for a moment, but eventually turned and made a new course for easier fare.

Over Chalmers's shoulder, Clyde could see Nicole getting out of the water. It splashed and trickled noisily, and then was silent. She took a large blanket and draped it over herself, and then she quietly padded out of the room with a sharp glance in Clyde's direction and tightly pursed lips.

When she was gone, Chalmers leaned his elbows on the countertop. 'So. The new recruit.'

'Yessir.'

'Having problems with him?'

Clyde gave a partial shrug. 'He's cooperative. To a point. But he doesn't want to talk about the group he came from. And I'm not sure the ... *alternative methods* are going to be effective.'

'Oh.' Chalmers stretched his back languidly. 'They're always effective. Just takes time. However, I understand your hesitation. After all, I've made this man your trainee. Your tagalong. So do you torture him and hope for forgiveness later? Or do you approach it with a softer hand?'

Clyde remained silent. Chalmers seemed to be mulling something over.

'Maybe it was a mistake to ask you to do this,' Chalmers said absently.

'I can do it,' Clyde insisted.

Chalmers held up a hand. 'Clyde, it's not a lack of faith in your ability. I think you were right to come to me. This man is a unique situation. And perhaps we need to come at him from a different angle.'

'Okay.'

Chalmers scratched his chest again, his fingers disappearing into the gray fur. 'I think I have a good use for Mr. LaRouche.'

LaRouche sat in the tent, very quietly. His hands remained folded in his lap. Shoulders slouched. His eyes affixed to the dirt. He was thirsty again. And his hunger was becoming a different animal in him. For a time, hunger makes itself known through physical pain. But after a while, it gives up on sending signals and hijacks your entire brain, so that all you can think about is what you might be able to eat. Leaves. Bark. Dirt. Anything.

LaRouche was still a ways off from that point of desperation, he thought. But he noted that the physical pain seemed gone. Now he just felt empty and couldn't stop counting the days since he'd eaten last. That was the majority of his thoughts, like the vast mass of an iceberg below water.

The tip of the iceberg – the more lucid thoughts – were of fear and dread and morbid curiosity.

Are they going to torture me to get me to talk about Wilson? I can take a beating.

Depends on what they're beating. And what if they have other ideas?

Prisoners in Soviet gulags would be tortured. They would beat their dicks with rubber hoses. Sometimes they'd shove glass thermometers into their cocks and break the glass with a hammer. Holy fuck. What if they do that to me? I can't do that. I can't handle that.

Everybody breaks. That's what they told me in training, right? Everybody breaks.

No shame in it.

But then you will have betrayed them twice.

Twice a traitor. You should feel double the shame.

God, I wish I was dead.

He was beginning to sweat, despite the cold. He could feel it at the small of his back. In the palms of his hands. There was a part of him that wanted to go, wanted to test and see if he was truly free to leave. But Clyde's words still hung on him like steel chains: *Where would you go? Would you go back to them? Would they take you back? Would they forgive you for what you did?*

We are your family now.

There was a part of him that was drowning. Flailing about and failing miserably at treading the waters of his new reality. Its head was underwater more often than not at this point, but every once in a while it would thrash its way above the surface, take a deep gulp of air, and shout, panicked, *This isn't you!*

And then it would sink into the water again.

And it would just be LaRouche, staring at a great emptiness, wondering where survival ended and morality began. At some point far behind him? Or had he yet to cross it?

Footsteps.

LaRouche's gaze sharpened and he looked up at the wall of the tent, where he could see the shadow of the man that was standing there, presumably to keep an eye on him while Clyde was gone. The shadow sidestepped and half-bowed. LaRouche heard a mumbled, 'Morning, sir,' and then two more shadows sprawled out onto the wall of the tent. Then the tent flaps were ripped back.

Clyde and Deacon Chalmers.

Here to torture you. To put glass thermometers in your cock . . .

Deacon Chalmers was holding a plate of something in one hand. Another bottle of water in the other.

A trick. Going to try to bribe me with it.

Before letting the tent flaps closed, Clyde leaned out and spoke to the shadow still hovering on the tent wall. 'You're good. Thanks.'

The shadow nodded, then disappeared.

LaRouche found Chalmers's gaze for a moment, but then couldn't help himself – he stared at the plate. The smell of it was filling up the tent now, and LaRouche swallowed as his mouth began to water. Seeing a possible end of its misery, Hunger stabbed at his gut again.

Chalmers walked to LaRouche, stood in front of him. He seemed to be sizing LaRouche up. Taking the measure of him as deliberately as a tailor fitting him for a suit. Closer now, LaRouche could see what was on the plate. Some sort of hash. Gray meat in strings and bits. Some starchy thing, finely chopped. Potatoes, possibly.

LaRouche was desperate for it.

Esau, prepared to sell his birthright for a bowl of soup.

But Chalmers made no deal with him. He placed the plate directly into LaRouche's hands, set the bottle of water onto the ground at his feet. LaRouche stared at it in disbelief. There was no utensil to eat with and his fingers dove into the food, grabbing a handful of it, then halting. He looked up at Chalmers, like a dog asking permission of the master.

Chalmers smiled. 'Please. Eat.'

LaRouche shoved the handful into his mouth. His stomach ached for it.

'I won't tell you what kind of meat that is,' Chalmers said, almost teasingly.

LaRouche chewed twice, then paused, looking at it.

Chalmers laughed. 'Don't worry, it's not human.'

And that was all LaRouche needed to hear. He continued cramming it into his mouth. Dog, cat, rat – he didn't really give a shit at this point. As long as it wasn't two-legged meat. The most instinctive taboo in the world. And on some level it reassured him that the Followers had not crossed that line.

While he ate, Clyde and Chalmers watched him. Chalmers with something like amusement. Clyde with something like impatience. LaRouche ignored them both. He ate so fast the food seemed to back up in his throat and he had to take a gulp of water to clear it, clutching the plastic with dirty fingers still coated in food. As some of the food hit his stomach, the urgency died and he became a little more aware of himself. And of the two men watching him.

He slowed, looking up at them from underneath furrowed brows. Chewed, swallowed, stopped, with still a bit left on his plate. He went back and forth between Clyde and Chalmers, and then down to the nearly empty plate in his lap. Then back to Chalmers. He cleared his throat.

'What is this?' he asked, his voice thick with disuse.

'It's food.'

'No.' LaRouche sat up a little straighter in his chair. 'I was told I wouldn't get any food until I'd been ... tested. Why are you feeding me now?'

Chalmers crossed his arms over his chest, his face taking on a serious quality. 'I am going to test you, LaRouche. That is true, and I will not lie to you about it. But the way that you'll be tested will be ... different.'

SEVEN

P Is for Plenty

THEY HAD PREPPED THREE of the five I-beams necessary for the second cut when the sounds of the first shots reached them. Wilson was halfway through negotiating himself to the fourth I-beam, Gilmore crouched behind him, holding the hooked pole and waiting for the next load of explosives to be sent down. The sound of the gunshots rolled up the river at them, effortlessly gliding against the flow of water, bouncing off the wall of trees at each bank.

It was the sound of the .50-caliber M2, chugging away.

Both of the men snapped their head in that direction.

'That ain't five miles out,' Gilmore said. 'I'd say that's within a mile of us.'

'Fuck my life,' Wilson completed his movement to the next I-beam. 'You think it'll give us enough time?'

'I have no idea.' Gilmore made a megaphone with his hand. 'Hey! Hurry the fuck up!'

From up top, Dorian yelled, his voice strained. 'It's on the way!'

The bag dropped behind them. Wrong side.

Gilmore swore under his breath. 'Other side!' he bellowed. 'We're on the fourth I-beam! Go to the other fucking side! Jesus!'

Cursing and shouts from up top.

The sixty-pound sack of explosives hauled up and away.

Wilson's right calf twitched and threatened to cramp. Perhaps he should have had some water when he had the chance. His mouth was dry, but in that cold, gummy way you get during a winter day. He squatted down and balanced on his feet, letting his hand off the frigid steel and blowing some warmth back into them.

Was there anything worse than waiting when you had no time to wait?

Yes. Probably. But not much.

Down the river, the chatter of gunfire continued. Was it closer now, or was that his imagination?

This is bad. They're coming. They're coming and I'm stuck under a fucking bridge. How much time do I have? Should we just go with what we have? Do we risk it?

Either way was a risk. Staying and trying to complete the charges was a risk. Going with a half-assed detonation was a risk. This was just pure, unadulterated *shit*. Damned in both directions, so you might as well pick one and run with it, but whatever you do, pick it fast and don't waste any time.

'All right.' Wilson ducked his head so that he could make eye contact with Gilmore. The other man's face was lined and tense. He was chewing his lip mercilessly. 'When we finish this fourth I-beam, I want you up top setting up the lines and prepping the detonation. Can you do that?'

Gilmore considered for a few beats. Then nodded. 'Yeah. Let's do that.'

'Should shave a few minutes off.'

'What if you're not done with the fifth I-beam by the time they hit the bridge?' Gilmore's eyebrows twitched up. 'What if you're not at a safe distance?'

'We'll figure it out,' Wilson said, dismissively.

Dorian's voice from the top of the bridge again: 'Coming down!'

The green bag swung down again, this time on the side closest to them.

'There we go.' Gilmore extended the pole and hooked the rope, then pulled it in until Wilson could get his hands on it. They wasted no time. As soon as Wilson got the bag open, he shoved all the det-cord over to Gilmore and then began smashing bricks of explosives into the side of the fourth I-beam. Gilmore had the other three beams already connected. He laced a new line of det-cord in with the others, then spooled it out and began wrapping the uli knot.

They worked to the background noise of gunfire.

They should be getting farther away.

Leading the infected away *from us, not* toward *us.*

Unless it's not working.

Gilmore must have noticed the closeness of the gunfire as well. He looked up from his work, peering down the river, trying to see if anything was visible. 'We don't have a lot of time here,' he mumbled. 'I'm not saying half-ass it, but I'm saying we need to hurry the fuck up.'

Wilson grabbed two bricks of C4, smashed them against the steel. 'Can't go much faster.'

'Just gonna have to finish it up sloppy,' Gilmore snapped. 'It's fucking explosives. Not rocket science. It's not fucking complicated.'

Wilson slid the remainder of the C4 over to Gilmore. 'You sure about that?'

Gilmore passed the det-cord. 'No. I'm not. There's a strong possibility we might fuck this up. But if we try to do it perfect, it ain't gonna happen at all.'

'We'll get it done,' Wilson said, but his confidence was shaken.

Down the river, the *chug-chug-chug* of the M2 fell silent.

They didn't stop working. Almost as though they had expected it and did not need to ruminate on what it meant.

'Out of ammo,' Wilson muttered, using his knife to cut into the C4 and stuff the uli knot in. 'Maybe they got their attention.'

'Yeah. Maybe.'

Wilson trailed the det-cord down and gave himself a length before cutting it off. 'All right, this side is prepped. Get up top and get the detonator ready.'

Gilmore swung under the I-beam and edged past Wilson. He grabbed up the rope and quickly untied it from the green seabag. Then he fashioned it around him, much like Wilson had done. Then he gathered the seabag into his lap. Wilson watched him for a moment as he gathered the other ends of the other det-cords and connected the newest two lines.

'Pull me up!' Gilmore shouted up top. There was a pause. In the silence, Gilmore looked at Wilson again. 'Don't waste time down here.'

'I got it,' Wilson nodded.

The sound of a diesel engine again. The slack was taken out of the rope and Gilmore gingerly lowered himself, trying to reduce the amount of swing once he was pulled from the cement pylon. Then he was out over the water, watching the last I-beam go over his head and making sure he didn't bang up against the substructure of the bridge as they hauled him up.

Wilson worked the det-cord frantically, but then all the lines were connected and he didn't have anything else to do until they sent the bag back down with more C4. He filled the empty time with all of the ways it could go wrong. He had just sent a man that he barely knew to do the detonation. How did he know that Gilmore wasn't going to freak at the first sign of infected and punch the detonator, blowing up Wilson right along with the bridge?

Shit, that's a damn oversight.

What if Gilmore did the opposite? What if Gilmore was so scared that he refused to detonate even when the infected were crossing the bridge in droves? What if Wilson got cut off from his group, huddled there underneath the bridge while the sound of millions of infected feet pounded the cement two feet above his head?

What if Wilson couldn't make it out from under the bridge in time? Did he really want Gilmore to punch it anyways? Did he really want to die for this bridge?

His stomach felt fluttery and weak. Fingers and toes tingled. Perhaps a little light-headed, which wasn't good when you were balancing twenty feet off the cold water below. Cold water with snakes and biting fish and ... and ... whatever the fuck else was in there.

Water moccasins.

Is that a snake?

He'd heard people mention them. The name sounded ominous.

God, I hope there's not water moccasins down there.

'Coming down!' Gilmore yelled.

The seabag swung down, heavy with explosives. Record time. If they'd worked this fast earlier then it wouldn't be flop-sweat time now. *If I make it through this one, it'll only be midday by then. Could we rush to the next bridge and blow it before dark? If we can do that we can buy ourselves a little time. Then we won't be under the gun so bad tomorrow.*

As it stood now, it was a neck-and-neck race.

Wilson didn't want to be in a neck-and-neck race with the infected.

He squatted down and reached, feeling his back and shoulder muscles complain as he snatched up the pole from where Gilmore had left in on the next pylon. Then he hooked the seabag and yanked it in. It felt heavier this time, maybe. Or maybe Wilson was just tired. Or maybe Gilmore had just thrown a bunch of shit into the bag without really counting out the poundage.

Can we afford to be this sloppy? Can we afford to be wasting C4? We barely have enough to blow all the bridges as it is ...

Once again the anger poked up. Anger at Gilmore, indirectly, and Colonel Staley, directly. They needed help. It would take a goddamned five-second fire mission from an artillery battalion to level this bridge to rubble. No race against the clock. No potential loss of life – for *them* anyway. And he knew for a fact that there was artillery stationed at Camp Lejeune, because Gilmore had mentioned it in passing. He had mentioned it, very blasé, too.

Oh. What? You don't have a battalion of 155 mm Howitzers?

Can you even kill a bridge with artillery? Wilson wasn't sure. But he knew they could send an air strike. He knew that shit worked because he had seen it with his own eyes. He knew it would be expensive and a hog on resources for them, but they wouldn't even have to do it for all the bridges. Just a few. Just to help Wilson get a leg up.

Did they not see the threat here?

He was slapping on C4, haphazardly, angrily. Uli knot. Cut the center brick. Stuff the det-cord in. Swing to the next side. From up top, blue det-cord swung down, wriggling and twitching like a live thing.

'Hook me up!' Gilmore shouted from up top.

Wilson gathered the det-cord that had already been chained together – deceptively heavy from all the other connections that had been made. He pulled it to him gently, not wanting to accidentally yank some det-cord free of the C4 it was intended to detonate. That would be just his fucking luck ...

Tires screeched.

The sound of a Humvee roaring up, then the overused brakes squealing.

Wilson was frozen under the bridge. He could hear Tim saying something, but even as he strained, he couldn't tell what it was. He could tell that Tim's blood was up. He could tell that there was urgency there and it made Wilson want to just grab that rope, get up top, and get him and the group to safety. Fuck it. He would rather fight on the run than die for the goddamned bridge.

Sorry, Lee ...

The voices on the top of the bridge became suddenly silent, as though they too were listening to something.

In Wilson's straining, the blood rushing past his ears, and the steady, omnipresent sound of the water flowing underneath him, he almost didn't catch it. But then a short, sharp bark echoed up to him from down the river and it seemed to break through to him, and then he could hear it.

The muted roaring sound.

Like a tornado bearing down on them.

Tim's voice, yelling over the side of the bridge at him: 'Wilson! They're almost here!'

Shit shit shit.

Cut and run or stay? Cut and run or stay?

He realized his hands were still working. Shockingly smooth for how jittery he felt. All the rest of him was a live wire, twitching and sparking. But his hands seemed possessed by another, steadier man. He was working. Still working. Getting all the det-cords hooked up. And that seemed to be the impetus he needed.

I'm gonna get it done.

Two full cuts. Nice clean demolition.

Just keep working smooth and fast. Focus on the work. Not on how close they're getting.

Close. They were getting very close. So close that he could hear them, and he bet that if he took his eyes off his work and looked down the river, he would see them splashing around in the banks, slinging water around and swinging around the trees that lined the water, crazy, stumbling, apelike forms, running forward and then stopping to sniff the air, to sniff out prey.

'Don't look,' he told himself. His thoughts now coming out of his mouth. 'Don't look. Don't distract yourself. Focus, focus, focus . . .'

He looked.

And wished that he hadn't.

Dorian stared out the opposite end of the bridge, facing southeast – the direction they were coming from. And he could see them. Along the banks of the river. Very close. And he could see the whole woods rippling with them, the bare-bones forest seeming to come alive with strange, jerky movements.

He could hear them. He could hear the roar of thousands upon thousands of voices. A noise that he had never heard before. At least not like this. He'd seen crowds, and he'd been in crowded places, and in a way, it was the same sound. But he had never been in the presence of so many. And the noise was like a physical thing, pressing at him.

He ran to the other side of the bridge, pulling his rifle off of his back. He began pointing at people from his group, shouting to get their attention, and then he was pointing to the southern side of the bridge. 'Get everybody off the bridge! Get off the bridge!'

Lance Corporal Gilmore had a big roll of blue det-cord and was running with it. It pinwheeled in his hands and the det-cord unspooled after him, leaving a trail where he had run. Here at the bridge, the main line of the det-cord had been shoved into a crack in the bridge abutment to keep it steady while it was unspooled. Beside where the det-cord was hooked, the black rappelling rope was also hanging over the side.

Dorian went to it and hung his upper body over the edge, yelling down. 'Wilson! Hurry the fuck up!'

'I just got a few more bricks . . . '

'Fuck the bricks! You need to get out of there!' Dorian screamed, his voice going up with stress. 'They're almost on the bridge!'

Behind him, one by one, the vehicles roared away.

All but the LMTV to which that black rappelling rope was attached.

'Come on, Wilson! Just go with what you got!' Dorian looked down the bridge to the safe side – a relative term – his eyes following the line of blue det-cord. Gilmore was already off the bridge, heading for more distance. The vehicles passed him by, and then the last one slowed, and he hopped up onto the tailgate as it was still moving.

Dorian felt suddenly very alone. Very afraid. His courage was like a thread stretched between him and the others, and the more distance they gained, the more frayed and tattered that cordage became, and now it was breaking, and he realized that his hands were trembling.

From under the bridge, Wilson's voice floated up, only breaking through to Dorian because of the urgency that it held: 'I'm on the rope! Pull me up! Pull me up before Gilmore fucking blows this thing!'

Dorian looked down, could barely just see Wilson's form swinging out from under the bridge, the top of his head, the dark skin, the eyes looking up at him, expectantly.

Pull me up before Gilmore fucking blows this thing.

Dorian glanced to the far side of the bridge and nearly fumbled his rifle.

Where before there had only been concrete, now there was a wall of bodies, hurtling toward him, all of them running in great loping strides, their voices mixing together in a blood-freezing ululation. The one in front, the one leading the others, was tall and lank and dark-skinned. Even across the distance, Dorian could see the flash of the thing's teeth, gnashing in the air as though it could already taste flesh.

Holy shit.

Dorian fired his rifle. The percussion of that first round seemed to deepen his trance. The next three rounds Dorian didn't even hear or feel. He was one hundred percent focused on the lead infected, sprinting toward him and the bullets that he was lancing out there, and he saw in intimate detail like a close-up, slowed-down, instant replay as the projectiles pierced the man's lower leg, shattered the shin bone, rippled through the calf muscle.

The man faltered, that one leg going out from under him.

The next projectile hit him in the right side of his chest, perfectly square on so that Dorian could see the shock waves of flesh rolling out from the hole that was spewing bright red arterial blood. Dorian didn't see where the last two rounds were, because the man that was sprinting at him collapsed, face-planting into the concrete, and he never moved again.

Behind the fallen infected, at that wild and dangerous end of the bridge, in a land stripped clean by the hordes of infected like a ruined farmer's field after locusts, the roiling, animated woods, closed in on the road, choking the blacktop with gray bodies.

'Dorian!'

He looked over the edge, saw Wilson again.

Thoughts, very clear: *If I pull him up, I will not make it out of here. If I leave him there, he will be blown up by the blast, but if I try to pull him up, I will be overrun by the infected. It is just me. Just me. Just me and nobody else. And I will be overrun and I will die. And Wilson will die either way – blown up or eaten. I could save myself if I ran, but I'm not going to do that, am I? No I'm not. I can't do that …*

'Hey!' Wilson had his knife in his hand. 'Get off the bridge!'

Dorian fixated on the knife in horror. The edge hit the rope and started sawing. 'No, no, don't do that!' He reached out like he might grab ahold of Wilson, though the man was ten feet out of his reach.

Then the knife made it through the rope, and Wilson was falling.

EIGHT

FAULT

SNAKES SNAKES SNAKES.

Wilson thought as he fell.

He hit the water. For a moment, it didn't make it through his clothes and then all in a rush it struck every inch of his skin and it was frigid enough to seize the breath in his lungs.

First thought: *It's so cold I'm gonna die.*

Second thought: *Too cold for snakes.*

His boots touched the ground. Full-blown panic exploded the air out of his chest. He tasted muddy water. How deep did he have to be to touch the ground? Would he ever make it back to the surface? *Oh, God, not the river bottom I hate the river bottom I hate the river bottom I don't want to touch it I don't know what's down here what in the fuck is down here?!*

He clawed for the surface.

Silt sucked at his boots. Branches that might have been skeleton fingers or the teeth of crocodiles scraped his legs. Then he was free and he could feel himself rising – or at least hoped that was the sensation he was feeling. Maybe what he was actually feeling was all the oxygen being depleted in his lungs and him drowning, still caught beneath the surface of the river.

He had an image so clear that he thought it was real –

himself, thrashing around in the deep waters, dragged along by the current, never able to come up for air, being caught on a submerged tree, tangled up, dying there in the dirty brown water.

His hands hit cold air. Slapped the top of the water. Then his face and head broke, felt the water sheen off. He spat, then pulled in all the air he could handle. He opened his eyes to a watery smudge. His legs were pumping furiously to keep him afloat. He blinked rapidly to clear his vision and looked around him, twisting in the water. The bridge was maybe twenty yards behind him. He could make out the top of the last LMTV – driven by Dorian? – hurtling across the bridge toward the southern bank.

The current was quicker than it had seemed.

He could see the southern bank sliding past his vision with surprising speed. There was a lot of water between him and that bank. A lot of muddy, silty river bottom, and a lot of clawing, submerged trees. Something grabbed at his back.

He cried out, but simultaneously told himself *It's just another tree.*

He twisted to push himself away from it.

Wild eyes. A dozen faces. Barking, reaching, grasping.

A tree branch swept into his view and he reacted too late, too sluggish in the water. The ends of it lashed his head, scraping across his face from left to right. An infected stood on the bank, knee-deep in the water and closer than the others, grunting madly at him, and trying to hit him with the tree branch that it clutched.

Wilson backpedaled, splashing loudly in the water and seeming to excite the infected on the bank. They inched closer into the water while the one with the branch took another swipe at him. What was it doing? Trying to knock him out? Or hoping that it could pull him closer to the bank with the branch?

Wilson couldn't force himself to turn away from them, and he tried clumsily to backstroke away, but the current of the river was pushing him toward the infected, and now more and more were gathering at the riverbank, drawn by the excited calls and the sound of Wilson's panicked splashing.

Not this! Not this!

You should have stayed on the fucking rope!

It would have been better to be blown up!

He was only a yard or so out of their reach. His feet hit mud. Squished down to his ankles.

The branch came again. This time Wilson warded it off with his left hand, while his right groped for the pistol he had strapped to his leg. He feared pulling his feet out of the mud and trying to swim. He thought that there was no way he could outswim the current, and then he would be pushed toward the infected and he would feel them grabbing his feet and that would be the end of him.

Eaten alive. Eaten alive. Do you want to be eaten alive?

He found the pistol and ripped it out of its holster. It breached the surface in a shower of white water and his finger was already pulling the trigger. He had no idea where the rounds were going, but the infected on the bank reacted by drawing back, one of them pitching over backward, though Wilson wasn't sure if it was from one of his shots or not. He'd only seen them recoil from gunfire a handful of times. Perhaps their discomfort with the water was making his gunfire more convincing. Frankly, he didn't give a shit what the reason was. He had them going in the opposite direction, and that was all that mattered.

He lurched out of the mud and propelled himself away

from the riverbank, swimming as hard as he'd ever swum in his life. Just taking one big breath and not worrying about taking more. He plunged his head into the water and spun his arms as fast as he could, kicking his legs until they started to burn.

When he couldn't go any farther without taking a breath, he lifted his head out of the water, gasping and spluttering, river water pouring into his eyes. He looked over his shoulder as he swam wildly for the other side. He had gained distance, but not quite as much as he would have liked. The infected were still crowding on the bank, prancing around with irritation, like hunting dogs under a treed animal.

He was maybe halfway across.

His pistol was still in his hand as he swam. He thought about dropping it, letting the river take it, but he couldn't bring himself to let it out of his hand, no matter how cumbersome it made his swimming. He didn't even know how many rounds he had fired, or how many he had left in the gun. For all he knew it was empty and had just failed to lock back – which wouldn't be the first time.

Ahead of him the riverbank loomed, the trees seeming monstrous from his low perspective. Their roots were tangled and serpentine and Wilson didn't want to go near them. But to get to the other side of the river, you had to go through all those tree roots ...

The world seemed to heave.

The sound hit him like a physical wall.

There was a sharp pain in his ears, and then a fluttery, waterlogged sound, like everything he heard was through the walls of a shower stall with the pipes running. Instantly, the calm river turned to white water. Wilson could feel himself being rolled over.

Rollin' on the river, he thought dazedly. *Ro-o-ollin' on the river.*

His free hand shot out through the water and grabbed the first thing he could find. His fingers wrapped themselves around decades of scum and algae that sheathed a tree root. His hand almost slipped off, but he held tight, feeling his body still drifting the way of the river flow, like a wind sock hanging loosely by a thread.

I don't want to touch that!

But he wanted to be *rollin' on the river* even less.

He looked up, feeling the cold water dribbling over his mouth and lips. Straight in front of him, maybe two hundred yards away at the most, the bridge was obscured by a massive dust cloud. He swallowed tangy and odd-tasting water, then coughed and pulled himself closer to the tree, his eyes wide with shock.

Holy shit, he blew that thing when I was only a couple hundred yards away.

The dust cloud had grown legs, like it was some fat-bellied spider unfurling out of a ball. The legs seemed to grow slowly, reaching out for Wilson, but in that microsecond of observance, he saw that they were in fact *rocketing* out of the dust cloud, arcing out over the river – hundreds of smoky tendrils – and then slamming into the water like meteorites.

'Fuck . . .' He put his head against the tree, his face pressed into the rough bark and the slimy sheen of algae and mildew that coated it. It smelled like must and swamp rot. The arm that still clutched his pistol curled up and over his head, and he hoped none of these concrete projectiles found him and punched a hole in his skull.

Please be lucky. Be lucky for one fucking day in your life . . .

All around him bits of the bridge as small as pebbles, and

some as big as his chest, were hitting the water, creating a cacophony of watery noises – *spliff, sploonk, splash*.

Splish, splash, I was takin' a bath . . .

Please be lucky.

He opened his eyes, peering from underneath his sheltering arm. He could see a small portion of the river that stretched out beside him. He could see the chunks of bridge, still raining. And things moving through the water. Floating down the river – *rollin' down the river* – like pine logs heading for a lumber mill.

Arms.

Legs.

Whole bodies, in some cases. But mostly just the parts.

He looked up, toward the bridge, saw the dust cloud clearing. His eyes went to the water again, which was beginning to settle as the rain of shrapnel petered off. There were more logs rolling down the river. Lots of them. And on the northern side of the bridge, he could see the infected beginning to bottleneck, could still hear the roar of them

In the water ahead of him, a body rode the river languidly, feet first.

Are they dead? Are you sure they're all dead?

He pulled his arm from over his head, brandishing his pistol.

The body followed the river flow until it tumbled into the bank of tree roots just a yard or two in front of Wilson and something must have caught it there. Lazily, it began to spin around so that its head was facing Wilson, just a wide, horrific arc that brought a pale but not entirely dead face into view.

Maybe it was dead.

Maybe it was just the water that was making it move.

It seemed like the mouth was working, like the thing was

trying to catch its breath. Blood was flowing rapidly from nostrils and mouth and empty, hollowed-out eye sockets. The river water thinned it into trickles and rivulets. The whole body undulated. Squirmed.

Wilson forced himself upright and away from the body. He thrust his gun out and pulled the trigger. The gun fired twice, and then the slide locked back. Neither shot hit its mark. But Wilson was clambering for his feet. Beneath the soles of his boot there were slippery tangles of tree roots and more silty river bottom, but there was also hard clay. Still slick under the water, but at least his boots didn't sink into it.

He realized suddenly how horribly cold he was as he stood up out of the cold water into the cold air, felt the wind trying to pull the moisture off him, leeching his already lowered body temperature. He was trembling badly, to the point that his teeth were chattering.

Go. You need to get moving. Don't stop until you get back to the convoy.

What if they left me?

Don't stop moving until you get back to the convoy.

Unsteadily, he picked his way out of the tangle of tree roots and thanked God sincerely when his feet hit solid forest dirt and layers of fallen leaves. He stood for a moment, shaking violently, but so overwhelming glad to be on solid ground. Then he thought about everything else that was on solid ground and he wondered why he had been so afraid of the river.

He started moving again, one hand clenched against the cold, the other still clinging to his empty pistol.

Dorian slammed the LMTV into neutral and yanked the emergency brake. He could still feel his heart pounding in his chest and his hearing hadn't quite returned to him. Everything seemed to be surrounded by an angry hive of bees – a steady, thrumming, buzzing noise. His vision was even sparkling a little bit and he wondered how much damage the shock wave coming off that bridge had done to his brain.

What if Wilson was closer than I was? He had to have been closer.

What if he's dead?

Dorian was already pissed, but that one thought circling his brain didn't help.

He was in the red.

He threw his door open and swung down from the tall vehicle, immediately looking for Gilmore. Looking for the man with the detonator in his hand. He walked as only angry men walk: with his hands clenched into bloodless fists, and in long, stiff strides, his head canted down as though walking into a gale of wind.

What if he's dead?

What if he's dead?

Gilmore killed him.

It's Gilmore's fucking fault!

Dorian saw him, standing at the back of the truck that he'd hitched a ride in. He was still holding the detonator in his hand. A grim look on his face, still staring at the dust cloud like he was waiting for it to clear and for Wilson to miraculously come striding out of it.

'Hey!' Dorian barked. 'What the fuck?'

The anger was making that Brooklyn accent creep back into his voice. He'd moved away a long, long time ago, and never really had a desire to go back. But the voice of it was still there, waiting for a little instigation to come out and broadcast to everyone that *this guy's a yank.*

Gilmore glared up at Dorian. One foot pivoted back, blading his body as Dorian continued to approach, not slowing down. The detonator dropped out of his hands. It didn't require a lot of thought to figure out why Dorian was coming at him.

Gilmore held up one hand, palm out. 'Dorian,' he said in a warning tone.

The two bodies reached that distance, just within arm's reach, where you either go for it or you back down.

Dorian slapped Gilmore's hand out of the air and lunged for his collar. 'What the fuck were you thinking? You fucking killed him!'

Gilmore pulled back, but Dorian had already got his fingers into the fabric and twisted it up. 'Back the fuck off ...' Gilmore said, his left hand posted on Dorian's chest, his right cocked low at his side.

But Dorian was still screaming. Not listening. 'You didn't have to blow him up! You could have given it a minute! We could have fought them off long enough for Wilson to get back here!'

Gilmore's voice was strained. 'No, we couldn't. Not that many of them.' The two sets of feet shuffled back and forth, side to side, like some strange and violent parody of a waltz. 'I'm serious, Dorian ...'

Dorian shook him. 'Motherfucker ...'

Gilmore's left hand looped around fast, striking the top of Dorian's arms and raking them off his grip on Gilmore's jacket. Then his right arm came in hard and low, slamming into Dorian's midsection, doubling him over. Gilmore's left hand came around again, took the back of Dorian's head, and then the Marine just stepped back and applied downward pressure.

Where the head goes, the body will follow.

Dorian watched concrete coming at him and his hands shot up just in time to catch himself from face-planting. And then he was on his hands and knees. Still mad, but somewhat embarrassed, and mostly just waiting for the breath to return to his lungs. His eyes were watering, the same way they water when you vomit. Dorian gulped for air, but his diaphragm still wouldn't allow it. Through the blur of his watery vision, he could see Gilmore's dirty old boots, just a few paces from him.

Gilmore's voice, heated: 'I told you to back the fuck up, Dorian.'

Dorian coughed, and that seemed to do the trick. His lungs opened up.

Fuck, that sucks . . .

Gilmore was speaking, more evenly now. 'I saw him drop from the line. I gave it as long as I could, but if I waited any longer there would have been too many infected for us to deal with.'

'He was under the bridge,' Dorian croaked.

'What?'

Dorian sat up, stretching his core out. The ache in his gut was a dull reminder to control his anger level. Still, he glared. 'He was still under the bridge when he came up for air. And then I drove away and you hit the detonator less than a minute later. There's no way he was a safe enough distance away from that.'

Gilmore looked away, rubbing his forehead. 'I don't . . . I don't know what you want.'

Dorian felt hands grab him by the arms and haul him to his feet. He looked to his left and found Tim there, and the others beside him, standing with Dorian and staring at

Gilmore like an imaginary line had been drawn in the concrete and they were choosing sides.

Dorian pointed at him. 'This is your fault.'

'My fault?' Gilmore said, incredulously.

Dorian raised his voice again. 'If you motherfuckers would give us the help you promised, we wouldn't be in this fucking position! We're having to wire these goddamned bridges under the gun, having to rush, and now that shit's caught up to us! What would it take for Colonel Staley to take out a bridge for us? Just one! Just one to put us ahead of the game! How much would that really cost him?'

Gilmore took a step toward them, his arms spread out, face beginning to flush. 'You think I don't know that, you dumb fuck?' He pointed to the single stripe beside his name on the front of his chest rig. 'You know what that means? It means my opinion don't count for shit! It means a colonel don't have to listen to a goddamned word I have to say! You think Staley chose me because I'm some personal confidant and he trusts my opinion? Is that what you think? You're an idiot.'

Gilmore shook his head, made eye contact with all the remaining survivors of their little group, the corners of his mouth downturned, the picture of bitterness. 'I'm here because I was the only motherfucker that volunteered to come with you. *Jee-zus.*' He turned away from them and swore at the woods.

Dorian sucked the gummy saliva out of his mouth. Spat. *Shit.*

He could feel the anger fizzling out in a cloud of steam.

Like pissing on a fire.

Looking out at the woods, Gilmore's head canted to the side, like he was trying to see something through the trees.

His hand went to the rifle slung on his back and almost whipped it around, but then halted.

Dorian found himself watching Gilmore, rather than looking for what was in the woods.

The Marine seemed to relax again into his bitter resolve. He rocked back on his heels, then threw a hand out at the woods. He looked over his shoulder at Dorian and the expression was purely vindication. 'There's Wilson.'

It seemed like he'd wanted to add something to that, but held it back.

Dorian looked into the woods.

Sure as shit, there was Wilson, looking muddy and soaking wet, trudging through the woods and spilling great gouts of steam out of his mouth, leaving trails of it behind him. He had his pistol in one hand – slide locked back.

Dorian took off into the woods, meeting Wilson halfway.

Wilson huffed and leaned on Dorian, exhausted. 'Holy fuck . . .'

'Are you okay? Are you hurt?'

'What?'

'Are you hurt?'

There was momentary confusion on Wilson's face and Dorian realized that Wilson was momentarily deaf – or maybe more than just momentarily. Dorian put both hands on Wilson's shoulders and overenunciated his words. 'Are. You. Hurt?'

'Am I hurt?' Wilson shook his head. 'No, I'm not hurt. But I can't hear worth shit.' Dorian noticed that the man's voice was trembling. Noticed that his whole body was trembling, actually. His teeth were showing and they were chattering together.

Dorian put an arm around Wilson and they began walking for the road.

Up ahead, the group stood on the right, huddled close together.

On the left, Gilmore stood by himself, looking livid.

Wilson glanced at Dorian. 'What happened?'

'Argument,' Dorian said loudly.

Wilson shook his head, a little bewildered. 'Seriously?' Wilson began pulling his sopping jacket off. 'Well, get the hell over it. We're on the move to the next bridge as soon as I can get some dry clothes.'

NINE

SHADOWS

ANGELA WATCHED AS LEE SLEPT.

Sunlight pressed brightly at the office window, casting shadows over Lee's face. Whether from the probing light, or the pain in his head, or perhaps his dreams, Lee's face was crunched into a frown as he slept. His face, lean and tired and overworked. The thickening beard hid much of the wear, but his dark, sunken eyes told the tale. Even when they were closed.

His dreams seemed to her a curse. They always seemed to be nightmares. She could not remember the last time she had seen Lee sleep peacefully for longer than ten minutes at a time. Always, he would murmur, or twitch, or his legs would kick about. Sometimes his voice would become very loud, but she could never quite make out what he was saying. And his exhaustion was so deep that he rarely woke himself up.

Angela had never asked him to, but he had moved his bedroll to the office inside the Camp Ryder building, knowing that his constant vivid dreaming at night woke her and Abby and Sam. Just before Eddie Ramirez had tried to murder him, Lee had slept again in Angela's tent, trying to cling to some momentary comfort, because no one liked to sleep alone under skies so dark they seemed alien.

It was odd, she thought, but they had never been physical.

Is it really that odd?

Perhaps not. Even on nights when they reached across covers and touched the other's hand or arm, it had never gone further. That touch was simply the reassurance needed that there was another person in the dark with you. That you were not simply adrift in an empty vacuum, alone for eternity.

There was some part of her that wondered about it. Perhaps was even a little taken aback that Lee had not even made an advance – *God, that sounds pretty conceited* – but there also seemed to be an understanding between the two of them. An unspoken agreement that neither would make the leap without the other being ready for it.

Or maybe that was all in her head.

But it *seemed* that they . . . they *what?*

Ah, now what word to use?

Love was a bitter and unrealistic word for her. Love was for girls and boys, with flower petals to pluck. Love, outside of her mother's love for Abby, was something she refused to contemplate. It was built of obsolete things like 'romance' and 'passion.' It was some mythical thing she was passingly familiar with when she'd felt it fleetingly for a man who had been her husband, who had cheated on her, who had been infected, and in his raging insanity, had tried to murder her and her daughter. A man whom Lee had shot dead right in front of her eyes. Right in front of Abby's eyes, and it seemed the little girl would never forget that.

Jesus, how screwed up are we?

No, *love* was not the word, nor would it ever be.

What there was between them was . . . something inexplicable. Some deep, familiar comfort that they found in each other. Each seeming to shelter the other in the ways that they could. Propping each other up. Maybe an outside observer could ascribe some word to it that they thought was fitting. All Angela could do was itemize the things that she felt.

She felt fear when he was in danger. She felt relief when he came back alive. She worried about his injuries. She worried about his dreams. She felt glad when he seemed in high spirits, and she felt grim on days when he seemed quiet and cold – which was often lately. She felt restless on days when he withdrew. Happy when he came back. Though she had proven to herself and everyone else that she could handle herself perfectly fine, she still felt better when he was around. When he tossed and turned and groaned in his sleep, as he was doing now, she wanted to lay a hand on his chest, and she wanted it to be enough to still his disquiet.

And sometimes it was.

Most times.

Was there a word for the sum of those feelings? Probably. Definitely.

Actually, there were most likely many words to describe it.

But Angela chose none of them.

It simply *was* what it *was*.

She knelt down beside him and regarded him, somewhat blindly, perhaps. Not seeing the sunken eyes or the lids bolted shut, or the scrunched downturn of his mouth. The scraggly beard. The haggard face. The greasy hair. The scars. Rather, she simply saw a man who gave everything and kept nothing for himself. And she reached out and put a hand to his chest and hoped that it would give him something to cling to.

He was in the Hole.

He could tell. He knew it from the plush carpet under his feet. From the clean couch, and the soft, electric lighting, and the kitchen with the still-running refrigerator. He stood in the middle of the small living area, staring at the vaultlike door to the outside world. Staring at it with his heart pounding in his chest.

And he could hear something beyond that door.

Something crashing, slamming down that long cement hallway. He could hear the red emergency lights that lit the way exploding with a sharp *popping* sound as whatever was in that tunnel drew closer and closer.

'You motherfucker!' it shouted, muffled through inches of battened steel. 'Come back to the land of the living, you motherfucker!'

There is no land of the living. There is no land of the living. There is only the land of death.

The valley of death.

The valley of the shadow of death.

And I fear the evil, because it is a part of me.

He was naked. His hands groped for his rifle, his pistol, his knife – anything. But there was only the cold, bony skin of his own emaciated body. He tried to back away from the door, but his feet were rooted to the ground. His blood felt thick and viscous in his veins. Muscles frozen and uncooperative, like rusted machinery.

Whatever was in the tunnel had reached the door now, and it was pounding on the other side. But instead of holding, as solid steel should, the hatch was buckling and caving in like thin sheet metal. 'Open the goddamned door!' the manic voice screamed at him. 'Open the door and come back with me!'

Gashes in the steel opened, then yawned like many growing mouths. Fingers came through – the hands of dozens of people. They reached for him and their flesh parted under the rough-cut edges of the steel and blood poured out of them. The fingers and hands ripped and tore and pressed at the openings, forcing them wider and wider so that Lee could see dark shapes moving in the red light of the single remaining emergency light in the tunnel.

'Open the door and come back with me, Lee! Come back to where you belong, you murderous piece of shit!'

Lee took a breath to scream, but his teeth began to fall out, cluttering his tongue, dropping down into his throat like coins down a well. He spewed them out, gagged, and he could not find his voice.

A face appeared in the jagged hole that was directly in front of him. He knew that it was Father Jim, but even as this recognition pounded over him, nauseating and head-splitting, Father Jim pressed his face into the hole in the steel and his skin tore open along his cheekbones, pulling away and revealing bloody bone underneath.

Father Jim glared fiercely, wildly. 'You sinner! You sinner! You sinning piece of shit!'

Teeth still falling out, all Lee could do was cough and spit them to the ground at his unmoving feet.

'You wanna quote the Bible, you blasphemous son-ofabitch?' Father Jim's marred face screamed. 'Here's a psalm just for you: "The Lord has forsaken you, and you are in want. He maketh you to run like the hounded animal you are. Your still waters have turned putrid. You have lost your soul."'

More teeth than Lee could have possibly had were coming out of his mouth. Like vomit made of bones. They *clattered* out of him, piling up on the ground. If he could have spoken, what would he have said? Would he beg for mercy? Would he beg for the thing he would not give others?

'"Yes, you are walking through the valley of the shadow of death,"' Father Jim continued, voice booming and venomous all at once. '"And you will be terrified of the evil because it has pervaded every part of your sorry soul. You are alone, and no can save you. There is no banquet to be prepared, because everything you have has been taken by your enemies. Your head is anointed with the blood of others, and your cup is filled with shame."'

Lee could not breathe, and he collapsed to his knees.

The hands coming through the door were reaching, lengthening, and they grasped him now, pulling him toward the door. Toward doom. And the red light in the tunnel beyond was the glow of fire. And everything he smelled was the stench of death.

Father Jim's breath, impossibly close to his ear: "'Surely your violence and brutality will follow you all the days of your life, and when you are finally slaughtered like a dog, you will go straight to Hell forever. Amen."'

Lee woke up, air coming through his clenched teeth.

Angela was there. Her hand was on his chest. She was looking at him with concern, but also a bit of a tensed look, like she was trying not to show pain. He looked down and saw that he was holding her wrist in a death grip.

He released her, all at once sitting up and folding himself up against his knees.

Relief. That the dream was over, and also that the agony in his head had dissipated. Like the headaches were some physical manifestations of bad things wanting to be excised. Pressing to make their way out of the cellar and into the house.

After a few breaths, Lee rubbed his face. 'I'm good. Headache's gone.'

Angela nodded. 'What was the dream about?'

Lee shook his head. 'Nothing. Didn't really make any sense.'

'Oh.'

The naked feeling would not depart, though. Lee found himself looking to make sure that his rifle was still lying on the ground beside his bedroll. His knife still strapped to the belt around his waist. He relaxed and let his head fall backward, staring at the ceiling. His neck muscles stretched in a way that was painful but also wonderful.

The window in the office showed a cloudless blue sky.

He looked around and realized Deuce was not with them. Lee didn't bother asking where the dog had gone. Deuce was given to bouts of patrolling. Like the dog had some internal clock that forced him to run the perimeter of wherever he was at. Lee knew that he had probably slipped out of the room when Angela had entered, and was out in Camp Ryder, trotting the beaten path along the inside of the fence. Smelling for danger. He would return in his own time.

Angela sighed. 'When are we gonna talk about what's going on with you?'

'What's going on with me?' Lee thought he sounded convincing enough.

Angela raised her eyebrows. They stared at each other for a while. But Lee was ceaselessly stubborn in ways that Angela was becoming intimately familiar with. Some of them were good, making him reliable, steady, loyal, honorable. But other times he could tell it truly bugged the shit out of her that getting the truth out of him was like wringing water from a rock.

'Okay.' She slapped her thighs. Settled back against the wall and crossed her feet out in front of her. She pulled her blond hair out of her face and pinned it behind her ears. 'You don't want to talk about what's going on with you.' She held up a hand, index finger protruding. 'I'll just say one thing and then we'll move on.'

Lee nodded. 'Say it.'

'It's eating you alive, Lee.'

... it has pervaded every part of your sorry soul ...

Lee forced a smile that came up grim and sullied. He took her hand in his, holding it tight. 'It's my problems, and no one else's. Not you or Tomlin, or Abby or Sam. Just me and mine. And I won't pawn them off on anyone else. Period.'

Angela's jaw stuck out. Clearly she wanted to say more, but she had promised one thing to say, and she had said it. She looked down at the ground, as though resetting the conversation. When her eyes rose again, the expression on her face was more neutral. 'Camp Ryder, then.'

'Camp Ryder,' Lee echoed.

'Bus is dead. Jerry is dead. Mr. Keith is dead.' She raked a single fingernail along her right eyebrow. 'Camp Ryder needs a leader. And this isn't an accusation, Lee, but you and Tomlin haven't exactly been there over the last few days. I don't think either of you have said anything to these people outside of closed-door meetings up here.'

Lee's tongue touched a patch of flaking skin on his lower lip. 'You asking me to step up?'

'You. Or Tomlin.' She nodded vehemently. 'Everybody feels like we're just floating in the breeze right now. I mean, I know that you're distracted with the mission to blow the bridges and making sure everything there goes off, but there's still *these* people *right here*. If you don't have the time for it, maybe Tomlin needs to be the one to step up.'

Lee tilted his head. 'Angela, me and Tomlin aren't going to lead Camp Ryder. You know that, right?'

Confusion. 'What? What do you mean?'

'That's not what we do. We're not supposed to come into

groups of civilians and take them over. That's not what the mission ...' He trailed off, his mind catching up to his mouth.

'Lee, there is no mission anymore. You said so yourself.'

He took a deep breath. 'The point remains the same, though. We're not taking over Camp Ryder. We're not taking over leadership of anyone. We're here to help. I was here to help Bus, and I'll be here to help whoever else takes control. But it's not going to be me.'

'Lee ...'

'What about you?'

'Me?'

'Yes,' Lee nodded. 'What about you?'

'Leading Camp Ryder?'

'Yes.'

'No.' She gave a violent shaking of her head. 'Come on, Lee. Half these people don't even know me.'

'And yet you talk to them. They talk to you. You have your finger on the pulse of the camp. You just said yourself how everyone was feeling. How'd you come across that information, Angela? Mind-reading?'

Angela couldn't really refute what Lee was saying, but she wasn't able to accept it, either. 'No. No way. I can't do that. I got other things to worry about. I can't ... I mean ... I just can't.'

Lee stood up laboriously, taking his time. 'Angela, whether you like it or not, you're already doing it. If you didn't say another word about leadership, in a week, you'd be the "unofficial leader" of Camp Ryder. Give it a month, and you'd be just like Bus. No one ever chose him to do the job. He fell into the role.'

'And someone hated him so much that they killed him in cold blood over it.'

That gave Lee pause.

'We could . . . ' Angela seemed to be calculating something. 'We could hold an election.'

Lee's immediate gut reaction was *hell no*. He didn't want this opened up to an election. God knew what sop they would elect if given the chance. He didn't want just any Joe Schmoe in Camp Ryder to suddenly be running it. He wanted someone he trusted to run it.

Angela was good, Angela was solid, Angela had the trust of the people of Camp Ryder more than she knew. And Lee was comfortable with her. He could deal with her. And she respected the things that he needed to do. What if someone else came in, and became another Jerry? Another proponent of sequestration, cutting Lee off at the knees . . . ?

Cutting you off from what, Lee?

From your mission? Your nonexistent mission?

So what if the next guy doesn't want to expand. Doesn't want to go out there and meet other groups of survivors. You don't have supplies to give them, and even if you did, would they want to be a part of what you've started? Directly opposing the acting president of the United States of America?

It was all academic anyway. He did *not* have the supplies. There was no reason for him to gather other groups of survivors. If someone else took control of Camp Ryder, Lee would be little more than a military advisor. Perhaps he would train volunteers to act as a military arm of the camp. But he could not support anyone.

'Okay,' Lee said, slowly. 'Do you think that's the best option?'

Angela considered it for a moment. 'Yes. I do.'

Lee finger's combed his beard and he was about to speak, but a knock at the door held any further conversation.

Lee regarded the door with some slight irritation, as

though the inanimate object were responsible for the interruption. He glanced at Angela and said quietly and quickly, 'You've got your work cut out for you on that, Angela.' Then he turned back to the door. 'Come on in.'

The doorknob rattled, almost hesitantly. Like it had sensed his irritation and wanted to cut its losses. But the door swung up anyway, somewhat slowly. At first he had thought that it would be Tomlin at the door, but even just the character of the way the door opened told him this was not the case.

The person that stood in the door made his whole body clench.

Then the ghastly expression on the person's pale face made his stomach plunge.

'Jenny.' Lee's voice was low.

She stepped through the threshold, both hands clutching a notebook. Jacob's notebook. The one that Lee had given her for some interpretation because he couldn't wade through the language of Jacob's medicalese. Her gait was stiff. Her whole body tense. Her countenance beaten.

She shook the notebook. 'I read it.'

Neither Lee nor Angela said anything.

She took two more paces into the room and extended the notebook out to Lee like she just wanted to be rid of it. He took it from her, and then her hands retreated to the pockets of her jacket. Her eyes remained on the notebook until Lee turned and tossed it onto the desktop.

The sound of it slapping down seemed to wake her up. 'You want Captain Tomlin in here for this?' she said, hollowly.

Lee's jaw clenched.

Angela spoke up. 'I'll get him.'

TEN

NOTES

THE FOUR OF THEM STOOD in the office of the Camp Ryder building. A place where bad news had been traded many times before, with Lee in the exact same position: standing there with his arms crossed over his chest, staring at the dirty linoleum floor. The peeling sides. The dingy, worn-out blacks and whites. An image synonymous in Lee's eyes with the hard, knotted feeling in his innards.

To his left and right were Angela and Tomlin. Angela had taken a seat on one of the folding chairs that inhabited the room. Tomlin leaned on the wall, near the door, his hands clasped behind his back. In the center of all of them, Jenny had also taken a seat, but she seemed more relaxed than the others. Not in the sense of being at peace, but relaxed as you are when you concede defeat.

Jenny folded her hands in her lap. Looked up at Lee and seemed bitter and old and used up. 'You already know what the notebook was about, right? Why Jacob was keeping it?'

'It's his notes,' Lee said, a guessing tone to his voice. 'About the infected he had captured.'

'The pregnant one?' Tomlin asked.

Both Lee and Jenny nodded.

Tomlin's foot wiggled. 'I was under the impression that he had killed her before he left the hospital.'

'He did,' Lee said.

'Then why are we worried about his notes on her?'

'Because he told us to.' Lee rubbed the corners of his eyes. 'He clearly felt that there was something in the notebook that held bigger implications for us. But I couldn't make out some of the stuff he was talking about. I figured Jenny, with her medical background, might be able to translate.'

Tomlin made a dubious face.

Jenny cleared her throat. 'Over the course of the week or so that he was studying her, he recorded daily – sometimes twice daily – her vital signs, as well as those of the ... baby.'

Lee grunted at the use of the word.

Jenny picked at her fingernails. 'He also made some notations about his previous research. Drew some conclusions based on what he'd found at the onset of the plague. It seems, from what I can tell of his writing, that he did not believe that a female who was pregnant before being infected could continue to carry a viable pregnancy after the onset of symptoms.'

Lee and Tomlin both frowned at Jenny.

She clarified. 'Back in June when all of this happened, he recorded incredibly high temperatures in subjects dealing with the onset of symptoms. It screwed with their metabolism in a way that he wasn't really able to explain. Or didn't bother explaining in his notes. A pregnant woman who runs a fever that high – I'm talking about fevers high enough to cause brain damage – is at a very high risk of losing her pregnancy. Add in the factors of the hyperactivity, violent behavior, and ... the things that they eat ... and it's highly unlikely that a woman pregnant prior to being infected could carry that pregnancy to term. There would just be too much going on in her body for the fetus to be able to adapt.' Jenny wet her lips. 'In Jacob's opinion, it was so unlikely that he called it "virtually impossible" at several points in his notes.'

'Okay,' Tomlin said, hoisting himself off the wall. 'So the female subject he captured got pregnant after the infection. I don't think that's too hard to believe. It seems like these infected are forming small colonies. They still have the instinct to hunt, gather food, protect themselves. It stands to reason they would have the instinct to procreate.'

'Yeah.' Jenny nodded. 'That's all very true.' She leaned forward, put her hands in her pockets. 'But if you accept that it's a *virtual impossibility* that the subject Jacob had captured was carrying a pregnancy from before the infection, then you're basically forcing yourself into a different fucked-up conclusion.' Jenny looked briefly angry as she said this. 'The fetus's heart rate was sitting steady at about a hundred and fifty beats per minute. He notates that this is high for what he assumed was a three-month-old fetus, but not outrageous given the possible fetal stress, and taking into account biological changes that the plague might have caused. But one of the last tests he did was due to the subject showing some vaginal bleeding. He did an ultrasound, took record of the heart rate – still around one-fifty – and he measured the fetus, which he hadn't been able to do before. He recorded the fetus as approximately fourteen inches long.'

Jenny stopped there.

Lee looked at her, couldn't quite read her expression but could see that he was supposed to draw some sort of conclusion from it. Then he looked at Tomlin, saw the same confusion on the other man's face that he suspected was on his own, and turned his gaze to Angela, who was apparently the only other person to understand what Jenny was driving at. Her hand was covering her mouth. Eyes sharply narrowed.

'What?' Lee asked. 'What does fourteen inches mean?'

'That's a six-month pregnancy,' Angela said flatly.

'Soooo ...' Lee extended an index finger, as though he were trying to connect two dots that he couldn't quite find. 'The fetus was conceived before the infection?'

Jenny looked noncommittal. 'If you call the pregnancy survival during the high-grade fever of initial infection a *virtual impossibility*, then no. Jacob cites in his notes that vaginal bleeding is possibly indicative of the subject's womb unable to keep up with the fetal growth. And the fetal heart rate ...' Jenny trailed off, rubbing her temples, then raking her hair behind her ears with a suddenly unsteady hand. ' ... Well, he calls it *abnormal fetal growth rate.*'

Tomlin bit his lower lip and hissed air through his teeth, making a steady *fffffffff* sound.

Angela's voice was clinical. 'If you accept that a pregnancy wouldn't make it through the infection, then you have to accept that the subject got pregnant sometime in the last three months, four if we're being generous. Which means the baby she has is twice the size that it should be.' She pressed her fingertips together until the knuckles were white. 'Is there any reason to believe that this is pervasive among all pregnant infected? Or is this just some freak, isolated incident?'

Tomlin nodded in agreement. 'Maybe he just happened to grab the one infected lady that was gonna have a giant fucking baby. Could be a deformity.'

'Could be,' Jenny said stiffly.

Lee said nothing. His gaze was somewhere else because he wasn't there at that moment. He was standing in a dark room, acrid smoke boiling around him, ears ringing from a grenade blast, looking at the silhouette of LaRouche going deeper and deeper into the room. And then he was looking down at the bodies. The torn-up, bloody bodies.

Swollen, pregnant bellies.

LaRouche, gut-shooting them, one by one, with a blank look of apathy on his face.

And Lee was thinking, *Is this what three months pregnant looks like?*

The bellies were terribly large in his memory. Stretched tight like they were already on the cusp of giving birth. But maybe that was just his memory, hyperbolizing the things he saw, distilling them down to their essences.

Or maybe that was just how the bellies on those dead bodies had looked. Because they were all three months pregnant with a six-month-old fetus. Because every damn one of them had *abnormal fetal growth rate*.

'There's just ...' Tomlin was saying, his voice tight. 'There's just no fucking way, you know? There's no fucking way we're seeing biological changes in these things. They're just people. Just sick people. Gone crazy. Sick, crazy people. That's it.'

'That's bullshit,' Lee said without much emotion in it. He looked at Tomlin. 'They've already changed. Their metabolism changed. Their physical abilities changed ...'

'That just how crazy people are,' Tomlin said. 'Like people on drugs. They can push their bodies harder than the rest because they're mentally disconnected.'

'How do you explain the hunters, then?' Lee quirked his eyebrows. 'You gonna sit there and tell me they're not physiologically different? Hell, they even look different.' Lee shuddered, thinking of the small but obvious ways they seemed to have changed. The way their fingers seemed more clawlike, their jaws just a little wider than they should have been. 'We've seen them climb walls. Jump shit they shouldn't be able to jump. Run faster than they should be able to run.'

Tomlin wasn't convinced. 'It's just mental disconnect.'

'It's unnatural,' Lee said, stubbornly.

Tomlin pointed a finger at him. 'So you want me to believe that a bacteria is causing genetic mutations in the span of three or four months?'

'I don't need to ask you to believe it,' Lee said, his voice rising. 'It's already been proven. Jacob said their metabolism was jacked up in ways he *couldn't explain*. In a modern fucking laboratory, in a CDC research facility, surrounded by a team of scientists, they couldn't explain what the bacteria was doing to these people. The question now isn't whether it's possible – we know it's fucking possible, because it's been observed! The question now is how far do these changes go? Jacob recorded subjects' bodies burning through almost twice the calories they should normally be eating and still losing weight. Is it that far of a stretch to say their bodies are growing or changing more rapidly? That a fetus would grow more rapidly?'

'So you think this isn't isolated,' Tomlin said.

'I'm saying we shouldn't dismiss the possibility.'

'Okay.' Tomlin held his hands up. 'Let's go down the fucking rabbit hole here. Let's say this is pervasive. Let's say every pregnant infected huddling in those dens has' – he searched for the words – '*abnormal fetus growth*, or whatever. What are the chances of them actually carrying to term? Having a live birth?'

Jenny fielded the question. 'Well, the subject that Jacob had was showing some vaginal bleeding. Which is never a good sign in a pregnant female. It shows there's some sort of stress there – fetal stress, or system stress. Like I said, Jacob believed it was indicative that the female's womb was unable to keep up with the growth rate of the child.'

'So this thing grows so big the female's body can't hold it, and she miscarries.' Tomlin raised his eyebrows, as though searching for affirmation that this was indeed a possibility.

Jenny shrugged again. 'Maybe. There's no telling. Vaginal bleeding is just a bad sign. It doesn't necessarily mean that the pregnancy is doomed. Plenty of women show some bleeding during pregnancy and don't lose their baby.'

'Humor me here,' Tomlin said. 'The thing keeps growing, and let's assume Jacob was right assuming that the female's body can't keep up. Eventually something is going to give and that things is coming out, right?'

Jenny nodded, a little unsure.

'So does it die because it's birthed five months too early? Does the female die? Do they both die?' Tomlin looked briefly hopeful. 'Maybe they're all just ticking time bombs. Maybe this whole issue will just solve itself.'

'I don't think we're dealing with gigantism,' Lee said. 'Meaning that I don't think the faster growth rate of the fetus – if it is actually pervasive among the pregnant females – means that it's going to be a larger ... specimen. Maybe it's just *maturing* faster.'

'Maybe it's the gestation period that has changed,' Jenny added. 'Maybe it's shorter in infected females.'

'Like animals,' Angela said.

'Like animals,' Jenny agreed.

'Okay.' Tomlin shook his head. 'We seem to be accepting a lot of theory as fact here.'

'You said you wanted to go down the rabbit hole,' Lee pointed out.

'So where's it end?' Tomlin asked. 'What's all of this mean for us?'

'Well, if it is like Jacob seemed to think it is, then I'd say the infected are not only propagating, which was bad enough, but they're doing it in half the time that they should.' Lee didn't quite know what to think, bouncing back and forth between *this is complete bullshit* and *what if it's possible?* 'And if they're growing and changing that fast, then you might reasonably assume that whatever the fuck comes out of that pregnant female will continue to mature faster. Possibly becoming a threat a lot sooner.'

'We need to figure out a way to deal with this,' Angela said suddenly, her spine straightening as she looked back and forth between Lee and Tomlin. 'Whether or not Jacob's theory holds true, this needs to be handled. Maybe we need to start hunting these dens . . . '

'We're overextended as it is,' Lee said. 'Most of the people I would trust to get that job done are already working on keeping the northern hordes from crossing into North Carolina.' He looked at Angela. 'I agree. It needs to be dealt with. But until we get some more manpower and equipment, we just can't foot the bill right now.'

Angela looked like she wanted to say more, but then seemed to become thoughtful. Rolling something over in her mind. She was inspecting the low-bitten nail of her index finger.

The next voice to fill the silence was one Lee hadn't expected to hear.

The radio cracked, hissed, and the voice spoke with urgency: 'Harper to Camp Ryder. Anyone monitoring?'

Harper half-stood, half-sat in the passenger seat of his Humvee, glaring out to where the winding driveway of the mansion disappeared into looming trees. Beyond that, the small town of Eden. And inside the small town, bad things. Many, many bad things.

He felt tweakish. His stomach jumping and jittering. His legs wouldn't stay still. His finger kept tapping on the handset he held as he waited impatiently for some sort of response. It was just him and Sergeant Kensey there. Everyone else was inside the mansion. 'Mingling,' possibly. More likely staring at each other like two cliques vastly opposed.

It's bullshit. It's fucking bullshit.

Kensey was also waiting for a response, but he was communicating with someone very different, and he displayed much more patience than Harper. Kensey held a satellite phone, the only method of communication between him and Camp Lejeune, where his command was centered. He had spoken very briefly a few moments ago and had since been silent with a blank look on his face.

On hold, was Harper's best guess.

Harper took a short, frustrated breath and was about to key up again to speak when his own radio speaker crackled and spoke.

'Harper.' It was Lee. 'You got me. Go ahead.'

'Lee,' Harper almost burst. 'Dammit, I got some bad news. Mostly. Mostly bad news, but possibly some good news. Or at least a fix.'

'Okay, buddy.' Lee's voice was cautious. 'Slow down and explain.'

'You know the squad that Colonel Staley promised us?' Harper caught a sharp glance from Kensey. He took a pause to gather his thoughts and choose his words more carefully. 'They arrived today. But ... *unfortunately* ... they weren't authorized to help us blow the bridges.'

Silence.

Silence for a long, uncomfortable minute.

Kensey was staring at the radio speaker in Harper's Humvee now. Harper wouldn't have characterized the Marine's expression as 'concerned.' More like he was just curious what the response was going to be, and was expecting it to be loud and full of expletives.

Instead, Lee's voice was focused and careful. 'Did they tell you why?'

'Apparently Staley doesn't want to commit resources until he's met you and given your plan his stamp of approval.' Harper bit the inside of his lip and wondered what was going on in that dark little office inside the Camp Ryder building. Was Lee cursing a blue streak on the other side of that radio transmission? Or was he just staring at the radio with his head in his hands, trying to figure out what the fuck they were going to do next?

When Lee did speak, his tone was clipped, his voice somewhat strained. 'Well, did they give any sort of idea of when Colonel Staley was going to be able to' – here his voice rose in volume – 'make time for us?'

Unbelievably, Kensey smiled when he heard this. Like it was a mildly funny joke.

His eyes don't smile, Harper noted. *Just his mouth.*

'Well,' Harper said, looking right at Kensey, 'apparently there's been some lack of solid intelligence on what's going on up north. So I showed them, and now the sergeant over here is trying to make contact with his command to relay the situation and hopefully light a fire.'

'So how much time do we have, Harper? Because it didn't sound like we had a whole lot last time I spoke with you. And now we're facing another fucking delay.'

Harper took another deep breath. 'No, Lee, it's not looking good. They came across last night – not all of them, but enough that it's gonna be a real bitch to try to take down the bridges in the center of town. Most of them are still on the east side of the river, but I think the forage is drying up over there. We keep seeing more and more of them showing up on the east side of town every day.'

This time Harper could almost hear Lee's voice, like he was in the office with him: 'Fuck, fuck, fuck … this is not good, Harper. Not good at all.'

But instead, Lee just said, 'That's our bottleneck, Harper. It's our pinch point. If we lose that city and can't close it down then it's just gonna make our job twice as hard and twice as dangerous when the hordes start hitting the gap.' The irritation in Lee's voice ratcheted up. 'Is the sergeant there with you now? Can he hear what I'm saying?'

Harper looked at Kensey, but then he straightened and his attention went elsewhere. Harper could hear the sound of a voice coming through on the satellite phone, barely audible to Harper. Kensey immediately turned away from Harper and faced the opposite direction.

'Yes, sir. It's Sergeant Kensey, sir.'

Harper hit the transmit button again. 'Hey, Lee, stand by for a second. The sergeant is speaking with his command right now.'

Silence on the radio.

Silence as Harper waited, like a guilty man waiting for the verdict to be handed down by the foreman of the jury. He realized his mouth was open and he closed it. Kensey huddled close to the mouthpiece of his phone, like he was trying to be discreet, but Harper could hear every word he said. He just couldn't hear what was said back.

'Situation is that I don't think they were exaggerations.'

Pause.

'No, sir.'

Pause.

'From what I can tell, the estimates are accurate and the concern is legitimate ... Yes, sir ... I would characterize it as urgent ... Within a day, tops ... That's up to you, sir. I'm just relaying what I've seen ... Sir, I think it's as good as any. And I'm not coming up with anything better off the top of my head ... Yes, sir. Standby.'

Kensey didn't disconnect the phone. Instead, he put it to his shoulder and turned to face Harper. 'Colonel says he wants to meet. Is that your man on the radio?'

Harper nodded, then keyed up. 'Lee.'

Lee's voice: 'Go ahead.'

'Colonel Staley has found some time for us.'

ELEVEN

RISK AND REWARD

TOMLIN WAS NOT HAPPY. He stalked alongside Lee, his hands out of his pockets and swinging with his rapid steps. Lee wasn't walking particularly fast, but he was walking with purpose, and he had a longer stride than Tomlin, despite the hitch in his gait.

'This is dumb,' Tomlin said, point-blank. 'Dumb, and I don't like it.'

The Camp Ryder building was behind them. Their footsteps were crunching through gravel. The sunshine felt good on Lee's face, but the air was still cold and he could still see his breath, even at this midday hour. Ahead of them lay Shantytown, the collection of ramshackle huts that sprawled out in front of the Camp Ryder building. There were more of them now than there had ever been. During the assault on Camp Ryder, and the subsequent attack from the infected hunters, several of the shanties had been destroyed. Now they had either been rebuilt or repaired. Old Man Hughes and his dozen or so folks from Dunn had moved back in to Camp Ryder for the time being – Lillington would have to remain abandoned for a while.

There was also a group of a dozen or so that had been with Jacob. A week or so ago, they had fled an attack on them from the Followers, met with LaRouche as he was going east, and were advised to try to make contact with the Camp Ryder Hub at Smithfield. Of course, this had been before the Camp Ryder Hub was broken apart by Jerry. And when that group of refugees reached Smithfield, they didn't find a welcome party.

What they found was a doctor that turned them away at the point of a gun.

And a 'kind of crazy-looking' scientist that 'stood up for them,' though the leader of that group – Brett was his name – didn't explain what that entailed. Just implied it with a grim look. In Lee's conversations with Jacob, he got the impression that Doc Hamilton and his two thugs had been killed, and Lee suspected that Jacob had done it.

'You've already voiced your concerns,' Lee said to Tomlin, keeping his tone even-keel. 'I get it. I do. But I'm fresh out of options right now, Brian. If everything goes perfectly, there's still a good chance that we're fucked in the long run.'

'Then why risk it?' Tomlin groaned. 'It's unnecessary!'

'No, it's completely necessary.' Lee stopped and looked at Tomlin. 'Our window of opportunity is closing pretty fuckin' quick, man. And once it's gone, it's gone. Then we're fighting a whole different battle, and' – Lee lowered his voice – 'it's one I don't think we can win.'

Tomlin digested that, but still didn't seem entirely convinced.

Lee pushed on. 'A few days ago you were all about getting Colonel Staley's help. Now he's offering to meet and you're blowing your fucking lid.'

Tomlin rolled his eyes and made a frustrated noise. 'He's offering to meet. After he has failed to give us the assistance that he promised us, which I think should at least make you question his trustworthiness. Now he's choosing the place and time of the meeting, which he wants in a *third-party location*, outside of Camp Ryder.' Tomlin shook his head, resolutely. 'I don't like it.'

Lee ticked his points off on his fingers. 'First of all, he never promised us anything. We told him what we wanted, and he said he would try to help where he could, provided he agreed with our plan. Anything we read into that statement was our own fucking fault – he never said he was sending a demolition team, or even enough troops to help defend Eden while *our* people demo'd the bridges. Don't get me wrong, I'm just as pissed about this shit as you are. But would you commit your resources before you've even met with the man pulling the strings?

'And second of all, and most importantly . . .' Lee punctuated his words with his hands. 'We don't. Have. A choice.'

'There's always a choice,' Tomlin said, stubbornly.

Lee shook his head and started walking again. 'You're right. But I refuse the other options. How's that?'

'What if he's in communication with President Briggs and the interior states?'

Lee thought about that for a few beats, but it was not like Lee had not already considered it. But in his considerations he had not been able to come up with a logical answer. Eventually, he just said quietly, 'It's a risk we're going to have to take.'

Tomlin half-sighed, half-growled. 'Fine. I voiced my opinion.'

'You did.' Lee glanced at him over his shoulder. 'By the way, there's something else you're not going to like.'

'What?'

They were interrupted by Devon, who jogged up to Lee's

side. 'Nate's on the way, and I told Old Man Hughes and Brett to meet at the Square. What's going on?'

'Just a bunch of shit,' Lee said.

'Oh.'

Tomlin nudged Lee in the arm. 'Hey. What are you talking about? Something else I'm not gonna like?'

Lee stopped again, motioned Devon to continue on to the Square without them. He turned to Tomlin. 'I've got something else I need you to be doing. For Camp Ryder. For everyone.'

'Lee . . . ' Warning tones.

'It's about survival of the entire state, which means survival for South Carolina, too.'

Tomlin closed his eyes. Swallowed heavily. Lee had struck the chord, which was exactly what he'd meant to do by bringing up Tomlin's once-upon-a-time responsibility.

Lee rubbed underneath his nose. 'We need to assume the worst. Let's assume we don't make a deal with Colonel Staley, or that his help comes too late – which is a good possibility right now. If that happens, we are going to lose Eden, our pinch point. The area between our blown bridges on the Roanoke River and the Appalachian Mountains is going to widen to an uncontrollable area of land. And the hordes will start slipping through that gap, and they will be too numerous to stop, spread over an area that wide. There's even a chance that if everything goes perfect and we still manage to hold on to Eden, we'll run out of munitions before the infected run out of bodies.'

Tomlin nodded, though he seemed hesitant to agree with anything Lee was saying at this point.

'We need more help,' Lee said simply. 'And Fort Bragg is thirty miles south of us.'

'Fort Bragg,' Tomlin said, like he was tasting the words.

Fort Bragg was a military base that Lee and Tomlin, as well as most members of the United States Army, were familiar with. Home of the 82nd Airborne, as well as US Army Special Operations Command, it was an infamous shit hole. Two hundred and fifty-one square miles of sand and pine trees, adjoining the city of Fayetteville, which was for the most part an old military town and had the same used-up look as all military towns.

'We've avoided it until now because I had Fayetteville categorized as a city too big for us to deal with right now. Which it still is, and the chances that there's a massive horde in there are strong. But Fort Bragg is right there, and there's also a chance that they mounted a good defense, and maybe even cleared Fayetteville.'

Tomlin just stared for a long moment, processing. His index finger and thumb found the corners of his mouth again. Wiped downward, slowly. Finally, he said, 'You're laying a lot of shit on me right now.'

Lee nodded. 'I know I am.'

They reached the fire pit in the center of the Square, around which was gathered Old Man Hughes, Brett, Nate, and Devon. They watched the two captains, the two old friends, the two onetime enemies, the two comrades in desperation.

'This conversation isn't over,' Tomlin said.

'I didn't figure it was.' Lee faced the gathering at the fire pit. Hitched his leg up on one of the cinder blocks that ringed it. 'We're meeting out here because I think some transparency would do us good. I think meeting in the office is a nice controlled environment, but it's also a great way to start rumors and have our people thinking that we're being shady.' Lee's

face looked drawn and serious when he said it, staring at the
ashes in the pit. Some small bones sticking up out of the ash.
White ash from the bones. Dark, greasy-looking spots where
flesh had melted and boiled.

They buried their dead, but they burned the bodies of the
infected.

'We can't afford another split like we had with Jerry,' Lee
continued. 'So it's transparency from now on.'

'Okay,' Nate said, speaking up first. 'So what do you need
from us?'

'Well.' Lee drew himself up. 'I've got a couple pieces of bad
news. No good news.' He looked at the men gathered there.
'And I'm gonna need some volunteers.'

The group remained silent, expectant. And after a moment,
Lee told them everything. He hid nothing. He told them his
suspicions, his interpretations of the data that Jacob had written in his notebook, as well as Jacob's own interpretations of
it. And he told them about the bad news from Harper and the
plan that wasn't going so well up north. The plan, the plan,
the one that was teetering so delicately on a razor's edge.
Looking less and less likely, though Lee kept his doubts to
himself. He was not there to open his heart and mind or
burden the people that followed him with the rancorous
doubts that he had day in and day out. He was there to relay
facts. And that was what he did.

Lee had his hands in the pockets of his jacket, his foot still
braced up on the cinder block. His eyes were locked with the
ashes in the pit in front of him. A set of three skeleton fingers
poking up from the grayish white miniature landscape.

'Colonel Staley has agreed to a meeting.' Lee looked briefly
irritated. 'I have no idea what Colonel Staley's mind-set is
right now. Whether he truly sees this as urgent or not. I would

hope that he believes it is urgent since he's trying to set up the meeting immediately ...'

You're editorializing.

Lee sniffed, then spat into the ashes. 'Anyways. The meeting is set to take place just outside of Mount Olive, which is a real small town just a few miles east of Newton Grove. We're already friends with the folks from Newton Grove, so it shouldn't be too hard for me to get to Mount Olive safely.'

Old Man Hughes's eyes narrowed. 'Forgive me, Captain. I ain't tryin' to do your job or nothin', but ... who decided on the location?'

Lee glanced momentarily at Tomlin, who was diligently avoiding eye contact with a secretive expression that said, *I told you so, you stupid sonofabitch.* Lee directed himself back to Hughes, feeling the back of his neck burning. 'Colonel Staley arranged the meeting place.'

'Why are we letting the guy we don't know decide the meeting place?' Hughes asked with some suspicion evident in his voice. 'Seems like we would want to err on the side of caution and be the ones to decide what happens where.'

'Yes,' Lee said, a little exasperation creeping into his voice. 'You're one hundred percent correct. However, that would be an ideal situation if we had anything to offer in this relationship. Essentially, anything that we get out of Colonel Staley is going to be a combination of charity and mutual benefit. He's the one holding the chips. Ergo, he calls the shots.'

'But we don't know him,' Hughes said, actually sounding a little confused.

'No we don't.' Lee drew his hands out of his jacket long enough to scrub them over his face. 'But I'm taking the risk anyway, because the options are limited, we desperately need what Colonel Staley has, and I don't think we have the time or the position to go into negotiations about this shit. We've got to take a leap of faith on this one. *I* have to take a leap of faith, actually.'

Tomlin broke in, almost stammering. 'You're going alone?'

'No.' Lee shook his head. 'It will be me and whoever volunteers to go with me. I only need a couple. Just enough to ride in the truck with me until we get to the meeting point.'

'Just a couple?' Tomlin asked. 'When he's probably bringing a whole goddamned platoon?'

Lee turned himself to Tomlin. 'He can bring whatever the fuck he wants. And frankly, no matter how many guys I take with me, if he decides to break bad, we're done. He's got air support, artillery, and a shitload more guns than we do. So if he wants us dead or captured, it's gonna fucking happen. Which is why I only want enough men to get me there safe. The rest is in his hands.'

'Whoo.' Hughes actually laughed, though it sounded humorless. 'You got a lotta trust, boy.'

'It ain't trust,' Lee said. 'But we are completely out of options. If he meant to put the screws to us by waiting to meet, then he succeeded, absolutely. We lose Eden? We lose a couple bridges over the Roanoke River?' Lee shook his head, the conclusion of disaster remaining unsaid. 'We're already the Dutch boy with our finger in the dike. We don't have the resources to plug any more holes.'

'I understand,' Hughes said, still doubtful. 'And if you need the help, you got me and however many of my people you need. I can speak for them right here and now. We're happy to help in any way that we're needed.'

Lee nodded, respectfully. 'Thank you. But I only need two

or three others. So, you plus whoever you want. I trust your judgment.'

Brett watched the exchange with some interest, words hanging just behind his lips. When Lee and Hughes seemed to be finished, he raised a hesitant hand. 'So what would you like the rest of us to be doing? Do you need anybody in reserve when you make that trip? You know ... waiting outside of Mount Olive in case things get bad?'

Lee shook his head. 'No, I need the rest of you to stay here.' The rest of his thought was left unsaid: *I'm not emptying out Camp Ryder again. I'm keeping a base of friendly folks here at all times. I won't let that shit happen again.* 'I may need a couple more of you for something else, but we'll talk about that at a later time.'

Brett nodded. 'Well. Anything you need, Captain. We owe Jacob our lives. And you.'

'There's plenty of work to be done.' Lee looked at Hughes. 'Talk with your people. Need them ready to go by tomorrow morning.' He turned to the rest of the men gathered there. 'I have some other things to discuss with Captain Tomlin, and then I'll be speaking with a few more of you.'

Devon half-turned away, then brought himself around again. 'Captain, are we going back to Harper's group?'

Lee considered it briefly, but shook his head. 'Not right now.'

Devon bobbed his head once. He exchanged a glance with Nate, and then the two of them set off from the fire pit, probably back toward Nate and Katie Malone's shanty, where Devon was laying his head at night.

Tomlin had his arms crossed, a perturbed look on his face. Always even-keel, Brian Tomlin rarely raised his voice, but though his expressions were usually subtle, he rarely made an effort to hide them, and to the friend that knew him, it was not difficult to read what Tomlin was thinking simply by the twist of his mouth, or the arch of his eyebrows.

'You wanna talk inside?' Tomlin asked. 'Or are we continuing with the whole transparency thing?'

'Nope.' Lee remained rooted to the ground. 'We'll talk here. Fuck it. Tired of sneakin' around.'

'Are you?' Tomlin had a little more bite in that comment than perhaps he intended.

Lee gave him a sharp look.

Tomlin met his friend's gaze, then his expression softened with a sigh. 'So ... Fort Bragg.'

'Yeah.' Eyes back to the fire pit. Then scanning around. 'Fort Bragg.'

'Do I get a choice?'

'A choice in what?'

'Whether or not to go.'

'Well.' Lee stretched his back. 'I don't outrank you.'

'But ...'

'But I would hope you see the merit in seeking out some additional help.' Lee said, plainly. 'As always, Brian, if you have a better plan, it ain't gonna hurt my feelings if you say so. This is the plan I have come up with. I'm not married to it, and if you've got a better way of doing it, then I'm all ears. But we need help. Even if Colonel Staley comes through for us, we're still going to need *more* help. If we're going to mount a united defense ...'

'Yeah.' Tomlin seemed to consider it for a few breaths. 'And you're not just talking about the infected, are you?'

Lee looked at his longtime friend and felt a tired ache somewhere down inside him. Like running a race with no idea how long it would last. Was it twenty miles? Fifty miles? One hundred miles? No one knew. And maybe it just didn't have an end. Maybe you would just keep running for the rest of your damned life and eventually die without ever having seen the finish line.

Or you could just drop out of the race.

Yeah … right …

Slowly, almost imperceptibly, Lee nodded. 'Yeah. You're right.'

Because there was no guarantee that President Briggs was going to leave them alone. Maybe stealing the GPS wasn't enough. And Lee just had to assume that eventually President Briggs would figure out that Lee was still alive. Still trying to resist the tidal wave coming from the north. Still trying to save these southeastern states from obliteration. And then what?

'No, I don't,' Tomlin said with reluctance.

'You don't what?'

'No, I don't have a better plan. You're right. We need allies. And you're right that I'm the best person to make those travels. But I'm not going out there alone. I did that shit before and I promised myself I wouldn't do it again. Almost died too many times.'

'How many people do you want with you?'

'Two,' Tomlin said with confidence. He'd clearly already considered the question. 'Two should be good. Enough to watch my back, but not so many as to be noticeable.'

'Who do you want?'

'Nate and Devon.' Again, with confidence. 'I worked with them a couple of times when we were hiding out near Lillington. They're solid.'

Lee nodded, considering whether or not it was better to send them with Tomlin or back to Harper. Tomlin needed the manpower and had chosen them specifically. Harper needed manpower as well, but in Harper's case, two bodies was hardly going to make a dent. Harper needed *real* manpower.

'Okay.' Lee pushed himself away from the fire pit. He turned so that the sun was on his face. He squinted, felt the warmth cover his skin, and for a fleeting moment almost smiled. 'Do you want to talk to them, or do you want me to do it?'

'I'll do it,' Tomlin said. 'When do you want us to move out?'

'As soon as you're ready. This is your op now.'

Tomlin flexed his fingers, blew warm air into his hands. 'Roger 'at.'

When Angela and Jenny made their way to the ground floor of the Camp Ryder building, they found it deserted. Usually there would be some people congregating at the tables that now stood where diesel trucks had once been stored and serviced. Perhaps it was the sunshine today that kept them outdoors – though the air was cold, the sun was warm enough that you could heat yourself up a bit by standing in it. Unlike the dark corners of the Camp Ryder building.

Angela slipped her hand onto Jenny's elbow and gently motioned for the far corner of the open main floor. They walked over and selected one of the abandoned tables, a weathered old wooden thing constructed like a picnic table. The wood was rough and cold when they sat on it, facing each other.

Angela wasn't sure how she felt. There were a lot of different things going through her head right then. But the baseline of fear was always there. Like a rule. She figured it never left her, but that she just became accustomed to it. She was inoculated to it, like an aching pain that just doesn't go away, but you just start to lose track of it because it's so constant. This is the gift of human adaptation. The changes had been swift and painful, but here was the approach of blessed homeostasis.

At least for her.

Some people were adaptable. Others, more brittle in their psyche.

And Angela feared that Jenny was one of those people.

Her eyes were dark and jittery looking. Like how Angela imagined an animal's eyes to be at the peak of the hunting season. She'd developed a nervous habit of rubbing and scratching at her neck, just beneath the collar of her jacket. She did it absentmindedly and when she moved a certain way that exposed her neck just above the collarbone, Angela could see bright red, irritated skin.

'Talk to me,' Angela said, folding her hands in front of her.

Jenny looked unfocused for a second. 'About what?'

'You. Greg. Anything you want.'

Jenny blinked at the mention of Greg's name. Her expression didn't exactly change, but it was as though every muscle in her face suddenly tightened. 'Why would I want to talk about Greg?' Her hand began to creep up to her collar. 'Why would I want to talk about that sonofabitch?'

Angela had no answer for her. She figured that Jenny probably knew why.

Jenny looked off, then up. Angela expected tears, but maybe those had been bled dry. Her eyes remained cold and dry. 'Greg.' She said it without feeling. Like a foreign word she did not know the meaning of. 'What can I say about Greg? Well ... Greg was a friend of Jerry's. Greg would sometimes come over to my place after his guard duty and we would fuck. Greg was a good manipulator. Greg would say whatever you wanted to hear to get whatever he wanted out of you. In retrospect, Greg may have been a sociopath.'

Her eyes found their dark way to Angela's again and in them was some sort of cosmic humor that Angela couldn't fathom. Jenny's hand had made it to her chest, her index finger rooting through layers of clothing like a weasel searching for a bug to eat.

'How's that for a eulogy?' Jenny asked. She leaned forward. 'If you're asking me how I feel about Greg ...' She seemed on the verge of revealing something. Letting something out. Like her hand was grasping a lever that would open floodgates. Then the look died. 'I've got nothing to say, Angela. And I'm not sure why you're even asking me about it. Seems like you have problems of your own you should be thinking about. Not trying to solve mine.' Jenny smiled and it looked bent to the point of breakage. 'My problems have already been solved.'

Angela shrugged, deflecting the offensive tone. 'If you don't want to talk, you certainly don't have to.'

Jenny just watched her. Unnervingly still.

Beneath her jacket, Angela felt goose bumps gathering.

Jenny's finger found her own flesh. Rubbed. Rubbed. Scratched.

Angela considered opening up in that moment, talking about the things that were bothering her. Leading by example, in a way. Maybe if she opened up to Jenny, Jenny would feel more inclined to open up to Angela. But looking into the other woman's eyes, Angela found something was not as it should be and then suddenly the concept of opening up to her seemed very disconcerting.

Jenny seemed to realize that the conversation – or the attempt to have one – was over with. She stood, her finger retracting from her collar so that her hand could push her up from the picnic table. She didn't immediately walk away, but instead held Angela's gaze for a while longer.

'I'm fine, Angela. Don't worry about me. I know exactly what I have to do. But you . . . you should open your eyes. Things aren't what they seem.'

Angela felt a flash of anger, though she wasn't sure why.

Stepping into dangerous territory, something in the back of her mind told her.

'How's that, Jenny?' she asked.

Jenny stuffed her hands into her jacket pockets and it seemed she was closing her gates. 'Oh, you'll figure it out, Angela. You're a smart woman. Smart and resourceful. You'll certainly figure out everything on your own. Once you quit lying to yourself.'

Angela couldn't help the anger leaking out this time. 'Lying to myself about what?'

Jenny turned and began walking away, and Angela didn't think she was going to answer, but when she'd gained a few paces of distance, she called a vague and flippant answer over her shoulder: 'About Lee, of course.'

TWELVE

PROOF

LaRouche was free, so it seemed. He had no ropes on his hands. He had no one covering him with an assault rifle. There was a guy with a rifle standing up in the pickup bed where LaRouche and three others were sitting, but it was unclear whether he was there to cover the four unarmed men, or whether he was just there as protection *because* they were unarmed.

The pickup truck was dark blue and old. Rust in the bed. Sounded like a cylinder was out of timing. They were the middle vehicle in a convoy rolling south through what LaRouche had to assume was Followers territory – no one seemed overly alert or cautious. It was interesting to him, but the infected seemed scarcer than usual. As the temperatures had continued to plummet, so had evidence of the crazed fuckers, running around naked. He thought about hibernation. Then he thought about exposure to the cold, and wondered what havoc it was wreaking on those packs and small hordes. Maybe that was why they'd seen so few of them. Maybe that was why this convoy proceeded so casually through the countryside.

The lead vehicle was a van, in which there were supplies. The rear vehicle was another pickup truck with more men in the back. LaRouche assumed that the others in the pickup beds were new recruits. They all had solemn, disastrous faces. They were all as filthy as he was. None of them spoke. LaRouche included. But between them all there seemed to be a tether. Some odd and unspeakable kinship that was found only in the doing of foul deeds. Because, at the end of the day, even when someone puts a gun up to your head, they can't force you to do anything you don't want to do.

Choices had been made. Each of the men in that truck had decided that they would rather kill friends and family than be killed themselves. And it stained them permanently, like each of them were marked with what they had done and recognized the same mark in others, somehow taking comfort from it. Because there was less shame when you could look around you and tell yourself, *See? All these guys did it, too!*

LaRouche was the exception, of course. No one had put a gun to his head and forced him to make a choice. No, he'd been the one pointing the gun. And he came to his decisions all on his own. He didn't need any help to be a filthy savage. Apparently that was just ingrained into him.

He recalled the muzzle flash in the complete blackness of the night. The way that it had illuminated Father Jim's face in that last, fleeting microsecond of his life. The expression that it bore ...

LaRouche tried to tell himself in his logical mind that there was no way Father Jim could have even registered the gun being put against his temple. Because LaRouche had pulled the trigger so quickly. There would not have been time for Father Jim to react. There would not have been time for him to look at LaRouche and show an expression. It was all impossible – Father Jim had been reaching for something, and then LaRouche had put a gun to his head and blew his brains out.

Simple as that. Nothing else to it. Father Jim hadn't felt a damn thing.

But sometimes in LaRouche's remembering of that microsecond as trigger released pin, and pin struck primer, and primer lit gunpowder, and gunpowder pushed bullet down a barrel, down, down, down a barrel and then through soft, thin layers of scalp, punching through skull and then into the jelly of the brain where it was *lights out, Father Jim* ... sometimes LaRouche remembered his expression being one of agony.

Other times it was an expression of betrayal.

Sometimes regret.

And the worst was when Father Jim's face strobed through LaRouche's mind and it bore a smile. Not a mean smile. Not a vicious smile. Just a smile. Like he'd heard a mildly amusing joke. Or maybe he was shaking hands with an old friend.

LaRouche found himself looking at the other men in the truck bed and thinking, *You're worse than they are. You're a worse human being. Because they had to be coerced into doing what they did, and you did it willingly. You are a sick fuck and you deserve what's coming to you.*

What exactly is coming to me?

Oh, I don't know. But karma's a bitch.

His gut burned. Bile and blood wrestling their way to the top of his throat. He didn't want to spew in front of the others. Instinctively, he knew that it could be bad to show weakness. Weakness would garner attention. Attention he did not want. So he kept swallowing, manically. Trying to lean his head forward in a way that would alleviate some of the uncomfortable roiling, acidic sensation hovering in his esophagus.

Time stretched in the back of the pickup truck. It was cold

and uncomfortable. The driver seemed to hit every pothole in the road, to the point that LaRouche would often look down and make sure that they were still even on a road. The wind roared over the cab of the pickup and it was the only thing that filled him until it was a hypnotic static that warped his perception of time.

By the time they reached the encampment, LaRouche almost felt a sense of relief. Then he thought about where he was and the feeling quickly faded. He had a general idea, but it was painted in broad strokes. There were four camps under Deacon Chalmers's command. Out of these camps the Followers launched their raids and took ground. The camps were made to be temporary and mobile so that when the raiding parties moved forward, the camps could pull up stakes and gain the ground. A leaping and bounding maneuver, so to speak. The camps stretched from north to south across North Carolina, and their slow, inexorable movement was west.

To LaRouche's knowledge, the camp that he'd been held at for the previous four days, the one that Deacon Chalmers had decided to make his headquarters, was the northernmost of the four camps. This one was the next one south. If he walked due west for long enough, he suspected he would run right into Raleigh. Or the clusterfuck that he was sure Raleigh had become.

Everything in this new camp was just as it had been at the last camp. The place was situated in a field that had once been cropped and now showed only some wheat stubble in the few places that it had not been trampled completely to dirt, or gouged out by tire treads. There were tents mostly, but some campers, too. Vehicles mixed in. Various types and colors, makes and models. Like some shitty used car dealership with a bad inventory and a bunch of squatters taking up residence in the middle of it.

When they came to a stop, the three vehicles in their little convoy began to unload. LaRouche stood and stretched. His muscles had taken on that stiff, achy jitteriness that seemed to poison them when his nerves were getting the best of him. The pain around his bullet wound smarted when he moved the arm, but he was surprised at how quickly it seemed to be healing. As he tried to stretch some normalcy back into his body, he looked to the pickup that was behind them and saw a familiar face getting out.

Clyde, wearing a thick black coat maybe a size too snug for him. His rifle slung on his back.

It was weird, but LaRouche felt better seeing him there.

They made eye contact and Clyde began to walk toward him.

Someone slapped the side of the pickup truck. LaRouche looked down and saw another man holding a rifle – not the one that had been in the bed of the truck with them – and he was looking up expectantly at LaRouche.

'You comin' with the rest of us, buddy?' the man asked.

Clyde reached the back of the pickup truck. 'I'll take care of this one.'

The man looked at him with some mix of confusion and suspicion.

'Trust me, friend,' Clyde said to the stranger as LaRouche swung his legs out of the pickup bed. 'You probably don't want to be anywhere near us right now. Deacon Chalmers sent us, and we need to speak to your commanding officer.'

The man actually took a step back. 'Uh ... '

'Perhaps you could point out where command stays,' Clyde said with a sigh.

It was obvious to LaRouche that accompanying him here had not been Clyde's idea, or his choice. Why Chalmers had sent anyone at all was a mystery to LaRouche. The impression that LaRouche had gotten from Chalmers was that he didn't really give a shit what happened to LaRouche.

How do you want me to do it? LaRouche had asked.

To which Chalmers had simply shrugged and said, *Figure it out.*

The stranger that clearly wanted no part of what they were up to pointed to a motor home. Nothing extravagant, but more than a Winnebago. He said nothing. His gesture was enough of an answer. Then he stepped out of the way and LaRouche began walking toward the motor home, Clyde in tow.

He ached for something to douse the fire in his stomach and throat.

But he had nothing and knew that nothing would be given to him. Not yet, anyway.

Why are you doing this? Why don't you just ... just ...

Die?

Yes.

Because I don't want to die.

You should.

I know. But not yet.

He glanced behind him. Clyde's face was exactly what he expected it to be: irritated. A man being forced to do something he didn't want to do.

There was no guard posted around the motor home, a sign of how things were so obviously going wrong in this camp. In fact, the disease of bad morale seemed to have pervaded everything around here. The camp LaRouche had come from had seemed busy. This one seemed dead. Withered. He had not expected military precision, but here the men sat around with bored expressions and eyed him and Clyde as they walked by. There were guards on watch, but they were clustered rather than spread out, and they seemed to be spending more time joking with each other than watching.

Lack of discipline, LaRouche thought, a doctor diagnosing a patient for whom he had little sympathy, but still felt responsible for. *Lack of discipline, and we all know why.*

At the motor home, LaRouche stopped at the door and looked at Clyde. 'Should I knock?'

Inside, they could hear someone being given a heavy-duty dressing down. The man that was yelling stumbled over his words, but his ire remained obvious even as his speech was unclear.

Clyde pressed his lips together, looking around. If anyone gave a shit that two strangers were standing outside their commander's motor home, they were doing a great job of hiding it. Finally Clyde just shook his head. 'No. Let's just go in.'

LaRouche's stomach heaved – more of a burp than a purge – and some of the biley-bloody mix hit the back of his tongue. He made a face and swallowed hard. He wished for the Tums that Wilson had given him. Wilson. Wilson, his friend, back in the time when he had friends.

Aren't these your friends? His own voice was sarcastic in his head.

He reached forward and yanked the door open, taking the two narrow and steep steps up into the motor home and looking left down a cramped corridor full of wood paneling. A pair of seats with a table between them. Two men standing up. One sitting down. A map laid out across the table. Weighed down by a half-full handle of whiskey.

The man sitting down was slightly older than the other two, balding on top and graying on the sides. He had a bulbous nose with ruddy gin blossoms in full bloom. He had an expression of drunken anger all over his face and he was looking up at the other two, the veins in his neck protruding violently. The entire motor home stank of bourbon.

The other two men were middle-aged and they had on their faces the expression of men that are being rebuked by someone they have little respect for. Still, like children that knew their punishment would be quicker if they acted sorry, they were staring at the floor.

When LaRouche and Clyde entered the motor home, all eyes switched to them. The two men standing and receiving their verbal thrashing seemed only mildly curious about who the hell these newcomers were. But the older man, whose face bore a drunken rage that LaRouche was well familiar with, stood up violently out of his seat.

'Do you fucking mind?' he bellowed. Then, as it seemed to hit him that he did not recognize either of them, his eyes narrowed, glittering like pig's eyes. 'Who the fuck are you two? Get the fuck outta my goddamned house! I am the commanding officer of this camp, I swear to God ...'

LaRouche began walking toward him. The other two men stepped back, not quite sure what was happening. Behind him, Clyde lifted his rifle and pointed it at the two men, shaking his head slowly, the message not to interfere coming across quite clearly.

The older man was staring balefully at LaRouche. 'Who the fuck do you think you are?'

LaRouche felt vomit rising again, but he was starting to be accustomed to it. He reached out and grabbed the bottle of whiskey that was sitting on the map. Quietly, he answered the drunken man's question, though the man was still yelling and cursing and LaRouche doubted he heard him.

'Chalmers sent me,' LaRouche said.

Whether or not the man actually heard him or not, he leaned forward. 'What did you say, you mumbling fuck?'

LaRouche swung with the bottle. It made a solid, heavy crunching noise as it struck the man's face. The man staggered out from behind the table, his hand flying to his face and his balance teetering either with drunkenness or with the force of the blow, or possibly both. LaRouche felt something dark and needy rising up in him. A shark in bloody water. He had never really considered himself a violent man, but there was something in the way the bone crunched when he hit it that satisfied him. He lifted the bottle again and brought it down on the back of the man's head, again to the gratifying sound-sensation of bone giving way.

The bottle was not capped and some of the liquid escaped, sluicing down his arm and filling his nostrils with the sharp, fiery smell of whiskey. A smell he had once loved and that now made him sick in his mind. The man hit the floor on his hands and knees, groaning strangely, and he rolled. LaRouche was hardly conscious of the two other men, edging themselves out of the way.

LaRouche had hoped that the bottle would break so that he could use it to open the man up. Because Chalmers had given him specific instructions: 'Kill the man with his beloved whiskey.'

'How do you want me to do that?' LaRouche had asked, incredulously.

And his answer had been 'Figure it out.'

All at once, that dark, fast-thinking, violent creature that lay coiled in LaRouche's brain came up with a way to do it. And he didn't think anything further. The idea came – not in words, but just an image. And LaRouche – no, not him, he didn't want to believe it was him – felt that it was *right*. It just seemed *right*, even if it was wrong.

He was flowing now. He was a tidal wave. He was there to crush and drown.

Drown, drown, drown.

Drown your sorrows . . .

LaRouche mounted the older man and if he had been able to see his own face, he may have been jolted out of his current state of mind and back into something more reasonable. But he couldn't see, and the wave that was him just kept on coming. He pinned the man's arms down with his knees and in the man's semiconscious state, he barely fought it off. Then he put the mouth of the bottle to the man's lips and upended it. Brown, stinking liquor splashed out of the bottle and over the man's face, some of it in his mouth, and some of it in his nose.

But that wasn't good enough for LaRouche. He put his palm on the bottom of the bottle and rammed it into the man's mouth. Teeth shattered and broke as the neck of the bottle forced the man's jaw open impossibly wide. LaRouche thought he heard it snap out of joint. The whiskey began glugging down the man's throat. That woke him up quick. His eyes went wide. He coughed and a volcano of whiskey spluttered out but that only made LaRouche bear down harder on the bottle, creating a tighter seal. The man thrashed underneath LaRouche but it was essentially useless. Blood and bourbon began to jet out of the man's nose as he tried to take hitching breaths, tried to breathe past the assault of alcohol entering his mouth, his sinuses, his lungs. LaRouche reached around and pinched the man's nostrils shut, taking away that one small airway that was probably ineffective anyway.

The man's eyes bulged, bloodshot. His face was turning from red to purple. His thrashing became more violent as it turned into death panic. LaRouche held on tightly, angrily, *furiously*, though he did not know why he felt so enraged. The man was bucking hard, but LaRouche was holding on harder. When his grip on the man's nose became slippery with blood and sweat and whiskey, he would simply reassert it. His entire upper body was pressing the whiskey bottle into the man's mouth. LaRouche stared right into the man's eyes and waited, almost breathlessly, for the life to bleed out of him.

I want you do die. I want you to die so badly.

And he did. Eventually. After an astoundingly long time. Drunk and old, perhaps. But he fought to live like a wild animal, and when he finally died and his chest gurgled and hitched its last hitch, the man's heels striking the ground one last hard time as the life went out of him, LaRouche climbed up onto his feet and his knees nearly buckled with fatigue.

He stood there in the stink of alcohol and the defecation of death, breathing hard and staring down at the lifeless mass at his feet. A man with a whiskey bottle jammed down his throat. Killed by his beloved whiskey bottle, just like Deacon Chalmers wanted.

Job well done, his mind said, again with the snarky tone.

Not really his mind, he thought. Some little splinter of his mind, hiding down deep, launching these guerrilla attacks on him. Trying to overthrow him. But even that part of him didn't know whose side it was on. It was just bitter. Lashing out.

The rest of him buzzed.

He felt alternately like he was in some deep, deep trouble, and then felt exultant for reasons he couldn't explain. If he were honest with himself, he could not explain any of it. He was confused. Lost. Without bearings and with no idea how to gain them back. Perhaps that was why he was so ... malleable.

When he had gained his breath back again, he looked at the two men that Clyde still had covered with his rifle. Though all three of them – Clyde included – were staring at the body on the ground, their eyebrows raised, eyes wide. Noses wrinkled. Shock and disgust.

How do you feel about that?

I'm not sure.

Of course you're not.

When he spoke, his voice was a croak. 'Which one of you is Beatty?'

They looked up at him. Blank eyes.

'Beatty,' LaRouche repeated, now with irritation.

The smallest of gestures, one of the men raised a single finger. He was the shorter of the two, somewhat stocky in build, with a shock of almost white-blond hair and a slightly darker, almost reddish beard. He was wearing a pistol, and it did not escape LaRouche when his fingers twitched toward it. Sure, Clyde might gun him down if he went for it, but it had to be better than having a whiskey bottle jammed down your throat.

But LaRouche had already completed his job. He'd passed his test.

He nodded to Beatty. 'Chalmers says that you're in charge now. He says that he trusts you to get this camp back in order.'

Beatty looked briefly terrified. But he drew himself up and nodded.

Then LaRouche and Clyde walked out of the motor home, leaving behind a mess for someone else to clean up.

They hitched a ride back with the same convoy that had taken them. While they waited for all the supplies to be off-loaded from the van, they sat outside of it in silence. Men from the camp passed them by and LaRouche got the distinct feeling that they had no business where they were apparently going, but were walking by to simply walk by and take a look at the two strangers.

Rumors were already spreading.

Good. Let them spread.

Once the supplies were out of the van, LaRouche and Clyde climbed in, taking a seat in the far back. There were no actual seats, and it wasn't much more comfortable than the bed of the pickups, but at least they weren't exposed to cold wind. It was heading swiftly toward dusk and the wind was kicking up from northwest to southeast, bringing even colder air down from the mountains. The temperature had already dropped noticeably.

It'll be below freezing tonight, LaRouche thought. And then, needling through the back of his head, a thought that didn't come in words, as though he were afraid to voice them even in the sacred privacy of his own mind. He pictured the girl with the green eyes. Pictured him sleeping in a mound of blankets, maybe with her beside him. There was no sexuality to the image. Rather, a keen desire for some human contact that was not born of conflict.

As the van trundled out onto the road, LaRouche studied his hands for a while. Across from him, Clyde was reclined against the wall of the van, looking out the back windows at the flow of the terrain as they passed it.

LaRouche ventured lightly when he spoke. 'What will you tell Chalmers?'

Clyde almost jerked, as though he had been half asleep. He turned himself to LaRouche, at first with a frown, and then with a blank look. A poker face. Clyde was hiding his true feelings from LaRouche. 'I'm gonna tell him that you did what was asked of you.'

LaRouche took another moment before speaking again. 'Are you going to tell him how I did it?'

Clyde shrugged. 'If he asks.'

LaRouche folded his arms across his chest and looked away, out the same back windows Clyde had been fixated on. 'Did I pass my test?'

'That's up to Chalmers.'

LaRouche wasn't sure if he actually wanted this. But did he have any choice?

There's always a choice.

Yes, there's always a choice.

Silence in the van, and for a time, silence in his mind.

Clyde seemed to have taken LaRouche's silence as worry for whether he had actually passed his test. The other man sighed, shifted his rifle in his lap. 'I can't think of any reason why he wouldn't think that you passed your test.'

LaRouche glanced back at his odd companion. He nodded once and then they were silent the rest of the way.

THIRTEEN

BAD DECISIONS

ANGELA SOUGHT ADVICE FROM the one person she felt had the best sense of Camp Ryder. She found her at a small folding table near a fire with two others – an older man and a younger woman – engaged in something she had rarely, if ever, seen her engage in: recreation.

Each of the three at the table was holding playing cards. There were more playing cards in the center of the table, some of them faceup. There was also what appeared to be a 'pot,' and the three players were literally playing for beans. Black beans, actually. Angela had never been much of a card player herself, so she had no idea what type of game they were playing, but Marie seemed to be the one that was winning, as she had the most beans piled on her side of the table and the other two seemed morose.

Marie took her eyes off her cards as Angela reached the small table. A big smile broke out across her somewhat extreme features and she put her hand of cards facedown on the table. 'Angela,' she said brightly. 'You wanna join us for some Texas Hold 'Em? Buy-in is fifty.'

Angela returned the smile but shook her head. 'No, I'm not much of a card player.'

The older man pushed in a small cluster of beans, seeming proud of himself, and then stared hard at Marie.

To Angela, Marie said, 'So, what can I do for you, hon?'

'I just needed to talk to you about some things.' Angela said it still wearing her smile, but Marie must have picked up on the tone of her voice.

Marie's own cheery expression dampened and she looked back to the game.

'Bet's to you, Marie,' the man said, his foot tapping over-eagerly under the table.

Marie quirked an eyebrow at him. 'Yeah, I fold, Hank. You're a horrible bluffer.'

Hank looked offended for a split second, and then recovered. He scooped the pot to him. 'Maybe I wasn't bluffing.'

Marie stood up from the table. 'Hank, Jess, I'll rob you blind another day.'

Rolling eyes responded to her.

Marie zipped up her jacket and she and Angela began walking. There weren't many places of privacy around Camp Ryder, one of the only ones being the office upstairs. But Angela had taken enough bullshit in that office for one day and she wanted desperately to be outside where the dark, motor-grease-stinking walls didn't seem so cloying.

Marie's game face seemed to fade as she walked. 'So, you seem very serious, Angela. What's on your mind?'

'Leadership,' Angela said simply and without hesitation. 'Camp Ryder needs someone to take charge of things here.'

Marie looked at her a little queerly. 'Are you uncomfortable with the job Lee is doing?'

Angela felt something go through her like the vibration of a tuning fork.

Jenny, saying over her shoulder, *About Lee, of course.*

'No,' Angela said, and she was pleased that she sounded sure of herself. 'Not at all. But I had a conversation with him earlier about this very same thing.' She rubbed her hands together and blew into them. The temperature seemed to be dropping rapidly. 'Lee and Tomlin don't want leadership of Camp Ryder, or the Hub, or anything else. Lee has made it very clear with me that he's here as a support. He doesn't want to take over.'

Marie seemed to be mulling something over in her head. 'I hate to presume, Angela, but if you were going to ask me ... ' She grimaced and began rapidly shaking her head. 'No. Not a chance. Not gonna happen.'

Angela took the other woman's arm and gave it a squeeze. 'Marie, I think you could lead this camp, absolutely I do. But I wasn't going to try to talk you into it. I was actually wondering how you felt, and how you think Camp Ryder would handle an election?'

Marie's pace hesitated, but she picked it back up. Eyes on the ground now. 'An election,' she said thoughtfully.

'Rather than having someone "step up," that maybe not everyone wants in a leadership position, what if we opened it up to a vote?'

'Nominees?'

'No, just a straight vote. Writing in the names.'

Marie did stop this time and looked at her friend. 'Angela, there are a lot of different groups in this camp. *Cliques*, you might call them. You've got all the original Camp Ryder folks – some of them supported Bus, and some of them supported Jerry. Then you've got the rest of the young people from Fuquay-Varina who were with Professor White before he disappeared. And the folks from Dunn who do whatever Old Man Hughes tells them. And then the people that came in with Jacob, the people that fled from the Followers. And their leader is pretty much Brett.' She looked at Angela very pointedly. 'They're all just going to vote for the person that they know best, and since all these groups are roughly equal in numbers, if you do a straight vote and let someone win with twenty percent of the vote, all you're going to do is piss off the other eighty percent.'

Angela had considered this, but only briefly. 'But we need someone calling the shots here, Marie. We're just wandering around in the dark with no one leading us. And we can't just appoint someone to take control of the whole damn camp. I feel like that would have worse reactions than if someone like Old Man Hughes was voted in with twenty percent.'

Marie didn't verbally respond, but she made a face that said, *Well, you've got a point there.*

'I don't want there to be any campaigning,' Angela said. 'It's just going to lead to more infighting. And we have to come up with something that is going to prevent us from . . . getting torn apart again.'

Marie nodded, her curly brown hair stirring around her face. 'You're right about that. But the only way you're going to avoid campaigning is if you hold a vote so quick that no one has time to do any campaigning.'

'Okay.' Angela waited, because it seemed that Marie was nursing an idea.

Marie looked thoughtful. 'Plus, whoever wins needs to win by a vast majority. We have to make sure that the *majority* of people in Camp Ryder want this person running things, if we ever hope to keep a split from happening again.'

Angela nodded in agreement as Marie spoke. Their conversation continued, as well as their walk. They eventually found themselves at the rear of the Camp Ryder building and for a time they were focused on the conversation and forgot the things that had happened there. As the talks went on the two women began to arrive at the same conclusions. Ideas were passed back and forth and some were discarded and some kept.

Gradually, they settled on the plan for how Camp Ryder would elect a leader.

As the focus of the conversation began to abate, the memories of the place where they stood seemed to creep back on them. The people that had been killed here. Some murdered, some simply died while fighting. All the bodies that lay buried in the ground not twenty yards from where they stood, the hills of earth marked by crude wooden crosses. Some graves had patchy grass and weeds growing over them, but some were fresh.

The two women stood in the quiet for a time.

Perhaps it was the unsettling mood of the place that brought to mind an earlier unsettling for Angela. She worked some moisture around in her mouth – the cold always seemed to dry her out quicker than heat did. Then she said, in an almost conversational way, 'You spoken to Jenny at all recently?'

Marie shrugged in a disinterested way. 'Me and Jenny never really . . . hit it off.'

'So you don't talk to her?'

'Well, I don't give her the cold shoulder or anything,' Marie said. 'But I don't make a habit of sitting down for long chats with her. I still say "hello" when I see her. And if I'm walking past the medical trailer I'll pop in and ask her how she is. I've done it a few times over the last couple days. Since I heard about the whole Greg thing.'

Angela nodded. 'How do you think she's doing?'

Marie made a face. 'Oh ... hell, I don't know. Are you asking me if she seems a little weird? Yeah, she seems a little weird. But what the hell do you expect, given what she's been through? She'll be all right with enough time. But honestly, you probably have a better idea of how she's doing than I do. You two were always a bit closer.'

Angela pursed her lips, hesitant.

'Why do you ask?'

Because she seemed a little ... unstable?

'Nothing,' Angela said, forcing a smile. 'Just checking on her.'

'Well, don't take my word for it,' Marie said, pulling her jacket around her. 'Go ask her how she's feeling if you want to know.'

'Yeah,' Angela said, but she didn't think that she would.

Jenny sat alone in her shanty. Alone in the dark.

It wasn't truly dark. Only dim. But it felt dark, with no windows and the tarpaulin door pulled shut against the world beyond. The sunlight was muted, but it still made the blue plastic glow with strange ghost lights that grew stranger as the time passed. In the darkness, her eyes played tricks on her, and often, her ears as well.

Beyond the thin walls of the shanty, the voice of nearly every person in Camp Ryder seemed to be audible. That alone might have been enough to irritate her at times, but she'd grown used to it and when it did bother her it was in flashes of impatience. But sitting there alone, silent save for her own breathing, oftentimes she would think she had just heard Greg's voice.

Greg, coming to pull her tarpaulin door open.

Greg, coming to fuck her after his guard duty was done.

Greg, coming to drag her into the office where Jerry could 'question' her.

Whenever she heard that phantom voice she wondered if she felt terrified or excited. Maybe it was both, and perhaps those two things were so closely intertwined that there wasn't enough difference to distinguish them. She'd read once that the areas of the brain that light up when you're scared are the same areas of the brain that light up when you have sex.

Sex and fear. Not much different in the animal part of their brain, it would seem.

Sex and fear and pain and all kinds of other stuff, just getting mixed around in a great big soup pot called her brain. She wondered what haywire receptors were going off inside her gray matter, what confusion of chemicals and electronic impulses were firing back and forth. She pictured it like sparks and arcs of blue electricity jumping through jumbles of copper wiring. Pure chaos.

She sat at the edge of what could be called her bed and wondered where box springs and mattresses and down comforters had gone. Why was she sitting on cardboard and dirty blankets that smelled strongly of a dead man's sweat?

Jenny looked off to her right, sniffing against her nose, which seemed to run perpetually in the cold. It was ridiculous, really. It never stopped. Cold, cold, cold, everything was cold and she was always cold and there seemed to be no real way to get rid of it. Except to wait for summer to get here. Months away. Long, long months that may as well have been years. No wonder earlier generations cursed the dark and cold of winter and longed for summer, no matter how hot it would get. Freezing temperatures were only charming when you had central heating.

On the right-hand side of her shanty, there was a pile of items.

Greg's things.

They hadn't been given to her, and she hadn't asked for them. But she'd gone into his shanty after the assault for Camp Ryder was over and she stood there for a while, wondering how she felt. Twenty-four hours before that point, she would have been crushed by the death of Greg, but that was before she realized that Greg didn't really give a shit about her and was just using her as a warm place to stick his dick every night.

Still . . .

Anger, sex, fear. Interesting cocktail, there.

Standing in his shanty, she'd kicked around his stuff, figuring no one would really care. She'd found some things, maybe some things he kept for himself, or didn't want anyone else to know about – she'd found them squirreled away in a jumble of old jackets – and she'd appropriated them, along with the jackets and anything else she could use. In her mind, she kept saying, *I might as well get some use out of the fucker*, but it was a cold, brash thing to think, and she knew that in her heart she really didn't feel that way.

She felt abandoned.

That was it. That was the fear and the anger part, anyway. Oh, she was pissed at Greg. She was angry at him, and he would never again draw a breath with which he could apologize, and for that reason she would never forgive him for what he did to her. Even if he could have apologized, forgiveness might have been beyond her. The way he'd made her feel, standing up in that office, feeling dumb and used like a fucking breeding heifer that wasn't good for calving anymore.

But there were other times. Times when he had looked at

her with actual tenderness, when he had spoken gently to her and seemed to love her. Yes, those moments were few, but they had been there nonetheless. And they had been there in a time when even those small things were needed so badly that they seemed monumental.

So how was she supposed to feel about Greg?

Conflicted, apparently.

She shook the object that she held in her hand, and it rattled noisily. It was a good sound. A full sound. She opened her fist and looked at the label on the orange bottle, but she already knew that it had been scratched off. Inside was just a mess of different things, like the inside of a kaleidoscope. Ovals and circles and triangles and rectangles, in white and pink and blue and yellow. She wasn't sure what they were, but she'd already taken two.

Two magic candies.

One she was pretty sure had been Adderall, and the other was a mystery.

She was well aware that many of the people in Camp Ryder had developed a taste for pharmaceuticals. Their lives were miserable, with no hope of getting any better. Why wouldn't they want to get high? People complained about their lives and got high when they were living in two-thousand-square-foot houses, watching fifty-inch TVs without a real care in the world. Why wouldn't this ragged band of survivors want to take a mental break every once in a while? And she was well aware that Greg had been happy to supply that habit. It was one of those things that most everybody knew about, but nobody really talked about for fear that someone like Angela or Marie or Lee would hear and put a stop to it.

Hell, they probably already knew anyways.

Maybe Lee was popping pills right along with the rest of them.

Greg kept most of his stash in their proper pill bottles, complete with labels so that if someone needed an upper, he could give them an upper or if they needed some antidepressants, he could give them that, too. But this particular bottle seemed to be the mystery box, filled with the dregs of other pill bottles that he didn't believe warranted being divided into individual pill bottles. Or maybe he'd become so used to them that he could identify what each pill was by sight.

She was beginning to feel the effects of the first two pills. For once, her blood felt warm in her veins. It was like she could feel it swishing through her bloodstream, in an odd, but not unpleasant way. Her chest felt light and her thoughts felt quick and sharp and she was beginning to feel overwhelmingly positive. Like she'd just done something wonderful. Like she'd just been declared the Greatest Person in the World.

Jenny opened the bottle and looked inside. There was a little, round, pinkish orange pill. She decided to try that one, too. She popped it in her mouth and swallowed it dry. Then she replaced the cap and shoved it under her blankets. *Three pills is enough, Girly-Girl. Let's not get carried away.*

Some time passed in her shanty. She began to fidget.

She wasn't sure what the third pill had been. She could not feel anything different from what she'd felt before, but it seemed to have intensified. And her thoughts were not quite as clear as they'd been before, or at least the decision-making aspect of them. She found herself 'deciding' to do things that suddenly seemed ridiculous.

I'm going to strip naked and play in the snow.

Except there was no snow. Just cold gravel. And if she

stepped outside her shanty stripped naked, everyone would think she had gone mad.

The guys would like it, though. Oh, yes, all the men that look at me like that when I do my rounds. I know what they're thinking. I know what they're picturing. Maybe they all wanted Greg dead so they could take a crack at me. Well, fuck Greg and fuck them.

Time passed. It was difficult for her to tell how much, but she knew that it had. Her head was buzzing, her chest was light. She was feeling optimistic, but the fidgeting was increasing and she found her heart rate and her respiration increased. *Doctor, you seem to have developed a slight arrhythmia, Doctor. Why, thank you for noticing, Doctor. I've also noticed you appear to be displaying some signs of distressed breathing, Doctor. Well, Doctor, do you think this requires treatment? Actually, Doctor, I believe we will just keep you for observation. That sounds like a great idea, Doctor, and might I say you look lovely today. Thank you, Doctor. Remember to get plenty of fresh air and exercise. Say, Doctor, you're not a real doctor are you? No, Doctor, in fact I am not. Well, what in the hell are you, Doctor, if you're not a doctor? I'm a third-year nursing student! Ha, ha, ha!*

She rose up from the bed and walked to the tarpaulin door. She flung it open and realized it was rapidly approaching dusk. More time had passed than she'd realized. She was amazed for a moment at the color of the sky, and then wondered if it was a trick of the drugs. The western sky was alight with oranges and purples and pinks. And then suddenly all those colors seemed as dull as concrete to her. It was not that her eyes saw them differently – they were still bright and vibrant as they'd been a moment ago – but the buzzing in her head seemed to make everything gray in a wonderfully inoffensive way.

She hung in her doorway, hands clutching the tarp. She

closed her eyes and breathed deep. Now *there* was something to set her right. The air was cold and crisp and jarring. But it couldn't really touch her. It was like the warmth coursing through her skin made a force field of heat around her body that the cold couldn't get through. But she could still taste the cold on her tongue, smell it in her nose. And she felt excited by it for the first time since she'd been a little girl and the smell of cold was the smell of Christmas and lights and presents.

She began walking, a half smile on her face. There was a path that went around the interior of the fence line. It hadn't been there when they'd arrived and taken over Camp Ryder, but hundreds of guard shifts had stomped down a narrow strip of dirt with yellow-brown weeds off to either side. Her shanty was near the end of the row, so all she had to do was hang a quick left and she was on the path, walking with the fence to her left.

Jenny stopped for a moment and looked behind her, aware that her current mood might be perceived as a little off to other people, and so she didn't want them to see her. But with dusk coming, everyone seemed consumed with the task of preparing meals or buttoning up for the night. Marie had started cooking the community dinners again, so plenty of them were heading into the Camp Ryder building for a bite to eat and some socialization.

It seemed very quiet in the camp, and with the western sky so boiling with bright colors, the camp below seemed dark by comparison.

She looked forward. The Camp Ryder building stood there, hulking over the rest of the camp, just a midnight-blue silhouette against the orange-washed sky. She could see the outline of the guard on top, standing and looking the other direction with his rifle cradled in his arms. Down below, the door to the building opened and inside was bright like a roaring fireplace and the sound of laughter drifted across to her before someone slipped in and closed the door behind them again, shutting off the sound and light.

She turned around, deciding to walk with the fence to her right, away from the building and into the less utilized section where a jumble of shipping containers sat, so far unused. As she walked she had trouble feeling her feet hit the ground. She stuffed her hands into her pockets and they felt warm there, like she was holding them to a fire. She felt simultaneously wired and drowsy. It was an interesting sensation. Absently, she considered the possibility of negative physical side effects from combining several medications that were probably past their prime. But in the end she decided that it would be okay. The worry that it took to consider the consequences of her actions seemed intangible. There was nothing to worry about.

Somewhere around the southernmost point of Camp Ryder, with all the empty and abandoned corrugated steel of the shipping containers to her left, and the fence to her right, and no one around, she got the distinct sensation that she was being watched. Maybe it was paranoia, but it's not really paranoia if it's true, right?

She stopped where she was, standing there and feeling the breath go in and out of her lungs, warm and frigid all at once. The buzzing. The ringing. The floating. The weightlessness. She looked at the fence, squinting at it like it had confused her. She could see all the chain links, but on the other side they had fortified it with all manner of flotsam. But there were gaps, because all these pieces of trash that they'd used to build their fence into a wall, none of it fit together like puzzle pieces. And some gaps were bigger than others.

There was a man standing in one of the gaps.

She stared at him, and he stared at her, and she wondered if she knew him, but didn't think that she did. Somewhere deep down inside her there may have been a little squirm of fear but she felt so far above little things like terror and death that it never really registered with her.

What did register was the fact that the man had only the barest tatters of clothes clinging to his body. She could see every rib, every muscle. His belly was distended, his face shaggy with a beard, and the beard was clumped and dreadlocked with blood and gristle. His eyes were wide and oddly clear. Very stark in his face. His skin seemed dusky by comparison, and the sunset that loomed behind her must have played a trick and lit up his eyes, making him almost appear cognizant.

'Hey,' she said. The word just kind of stumbled out of her, like a drunk coming out of a bar.

The man's wide eyes blinked, glittered.

He was pressed up against the fence, his fingers curled around the links. She looked at his overgrown fingernails and could see black crud underneath them. Dirt and blood and guts, probably. But aside from the single blink, he didn't stir when she spoke, just kept staring at her.

Jenny looked behind her to see if anyone else was there. There wasn't. She was alone.

She knew what she should have felt, but the sensation of well-being was overpowering. Logically, she knew that chemicals in one of those pills she took were intercepting the stress hormones, or possibly inhibiting them by blocking the receptors. Her body might have been sending out the panic signals, but the brain wasn't getting them.

Instead, she looked back to the creature clinging to the

fence, and she shuffled to the right, and then to the left. The
man's eyes followed her quickly. He was there, thinking something inside that broken-down brain of his, but what it was
remained a mystery.

'Are you one of the good ones?' she asked, wondering why
he wasn't growling. Why he wasn't screeching at her and
clambering to try to get over the fence at her. She took a step
forward, locking eyes with him. 'Are you one of the ones that
don't like to eat people? Well ... it looks like you've been
eating something, that's for damn sure. But hey, I won't
judge. We all gotta live, right?'

The man was staring right back at her. Right into her eyes.

What was it about any animal in the kingdom that they all
knew what eyes were for? How did they all know to make eye
contact? To look back when they were being looked at? How
could something insentient have any concept of what the eyes
meant?

She took another step forward and she was close enough
that she could hear his breathing now. It was a steady, rhythmic sound. His mouth was closed. He was breathing slowly
through his nose. His eyes remained on hers. Her own breathing was elevated, but was that from fear or drugs?

'Hey, big boy ... ' Her left hand went to her pants pocket
and withdrew the knife. The man on the other side of the
fence seemed not to take notice. 'I bet you're one of the
nonaggressive ones, aren't you? Can you understand what I'm
saying? Can you nod or something?'

It remained still.

'Okay, that answers that.' She smiled. 'But you don't seem
so crazy right now, do you. You like it when I talk to you?
How long has it been since you heard someone talk to you
normal? Most everyone probably just screams and runs away

and shoots at you, huh? You know what I wonder? I wonder
what you'd do if I touched you. Would that wake you up a
bit? All the men seem to like it when I touch their hands.
Wouldn't that be fancy. Just like a fuckin' fairy tale, huh? I
touch your hand and you transform from a hideous beast into
a handsome prince.'

Jenny raised her right hand, and when she did, she watched
the man's eyes jag down to it for just a split second, and then
they were back, fixated on her eyes. That was interesting. It
was seeing what was going on. It was processing. So if it was
nonaggressive, what would it do if she touched it? So far it
hadn't done anything but stand there.

For some reason she had this image in her head of the men
on the nature documentaries, the ones that swam with sharks
and walked up to prides of lions and wrangled alligators. She
always wondered how they did it. Maybe animals just
responded differently to them. Maybe they had some sort of
power. Maybe it was more scientific – maybe they gave off
nonthreatening.

She kept picturing that – the guy swimming with sharks,
rubbing their bellies – and she wondered if she actually had it
in her to reach out and touch one of these infected. And what
if she did? And what if it was okay with the physical contact?
Hell, what if it *liked* the physical contact? That was another
weird thing about animals – they all seemed to like having a
human pet them.

Well . . . at least when they got over the desire to maul you.

*But is this an animal or a person? And does it even make a
difference?*

Her thumb flicked the blade from the folding knife. It
made a quiet *snick*. This time the man on the other side of the
fence didn't notice. And Jenny's other hand was still hanging

in midair, drawing closer to him. She held his eyes for a time, and then she looked at the hand, the filthy hand, that hung with hooked fingers through the chain link fence.

She could touch it. He would let her. She could feel it. She could sense it like you could sense when an animal was going to strike at you and when it wasn't. And this one, man or animal, was docile. He would not hurt her and this would be uncharted territory. What do you do with an infected when he's not aggressive?

Her index finger brushed his fingers.

She had expected them to be cold, but they were oddly warm to the touch. The plague, still making the bodies run hot. The man's finger twitched when she touched it. Then they were still. Jenny's fingers were still touching his. He was looking at her hand now, but still didn't move or lunge at her.

'There you go,' Jenny said softly. 'What do you think about that?'

His fingers extended, but they did it slowly. Then they curled around hers. Maybe if there had not been so many chemicals coursing through her brain, cutting off and preventing the warnings of fear from coming through clearly, she would have felt a sudden tug of apprehension, but she just stared dumbly with a half smile on her lips.

And then the fingers were wrapped around hers and before it truly registered with her, they had clamped down like iron bands, crushing her fingers into the fence.

She let out a muffled cry and tried to yank her hand away.

The man on the other side of the fence had changed. His mouth was yawning open, the teeth bared like fangs, his eyes crunched to squints. His gaping mouth reached for her hand and his hot fingers were trying to claw them through the chain links. She could feel the fingernails breaking through her skin.

She couldn't scream because her breath was caught in her chest with the strain of trying to break free. And she couldn't be heard, couldn't be seen, no one in the camp knew where she was and what she was doing and she could never let any of them find out because ... because ...

No! No!

She felt the bones of one of her fingers crack but she kept herself from crying out in pain, though, honestly, the pain was muted. She bared her own teeth and lashed out at the fingers that were clutching her, slashing at them with the knife. She dared not scream because what would she say to anyone if they found her? So instead she just groaned with effort, mumbling in a panic, 'Let me go! Let me go!'

The knife kept coming down. Short, quick strokes. The infected was growling now, trying to get its other hand through the fence to grasp her. The knife was opening splits in his skin and bright red blood was pouring out, even hotter on Jenny's hand's than the infected's inflamed skin had been.

She was striking wildly, not even looking, just pulling away, with one foot up on the fence, trying to yank herself free, and the pain in her fingers was sharp and dull at once and true fear was finally coming through from the drug-induced haze of well-being: *What if he bites my fingers off? What if he bites me? I can't let him bite me!*

And then with one stroke of the blade she felt his fingers loosen, and with the next, she was free and tumbling backward into the dried grass. She scooted away from the fence, breathing heavily, still clutching the bloody knife in her left hand, her broken right hand pulled into her chest.

The thing on the fence stared at her and gave the fence one last angry shake, and then he was gone. She could hear its footsteps running through the woods.

She sat breathlessly in the grass for a second. She looked down at her hand and felt elated to see all five fingers still there. Her hand was covered in the thing's blood. She wiped it hurriedly on her pants, feeling the stickiness between her fingers. Her middle finger throbbed and she could see that it wasn't sitting right. How would she explain that? She would have to think of something.

She stood up shakily, deciding that she was done with her walk. She was done with being outside. She needed to clean and set her hand and then she thought she should probably spend the rest of the night in her shanty, thinking of how she was going to explain the broken finger to everyone that asked. It wouldn't be too hard. There was plenty of manual labor around the camp that regularly resulted in broken toes and fingers and small injuries of the like. She was trying to hammer up a center beam to reinforce her roof and missed the nail and hit her finger.

There. That was a perfect excuse.

She looked down at her hand again.

Fresh blood was rolling across it.

She stopped, staring down at her hand.

Oh, fuck. No. This is bad. This is very bad.

In the moment she had not felt the cut on the back of her hand – about an inch long but deep. The pain of her broken middle finger had disguised it, but now as she stared at it the pain became a real thing and differentiated itself. One of her rapid and sloppy knife strikes had gone off target and slipped through her own skin. The wound was wide open and all around it was not only her own seeping blood but the stain of the infected's blood that she'd wiped off.

This doesn't mean anything. It doesn't mean I'm infected.

Blood to blood is the most likely method of contracting FURY.

No, I don't have it. I can't have it. That's ridiculous. You've made it this far, you're in a relatively safe place, you've survived all kinds of disasters and attacks from people and infected alike. You are not going to catch the plague because ... because you were HIGH AND NOT THINKING CLEARLY!

She was mumbling curses under her breath. She realized that her legs were moving again. She needed to clean it. She needed to stitch it up. What would she say about the cut when people asked? Because the hammering nails story wouldn't work for that. She would have to come up with something else.

She needed to clean it. Clean it very good. Maybe that would make a difference.

She heard the words coming out of her mouth, unsteady and wavering. 'What am I gonna do? What am I gonna do?'

FOURTEEN

THE GIRL

LAROUCHE STOOD ON THE front porch of the farmhouse that Deacon Chalmers had commandeered. He was standing there, facing out into fast-approaching dusk. The sun had already dipped below the top of the trees that surrounded this little property, and it was glaring through the empty branches in ribbons and spears. The growing night smelled like winter chill and wood smoke.

LaRouche's back was to the door of the farmhouse. Behind him, he could hear a quiet conversation occurring inside. A conversation between Chalmers and Clyde. A conversation about him. What were they saying? He had no clue. He'd been given a task. And he'd completed that task.

Why?

Because that's what you're good for in this world.

Doing people's dirt. You did dirt for the US government, and you did dirt for Lee, and now you're doing dirt for Chalmers. It's just what you do. Don't overthink it.

The door behind him opened and he looked over his shoulder. Clyde stood in the doorway. They made eye contact, but if what was coming to LaRouche was good or bad, punishment or praise, Clyde was not revealing it. He motioned LaRouche inside.

They found Chalmers in the living room. Standing.

The fireplace was crackling warmly. Chalmers was looking into the flames. A diviner seeing visions. He seemed thoughtful.

I did what I was told.

Blood and snot and whiskey spurting out of the old man's nose – that was the image that came to LaRouche in that moment. It was by far not the worst thing he had seen, but for some reason it made his throat tighten. Perhaps because he had not expected himself to do it. It was like watching something take over his own body. Something acting of its own volition. Something dark that was inside him, and completely capable of hijacking the whole system whenever it chose to.

LaRouche stood still and silent, and tried not to care.

Chalmers cleared his throat. 'I heard how you' – careful consideration here – 'dispatched the old drunkard.' Chalmers was nodding. 'It was quite a nasty thing to do, LaRouche. Very nasty. But then again, killing is nasty, and at the end of the day, dead is dead, isn't it?'

LaRouche absorbed the words for a while. Then he nodded. 'Yes, sir. Dead is dead.'

A half smile played on Chalmers's lips. His eyes twinkled darkly. Like a candle thrown down a mineshaft. 'You know, I find it interesting the level of importance people put on the method at which one expires. Shot in the head is stabbed in the heart is drowned with your own bottle of whiskey. It's all the same.' He took a step toward LaRouche and rested a hand on his shoulder. 'You did exactly what I asked you to do, LaRouche. You made your oaths, you fasted the fast, and did as you were instructed, not only faithfully, but efficiently. You have passed the test.' His smile widened. 'I'm proud to call you a part of our family. The Lord's work is long and difficult and never ending. But we will discuss that tomorrow. For now, enjoy this night that God has given you.'

LaRouche did not respond. He only stared back, trying to keep everything off his face. The disgust. The bitter sense of irony that would have cracked him into mad laughter.

Clyde turned to him and pointed for the door. 'Come on, LaRouche.'

Chalmers said nothing else as the two men left the farm-house.

Outside, with the house behind them and steadily retreat-ing as they took the footpath back to the center of camp, LaRouche finally spoke. 'What happened back there?'

Clyde didn't look at him. 'What do you mean?'

'I saw how you looked when we went in there.'

This time, Clyde gave him a sharp glance. 'It's nothing,' he said, cautious as a man who doesn't know the discretion of the man he speaks to. 'Deacon Chalmers ... likes things done a certain way.'

'Did you think he was going to kill you?'

Clyde sniffed. 'Not me.'

LaRouche nodded and left the conversation where it was.

They left the footpath and headed down the dirt road that had once been a farmer's long easement. A drive that would have taken that farmer to a place that he thought was removed from the dangerous world beyond. But not removed enough, apparently. It had come for that farmer in the end. As it had come for everyone.

As they walked, LaRouche looked to his right and found himself staring at a woman, standing next to an open tent flap. The tent was one of the heavy, canvas constructions with an aluminum chimney that fed down through the roof of the tent to a wood-burning stove. The stove glowed warmly, but there were other lights on inside the tent, and LaRouche could see through the open flap that there were several other women inside. They seemed at ease, reclining on bedding, some even having mattresses, and all of them having warm blankets in what looked like a very warm tent. There was even the sound of light laughter and it almost jarred LaRouche when he heard it.

'LaRouche,' Clyde said.

LaRouche looked at him and realized that he had stopped walking. He moved his feet under him. 'None of those women are restrained,' he said, and he was disgusted at how confused he sounded. As though it were normal for them to be locked in cages.

'No,' Clyde said, indulgently. 'They're the ones that the Lord has blessed.'

'They're pregnant.'

Clyde sighed and nodded.

'Why don't they run?' LaRouche asked, plainly.

This time it was Clyde who stopped. He turned on LaRouche and leaned forward so that their faces were close and he was able to whisper his words and still be heard. Though whispered, they came out harsh and sharp-edged. 'You should watch what you fucking say, LaRouche, or you're going to get yourself killed. And me for that matter, since I'm in charge of you. You wanna have an honest conversation? Fine. But not here in the middle of the fucking camp with God-knows-who listening.' His voice lowered again to barely a mumble. 'For now, all you need to know is that those women were blessed by God. They carry the seed of the Lord's Army. And they are treated with the respect that they are due.'

LaRouche stared at the small man before him that was

giving what amounted to a dressing down. For a brief moment, LaRouche could feel it like thunder in the distance – a faraway desire for violence. To take offense to the tone and to deliver something painful. But there was also something in Clyde's eyes that LaRouche recognized as not necessarily being a rebuke. More of a caution.

LaRouche held up a hand. A gesture of surrender. 'Sorry.'

Clyde turned away and began walking again. His irritation seemed to be deflating and he spoke to LaRouche over his shoulder as they approached a section of camp that was made up of pickup trucks and tents, and a few tents inside pickup truck beds. His tone was flat. A man delivering instructions. 'You'll choose one of the women tonight. From the general population.'

From the cages, you mean, LaRouche thought but had the sense to hold back.

'Everyone goes to bed with a woman,' Clyde said. 'It's how we're going to repopulate this country. Build up a nation of children with strong beliefs in what's right.'

LaRouche almost choked. *What's right?*

Clyde didn't notice, and kept going. 'But tonight is the only night you choose. Every other night one will be given to you randomly' – when he said this, he gave a secretive glance at LaRouche, like there was something more he wanted to say, but wouldn't – 'but tonight is a special night. You're being welcomed into our family.'

They stopped now in front of the cages. The frames of the cages were overlaid with white canvas, like the tents that the pregnant women were in. The fires were on either side of the rectangular construction and they burned warmly and were stoked by men with rifles on their backs who seemed there to guard the women. Or to keep them from escaping.

LaRouche wanted to ask what would happen if one of *these* women tried to escape. But he didn't think that Clyde would appreciate the question. At least, not until they were in a location more conducive to 'honest conversation.' He suspected that those that tried to escape were made an example of. The people in that cage, the women with the blankets wrapped around them, huddling together because of the steadily deepening cold of the night, their options were reduced to nothing. You complied or you died. You could fight, but in it would only be pain, and likely death. Or you could go along, and be treated well. All you had to do was conceive.

What about the women who have trouble getting pregnant? LaRouche wondered. *What do they do when a woman doesn't get pregnant for a long time? Do they discard her? Do they just throw her away like a broken machine? Or do they kill her? Would it be more merciful for them to kill her or to simply abandon her?*

LaRouche realized that Clyde was watching him carefully.

Clyde's voice was so low, LaRouche could barely hear it. 'Just go along.'

LaRouche turned back to the cage and the women there. He felt no desire. Only a cringing sort of pity, a sort of sickness that went past his stomach and reached for something much deeper. He felt a sense of shame also, but muted. *This is how it has to be.*

He looked for the girl with the green eyes. His gaze floated over many of the others, but just like the time that he had spent in his own cage, sitting across from the women and watching them, all but the girl with the green eyes seemed to be dead inside. She still had a little fire left in her, and that was what drew him to her.

He found her huddled in a corner, watching him and Clyde.

'Her,' LaRouche pointed to her. 'The girl with the green eyes.'

Clyde tilted his head slightly, regarding the girl with a quizzical eye. LaRouche was about to ask him if there was some reason he could not pick that girl, but Clyde spoke first. 'She's plain,' he said without conviction or emotion. 'Are you sure you wouldn't want to choose one of the better-looking ones?'

LaRouche glanced at the others, but more just to humor Clyde. 'No,' he said. 'I'm sure.'

There was no privacy in the camp. Even if you had a tent to yourself, which few people did, you were still only a thin nylon wall and a few feet away from others. It reminded LaRouche of how closely packed everyone had been in Shantytown at Camp Ryder. But even a shanty was better than a tent.

LaRouche had neither. He had two large, musty-smelling blankets and a corner of a large box truck that had once been used to move all of the people's belongings. Now it contained six mounds of cloth – quilts and wool and woven fabric – and underneath the layers, soft voices murmured and bodies moved. No one had come out from their blankets when he had pulled up the rolling door. None of them cared.

He had closed the rolling door of the box truck as far as it would go. A piece of two-by-four kept it a few feet from closing completely, to keep them from being accidentally locked in, LaRouche supposed. The interior was dark and he waited a while for his eyes to adjust. In the darkness he only heard the quiet mumble of voices. The sound of people ... making love? No. LaRouche didn't think that was the right phrase. Simply *fucking* seemed more appropriate. The inside stank. It stank like old sweat and new body odor and the same mustiness that clung to the roll of blankets he now held, and the rank smell of the activities the others were engaged in.

Beside him the girl with the green eyes shifted and he could feel her tension coming across like a buzzing electrical field. He wished he could speak, to say something to calm her, but he did not think this was the right time. Like Clyde had said, if you wanted an honest conversation, this was not the place to do it in.

The walls have ears, LaRouche used to tell his guys when instructing them on being discreet. Particularly when talking shit about their commanding officers. Same situation here, except the consequences were much worse than extra PT or guard shifts. Here the consequence for everything seemed to be death. Everyone walking a constant tightrope on which either side was your destruction.

Don't lose your balance.

He thought about reaching out and taking the girl's hand, but he knew it would be construed wrongly. She might not jerk away from him, but she would think he had other things on his mind. Which he did not. Inside of him wasn't dead, but it was alive with different things. Molten things. And they scorched all the other things black.

When his eyes had adjusted to the dark and he could pick out the twitching, moaning piles that were strewn across the floor of the box truck, he started forward, picking his way through. He could hear the rustle of fabric behind him as the girl followed and he felt an odd thrill go through him from his neck all the way down his back. A sensation of danger, like having a strange dog lurking behind him. He kept thinking of the harsh light in the girl's green eyes and he wondered if she would be the type to hide a knife or some other homemade shank in her clothing, and maybe use it now to punch his kidneys out and make a run for it.

He almost wanted her to do it. Maybe that was why he let her walk behind him. Maybe that was why he refused to turn around and ruin the opportunity for her.

He made it to the back end of the box truck without being knifed. He found an empty spot big enough for them to lie down into. They had no mattress or bedding, and the floor of the box truck was cold wood, but he supposed it was better than the ground. He laid one of the blankets down as a thin cushion and then sat on it. In the dark he looked up at the girl. He could not see the color of her eyes, nor the expression of her face. She simply stood there, as still as a tree, and he could tell that she was looking at him, but the light was muted and only lined the side of her face. She could have been looking at him with pure hatred and loathing. And he figured that was not far off the mark.

LaRouche waited for a moment before he gestured to the space at his side and spoke very quietly, barely audible over the sounds of the people around them. 'Sit with me.'

She took a half step forward so that she was on the blanket he had laid out, and then she sort of melted to her knees and sat back on her heels. *Resigned* was not the right word for how she seemed. More like steeled for something she didn't think she would be able to stop. She reached up and began to unzip her jacket, this time her face focused on the zipper, rather than looking at LaRouche.

He reached out and put his hand on hers, staying it.

She glanced up at him, again, her expression a mystery.

LaRouche shook his head. 'Just lie down.'

A moment passed, him staring at the dark shadow-mask of

her face. Finally she put her arms out and lowered herself stiffly onto her side, facing him, and then he saw the muted light fall over her features, but they may as well have still been in shadows. There was nothing there. She seemed gone to another place in her mind, and her eyes would not hold his, but rather fixed themselves on the ceiling.

LaRouche looked around at the steadily moving mounds all around him, one of them moving more rapidly and the voices becoming hoarse. He was looking for anyone that was above the covers, maybe looking at LaRouche – the new guy – and wondering what he was up to. But once again, no one seemed to be paying him any attention.

He put the blanket at his feet and then rolled it out over the top of himself and the girl, pulling it over their heads, where his face grew warm with the sudden heat of their bodies and breath. In the stifled silence underneath that blanket, he could hear that the girl's breathing was fast. The warm air was thick with his own smells – his dirty clothes, his stale breath, his unwashed body. He could smell her as well, and that was discomfortingly intimate to him. A lighter smell than his own, and much less offensive, he thought.

He wondered what was going through her head in that moment.

Through the veneer of *unfeeling* that had covered him like a dense, whitewashing snow, he sensed a jutting of pity, and of shame. Pity for this girl, and the situation that she was in. And shame? Yes. Shame for what he was sure she thought of him.

The loudest of the coupling had subsided now to heavy breathing, and it seemed the noise that had shielded him was dying down and the night was growing quieter. So he pulled himself closer to the girl that was next to him and he could feel her body stiffen, but only very slightly. If he was drunk, or of a bent of mind that he cared very little about her consent, it would not have bothered him at all.

He was close enough now that he could feel strands of her hair tickling his face.

His voice was the barest of whispers. 'What's your name?'

He heard a slight brush of fabric, and imagined she had turned her head toward him. Perhaps a look of concern on her face. *What kind of sick fuck are you?* she might have been thinking. *You have to know my name?*

'Claire.'

LaRouche absorbed that for a moment. For some reason the name tweaked at him. It bothered him that she had such a delicate-sounding name. A decent name. The name of a girl he'd known in grade school who was a pale little thing with a kind smile and never a harsh word to anyone. He wished that her name had been something stronger.

Doubt overtook him momentarily.

But still, he pressed on. He could feel the warmth of his own breath against the side of her face, but still he wished he could speak closer, at a lower whisper than he was already. His heart quickened its pace because he feared being overheard.

'Claire, if you had the chance, would you run?'

FIFTEEN

OVERRUN

THE LAST COFFEE TABLE was long burned to ashes. But the night was still falling, and the temperature was dropping again. Harper scrounged for more wooden furniture, prowling the second floor of the big house with a hatchet in hand.

After one giant crash and a lot of banging and cracking, he came back down to the living room with large chunks of an old cherrywood armoire he'd found in the master bedroom.

Everyone was huddled in the living room, bedrolls laid out as close to the fireplace as they could manage. The downstairs was too large for the fireplace to heat the whole area, but in the living room, next to the fire, you could barely sense the chill. Elsewhere in the house, you could see your breath. The ornate thermometer that clung to the outside of the kitchen window showed the mercury already dipping below freezing. Harper guessed it would be in the twenties before the sun came back up.

Kensey had already curtly informed Harper that his Marines would handle the night watch. At first reaction, Harper was almost a little miffed that Kensey clearly lacked trust in Harper's people. But after he pushed his pride away, he realized he would get to sleep the entire night, as well as the rest of the people in his group. He didn't think he remembered

the last time any of them slept an entire night. Probably sometime back at Camp Ryder.

Kensey posted two of his Marines outside. Their bivy sacks
sat empty. Harper peered through the glass doors leading outside, but he could see nothing beyond those panes but the
mottled shapes of darkness and midnight shadows. The moon
gave a cold, silver cast to everything. It stared down at them
from a cloudless night sky.

Kensey was slouched in a plush chair when Harper entered,
holding a quiet conversation with one of his men. Dylan was
propped on the hearth, dishing out something dubious he'd
made in a pot by the fire. He and Charlie chattered noisily,
and Julia was sitting in another chair, pretending to listen to
Dylan and Charlie's antics, though she was watching Kensey
closely.

It almost brought a wry grin to Harper's face. But Julia had
been ... confrontational lately. He wasn't sure why, or what
was brooding inside her, but he didn't like it. He loved Julia
in some cross of fatherly and brotherly feelings. But he missed
the Julia he'd met three months ago. She'd been as headstrong then as she was now, but with benevolence.

Now she just seemed headstrong and reckless.

If Julia wasn't careful, she could drive a wedge between
Harper and the Marines. And they needed the help. They
weren't going to get this done on their own, and Harper
didn't see anyone else around with the resources to help. So
the situation called for a bit of politicking. Not Harper's
strong suit, but you don't get to be vice president of a bank
without some schmooze in you.

Harper dumped the load of cherrywood on the ground
next to the hearth, causing a clatter. Then he reached down
and threw a few medium-sized pieces into the dimming fire.

He shook out his arms and stretched his back. The others were looking at him, as though he'd been purposely noisy to gain their attention.

'Armoire,' he said casually with a nod at the pile of wood he had brought. 'Full of fur coats. Kensey, you seem like a man who might look good in a mink coat.'

Kensey humored him with a smile.

His Marines chuckled behind him. One of them called quietly, '*Pimp.*'

Kensey shook his head and tilted the brim of his cap back. 'Only if it comes with a top hat and a cane.'

Harper shrugged. 'Sorry, I'm keeping those.' Harper took the opportunity to find Julia's gaze. 'Would you mind helping me with the rest of it? There's just a bit more than I can carry.'

She raised an eyebrow, then hoisted herself from her chair. 'Yeah, I kinda guessed there would be.' She looked at Charlie and Dylan. 'One of you want to help?'

Harper interrupted. 'We should be able to get it all between you and me. Dylan, you keep dishing out whatever you made. It smells good and I'm fucking starving.'

Dylan, who was half on his feet, looked hastily between Julia and Harper, then settled himself back to his seat and his task. 'No problem.'

Julia eyed Harper with something like suspicion, but followed him when he delved back into the darkness of the house. They stepped into the large atrium. The twisting staircase that rose up to the second floor. Tile floors. Expensive-looking wooden banisters following it up. A monstrous chandelier hanging dark and looming over the whole thing, seeming more like a death trap now. Harper kept eyeing it, waiting for it to crash on him, skewering him in a million places with brass and crystal.

But it didn't fall. It hung silently, as the whole house was silent except the living room directly in front of the fire. They took the stairs, stepping lightly without meaning to. When you were squatting in another house, and the darkness was around you and all was silent, it could make any man feel like a thief in the night, and even if their business was honest, they hunched their shoulders and padded lightly.

Harper had a small flashlight that he used to light their way. The glow was dim and yellow, but bright enough to guide them into the main bedroom. It was a fairly large thing, but not overly extravagant, Harper thought. Despite the ominous chandelier and the fur coats in the massive armoire, he had not seen a lot in the house that indicated extravagance. Whoever had lived there had definitely not been afraid to spend their money, but they seemed more like the horse-and-acreage type of wealthy, as opposed to the matching-Maseratis type of wealthy.

The bed was king-sized – naturally – but Harper avoided looking at it. It was the one spot in the house where there was evidence of something bizarre and horrible happening. The sheets were tousled and ripped off the bed. The mattress was torn open. There were dark stains that looked like blood to him, and splatters of it on the ceiling directly above. But as far as he could tell, the rest of the room was spotless.

Two nightstands. Two lamps. Two dressers. Pictures of a man on one. Pictures of a woman on the other. Pictures of both of them on the walls. The man with a bored, pacifying look in his eyes, the woman with a twinkle in hers, as though she were already thinking of where she would frame the photos and hang them on her walls. Happy couple, at least for the photographer. No kids, it seemed like. A chocolate Lab in one of the pictures, but it was the only evidence of an animal

Harper had seen and it made the presence of it in that pho-
tograph seem like a prop.

Harper turned his back to the disturbed bed. The destroyed
armoire lay in pieces at his feet. He shut off the flashlight to
save batteries. They could see by the light of the moon
coming through the windows, although just barely. Julia was
facing him, hands in her pocket, half her face illuminated by
the bluish, mercurial lighting. But the one side of the face
showed that she wanted to know why Harper had pulled her
aside.

'Is everything okay?' she asked.

He smiled, but tiredly. 'Okay? Rarely. Not with us, anyway.
We don't have that kind of luck. But I guess if you're asking
me if everything is status quo, then yes. We are still afloat . . .'
He took a breath and shifted his weight. He had trailed off,
and now he just stared at her for a long moment, watching her
face become more and more expectant. Waiting for him to
finish his sentence. But that sentence was dead in the water.
He went in another direction. 'How are you?'

Her teeth seemed to glow. He couldn't tell if it was a smile
or a grimace. 'How am I? Why, I'm fine, good sir. And yourself?'

'I'm serious,' he said, and his voice was very serious indeed.
'I'm worried.'

'You're worried.'

'About you,' he clarified.

'How so?'

'Julia.' Harper's voice took on a cautious tone. The voice
of a wise man treading lightly. 'I'm not trying to start an argument with you. But that kind of goes to my point.'

Eyebrows up.

'You seem . . . very confrontational,' he said.

She huffed, a sound of pure defense. 'I don't think I'm any more confrontational than usual.'

Harper shrugged, not wanting to push it. As he had said to her, he didn't want an argument. He'd simply wanted to give her a chance to clear the air, if she wanted to. He certainly wasn't going to drag it out of her. But then he thought about Nick. He thought about how he'd given every warning sign and signal and Harper had ignored them all because *they were all stressed out. What made him so special?*

And then Nick had shot his wife to death, because he didn't want her to have to live in this world. And then he stuck the barrel of his rifle in his mouth and scattered his brains across the side of the military truck they'd commandeered. Harper thought about it often and with remorse. He thought that if he might have intervened, might have put a stop to whatever was going on inside Nick's head, if he'd only gone and talked to him, he could have kept him from going over the edge.

Was Julia like Nick? He didn't want to give her the chance to become like him, though. If there was something growing black in her mind, he wanted to nip it in the bud now. Figure out what was bugging her – *What's fucking bugging her? Try the whole goddamned world. You act like you're removed from it all, old boy, but you're just as fucked as everyone else. Perhaps you should remove the log from your own eye ...*

'Look ...' Harper rubbed the bald spot on the top of his head once again, like he was checking to see if it was still there. Then he stooped for a stack of wood. 'I didn't mean anything by it. If you don't feel like talking, I ain't gonna force you. You just seemed a little outta sorts. That's all. Forget I said anything.'

He gathered up an armful, avoiding tacks and nails that protruded from the wood. It still smelled of musty old fur coats. Harper had never liked that smell. Reminded him of dusty attics and crumbling relics and his grandfather, who drank too much and never had a kind word during their yearly forced visits for the holidays.

He straightened, hugging the load of wood to his chest. Julia was still standing there. She had not gone for any wood, but was simply regarding it like she might be trying to come up with a game plan for how she was going to gather it. Or maybe she was considering other things.

'You gonna help me with this or what?' he asked quietly.

When she looked up at him he could just barely make out that she was looking right into his eyes and there was the slightest silver glimmer at the bottom of the one eye that caught the light. She blinked rapidly. Harper stared back, quietly shifting his grip on the wood.

'You remember the night at Camp Ryder, right before we left for Sanford? Before we lost Jake and before Lee found that den?' she said, her voice low, almost tremulous. 'We were all around the fire that night. Do you remember that?'

'Yeah.'

'I think you'd already gone to bed. But it was me and LaRouche and Lee and there was just a little bit of whiskey left in this bottle and we were passing it around and it was really quiet. And then LaRouche said something. He said, "I don't think I'm gonna make it."' She smiled but she looked terrified. 'He had a feeling, you know? He just knew. And now he's gone.'

'Julia . . .'

'And I had that same feeling. I had it then and I've had it ever since. Like I'm walking a tightrope and I don't know how long I can keep my balance.'

'You're not going to die.'

Julia looked fierce for a moment. 'Don't you fucking say that, Harper. Don't ever. And don't tell me that you're watching my back or some horseshit like that. You think LaRouche didn't have people watching his back? What about Jake?'

Harper nodded and spoke softly. 'You know what, Julia? You're right. I can't tell anyone that they're not going to die. Because how it happens seems to be completely fucking random to me. And I don't think it's beholden to gut feelings and hunches.' He paused to take a breath and moisten his lips. 'Lee ever talk about his parents with you?'

She seemed unsure where this was going. 'No.'

'Did you know that they both died?' Harper laughed, humorlessly. 'Both of them died in the same car wreck. And do you know when this happened? When Lee was deployed to Afghanistan. He told me it was one of the bloodiest months for US troops in that war. He was in firefights almost every day of the week. Never got a scratch on him. On the other side of the world, in the safest country on Earth, his parents get crushed by an eighteen-wheeler on the interstate.'

Julia pursed her lips. 'While that's an uplifting story . . .'

'My point is that you don't know when it's going to happen, Julia. It happens when it happens. It's not your job to try and guess when your clock runs out. It's your job to keep fighting until it does. Just because the world has gone to shit doesn't mean that you're destined to die young. Just like when the world was safe you weren't guaranteed a full life. You know, I wake up some days, and I have the same feeling? I'm one hundred percent positive that today is my day. It's happened more times now than I can remember. But somehow I'm still here. So if you think there's something to your gut feeling, you're fucking wrong, Julia. You're completely wrong. And I don't want you being reckless and rash and constantly picking fights because you think you don't have much time left.'

She made a sucking sound with her teeth, but finally she nodded. 'Fine. But if you think my dislike of Sergeant Kensey has anything to do with this . . .'

'Does it not?'

'No.'

'You just don't mesh?'

She shrugged. 'Sure. You could say that.'

'Okay,' Harper said, rolling his eyes. 'Well, regardless of your personal feelings, he's relayed what he's seen to Colonel Staley and it sounds like they're meeting tomorrow to hash things out.'

'You don't think it will be too late?'

Harper shrugged. 'It'll be too late when it's too late.'

An amused smile. 'You're very Zen about everything.'

He used his leg to hoist the wood back up high on his torso. 'Yeah, well . . . it's that or go apeshit.'

'Am I apeshit?' She stooped and began to gather wood.

'No.' Harper shook his head. 'You're just crazy. But that's okay. You can come back from crazy.'

He looked for a reaction from her – hopefully a friendly one – but she seemed involved in her task now. Harper thought he might point out that it was a joke, but then figured she knew that. He waited for her to gather the rest of the shattered armoire, his own load beginning to weigh uncomfortably in his arms. When she had the rest of it save a few bits and pieces, they started down the dark hallway again.

As they descended the stairs, Harper could hear the slight creak of the back door opening. There were hushed voices and then the sound of a quiet scrambling. Harper craned his neck back toward Julia and he could see from the look on her face that she had heard it, too. He picked up the pace, hurrying to the bottom of the stairs, where he had a clear view into the living room.

Charlie and Dylan were standing there, rifles in hand. All the Marines had posted up on windows that faced the back and the driveway, their rifles in hand. One had his helmet on, a set of night-vision goggles rocked down over his eyes, scanning through the lower corner of a large window. Sergeant Kensey was closing the steel doors to the fireplace, hissing and baring his teeth as he negotiated the hot metal.

He's hiding the light, Harper knew with sudden certainty. *So somebody doesn't see it.*

Kensey saw Harper and Julia approaching with their bundles of wood and he held a finger up in front of his lips and with the other hand out, palm down, motioned for them to put the wood down. Harper knelt on crackling knees, wincing as sore muscles and aching tendons complained against him – morning and night were the worst – and he slowly, carefully, released his pile of wood onto the ground. It wasn't loud by any means, but in the sudden, breathless silence, the muted clack of a few boards on the floors sounded like gunshots.

'Get behind something,' Kensey said, the words just breath coming out of him.

Harper glanced over his shoulder and saw that Julia had freed her hands up as well and was slinging her rifle off her back and into her shoulder. Harper followed suit, getting down into a crouched position and duck-walking to where Kensey was kneeling behind one of the plush chairs.

The Marine looked at him, eyes wide. 'Stop moving!' he hissed.

Harper froze. In the dark. The warmth of the invisible fire

still playing on the left side of his face as he stared at the glass back door with everyone else. He summoned enough air into his lungs to whisper so quietly that he barely even heard himself. 'What the fuck is going on?'

He wasn't sure whether Kensey actually heard him, or whether the other man had just figured that Harper might want to know, but Kensey turned to face him, moving slowly and steadily. When they made eye contact, Kensey pointed very deliberately toward the back door. 'Infected. A lot of them.'

Harper felt his pulse throttling up. His legs began to tremble. Partly from the strain of his squatted position, and partly from the sudden dump of adrenaline through his system. 'Do they know we're in here?'

Kensey just shook his head, then turned back around, welding his rifle to his cheek.

Harper's head was almost lost in a sudden cloud of panic. He didn't like the term *panic*, because it made him feel like a bitch, but that's what it was. His mind couldn't seem to focus on the task at hand. His body felt like it was getting ready to explode on him. He had an almost irresistible urge to run while they were still out of sight, and it butted heads with the part of him that wanted to hunker down because he knew that with his luck the second he stood up to run, those *things* would suddenly appear and give chase. Besides, he couldn't run, could he? No. Even if he'd been by himself and didn't have a responsibility to Charlie or Dylan or Julia or any of the others, he still could not have run. Because he was trapped in this house. Trapped like a fucking rat. The only solution was to lie very still and hope to God the bad things didn't see you.

Bad things. Bad things. Like a kid trapped on his bed because of what's underneath it.

Some analytical part of him managed to shrug off the soaking of stress chemicals coursing through him. It seemed to calmly raise its finger with a question. Very politely. *Excuse me, when you're done having a panic attack, you may want to address what is going to happen if the infected try to get into the house.*

Harper forced his breathing in and out, steadily.

We hope they give up and go away, he told himself.

And if they get in? If they see us? Let's go worst-case scenario here, Billy-Boy. The fight's on. What are you going to do?

What am I going to do?

What can *we do?*

Through the glass door, framed by the statues of two Marines, rifles held at a low ready, Harper could see the back driveway and the woods beyond. The blackness, and the vertical stripes of tree trunks. Everything looked monochromatic. Just blacks and grays and stillness.

Were they out there?

If we get attacked, we can't stay on the ground floor. There's too many ways in. They'll have us surrounded. At least on the second floor we only have to watch the stairs. Choke points, Lee would call them. But do you really think you'll be able to hold them off? And for how long?

Guess it depends on how many there are.

Movement caught his eye. Something out beyond the driveway, out in the trees.

One of the Marines muttered something and slid down farther into concealment.

Harper's grip on his rifle felt sweaty.

Something in the fire cracked loudly, making Kensey twitch.

'How many were there?' Harper whispered.

A slight shake of the head. 'Reilly said over a hundred, easy.'

Something stepped into the center of the driveway. Harper's gut twisted up when he saw how close it was to the house. And then there was another, and another after that. They were close, but still too far to see details. Rail thin, though. They seemed to huddle together closely as they moved. Drawing body heat from each other, Harper thought, and it disturbed him. It was almost like they were clinging to each other. It was almost something to pity, their hunched forms like starving waifs in some war-torn country.

And he almost did pity them, but his heart was hammering and his skin was prickling and his vision was dancing at the very edges, and he could not comprehend a feeling like pity in that moment. Just fear and necessity.

The ones in the driveway paused for a long moment, looking around them. They seemed to be scenting the air. Harper could see the plumes of their breath drifting up and creating a cloud that hung over them. What were they smelling? The sweat of people? Could they distinguish that over the smell of their own legions of filthy bodies?

Perhaps it was wood smoke that they were smelling.

Maybe that's what had led them here.

More and more kept coming out of the woods. They were oddly silent. No hoots and hollers. No barking or yapping. Harper didn't know what they were looking for, but he figured it was what every other animal was looking for – food. They seemed to mill around for a moment and then the milling became more purposeful, and almost as though they shared some collective conscience, the uncountable, dreadful faces of the horde turned toward the house, almost in unison.

'Fuck ...' Nothing but wind through Kensey's clenched

teeth. He sidled down into the plush chair that he was using to hide himself, now completely out of view.

Harper no longer wanted to look at the creatures in the driveway. Because if he could see them, they could see him. So he lowered himself down, almost prone, so that his body was hidden by the same chair that Kensey hid behind, as well as the ottoman next to it.

It was worse. Not being able to see them.

Harper stared at the floor. The darkness on him, stifling, and yet completely clear. Transparent. Nothing there to conceal him from prying eyes. The floor was wide-planked hardwood. Mud from their boots was caked and scattered over the floor. Bits and pieces of wood particles from the coffee tables they had demolished for firewood. These were the things he focused on as he lay there on the ground, the cold floors pulling the heat out of him, right through his jacket.

His finger danced outside the trigger guard.

He made it lie still.

Where were they? What were they doing? Were they going to surround the house? What if they looked in the other windows at the front of the house? Would they be able to see all of them then? Would they attack if they saw, or would they ignore them unless they moved?

His abdominal muscles ached from being tensed, though he didn't even realize he was doing it. He very slowly craned his neck so he could see over his shoulder and behind him. Julia was there, lying prone next to his feet. Her eyes were closed. Jaw locked. Lips tight. Her rifle was pulled in so close to her that it seemed like she was hugging it like a long-lost lover.

Go away. Just fucking go away.

Something thumped at the back door.

Harper couldn't help himself. He rolled carefully so he could see underneath the legs of the ottoman and just barely see the bottom of the back door. In the silvery moonlight, he could see pale, malnourished legs out there. They were covered in mud and deep, crisscrossing cuts on the outside of the thigh, like the thing had run through a briar patch. But that was as high as his vantage point could see.

They're at the door.

The knob rattled, just slightly. A tiny sound, but the only one in the house.

Did they lock the door? Did they remember to lock the door?

He had an image of it just casually drifting open in front of the infected, and the entire horde just meandering their way in. More than a hundred? How many more? Would they be able to handle them if they attacked?

He cursed himself for letting them stay here in this house. He cursed the house. That logical part of him tried to say that the house was as safe a place as any to stay and that this was just one of those unfortunate circumstances where you found yourself unexplainably *fucked*, but with no real cause to blame. It didn't matter, though. Harper still cursed it all.

Like a claustrophobic man caught in a dark cave. Cursing the little place where you found yourself would do no good. It would not free you from your prison, or make the millions of megatons of earth and stone that sat over your head go away. But you cursed it anyways, because when you're completely powerless all you can do is shake your fist.

The last respite of the trapped man.

Just go away. Please, God, make them go away.

He remembered what he'd said to Julia only moments ago. And it had all been true enough, but it felt like foolishness on his lips now and it tasted bitter. *Zen*, she had called him. But not now, with his heart and his body thundering with the fervent desire to be someplace – anyplace – else.

The glass. Something was tapping at the glass.

Then the slow, whining sound of a hand being dragged across the glass. Except it wasn't at the back door. It was at one of the other ground-floor windows. The house was suddenly filled with the bumps and scratchings and squeaks at the windows and doors. Everyone inside was frozen to the point that they held their breath.

If the infected started to break through into the house, Harper wondered, would they even get everyone up the stairs before the horde completely enveloped them? Success seemed unlikely. Their fate was suspended by a thin filament of chance.

It seemed like a long time passed.

Harper's lungs began to burn and he hazarded some slow breaths out and in.

The fire popped again, seemingly louder than before.

The cacophony of noises all around them seemed to go on forever, even growing in intensity until that was all that Harper could think about. He just kept picturing one of them finally putting its fist through a window and sparking a frenzy. But then, very suddenly, the sounds died off around them. Like a rainstorm that falls furiously for twenty minutes and then abruptly passes on.

For another minute, perhaps two, no one moved.

Slowly, Harper and Kensey moved at the same time, Kensey peeking out from behind his chair and Harper once again peering under the legs of the ottoman, both of them looking at the back door. The glass seemed like a view onto an empty stage. The driveway stood abandoned where only minutes ago it had been filled to the brim with throngs of bodies and the steam that rolled off them in clouds. The woods beyond the driveway were once again dark and motionless. The house was completely silent.

The only evidence that anything had happened at all were the streaks of filth that covered the back door, and as Harper rose he could see that it was on the windows as well. Muddy, bloody, greasy handprints and smudges where faces had been pressed up against the glass as though the infected had been trying to see inside and determine whether this nut was worth the effort to crack.

It seemed that everyone decided to release their breath at the same time.

Charlie actually laughed, but quietly.

Julia swore and stood, only to collapse into one of the chairs that circled the fire.

Kensey was shaking his head. 'I can't believe they didn't come inside.'

Harper had to agree on that. 'What were you gonna do if they got inside?'

Kensey looked at him, his eyes odd in the darkness. 'Start shooting. A lot.'

Harper nodded. Apparently the Marine's plan of action wasn't much better than his own.

Kensey rubbed his face like he was reassuring himself it was still there. 'How many was that? Couple hundred?'

'Probably more,' Harper said, faintly.

'I'd guess closer to a thousand,' Julia spoke up from where she was slouched in the chair.

No one argued with her. And Harper considered her words. It was a lot of infected, but it certainly wasn't the entire horde that had been gathering at the eastern side of Eden for the last few days. Still, it was much more than the couple dozen they'd seen leaking across the bridge into western Eden in dribs and drabs.

'I think they pushed over the bridge tonight,' Kensey said, interrupting Harper's thoughts with something that had already occurred to him. 'I think that was just the first little bit of the horde that we saw. Just passing on through.'

Harper had nothing to say, but Kensey was looking at him as though it required a response. So he just swore. It was the best he could come up with.

'Harper, we've officially lost our hold on Eden. There ain't no fuckin' way we're gonna hold it now.' Kensey stooped to grab his pack. 'And we need to get the fuck out of here. Tonight. Now.'

'What?' Julia was on her feet in a flash. 'We can't fucking leave!'

Kensey seemed to care very little for her opinion. 'And what are you gonna do, ma'am? I'm all for some guns-blazing, heavy-combat, Marines-don't-know-the-word-*retreat*, motto bullshit, but at some point in time you have to be able to recognize when it's time to back the fuck off.' He hoisted his pack onto his shoulders. 'Shit. If staying here and fighting and dying meant that we were actually doing some strategic good? I'd stay and I'd fight. But staying right now would just be stupid. We're not holding the line until reinforcements get here. And we're not fighting an enemy that is going to be disheartened by our resolve. All we've be doing is killing ourselves. Stupid.'

'Because you motherfuckers didn't send us the manpower you promised!' Julia was almost shouting.

Kensey stopped what he was doing and looked at her as though he might like them to come to blows.

Harper stepped in, his voice tight, but level in its tone. 'He's right, Julia.'

'You don't know that he's fucking right,' she spat. 'He's just guessing. Until we put someone on that water tower and put eyes on Eden, we won't know what the fuck that was.'

'No way.' Harper shook his head. 'Not with a horde rolling around out there.'

Julia's eyes became somewhat deadpan. 'Fuck that. I'm going.'

Harper was so surprised that he couldn't speak for a brief moment. Then he spluttered. 'Uh ... going where?'

Julia had already crossed to the back door. 'I'm going to the water tower.'

'Julia ... '

'No.' She shook her head and pulled open the door and then she was gone through it.

SIXTEEN

BROKEN

JULIA HIT THE WOODS FASTER than she had intended and it was only the loud crunch of leaves beneath her feet that halted her for a single beat of her heart and forced her to go slower and more quietly. But she felt like charging through, heedless. She was livid. Her blood felt scorching in her veins.

That motherfucker, she thought, picturing Kensey in her mind. How dare he just leave them? Without waiting to see if Eden was actually lost. Just expecting them to drop everything they had risked their lives for because it was *his opinion* that Eden was overrun. Why not give them the chance to check? Why not afford them the hour that it would take to make sure before they abandoned the whole goddamned thing?

In the back of her mind there was a quiet voice that kept saying, *You're alone. This is dangerous. You shouldn't be alone out here. It's too dangerous.*

The truth of the voice did nothing to stop her from squashing it down. Anger kept her feet moving forward, though fear was beginning to slip through, like rain through a leaky roof. The woods still stank of the horde that had just passed through them, she realized. And what if Kensey was right? What if the horde that had surrounded them for those brief, terrifying moments had just been a smaller satellite arm of the larger horde of millions?

What if Eden was truly lost?

You don't know until you know.

Just like Harper said.

It's too late when it's too late.

All she knew was that people had died to get them here. Lee had come up with a plan – a damn good plan and the only one she thought was reasonably achievable and would still be effective against a threat so widespread – and they had sacrificed lives to make it happen. Now the people that were supposed to be helping them were dragging their feet, and some know-nothing sergeant whom she pictured spending the last four months in the relative safety of a guarded military base was telling her that it had all been a waste.

Never mind Gray.

Never mind Nick and Torri.

Never mind all the little bits and pieces of herself that she'd murdered just to stay sane enough to make it here. The decency she'd once clung to, the sense of honor, of right and wrong that she felt could still be a part of this world if she just *tried* hard enough . . .

Now those concepts stank of decay in her mind and the rotting of them soured her stomach.

And all of that was just supposed to be swept aside because Sergeant Kensey had never come into contact with a horde before and was scared out of his mind? Was that it? He seemed green to her. She didn't give a shit about what wars he'd fought, if in fact he'd fought any. This was different. This was here and now. This was home. And this wasn't for the interests of politicians and the international economy. It was for survival. And she knew this war. She'd fought this war. She had blood on her hands and damage in her heart for the things she had seen and done.

And now this guy? This guy that she didn't know? Telling her to drop it all?

Hey, little lady. Why don't you calm down and let the men figure out what's best for you.

Fuck you, Sergeant Kensey.

If he didn't have the balls to make sure that the threat was real before he tucked tail and ran, then she would do it for him. And if she climbed that water tower and looked out over Eden and saw the streets filled to the brim, if she saw that any effort to punch through and demolish the bridges would be a waste of life, she'd be the first to take her lumps and admit that Sergeant Kensey was right.

But she needed that proof.

She stalked the woods. Just like her father had taught her when he'd taken her deer hunting. Slow, cautious steps. Take a few, then stay quiet for a minute. Listen to the forest around you. Behind her she could hear the steady rustle of someone else's feet through the leaves – not quite as cautious as hers – and she wondered if it was the infected or Harper coming after her.

She kept pressing forward. Standing in the middle of the woods trying to figure out who was tailing her wouldn't do her any good. If it was Harper then she didn't care. If it was the infected, she needed to keep moving forward anyway.

The quiet voice again: *This is a bad idea.*

Shut the fuck up.

Maybe Harper was right, after all. Maybe she was being rash. Maybe she was having a hard time controlling her anger lately – *Maybe people should stop making me angry* – and maybe, just maybe, she was making these decisions because there was a part of her with a death wish.

She wished her sister was there. Marie had always been the more levelheaded one. She'd also always been more honest. Brutally honest at times, though rarely mean-spirited about it. She could rely on her sister to tell her how things really were.

What do you think Marie would say? Would Marie agree with Harper? Would she tell you that you were being rash? Making bad decisions? Would she give you that look and say, 'Come on, Julia'?

Julia didn't have the answer to that question. Marie was a long way away, dealing with piecing Camp Ryder back together. She was not there and would not be able to lend her younger sister any of her advice. So it was just up to Julia to figure things out. As it had been for a long time.

In that moment she felt utterly alone.

The fear was almost as strong as her anger now. But it was a bit late for caution. She was almost to the water tower. Or at least she hoped she was. She didn't make a habit of being in the woods after dark and she found it to be disorienting and oddly frightening on some primal level. Like her animal brain was telling her that the woods and darkness did not mix.

Keep on going. You're almost there.

The clawing fingers of winter-dead trees suddenly opened and she was standing on the edge of the clearing, the bulk of the light blue water tower rising up in front of her like some alien structure. She stopped there at the edge, surprised to find herself breathless, as though she had been running. She forced herself to breathe through her nose and felt her sinuses sting with the cold of it. The saliva in her mouth seemed thick and gummy. She spat on the ground and then remained still for a moment, listening.

Behind her the rustling continued, seeming to follow her tracks. But no voice called out to her, though she doubted that Harper would have called after her – it would be an invitation for unwelcome company. She found it difficult to judge the distance of the rustling. One second it seemed it was right on top of her, and the next it seemed very faint, like it might be heading away from her.

Maybe it's not Harper after all ...

The thought spurred her forward. She moved quickly across the circular clearing to the chain-link fence and slipped quietly through with only a slight metallic snickering sound from the fence as she negotiated her way through the cut. On the other side, she looked behind her, half-expecting to see a pack of infected come hauling out of the woods, raising their skin-crawling howl that was neither human nor animal.

The woods remained motionless.

Back to the tower.

She jogged smoothly to the ladder, slinging her rifle onto her back as she went. She took the first few rungs with a jump and a swing. The ladder groaned but held as it had every other time. She barely noticed now. She felt exposed as she gained height. Not only was she in the open, but she was high up now. Obvious. The water tower like a stage with spotlights.

Bad idea, Julia.

Too late to turn back now.

It's too late when it's too late, right?

She was almost halfway up when the rusted ladder finally betrayed her. The metal was icy to the touch and covered in a thin layer of frost, making her hands numb and slow to respond. So when the rusted rung in her grip *popped* and yanked free of the ladder, her unwieldy hand slipped right off.

Her heart went into her throat and she lurched out for another rung.

Her cold, numb fingers didn't open and close as fast as they needed to. She struck the next rung up clumsily, skinning her knuckles across it, and then she had no grip at all. Her body weight swung her out, pivoting on the one hand she still had fixed to the ladder, but she wasn't able to hold her grip with her entire weight on it.

Please hold on! Please hold ...

She was falling. The ladder rungs were whizzing by her face, it seemed. Close enough to reach out and grab, but when she tried her arms were not long enough. She had time to think that maybe she hadn't climbed up that far. Maybe the fall would not hurt her.

She didn't feel the impact. Her body felt like it was made of dense rubber. She could tell she was rolling, and it seemed like she was rolling for a long time to have fallen straight down. The tower and the ground swapped places a couple of times, and then she was still. Staring up at the sky. The stars were incredibly clear. She could see the Milky Way, a pale band across the sky.

She tried to breathe and nothing happened. Her chest seemed to be seized.

Still, she didn't feel much fear.

I'm still here. I'm okay.

Her stomach ached dully. She felt a numb warmth spreading over her legs. No, not both legs. Just her right leg. She tried to lean up, but couldn't quite manage it – God it was hard to move when she couldn't seem to take a breath. Then she tried to lift her legs and couldn't manage that, either.

That was when the panic hit her.

Paralyzed. Paralyzed. I'm fucking paralyzed.

It was the panic that managed to break through her shocked diaphragm and pulled air into her lungs. At the same time she rolled onto her side and her body curled up like a pill bug and she could look down at her numb legs that were becoming not-so-numb. She could feel her right leg and it felt weird to her. Loose, like a limp noodle. Disjointed. She could feel the skin bending in ways it had never bent before.

She managed to move her right leg.

The thigh and knee moved naturally. But everything below that *flopped*.

Her eyes went wide and she could feel the cold air on them. She thought she might vomit.

'Oh. Oh,' she whispered. Tears now mercifully blurring the image of her oddly bent leg. Unmercifully, the shock was dissipating like a fog and the numb, weird feeling in her leg was turning into agony. 'Oh, no. No.'

Then she clamped her hand over her mouth and her hard-fought breath came out of her in a stifled sob. *Don't scream. You can take the pain. Just don't cry out. Don't attract attention.*

But who was going to find her if she didn't cry out? What if it wasn't Harper coming through the woods after her? What if her final bout of incredibly stupid temper had led her out of the house and into harm's way and Harper had just shook his head and decided to let her figure it out on her own?

Lee had a phrase to describe when stupid people did stupid things that got them hurt.

'Self-correcting injury.'

Good job, Julia. Way to fucking go. You figured it out.

Self-correcting injury.

Then, *What are you going to do?*

She craned her neck at the woods and almost couldn't focus on what she was seeing. The pain was a white-hot curtain hanging in front of her eyes. She tried to listen but her blood was rushing in her ears and it was all she could hear in that moment. Blood in her veins and air in her throat. Adrenaline and pain muted everything else.

She blinked rapidly and felt the moisture on her eyes and rolling down her cheeks, at first warm and then ice-cold. She kept one hand clamped over her mouth to hush the scream that kept trying to come out and the other she reached down and clutched at her leg, just below the knee where the pain was intensifying.

'Okay. Okay. Okay.' Her voice was threadbare. She clenched her eyes shut and heaved herself onto one elbow. 'You can't sit here. You have to move.' The pain was bad, but it would only be worse if she got tracked down by some starving creature and torn apart while she was still alive. That was her sole motivation.

She began to drag herself toward one of the big steel pylons of the water tower. It was all she could think of. The area was bare of any sort of concealment except for hiding behind one of those four supports. And she needed to hide. There wasn't a chance in hell that she was going to drag herself through the woods, trying to get back to the house. And she would not call for help because she knew that help would not come – only many, many hungry mouths.

So she had to hide.

Fuck, it hurts so bad! She couldn't believe how bad it was. She'd broken a bone as a kid, but she didn't remember the pain being so bad. The throbbing was horrendous and she wondered if parts of her bone were beginning to punch through her flesh, too. Because the pain had a sharp edge to it now. She pictured her leg bones, all white and glistening, edging through muscle and skin with each movement she made. But there wasn't enough precision in the pain to know about the specifics. It was just a fiery riot below her knee.

Trying to control her breathing, she looked down to her strangely twisted leg and stared at the cloth of her pants, trying to see if it was getting dark with blood. She couldn't quite tell. There was a dark smudge, but maybe it was just dirt.

She continued pulling herself along the ground, and gradually her mind came back to itself, able to acclimate through the pain to a certain degree. Just the basic functions. Her blood wasn't roaring in her ears as bad as it had been. The world didn't seem so white and sparkling in her vision. She was able to see what she was crawling toward with clarity, and she was able to hear behind her.

In the woods.

The sound of feet in the leaves.

More than one pair, she was certain.

'Don't let them get me,' she said to no one in particular. *Sitting duck, you stupid idiot. You dumb bitch. Nice self-correcting injury you got yourself there. Had to prove a point. Had to be the big girl. Had to show off your dick. Christ, sometimes you're worse than the boys.*

All she knew was that she didn't want *them* to get her. If she had to wait in the freezing cold for hours, if she had to wait all goddamned night, that was what she would do. It was cold enough to freeze a person to death, but there were tricks, like tensing your body and your abdominals to increase core temperature. If she could manage it. Being injured wouldn't help. It would sap her strength. But she was having trouble coming up with a better plan.

Wait. Just wait. Harper knows where you went. Eventually they'll come looking for you.

Won't they?

Of course they will.

But then another part of her wondered if they were all rolling their eyes when she stormed out of the house, happy to be rid of the Troublemaker. The one that kept making rash decisions. Like the decision to bolt out of the house with no help and to march through the woods, alone, in the dark, to the tower, only minutes after a horde had passed them by. Maybe they were relieved that she was gone. Maybe they would be in less danger that way.

The thought horrified her, but her mind wouldn't let it go.

She reached one of the pylons and she scooted up on it, her back to it. Behind her came the footsteps through the woods, much closer now. Getting ready to hit the clearing, she thought. Hit the clearing and then sniff the air and maybe smell her out like prey. Maybe root around the edges of the fence until they found the hole. And then what?

She yanked her rifle out from where it was slung on her back. It took some effort and some extra pain as she unintentionally leaned weight on her leg and nearly passed out from the pain that it caused. But she got it in her hands. She had it. Thirty rounds in the magazine.

Best-case scenario: if she was a real Cool Hand Luke, she might take down thirty of them before they ripped her to shreds. More realistically? It would take three to four rounds apiece to put down. So ... maybe ten.

Through the grim arithmetic she was still picturing Harper and Charlie and Dylan standing next to the fire, with Sergeant Kensey and his Marines standing behind him. Laughing and joking. All of them quite jovial with each other now that she was out of the picture.

'Well, that's a relief!' Sergeant Kensey would chuckle.

Harper would nod. 'She's been out of control.'

Charlie, giving Harper a slap on the back. 'If she wants to go, let her go.'

And Dylan would agree. 'She's only been causing problems for us, Harper.'

'She's rash,' Kensey would point out.

'That's what I told her!' Harper would say, with a laugh.

No, that's ridiculous, Julia told herself. And yet she kept picturing herself still under the water tower come dawn. Either as a big, black patch of frozen blood, or half frozen to death. Icicles hanging off her chin and nose. Skin a pale blue. Like a cartoon.

A hiss in the darkness. 'Julia!'

No more of your bullshit imagination . . .

The fence rattled. 'Julia, are you in here?'

Julia turned her shoulders, grunting against the strain it put on her. She could almost feel the separated bones grinding together. The thought made her nauseous. She looked out over the overgrown but otherwise cleared area at the bottom of the water tower and she saw a figure standing at the fence. Her heart went into conniptions.

Wait . . . that was . . .

'Charlie!' she snapped. 'Get the fuck in here and help me out!'

Charlie's figure seemed to triangulate on her voice. Another figure appeared, and she knew it was Dylan. 'I see you,' Charlie said, probably a little louder than he had intended. Worry was coming out of his voice and Julia realized he hadn't come expecting to find her crouched behind one of the water tower pylons.

Anytime something unusual was happening, it was usually bad.

That was a rule to live by.

Dylan's neck stretched, trying to see her. 'What's she doing on the ground?' he whispered.

Charlie just swore at him and told him to hold the fence.

Relief managed to overcome some of Julia's pain. It was still there, hard and resonant like iron hammers on steel drums, but at least there was someone there. She wouldn't be left alone under the water tower to freeze to death or be ripped to shreds.

Charlie made it through the fence and was too focused on getting to Julia to hold the fence for Dylan, who came through more noisily. Charlie's head swiveled around, his eyes darting one second, and then locked on to Julia the next.

'What's wrong?' he asked. 'Are you hurt? What happened?'

'I'm hurt,' she said. She forced a ghastly grin. 'Self-correcting injury.'

'What?' Charlie looked confused.

Julia closed her eyes and shook her head. 'Nothing. Help me up.'

'Holy fuck!' Dylan's voice. 'Your leg!'

It took a second for Charlie to react. 'Oh my God, Julia . . . your leg. It's broke.'

'No shit it's broke!' She stifled her voice because it reached for volume – that scream still trying to make its way out of her. 'Help me up, Charlie.' She thrust her right arm out to him, her left holding her rifle.

Dylan shook himself into action and crossed to the other side of her. They stooped down, each of them grabbing her by the upper arm. Charlie looked at Dylan and nodded his head. 'Ready? One, two, *three*.'

It was inevitable that her leg moved when they pulled her to her feet. It felt like the bone was bending again, trying to cut through her flesh. She tried to relieve the pain by holding her leg up, hoping the broken parts would hang naturally and not so painfully, but it only made it worse. She managed to control her voice, but her mouth still shot open and a little *Aaaahhh-aaah* noise came out of her.

They began moving her carefully toward the fence. Charlie and Dylan's eyes were constantly up and scanning as they did so. Julia stayed locked on to the cut in the fence, her teeth clamped down so hard that she thought one of them might crack under the strain. She wanted nothing more than to have never walked out of that house. She just wanted to be back in front of the fire, unbroken. Then she thought about why she had even left the house in the first place and she thought about the water tower and the view it would provide into Eden, where she could confirm or deny what Sergeant Kensey had held to be gospel truth.

Was Eden overrun?

They were halfway to the fence when a new sound reached her. One that she had not been expecting.

Tires on gravel. The roar of a diesel engine.

' . . . the fuck?' Charlie stopped dead in his tracks, staring at the gravel utility easement that led out to the main street. Julia followed his gaze and saw the blaze of headlights. She knew the shape of them well enough. It was a Humvee. One that was traveling fast.

It ground to a stop, causing gravel to skitter out in front of it. She could not see who was driving, but it was Harper that came out of the passenger side, leaving his door open behind him as he ran for the fence, waving for them to hurry up and not quite shouting, but not quite whispering, 'Let's fucking roll! Big horde's coming right at us!'

Charlie and Dylan swore in unison and began dragging

Julia for the fence. The boot of her broken leg caught and dragged her, but the two men on either side of her gave it no mind. They kept moving for the fence, even as Julia's entire body locked up with the strain of trying to find some momentary relief.

Harper was on the other side of the fence now, rifle in hand. He stared at Julia. 'Holy shitfire! Julia. What the fuck did you do to yourself?'

Charlie answered for her. 'She broke her leg. Open the cut.'

Harper swore again and grabbed the chain-link sections and pulled them apart like a curtain. 'We don't have time for this. We don't have time. You need to hurry.'

'We're hurrying as fast as we can.'

'Hurry faster!'

'I'm trying!'

Julia was being passed through the cut in the fence amid grunts of strain and effort and her own noises of misery. Then all of the sudden she was horizontal, Charlie and Dylan on her arms, and Harper holding her legs, on the thigh. It hurt, but not as bad as when she'd been vertical. But now there were other things to think about.

'Where are they coming from?' she choked out, trying to get her rifle up, but it was difficult with Dylan and Charlie on her arms.

Harper's response was clipped. 'Eden. Where else?'

'How many?'

'Fucking all of them.'

In her vision the dark shape of the Humvee, crowned by its own halo of headlights, was jerking and jumping back and forth with the hectic movement of the three men hurrying her along. They were breathing hard, all three of them. Actually, she was breathing hard, too, but for different reasons. She had to keep clenching every muscle in her body, as if doing so helped squeeze the pain out of her.

Another sound reached them and it split the late-night air like a crack of lightning and for a moment it spurred a burst of adrenaline that blocked all pain. It was the sound of a single voice lifting in a howl, eerie and ululating. And then it was answered by others. Many others. *Hundreds* of others, and it seemed the woods all around them were suddenly alive.

We're fucked. We're so fucked.

It's your fault. You did this.

Please don't let anybody die, because it would be my fault ...

They reached the Humvee and doors were ripped open. Someone in a familiar uniform was crouched inside. Calculating eyes already assessing her. Dirty old cap tilted back on his head to keep it out of the way.

'Careful, now. Don't bump that leg. You banged it up good, didn't you?'

'Kensey?' Julia said, feeling a little confused. Afraid. Exhausted. 'I thought ...'

'Yeah, you thought.' He pulled a pack up close to him and began unzipping the compartments. He was crouched in the back of the Humvee with Julia, while Charlie and Dylan piled in, slamming the door shut behind them. Harper took the front passenger seat and then the Humvee was tearing a wide U-turn, spitting gravel into the wheel wells.

'Are you a doctor?' she asked, lamely.

'Corpsman, once,' he answered. 'But that's about as close as you're gonna get.'

In the front, Harper was holding the radio handset and looking into the back. But he wasn't looking at Julia; he was looking through the back, into the woods behind them, his eyes searching the trees for the telltale movement.

'Come on. Get us the fuck out of here.'

They spun off the gravel and onto blacktop. The other four vehicles in their convoy were there and already rolling. Julia was able to see them by craning her neck up and around Reilly's body to see out the side window of the Humvee. And for the briefest of moments before the Humvee fell in beside the other vehicles, she could see the road toward Eden and the throng of gray movement, pouring toward them like a ghostly wave in the moonlight.

Then they were on the road, heading in the opposite direction.

She moaned a low, miserable sound.

'I'll give you something for the pain in a minute,' Kensey said, mistaking her moan for one of pain.

But it was simple despair.

Eden was lost.

SEVENTEEN

INSIGHT

LARouche SLEPT SOUNDLY FOR the first time in a very, very long time. And perhaps that was why the first gunshots did not wake him up, or even enter into his dreams. It was like his mind had been searching for a path where it could disconnect itself from reality, and had finally found its way out of the briar patch and could not be called back. It was off in another realm.

But like a dog on a leash, it was eventually yanked back. Freedom was just a cruel illusion.

His eyes shot open, cognizant that something was happening and he was missing it.

Claire was beside him, both hands on his chest, shaking him violently and yelling. 'Wake up! Wake up! We're being shot at!'

The interior of the box truck loomed out darkly in front of him and he could see out beyond the half-closed door. It was dark out but there was fire and flashlights blazing. The shapes of men swept shadows over them. The gunshots were rapid, obliterating, overpowering.

They popped and boomed all around and then something that felt very near to the box truck exploded, heavy and resonant, poking his eardrums even inside the truck and the concussion hitting him all at once. He watched the view from the small opening at the back end of the box truck and it flashed bright silver. Shrapnel peppered the side of the box truck, a few of the larger pieces punching jagged holes through.

Claire cried out and lurched onto LaRouche, twisting around, one hand trying to reach around to her back. LaRouche's mind was still a foggy blank. He knew what all of these things meant – the answer was dawdling around in his brain somewhere – but it wouldn't come to him in that moment, so it was almost like none of it was happening. It felt dreamy.

He pulled himself upright and hunched over Claire's form, as calm as though this were some simulation that he knew he could not be hurt from. He took her by the shoulder and rolled her onto her belly, where he could see what she was trying to reach for. It took a moment for him to find the tear in the fabric of her clothing. The blood had not begun to seep through just yet. Hot shrapnel sometimes was like that. It lodged like a cork and sometimes seared the blood vessels closed so that only a little ooze of red escaped.

But he found the wound. It was on her left shoulder blade. Not deep, or large, he thought. Most shrapnel couldn't make it through bones as easily as bullets could. It didn't stop it from hurting, though. Claire was writhing under his hands.

'It burns! Holy Jesus it burns!' she sobbed.

'You're okay,' he said in a voice that didn't sound like his own.

Something is happening. What's happening?

We're being attacked.

Yes, but . . .

Another enormous explosion rocked the world around

them, but it was not as close as the first. Again his eyes went to the box truck and saw that some of the others were hunkered down, lying prone with their hands over their heads. Some of the women were screaming, as well as some of the men. Others were surging out of their piles of blankets looking like madmen, half naked, anger glistening in wide-open eyes as they scrambled for their weapons.

Pap-pap-pap-pap-pap-pap.

Spears of dull red light shot through the side of the box truck. The men that were standing tried to hunker down. Some of them made it, others twitched and crumpled. It was hard to tell if they were hit until they didn't get up again. The ones that were still alive started crawling for the open door.

The sound was sharp, staccato. But controlled. Not some asshole laying on an automatic trigger. *Controlled bursts*, LaRouche thought. He could feel the connection being made in the back of his brain, but the fog of sleep and panic were muddling things. He was already moving toward the open back end of the box truck with everyone else and he realized with something like relief that his hand was latched on to Claire's and she was moving with him.

Just get the fuck out of here.

That was the first time that the reality of the situation started to dawn on him, breaking through the grogginess of his sleep. He was aware of the tin box he was confined to, aware of the bullets ripping through, putting down men in front and behind him, and he thought of the term *death trap*, and that was when it came home.

I've got to get out of this death trap.

Two of the men in front of him made it out. Two out of how many? A dozen, maybe? LaRouche wasn't sure whether that terrified him, or brought him some vindictive sense of joy, or maybe it angered him. Maybe it did all three.

Just go.

He made it to the end of the box truck and slid, down onto his side and off the tailgate in a tumble. Claire landed next to him. She let out a yelp and she had her eyes closed, though he couldn't tell if it was with pain or fear. In front of him lay a dead man, just outside arm's reach. All around him was shouting and cursing and gunfire and the smell of spent propellant.

Gunsmoke.

A scent that brought him back like smelling salts.

Yes. Controlled bursts. The rapid tattooing chatter of an M249 SAW. The fury of the fight. The sound of haphazard suppressive fire, punctuated with the well-chosen shots of those that had found cover and concealment. He knew all these sounds very well, but a cohesive thought still eluded him.

The dead man in front of him held a rifle. It was some black, synthetic thing with a magazine. LaRouche didn't have the foggiest idea of the make or model. It didn't matter. It was a weapon. He only hoped it had some rounds left in the magazine.

He crawled for it on his elbows, skinning them on the gravel and rocks.

The sound of the gunfire seemed to abate for a brief moment, only to energize itself again, but this time farther away. Still close enough that LaRouche could hear the bullets whizzing over his head, though. Close enough that they were kicking up dirt into his face and making him swear.

He snagged the rifle lying next to the dead man and retreated to the box truck. Claire had brought herself up and was sitting with her legs curled up to her chest, taking cover behind the rear tire of the truck. Good. That was the perfect place.

LaRouche slipped into the cover with her, squatting in front of her while he fiddled with the weapon in his hand, trying to find the magazine release.

'What's going on?' she shouted at him. The sound of a person who couldn't hear her own voice. 'Is someone trying to kill us?'

He looked at her earnestly and wondered what was going through her head in that moment. Did she hope against hope that it was someone coming to save her? Was she cursing him for taking up a weapon? Or did she think that this was just something worse, because things were always getting worse for her? Maybe this was just a rival gang of thugs, trying to lay claim to supplies and they would just murder everyone whole-sale, including the women.

He didn't answer her, though he knew. He didn't answer because he didn't know how she would take it. He didn't know how she would react. So he just put a hand on her shoulder, their earlier conversation rolling through his brain pan like a ricocheting bullet.

'Stay here,' LaRouche said, his voice low and serious. 'Don't fucking move from this spot. You hear me?'

She nodded, wincing. 'Yes.'

He left her there and he hoped she would be there when he returned. At the very least he hoped that she would be alive. He worked his way around the front of the box truck, cross-ing the distance between the two sets of tires quickly so that low-ranging rounds wouldn't take his knees out from under him. He paused at the front tires and then swung around, using the engine block for cover.

He finally managed to get the magazine out. He didn't see brass, but steel. Steel cartridges. Cheaper, and less reliable. But beggars could not be choosers. He slammed the magazine back into the rifle and fought to see if the safety was engaged. He couldn't seem to find a safety. He thought about just cranking off a round to see if it was ready to rock and roll, but then thought better of it. He hoped the previous owner had flicked it off before he'd been taken out.

He registered someone's voice, shouting at him. 'LaRouche! LaRouche!'

He looked up from the weapon and scanned the dark, fire-lit camp. In the darkness of the countryside that surrounded them, he saw the sparkling of muzzle flashes but he couldn't tell if they were aimed in his direction. They made him cringe back into cover, but he didn't hear the *buzz-snap* sound of rounds passing close to him.

A voice cried out again, but it was not the same voice, and this voice was simply screaming in pain. It was calling for help, and apparently not getting it. Then it just trailed off and was quiet again.

'LaRouche!'

He leaned back out from the cover of the engine block and looked again at the scene before him. One of the tents was on fire, nearly burnt down to nothing but blackened tent poles. There were two cars that didn't have a solid window between them. It was between these two bullet-riddled vehicles that LaRouche saw the dark form crouching.

It was Clyde.

'What?' LaRouche barked.

Clyde waved to him. 'Get the fuck over here!'

Why do I have to move out of cover? LaRouche thought. But then he was running. The distance between the front of the box truck and the two vehicles where Clyde was taking cover was no more than ten yards, but still it seemed that every shot doubled in volume and LaRouche got the disconcerting sensation that they were all directed at him.

He took the ground on his knees, ripping his pants and the skin beneath them, though he barely registered it. As he slid into cover beside Clyde, a round pecked at the dirt where he had just been and another gouged a trench out of the hood of the car just inches above their heads.

'Fuck!' Clyde was breathing heavily, sweating heavily, and looked sick. He stank of bourbon in a way that called to mind an old bald-headed man with mucous and blood and whiskey shooting out of his nostrils, sliming LaRouche's hands. And without the shield of anger, the memory made him want to gag. He wanted to wipe his hands on his clothing to remove the sensation of the snot and blood and liquor. Instead, he pulled himself closer to Clyde, because the stink of him was better than a hole in his head and the engine block was not quite enough cover for two men.

LaRouche didn't mean to shout in Clyde's ear but he did. 'What the fuck is going on?'

Clyde didn't react to the volume – maybe he was half deaf from the shooting anyways – but he gave LaRouche a queer look, as though he expected LaRouche to already know. 'We're being attacked. Come with me.'

Clyde started to rise, but LaRouche caught him by the shoulder and put him back down. 'Attacked by who?'

Why are you asking things you already know?

Clyde must have had the same thought, because he just threw LaRouche's hand off his shoulder and started moving to the back of the two vehicles, out of the safety of the engine block. 'I think you fucking know who, LaRouche. Another one of their fucking scouting parties poked our western sentry. He was able to sound the alarm. But I don't think he made it.'

At the trunk, Clyde poked his head up and LaRouche fully expected the top of it to pop like an overpressurized bottle. He scanned around for a moment, then ducked back down. 'Okay. You ready?'

'Where are we going?' LaRouche demanded.

Clyde bared his teeth. 'Don't fucking ask—'

LaRouche grabbed the other man sharply by the arm of his jacket.

Clyde's eyes snapped to his and LaRouche saw the truth of them in the flickering glow of firelight. They were empty glass, just like LaRouche's. Windows into an abandoned house. Clyde's mouth was open, spewing bourbon fumes into LaRouche's face. His tongue played at his bottom teeth, slipping across them like he was tasting blood.

LaRouche released him. He sat back on his haunches. 'Tell me where we're going.'

Clyde gave LaRouche a withering glare. Adjusted his glasses. Then he pointed to a van. 'There's a PKM in there. I'm getting on it. You're going to help me get it up and then flank them while keeping their heads down.'

'A PKM,' LaRouche said, his voice lacking any inflection of opinion. He wanted to tell Clyde to go fuck himself, but to be honest, he couldn't find anything wrong with what the other man was saying. It was a basic tenet of modern warfare. Apply suppressive fire. Move when the heads are down. Apply fire from multiple angles.

Clyde nodded emphatically. 'You ready?'

No. 'Yes.'

And then they were moving.

Clyde was up first, sprinting. LaRouche came up off his

knees and onto his feet, still crouched behind the vehicle. He peered and sighted over the top of the car. The hood of it was worse off than LaRouche had originally thought. It was studded and cratered with dozens of bullet strikes. Beyond the hood, the scene was one of chaos and fire. He was facing a far wood line that rose up into a hill so that the trees seemed to tower over them. There were a few campfires still burning, but most of the red glow of fire came from a vehicle that was just beginning to burn down, the husk of it like a skeleton picked clean. It threw dull light onto the lowest branches of the trees on the wood line, but above and beyond that it was darkness, except for the muzzle flashes that seemed to be racing for the top of the hill.

The sound of the battle still seemed angry and close, but LaRouche knew something that Clyde did not. He glanced off to his right and saw Clyde crouched at the back end of the van, flinging the back doors open. The angle of the van was so that he was concealed from the direction of the attack. He reached into the back and pulled out the PKM, a long-barreled, belt-fed cousin of the AK-47. LaRouche briefly wondered where in the hell they had come across it.

LaRouche turned back and saw that the muzzle flashes had reached the crest of the hill. A bullet pinged the ground but it was well away from him. As the muzzle flashes sank to the other side of the hill, the sound of then suddenly became muted.

Clyde slid in beside him and heaved the machine gun up onto the trunk of the car, then racked the charging handle to prime the belt. He settled into the stock, his face glistening though it was cold out. His eyes feverish and intoxicated.

'Stop,' LaRouche said, holding out a hand. 'Save your ammo.'

Clyde looked at him angrily. 'What?'

LaRouche put a hand on the side of the car and found the metal cold and frosted on his hands. He leaned on it. 'They're military, aren't they? The people that attacked?'

Clyde only nodded.

LaRouche felt suddenly sick to his stomach. It was the same feeling he'd had after he'd fought with Father Jim. After he'd pulled his pistol and put it to the other man's head. After he'd pulled the trigger and thrown himself down a path completely dark and unfamiliar to him. It was the sensation of realizing you are not who you thought you were.

US troops? he thought. *Am I fighting them? Am I fighting soldiers? Marines?*

But for some reason, his mouth was moving without the permission of his brain. While his heart told him *Traitor!* the rest of him just kept going down that path. It was a steep path, and it went only one way.

'We need to get the fuck out of here.' LaRouche realized he had stood up and was looking around for someone in authority. Chalmers, he supposed. 'Trust me, Clyde, we don't want to stay here. Things are gonna get real ugly.'

Clyde's eyes were wide, though the PKM in his arms had now been laid to rest. 'What the fuck are you talking about? We got 'em on the run!'

LaRouche gave him a hard look. 'You got the scouting party on the run, you dumb shit. That's what they do. They probe and then they run. And do you know what the fuck they're doing right now? Calling in the big guns. I don't know who these people are or how much equipment they have, but I promise you that we don't want to wait to find out.'

Clyde looked between LaRouche and the firefight that was

fading now, only a few muffled pops from the top of the ridge as the Followers' sentries pursued over the hill and then, getting away from camp and backup, would likely stop and come back, waiting for further orders. He mumbled something under his breath and then stood up fully, the big machine gun hanging in his arms.

LaRouche looked at him questioningly. He was beginning to feel the urgency of what he had said ticking through him. The thought of fighting against actual US troops made him nauseous, but he also had no desire to be killed by them. They needed to leave this area.

Clyde shook his head. 'It's not my call to make. You gotta find Deacon Chalmers and talk to him about it.'

They found Deacon Chalmers only a few minutes after their last exchange. He had only his massive revolver strapped to his hip in its leather holster and LaRouche could not see any other weapon. He was consumed with the task of gathering dead. LaRouche could see it in his eyes just as clear as the fire that consumed the car – Chalmers was enraged.

He was not a large man, but he did the work of two, stooping down into a squat and worming his hands underneath the armpits of a dead man with no face. He hooked his arms there, his hands grasping at the dead man's chest and hoisting him up off the ground. Chalmers seemed heedless to the bloody caul that flopped against his neck and face as he straightened and began to drag the body toward a gathering of others. There were only a few lying in a tight row. It seemed no one else had finished with the fighting and chaos just yet and Chalmers was the only one determined to begin gathering the dead.

Clyde hurried forward to help, but LaRouche did not

quicken his step. He stared at the short man with the gray beard and the cold and hot eyes that glared at nothing. He looked at the body that he dragged and the others that lay scattered around, crumpled over their wounds. Most seemed childlike in their deaths. The way they curled in on themselves. The fetal position instinctive.

LaRouche had a hard time figuring how he felt about it.

Knowing what he knew.

Being who he was.

None of it made any sense at all.

Clyde grabbed the dead man's legs and lifted them off the ground, and he and Chalmers carried the body. Chalmers gave no indication of thanks for the assistance, and even seemed not to notice that Clyde had come to help. He just kept staring and LaRouche couldn't really tell what he was looking at. The dead man's feet, perhaps. Or perhaps something none of them could see.

LaRouche followed along, still holding the unfamiliar rifle and wondering if they would take it from him. Did he have a right to a weapon in their eyes? This was a peripheral thought as the impatience crawled around his legs like grasping briars, prickly with the importance of his message. Would Chalmers listen to him? Would Chalmers listen to anyone right now, or was he too incensed to see reason?

They dropped the body with the others. Clyde carefully laid the feet down, but Chalmers did so without ceremony. He didn't stoop to lay the dead man's demolished head down. Instead, he just released it and it dropped there onto the ground with a muffled thump and a queasy-sounding crack, like maybe the skull had struck a stone.

Now Chalmers looked at Clyde and LaRouche. He seemed not to know them for a second and LaRouche watched his hand drift to his revolver for a moment. Almost an involuntary twitch. Then the deacon appeared to remember himself. He blinked twice, then furrowed his brow.

Realization did not mean a change in mood. Chalmers was still sour. 'What the fuck do you want?'

Clyde deflected to LaRouche with a look and a gesture.

LaRouche was not afraid of Chalmers, per se. Not in the way that Clyde and the others seemed to be. They approached with caution and did everything but cower. LaRouche understood the man as someone that was erratic in his temper, and often brutal with his decisions. Neither of these things made LaRouche uneasy, though. He had the same sensation standing before Chalmers that he'd had when he'd walked in front of Claire and wondered and almost hoped that she would stab him to death.

If you want to die so bad, there are many ways you could do it, he reasoned. *You could just not say anything and let whoever that was that attacked us blow this whole fucking camp up. You could go up in flames. Or maybe take a few 20 mm rounds to the chest that would turn you into pink jelly. I doubt you'd feel a thing.*

It was true. His life held little value to him. Yet he clung to it anyway.

'Did you have something to say?' Chalmers asked sharply. 'If not, then help me gather the dead.'

'You should leave the dead,' LaRouche replied. 'And we should leave this area. Immediately.'

Chalmers stared, his thoughts and expression a mystery.

'Who are those people?' LaRouche pressed. 'The ones that attacked us?'

'United States Marine Corps,' Chalmers answered, flatly. 'Out of Camp Lejeune, I believe.'

Like a tumbler lock, things suddenly fell into place for LaRouche. He'd known that they were US troops from the first barrage of gunshots that he'd awakened to. He'd known it from the controlled ferocity of their fighting, from the familiar sound of their guns, from the chatter of the automatic weapons and the explosion of well-placed grenades. But when 'Marines' and 'Camp Lejeune' were said, then other things far beyond tonight suddenly made sense.

'You've been fighting with them for a while, haven't you?' LaRouche asked, his voice quiet and earnest. 'They're hunting you guys down – hence your aggressive expansion westward. You're trying to get away from them.'

Chalmers's jaw muscles bunched. He did not like what LaRouche was saying, but he wouldn't deny it, either. He tilted his head back, looking down his nose at LaRouche. 'We are not trying to get away from them. The Marines that fight us are a vestige of the old world, the old government that ruled this land. God has sent us to conquer this land, but first we must gather our strength. Even after the fever has broken, a sick body needs time to marshal itself.' He pointed at LaRouche with a trembling hand, the finger almost touching LaRouche's chest. 'The Lord's Army does not *flee* from the Marines that so aptly call themselves *devil dogs*. We are gathering our strength and when we are complete we will return and wipe them out and claim the land that God has promised us.'

Do you really believe this crock of shit? LaRouche thought, but managed to hold his tongue. What he was picturing was not his own body being destroyed as gunships roared in and 20 mm Vulcan cannon belched flame and ripped earth and flesh alike. It was the girls and the women that had no choice but would still die along with the rest of them.

Thinking of them, he chose his words carefully. 'We need to move on from this place, and we need to do it quickly. When they come back it won't be to exchange gunshots with us. It'll be to exterminate us. Wipe us out completely.'

Chalmers glared. 'How do you know what they're going to do?'

'Because I was military. I was infantry once. And that's what we did. We patrolled forward and when we encountered resistance we held our ground or we fell back, but either way we didn't just duke it out. We called in an air strike. Or we called in an artillery barrage.'

For the first time the look of rage seemed to cool in Chalmers's eyes.

'Has this ever happened before?' LaRouche asked. 'Them probing your lines?'

Chalmers shook his head. 'Our base has never been attacked before. They've hit our supply lines and raiding parties many times, but never our bases. We usually don't stay in one place long enough for them to find us.'

'Well, then this is their golden opportunity, isn't it?' Movement caught LaRouche's eye and he looked to his right and saw Claire, perhaps fifty yards from them, kneeling over a woman that was lying on the ground. LaRouche wasn't sure if the woman on the ground was dead or not. She didn't appear to be moving. Back to Chalmers. 'They're ranging us. This is what they do. This is what *I* would do. Poke at your lines, get an idea of numbers, and then call in a strike – probably air. And I give it twenty minutes tops before they're all over this place and this little clearing is nothing but dead bodies and burning rubble.'

Chalmers looked out of it for a moment. He frowned, reached up, and touched the left side of his face with his fingertips and when they came away they were smeared with half-dried blood. He stared at them in the firelight and then rubbed his thumb across them, at first softly and then vigorously. Finally he looked at Clyde, ignoring LaRouche.

'Clyde, tell everyone to gather every weapon and piece of ammunition they can find, but be ready to roll in ten minutes. Send a runner to the other groups along the western front.' He looked intensely at Clyde, his words full of hidden meaning. 'Have them tell the others that now is the time. Tell them to meet us in the place we spoke about. Do you know what I'm talking about?'

Clyde nodded.

'Pass it on,' Chalmers ordered. As Clyde disappeared at a run, Chalmers fixed his eyes on LaRouche. 'I still don't know about you, LaRouche. I'm concerned about where your heart is. But for the time being I want you with me.' He pointed to the rifle in LaRouche's hands. 'And find yourself a better weapon than that.'

EIGHTEEN

TALKS

LEE AND HIS SMALL group left Camp Ryder when it was still dark. They did so quietly and without fanfare. The camp around them was dead quiet. The fires smoldered and the predawn hour was the coldest of the night. Lee's companions were an old man named Hughes, a brown and tan dog named Deuce, and two men that Lee had only just been acquainted with: Jared and Noah.

Jared was a short, pale man of perhaps thirty years with a bulbous bald head and scraggly bright red hair that attempted to grow along the bottom of his skull, like a wreath around his head. He seemed odd, but he was generally pleasant and quick to laugh. Noah was younger and seemed a wolf-man compared to Jared's relative hairlessness. He had thick brown hair and an almost black beard that seemed to consume his entire face. He was a serious man with suspicious eyes and love for no one but his fellow survivors from Dunn. He appeared to treat even Lee with some caution.

The only others that were awake that early morning were Angela, Tomlin, and his chosen two, Nate and Devon. Angela was there because she would not sleep after Lee had left – they both knew it. He had tried to rise as silently as possible. In his better days, he would have succeeded, more or less. But the injuries of his bodily abuse plagued him worse in the mornings, when the air was coldest and the joints were stiffest, and he found himself ever so slightly clumsy. Neither Sam nor Abby stirred when he gathered his things. But Angela lay there, wide awake, staring at his dark figure and feeling the heat of the blanket next to her slowly drain away. When he had grabbed his rifle, she had pulled the blankets off her and yanked boots on her feet and accompanied him outside.

Tomlin, along with Nate and Devon, were awake because they were preparing to leave at first light. Where Lee and his three men and a dog would stick mostly to known roads that wormed through the Camp Ryder Hub, Tomlin, Nate, and Devon were slated for a journey south and slightly west, which took them on roads that they had yet to travel or even scout. They did not want to navigate them in the dark.

The farewells were short and quiet and perfunctory.

Lee's hand lingered momentarily on Angela's arm, but then he was climbing into the vehicle that they would take. It was the same old Ram truck that Lee had once borrowed from the late Keith Jenkins. The other option was Arnie's little red Geo. Lee had offered Tomlin the truck, but Tomlin said he preferred the Geo because it was less noticeable. More incognito.

Old Man Hughes drove the truck, and Lee took the shotgun seat. Jared was behind Lee, and Noah was behind Hughes. Deuce was behind them all, in the bed of the truck, but tucked close to the cab to get out of the cold wind. Still, his snout protruded, always testing the air.

Now, on a long, winding back road that took them due east toward the town where they would meet Colonel Staley, Lee leaned forward and looked up at the sky through the windshield. Above them, stars shone starkly, but to the southwest, in the direction that Tomlin and Nate and Devon were heading, the sky was gray and dull as gunmetal, and the fire of dawn caught the edges of clouds and gave them away. A thick, ugly storm was coming in with dawn, and already the trees around them were beginning to sway as the wind picked up and the temperature started to rise. The bigger storms always brought warm winds with them. It would feel like the beginning of spring for a few days, and when the storm had passed, everything would freeze over, colder than before.

It was full light by the time they neared the meeting spot. It was not the actual town of Mount Olive that they were heading to, but rather an intersection just outside it, where Suttontown Road crossed Highway 55. That was the location that Colonel Staley had selected. Lee wasn't sure about the significance of this particular intersection, if there was a significance at all. He suspected that it was more a random selection.

The roads in this area of the country were flatter and straighter than in the Piedmont. The terrain had less contours for the roads to work around. As they were about a mile out from the meeting point, Lee waved for Hughes to stop.

Hughes obliged, but gave him a look.

Lee cracked his door, then looked into the back. 'Noah, come with me.'

Noah slid out of the pickup without question.

'Where you goin'?' Hughes asked, tapping the steering wheel steadily.

'Just sit tight here,' Lee said as he swung his legs out. From the truck bed, Deuce scrambled over the side and shook his coat out, ready to accompany Lee on whatever journey was planned. 'I'm going to push up ahead over that rise to the north. Hopefully get a look at this meeting spot.'

'I thought we were going to trust them.'

Lee grunted. 'We're here, aren't we?' He closed the pickup door behind him and crossed to the northern side of the road, Deuce finishing marking territory that he would never be able to hold and then following. Noah stood at the shoulder, scanning the flattish lands around them. As Lee reached him, he touched his shoulder and spoke as he moved past. 'Stay low and quiet, and about fifty yards behind me. Okay?'

'Okay. Got it.'

The rise seemed the only terrain feature in sight. There were small lines of woods, but Lee figured the hill and the brush that lined the top would be better for their purposes of staying hidden and trying to get a good vantage point on the intersection where they were supposed to meet the Marines.

There was risk any way you cut it. Lee was cautious. Colonel Staley was cautious. In all likelihood, Staley had lookout posted on a wide perimeter around the meeting point, and even doing the careful thing of reconning the meeting point ran the risk of stumbling on one of those Marines. But Lee also wasn't willing to step in blindly. His trust could only be stretched so far. It seemed the better risk was to run into a sentry.

Lee had read once that the best way to win at poker was to be the cautious player. But if you found yourself matched up against another cautious player, then neither would win. The game would just keep going. Stalemate.

Someone needed to take risks. Break inertia. Get the ball rolling.

They skirted the rise where gray-brown weeds stood at chest height. Deuce nosed through them, threading his way through thicker stands on a serpentine course, but always staying close to Lee. At the top, Lee knelt, looking out through the weeds where he could see blacktop crossing over blacktop.

Lee saw why Colonel Staley had selected this particular intersection. There was nothing there, save for a single house at the northwestern corner. The house was barely there anymore, just the brick façade standing, while the rest had crumbled and burned away. A few massive oak trees stood on the property and it seemed that one of them had fallen and taken out the back of the house.

Parked in the front yard of that house were two MATVs, the all-terrain vehicle that had begun to replace the Humvee on the battlefield. To Lee it had the look of a technical rather than a military vehicle. But he'd never rode in one and had heard they could take much more of a beating than the Humvee. These two were desert tan in color and seemed even from a distance to be well used. One bore an M240 machine gun on top, and the other a Mk-19 grenade launcher. Both the turrets were manned. Aside from the Marines in the turrets, Lee could not see the others, though he was sure they were there. The scene gave him an eerie, out-of-his-depth feeling.

What am I to these guys? I have no guns, I have no supplies. I'm just some random yokel who claims he's in the military as I pull up in a beat-up pickup truck along with a few civilians. His lips were set in a grim, frowning line. *I wouldn't even believe me.*

Lee knelt there in the tall weeds, the wind rattling through them and swaying the bearded tops. He watched the meeting spot for several long minutes. Keeping his eyes unfocused, looking for movement and not finding it. If they had snipers and sentries on the perimeter, they were well hidden.

But he expected that they would be.

Noah had sidled up next to him. 'Looks like a trap to me,' he whispered.

Lee frowned down at the intersection, probably about a third of a mile distant from them. 'I dunno. If I was in Staley's position, I'd being doing the same thing. Certainly wouldn't be showing up without weapons, waving a white flag of truce. If it were me, and I had his resources, I'd have a whole lot more than you see, parked just around the corner. Snipers in the woods. QRF ready.'

'So . . . ?'

Lee chewed the inside of his lip, considering. 'We go back and do what we planned to do. We show up at the meeting and hope for the best.'

They slunk back from the ridge, staying low until they were out of view, and then they stood and followed their own path of crushed dried weeds back to the road. They made quicker time going back than they had coming in.

'They're just out of sight of us,' Lee said when he climbed back into the pickup truck.

Hughes eyes him. 'So what's it look like?'

'Looks like a trap,' Noah asserted again.

'Looks like they're being cautious. Which is smart.' Lee pointed down the road. 'Go ahead and roll us in. But go slow. And be ready to book it if shooting starts.'

Hughes took in a big breath and let it slowly out of his nose. Then he picked his foot up off the brake and the truck started forward.

Lee didn't take his eyes off the road ahead of him. 'Let's open our windows and hang a hand out. No pointing guns.'

Behind him, the two back windows whirred down and Jared and Noah put their hands out the windows. They stayed quiet, as they had been for the vast majority of the trip. Hughes rolled his own window down and shoved his own hand out the window, although he seemed begrudging.

The intervening mile slid past, a thinning safety tether, and then they made a bend in the road and caught sight of the intersection ahead of them, and the two big MATVs that sat in the lawn of the defunct house. And then the safety tether was gone. They were there. They were committed.

Being on a level with the two MATVs, the one with the M240 and the other with the 'ma deuce,' sent a little sliver of fear through Lee. He swallowed it down, jagged and scraping, but he just forced it down. Settled it. Kept on going.

Hughes had unconsciously taken his foot off the gas and the truck was slowing to an idle. Lee looked at him and the older man seemed to realize it. He lowered his head and accelerated again, but very slowly. It would not do to appear like they were charging in.

As they rolled forward, the M240 turret tracked them. All that Lee could see of the Marine that was manning it was a helmeted head staring at them from between two pieces of armor plating that framed the machine gun.

If they wanted us dead, we'd be dead, Lee kept telling himself. But it didn't change how uncomfortable he was with this situation. *Maybe they want us alive ...*

But why would they want Hughes and Jared and Noah? They wouldn't.

But it was possible they wanted Lee.

An image flashed through Lee's head, his own imaginings gone dark and rogue inside his skull: well-placed shots snapping back Hughes's head, then Jared's, then Noah's. Blood splashing on the back glass and spattering Lee's face. Old Man Hughes slumping forward on the wheel, eyes dead as marbles and staring at Lee and through him. The doors opening and men in familiar uniforms hauling him out and slamming him on the ground ...

That would be the third time. The third time I've been captured.

And then another little movie played. Most of it was the same, but when it came to looking at Old Man Hughes's cold, dead eyes, Lee took up his rifle, heedless of the firepower pointed in his direction, and shoved it out of his door as the men in familiar uniforms yanked it open, and he fired, even as they fired back. He could almost feel the impact of big, heavy bullets ripping open his chest. But he'd keep shooting until his attackers were dead, or he was dead, or both.

There were no games left to be played.

His life was an all-in hand.

Show your cards and wait for the river.

'Stop there,' an amplified voice said.

Lee glanced about, the morbid visions dancing in front of his eyes clearing and he saw the scene for what it was. Death, or not death. Depending on how Colonel Staley wanted to play it. A bit of a quandary, he thought. Good possibility of being fucked if you show up at the meeting. Better possibility of being fucked if you don't. So you show up and you say your prayers and you hope for the best.

Behind an armored door panel, a Marine was standing with a bullhorn up to his mouth, speaking to them. Old Man Hughes complied, stopping the vehicle. The man with the bullhorn told them to put it in park and turn off the ignition. In response to this, Hughes looked at Lee.

Lee just nodded. 'Do it.'

The shifter was shoved into park. The engine died. Old Man Hughes took the keys from the ignition and put them on the dash.

'Throw your weapons out the windows,' the voice said.

Lee immediately shook his head. 'Don't do that.'

He could feel the other's abrupt tension like a charge of electrostatic energy hovering in the air. The feeling he thought you might get when you're standing in the path of a lightning bolt. He shoved both of his arms out the window, displaying his open hands, and then he unlatched the door from the outside handle and stepped out.

The Marine's voice bore an edge to it now. 'Get back in the truck!'

Lee's rifle dangled on its strap, heavy on his chest, but he would not take it off, nor would he get back in the vehicle. He held his hands high above his head as he stood to the right of his open door and raised his voice, feeling his own hammering heart play with the strength of his voice.

'We're not going to put down our weapons!' he shouted.

'Get back in the truck or you will be fired on!'

Lee shut his eyes. 'We are coming to this meeting peacefully because it was requested by Colonel Staley! But we are not going to do it unarmed! Where is Colonel Staley?'

'Comply or you will be fired on!' the Marine called back.

Someone in the truck swore.

Was it really worth it? What would happen if they threw down their weapons? Would they be better off keeping them than throwing them away? They were outgunned as it was, so holding on to the weapons was more symbolic than anything. And yet Lee couldn't bring himself to just surrender them like that. Because if he put down his weapons and Marines rushed him with flex cuffs and a burlap sack to put over his head, he wouldn't be able to do shit about it except fight and most likely get his ass beat. But at the end of the day he would still be alive, and he would be captive for the third time. Held for ransom, he figured. Or as a hostage to make Camp Ryder more agreeable in whatever negotiations they had planned. In either case, Lee was more useful to his people if he was dead, and more hurtful to them if he remained alive. If he was alive, he could be used to manipulate, and his own life would be one of misery far worse than he had known.

But should Old Man Hughes and Jared and Noah pay the price along with him?

Maybe he should have been clearer with them. Maybe they should have known that Lee was going to play this one like a man with nothing left to lose. Maybe that would have changed their decision to come along.

Maybe, maybe, maybe.

Too late now . . .

Lee's gaze was fixated on the muzzle of the M240 and he saw that it was staring right back. He kept waiting for that muzzle flash that would be the last thing he saw.

'I want to talk to Colonel Staley!' he called one more time. 'This is Captain Lee Harden with the United States Army. Colonel Staley asked for this meeting and now we're here! Let's talk!'

The Marine with the bullhorn lowered it from his mouth. He had nothing left to say. He turned to the gunner on the M240.

Movement from the front of the demolished house. The brick façade still bore the front door and the porch. A man stood at the door. He wore the same uniform as the rest of the soldiers, but he wore no helmet. He glared out across the distance, right at Lee. A slender man whose eyes Lee could not see behind a pair of sunglasses. He had thin hair on the top of his head that seemed as gray as it was brown and matched the desert colors of his uniform like he had been born and bred for the job he had taken.

He held up a hand. 'Hold your fire,' he said. It wasn't

shouted, but rather projected, his voice carrying without being pushed, forceful without being strained.

Lee looked back at the M240, still waiting for that little yellow bloom.

Stop and smell the roses, he thought, somewhat madly. *Stop and smell the gunpowder.*

'You.' The voice carried over to Lee and he turned his eyes to the man on the front porch. The figure stood there with one hand on his hip, the other pointing at Lee. Then he waved. 'Come on.'

Lee heard a whine and a growl, and claws scraping across bed liner. He looked behind him and found Deuce halfway out of the truck bed. He pointed at the dog. 'No. You stay. Stay,' he said sternly. He'd been working on that one command, but it was still iffy. Deuce was a very independent dog and liked to make up his own mind about a lot of things.

This time, though, the dog stilled. But he kept on staring at Lee, his eyes wide with something like concern, ears as forward as they were physically capable of being. The picture of intensity.

To the men in the truck, Lee spoke quieter. 'Back way the fuck up. Don't do anything stupid. If things go bad, just go back home, you got me?'

'Lee—' Hughes started.

'Do what I say,' Lee said, and then started walking, still holding his hands up and away from the rifle on his shoulder.

The engine started in the pickup truck.

There seemed to be a stir. Lee noticed a few more Marines that had escaped his view before. One of them was prone amid the rubble of what had once been the back of the house. Another was crouched in the ditch beside the driveway. Both had bits of brown burlap tied to their helmets and uniforms and held Remington 700 rifles. Designated marksmen. Or maybe Scout Snipers, like Jack Burnsides. Absently, he wondered if they knew the man.

Lee called out to the man on the porch. 'They're going to wait down the road a bit. Your welcome party has us a little concerned.'

Through the black sunglasses he wore, Lee could not tell whether the man on the porch was looking at him or the pickup truck as it slowly began to back away. But he gave no reaction. He just stood there, both hands on his hips now, and he waited.

Lee kept walking forward. He wondered if they were going to attempt to search him, maybe to see if he had a bomb strapped to his chest, but they let him pass by. It seemed like they were waiting for the man on the porch to tell them what to do, but he seemed to be finished with security protocols for the time being. If Lee were being honest with himself he knew that they were on opposite sides of the same coin. Both had to show a little bit of trust in order to make anything happen. That the man was willing to set aside his own security protocols for Lee meant that perhaps there was more to this deal than an act of charity. And Lee did not know whether that was something that he should take comfort in or whether it should make him more concerned.

As Lee reached the front porch of the old house, he stopped and looked up at the man before him. 'Colonel Staley?'

No expression. 'Captain Harden?'

Lee smiled.

The man pushed the front door open. It groaned and the corner of it scraped across the hardwood floors on the inside of the house. Lee realized the door was just barely hanging on its bottommost hinge. The man extended his hand to Lee. 'I apologize for the harshness of our first meeting, Captain Harden. I'm sure you understand. Times being what they are.'

Lee took the offered hand and looked the man up and down. Colonel Staley was about a head shorter than Lee. He was older, as most people of his advanced rank were – full bird, Lee noted – but he held himself in a certain relaxed way that belied his command, and his conversational voice was soft, with the slightest hint of a southern drawl.

Lee gave the colonel's hand a single pump. 'I understand,' he said, though he found his voice slightly stiff. For a moment it felt strange shaking hands with a colonel he'd just met. There was a time when he would have observed military decorum in this situation, but it felt like a far-off concept and it only ran through his head fleetingly. Here was not an officer and a subordinate, but rather two men with interests unknown to each other and some issues to work out.

Staley motioned Lee through the open front door. Lee stepped through, eyes quickly scanning. There were three Marines inside, both in full-battle rattle. Lee stiffened when he saw them, but neither made a move toward him. One stood at a crumbled section of wall, around which you could catch a view of Highway 55. He looked over his shoulder at Lee with some curiosity, but mostly apathy. The second stood at a table with two chairs. He watched Lee impassively.

The third was older than the other two, but younger than Staley. Somewhere in his forties, Lee guessed. His hair was a bland color of brown with a heavy sprinkling of gray. He matched Lee for height, but was more thickly built, particularly in the chest. He wore the designation of a first sergeant. He had a rifle strapped to his massive chest, but his hands were clasped cordially in front of him. Casually calculating

eyes tracked Lee as he entered what was left of the house.
They were the eyes of a large and powerful predator. They
were confident, and they seemed to divide all things into two
categories: *Prey* or *Miscellaneous*.

Lee stopped in the middle of what remained of a room. It
was difficult for Lee to tell what the room had once been – a
living room, he supposed. Most of the furniture was burned to
cinders and then soaked with rain. The table and chairs were
dirty, but unburnt. Lee wondered where they had come from.
Here he could also see the majority of the old oak tree that had
crashed down into the house. It was a blackened skeleton.

The door groaned shut.

Lee turned partially and looked at Staley as he shoved the
door closed. The older man removed his sunglasses, folded
them, and used them to point at the door. 'I know. It doesn't
make much sense to close the door when half the house is
missing.' He moved around Lee to the table. 'But there's
something about a door hanging open that annoys me.'

Lee didn't respond.

Staley gestured to the barrel-chested man standing at the
table and chairs. 'Captain Harden, this is First Sergeant Brinly.
My senior enlisted man. Will you sit with me, Captain? We've
got a lot to talk about.'

Without the sunglasses on, Lee could see the colonel's
more Icelandic features. The thick eyebrows. The squinting
eyes and the wrinkles in the corners that seemed to say that
Colonel Staley had spent the better part of his lifetime in deep
concentration. A man that did not make decisions lightly.

Lee crossed to the table, watching Staley and Brinly for a
sign of what was to happen next. But neither man was giving
anything away. They seemed placid, but focused. It struck Lee
that both of them might be waiting for him to speak, though

Lee had no intention of being the first. Speaking was showing your cards, and he wanted to keep his secret. It was his only defense. After all, they had called the meeting. They chose the time and the place. They could be the first ones to show their hand.

Lee took a seat, slowly.

Staley followed suit.

Lee sat stiffly erect, his feet wide, ready for movement, his hands not far from the rifle on his chest, but making sure that he wasn't touching it. Staley, on the other hand, leaned back in his seat, one hand resting on his lap, and the other on top of the table, still holding the folded sunglasses.

After a moment, Staley seemed to sense that Lee wasn't going to be the first to speak. He tilted his head and took a breath, seeming to choose his words very carefully. When he spoke them, they were deliberate and measured, like combining volatile liquids in a beaker.

'First, I want to thank you for making the trip to meet me here. I understand that safe travel is a little more challenging when you don't have armored transports.'

Lee gave a fractional nod.

Staley continued in the same cautious tone. 'In the interest of full disclosure and speaking on even terms, I'm going to say something to you. And when I say it, I would simply ask that you not react poorly, as we're both here under truce. I don't mean to harm you, and I hope you feel the same.'

Lee was still as stone.

Staley's eyebrows lifted. He leaned forward, putting both his elbows on the table, his hands clasping together around his sunglasses. 'What would your reaction be if I were to mention the name "President Briggs"?'

NINETEEN

TENSIONS

LEE'S PULSE SUDDENLY FELT like a swarm of bees, buzzing through his veins, rattling around in his head. There was a ringing in his ears. He tried to maintain a poker face, but couldn't help his eyes jagging to the left, where First Sergeant Brinly stood just a single pace away from the table, watching him. The best Lee could manage was not to grab his rifle. He remained still.

Take a breath.

If they want you, there ain't shit you can do about it.

But they'll have to take a dead body.

Staley didn't move much, but his hands spread out, showing both palms. 'We're just talking. No need for action right now, Captain Harden. Just talking stuff out.'

Lee looked at him hard. 'Then talk. It sounds like you have plenty to say.'

Staley retracted his hands from the table and leaned back. 'Honestly, there isn't much that I can say. I take it from your reaction – as controlled as it was – that there is no love lost between you and President Briggs. Is that correct?'

'*Acting* President Briggs,' Lee corrected.

Staley smiled, fleetingly. 'I guess that answers the question, doesn't it?'

'What are we doing here?' Lee shifted in his seat. His index finger touched the polymer grip of his rifle. It was very close, but so was Brinly. And the other Marine standing off to the left. And the one behind him, standing at the collapsed wall. He could hear their breathing all of the sudden, like his ears were suddenly keener. He could hear the creak of rubber boot soles on the hardwood floors. The brush of their uniform fabric as they shifted ever so slightly.

Could I take them?

Sure, I could take them.

But what about the others outside?

'I can see the wheels in your head turning.' Staley shook his head, an almost unnoticeable gesture. 'Please. I promise you that we're not here for you. We're here to talk. *I'm* here to talk. To meet you. To figure out the other side of the story.'

'What story?'

'Briggs's story.'

'How long have you been in contact with Briggs?' Lee tried to keep the tension out of his voice. It came across flat and without inflection.

'Well.' Staley picked at something that was stuck to the tabletop. 'We've been in contact since the beginning, but that implies something worse than the truth.'

'And what would the truth be?'

'The truth is that our communication has been spotty at best. The equipment has failures that are often ... convenient.' The corners of Staley's eyes wrinkled, like he wanted to smile, but wouldn't let himself. The inference was clear, though.

'So your comms work when you want them to work,' Lee clarified.

Staley answered in a roundabout way: 'They're down more often than not.'

'And when they're up? When they're working?'

Beside the table, Brinly spoke for the first time. His voice deep, and accented with someplace in the northern interior. 'I think our comms have been down for, oh, two months now?'

Staley's mouth twitched. Behind his lips, his tongue seemed to be scouring his teeth, like it might find the appropriate words there. 'I'll simply say that this meeting has been a long time coming. Your name has been whispered for so long that some of the men say you're just like Bigfoot. People have stories, but no one's ever seen you firsthand. Needless to say, I was surprised to be speaking with you directly on the radio last week. And somewhat dubious.'

Lee didn't take any of what Staley had said as a compliment, nor was he certain that it was meant that way. Staley did not seem the type to flatter. This was a simple statement of fact. 'So what's being said about me, Colonel? Maybe I can separate some fact from fiction.'

'Well.' Staley rapped his knuckles on the tabletop. 'The facts I gathered from the first few communications with Colorado – that's where President Briggs is, did you know that?'

Lee nodded, curtly.

'The facts I gathered were interesting and a little incongruous. Special Forces soldier, Navy SEAL, or some other secret government operative – no one was very clear on that point. But what they were clear on was that you had' -- he put air quotes here – '*gone rogue.*' Staley waited for a reaction, but received nothing. So he continued. 'You had access to large amounts of weapons, ammunition, and ordnance. Various war-fighting materials. You were in direct opposition to the government of the United States. You were fighting a guerrilla campaign against government entities inside North Carolina.

And you needed to be killed or captured immediately, and it didn't matter which.'

Lee's mouth had gone dry, but his expression remained impassive. He worked some moisture onto his tongue and swallowed. He realized he was incredibly thirsty, but he kept himself focused on the task at hand and kept his eyes locked on Staley's as though to look away would be instant death. 'So can I ask you why the might of the United States Marine Corps hasn't come crashing down on my head already? Why are we sitting here talking?'

'Because there were other commands given,' Staley said plainly. He leaned forward onto his elbows, his fingers interlacing. 'Things that I didn't agree with. I was ... uncomfortable accepting as fact the positions that certain people were claiming for themselves.'

'Such as the presidency.'

Staley nodded. 'And when you don't want to get cow dung on you, you should probably stay away from things that smell like bullshit, isn't that right?'

'I suppose so.'

'So now.' Staley's eyes narrowed. 'What's bullshit and what's fact? Gimme the Gospel According to Captain Harden.'

'I'll give you the truth.'

'That would be rare.'

Lee looked to his left, made brief eye contact with Brinly. Then he twisted and could see the shape of the second and third Marines out of the corner of his vision. They were all in the same places. In the back of his mind he kept thinking about them and kept having to tell himself that it didn't matter if he could get away from them. He wouldn't be able to get away from the ones outside.

And what about Colonel Staley? Could you take him?
And First Sergeant Brinly?

Lee didn't hold a special place in his heart for high-ranking brass. This one seemed a little more steely than most, but you weren't awarded rank according to your skills on the battle-field. It was time and politics, mostly, and sometimes ribbons. But mostly time and politics. Colonel Staley might command Marines, but chances were his tours were done in safe zones well out of the range of gunfire and mortars, and he'd prob-ably spent the last few months in the relative safety of the Camp Lejeune Military Preserve, surrounded by protective details similar to the ones around them now.

First Sergeant Brinly seemed like he would be the one to fight. Lee could see it in the way he watched Lee. He had predator's eyes. Very confident. Very still. Always waiting. And when he struck, if he struck at all, it would be fast, and ugly, and devastating.

Lee was by no means overconfident in himself. But he knew his capabilities. Brinly was a hard man, but not the hard-est. Not even the hardest that Lee had killed. When Lee looked at him he saw his huge chest and thought *top-heavy*. A man that had much faith in brute strength. Lee probably couldn't outmuscle him. But if he could break his balance, he could put him on the ground, and once he had him on the ground, he could take a half second to shoot the other two Marines and Staley, strip Brinly's rifle, and either shoot him or stomp his throat in before making a run for it.

If the need arose.

So far, things teetered but held.

So far . . . but Lee had yet to tell the truth.

'I'm not SF and I'm not SEALs,' Lee said. 'Not a covert agent or anything like that. Just a soldier. Me and forty-eight others were given this ... doomsday mission, I guess you could call it. Wasn't supposed to ever be used. Just a contingency.'

'And yet here we are.'

'Here we are.' Lee looked over Staley's shoulder at the blackened remnants of the oak tree. 'The mission had specific parameters. I won't lie to you, I went outside of those parameters. Not grossly, but ... ' He trailed off.

'You broke the rules.'

Lee looked at him, his voice cold. 'I left a bunker. I left a steel box in the ground to see what the fuck was going on outside. Communication with any sort of command was non-existent and had been for nearly a month. I needed to know what was happening. So I left the fucking bunker. Yes, I broke the rules.'

Staley considered this. 'Seems like a minor infraction.'

'I was declared a nonviable asset,' Lee said flatly. 'Or "gone rogue," to use your words. I was blissfully unaware of this until a few weeks ago, when people started trying to kill me. Come to find out I rubbed some people a little wrong. Mostly Briggs. The whole time I thought I was playing for the home team. Come to find out I'm kicking at the wrong goal.'

'What was the goal they wanted you to be kicking at?'

'Abandon everyone and everything. Hightail it to the interior states. Leave the coastal states to be overrun.'

Staley took a deep breath through his nose and seemed to be mulling something over in his mind.

Lee leaned forward. 'And if you've had any contact with Briggs, I'd bet he gave you similar orders.'

Staley didn't directly answer, though he didn't deny it, either. 'You mention the word *overrun*.'

'Yes.'

'Can you explain?'

'A while back we made contact with a microbiologist from the CDC. Name of Jacob Crane. He was coming out of a research facility in Virginia where some tests were done. Some computer models run. Et cetera.' Lee felt heavy speaking of Jacob, like the words themselves were formed of lead. 'He was also speaking from experience. He said there were hordes of infected people coming out of the major northeastern cities, some of them numbering in the millions. He said that they were following the path of least resistance, moving south and consuming everything they came across.'

'Like locusts,' Staley said.

'The comparison was made.'

Staley absorbed the information with little reaction. Lee waited for something, some sign of where the colonel's head was at, but the man kept his thoughts hidden from Lee, his expression enigmatic. 'I understand that this is the reason you are demolishing the bridges along the Roanoke River. At first I was . . . hesitant to believe it. Partly because it makes things difficult for me.' His voice took a different tone, and here for the first time Lee caught a hint of anger. 'I'm already fighting a war on two fronts. Camp Lejeune isn't just full of Marines. It is full of their families, as well as refugees from Jacksonville. We've secured the perimeter of the compound as best we can but it's a constant push on our fencing from the infected. We've been lucky lately but for a time they were getting through almost daily.' His voice darkened yet again. 'And then we have another problem that we've been pushing away from us. Some whacko, fringe religious group calling themselves the Followers of the Rapture.'

Lee raised an eyebrow. 'I've heard of them.'

Staley didn't look at Lee. Rather, his eyes remained focused on something that was on the tabletop. 'Apparently they originated out of the New Bern area. When this whole thing went down they came out of New Bern, trying to push south, and ran right into us. Which was bad for them.'

'I can imagine.'

Staley was silent for a long moment. He seemed to wake up with a breath and then pressed on: 'We've been pushing them westward, away from us. They're slippery fuckers, always on the move. And between manpower issues trying to keep the base secure and everyone inside fed, we haven't been able to pursue them as hard as we would have liked.'

Lee watched Staley carefully. 'Why pursue them at all?'

Staley made eye contact with Lee and held it. There was something else there, but it was staying unsaid. Lee wanted to pry the truth out of him, but thought it was best to let this one die. Staley didn't seem like a man that liked prying.

'Anyway,' Staley said a little brusquely. 'All of that is to say that when I heard about your plan to blow the bridges, I was a little dubious. I didn't want to be involved in another man-power drain, if you'll pardon my word choice. However, I've received some reports over the course of the last few days from some of the men I attached to your groups and it seems that the threat has been verified.'

Lee felt some heat rising underneath his collar. 'If you had doubts, it would have been nice to hear about them earlier.'

'You're hearing about them now.'

'And what is so convincing about these reports?'

'Lance Corporal Gilmore is attached to your man Wilson. We stay in contact via sat-phone and his reports are given on a nightly basis. He's impressed upon me the seriousness of the threat and says they are struggling to stay ahead of the hordes.

It's come to my attention that he has, on several occasions, seen these hordes with his own eyes.'

'They are,' Lee confirmed. He'd received his own reports from Wilson. They were running ragged. Sleeping four hours at night and then running to the next bridge. It seemed no matter how fast they moved, the infected were right there with them. Maybe it wasn't the same horde. Or maybe it was. Maybe it was so vast that they couldn't outrun it. 'We could use some help getting ahead of them.'

'So he says.' Staley moved on. 'My other man is Sergeant Kensey. He's with an entire squad that went to your man Harper in Eden.'

'I'm aware.'

'Sergeant Kensey gave his most recent report early this morning. Around five o'clock. Did you receive a similar report from your man?'

Lee stiffened. He didn't like Staley's tone. It was the sound of a man broaching the subject of bad news. 'No, we were already on the road at five.'

Staley dipped his head. 'I understand that you were holding Eden as a sort of pinch point. Bottleneck the hordes into a smaller geographical area. Good plan. Unfortunately, Sergeant Kensey reported to me this morning that Eden has been overrun and that they had to pack out.'

Lee's right hand didn't know what to do with itself. It found the strap of his rifle and clutched it. He had to force himself to remain seated and think calmly. 'What about my people? Harper's group?'

'They pulled out with Sergeant Kensey's squad. Like I said ... the city had been overrun.'

Lee realized his face had formed into a harsh grimace. He tried to relax. It wasn't working. He suddenly despised Staley for knowing what he did not. He didn't want to hear about his people's status through the mouth of someone he barely knew and wasn't even sure was a friend. It was only a blow to his pride, but still it chafed him.

Lee's hand worked at the rifle strap. 'I can't help but feel that we might have kept a foothold in Eden if we'd received the assistance we thought we were going to get in the first place.'

Staley smiled without humor. 'Yes, hindsight is always twenty-twenty.'

Lee leaned forward abruptly and put his fist on the table. He hadn't meant for it to be aggressive, but it hit the table with a loud thump and he heard the Marines shift as though getting ready to interfere if things got violent. 'So knowing what you know, are you still sitting on your hands or can we expect a little fucking help?'

Staley didn't even blink. 'Captain Harden—'

'No.' Lee jammed his index finger down into the wooden tabletop. 'I'm done with word games and bullshit. There's no time for it and I'm not inclined to play politics.' He gave a deliberate look at Brinly. 'You got your men here and mine are too far away to do any goddamn good for me. If you are gonna do something with me, then do it, for chrissake. If you're gonna help, then help. I can give you a fucking laundry list of things we need. But if you're going to sit there on the other side of that table and contemplate whether or not it's *worth it* to come out from behind your fucking barbed wire fences and actually *do something* before we're all slaughtered, then I think we're done talking.'

For the first time, Lee felt like his words were punching through Staley's veneer.

Lee pointed at him. 'You know what's out there now. You

can't plead ignorance. The situation is exactly what I told you it was. The needs remain the same. There is nothing left to discuss. You're either here to help me, or you're here to hurt me.'

'I can promise you that we're not here to hurt you or any of your people,' Staley said, his voice rising.

'Wasting my time hurts me,' Lee spat. 'Give me the help or let me go.'

'I'm generally not fond of ultimatums,' Staley said. 'However, I see our situations entangled. So far as I can tell, neither of us is willing to submit to the command and control of President – or *Acting* President – Briggs. Additionally, it appears that what you have told us about the size of the infected hordes from the north is true, or at least true enough to pose a serious threat. Your plan for the bridges over the Roanoke River concerns me, but in all of the time I've considered this, I can't really come up with a better option. If they truly are numbering in the millions, then we simply don't have the resources or the manpower to fight them off in a widespread offensive. So the bottleneck is necessary. Which means that our interests are the same. And allies are sparse enough these days.'

'I've heard this before, Colonel.'

'What happened to your bunkers?'

The question was so sudden and out of the blue that it rocked Lee back. He'd told Staley that he'd been in a bunker, but never mentioned anything about having more than one. And yet Staley was clearly asking in the plural. Was he just making an intuitive leap because of Lee's mention of supplies and a 'doomsday mission'?

'Who told you about bunkers?' Lee asked quietly.

Staley shook his head. 'Could've been Briggs, could've

been someone else. Hell, maybe I knew about it all along. The fact of the matter is this: I'm the bank, and you're the guy looking for a loan. The currency is beans and bullets and boots on the ground, but the situation remains the same. Before the bank makes a loan, it always wants to know what happened to *your* money.'

Lee stewed on that for a moment, and Staley let him think it over in silence.

'Briggs has control of them,' Lee said, finally. 'He sent one of his men after me. They worked their way into my camp, got a little close to me, and then when we were out beyond the wire by ourselves, he shot me in the head and stole . . . something from me.'

Staley's eyes shot up to Lee's scarred head. 'I was wondering what happened there. What was the thing he took?'

'The only way to find and access the bunkers.'

'I see.'

'Colonel Staley,' Lee said with a heavy breath. 'My mission here was very simple: find survivors, band them together, and start to rebuild something. Make sure that what popped up was built on American principles. But Briggs thinks that's a waste of resources. He thinks we're already doomed and he's written us off.' Lee made sure that he had eye contact with Staley. 'But the reason he took that thing is because he wants those bunkers for himself. Eventually the problems at his doorstep won't be that big anymore and when that happens he will come knocking and anyone that opposed him now or in the future is going to have to make a decision. I've already made my decision, and I'm fully prepared to deal with the consequences when they come – and they will come. But what about you, Colonel? Where will you stand when Briggs comes knocking?'

Staley stood. 'Captain, I'll cross that bridge when I come to it. For now we have a common enemy, and a common goal.' He extended his hand across the table. 'Let's work on that.'

Lee wanted to think about it. The words that Staley had said worried him. He did not want a temporary friend that he would always have to look over his shoulder for, wondering when the knife in the back would come. He wanted to be able to trust Staley, but after those words had been spoken, it seemed that ship had sailed.

But then, he didn't want the hand to retract.

Like it or not, he needed Staley's help.

He reached out and grabbed it. 'Deal.'

TWENTY

Edges

JULIA THOUGHT THAT THE pain could not be worse.

But as the adrenaline of the moment faded, she realized that it can always get worse. And it did. She had broken her arm once when she'd been a little girl. In the old barn that sat back from their house where Dad used to keep the lawn mower and store the majority of his tools, she and Marie had played Don't Touch the Ground, hopping from workbenches to the dusty seat of the old Cub Cadet rider, then to five-gallon buckets filled with joint compound that their father would probably never use. And then Julia had decided to go higher up and started climbing up an old, metal shelving unit full of toolboxes and worn-out power tools. Marie was perched on one of Dad's sawhorses and she'd been giggling at first, but then she got quiet. Julia, caught up in the moment, kept climbing.

'Jules, don't go up that high,' Marie had said in her big-sister voice, which would often come on suddenly when she decided they might be doing something they would get in trouble for. 'Dad's gonna kill you if you knock that over.'

But Julia was still laughing, working her way up the shelving unit and dangling off it dramatically, trying to get a rise out of Marie.

'Serious, Jul-ee-*uh*!'

'It's fine,' Julia snickered, reaching for the top shelf. 'It's sturdy.'

Then she had decided to shake the shelving unit to demonstrate that it was sturdy and put her worrywart sister at ease. But when she shook it, all of the sudden it didn't seem so sturdy. And a big black case that held one of Dad's circular saws went tumbling off the back of the shelf and all of the sudden there wasn't enough weight to counterbalance even her small frame. And the shelving unit was tipping over.

The rest was a lot of crying and sobbing and profuse apologizing and screaming for Mom (but not Dad, for God's sake; Marie, don't call Dad, he's gonna kill me!). To this day Julia remembered the sick feeling of surprise, right along with the sick feeling of knowing you were in deep, deep trouble. She remembered the taste of dust in her mouth and the sharp pain in her forehead where the cordless drill had slipped off and pegged her in the head. And she remembered the *concept* of the pain in her arm, but the memory of it was so far away that it didn't seem so bad.

But this was bad.

This was different.

This was here and now.

Their little convoy had fled the water tower and hauled ass down the highway, looking for an out-of-the-way place where they could find some refuge. Like a little herd of hunted deer, trying to find a place to bed down. Like refugees they ran, looking at places as they drove by at fifty miles an hour and deciding in the span of seconds whether it was safe or not. Could they stay the night there? Were they far enough away? Would they be able to hear the infected horde if they came upon them?

And like those running deer, they followed the paths of least resistance and they instinctively went with the things that they knew. For the entire time they'd been on the road, small industrial parks were the safest places that they'd found. They were usually set out of the way of the main highways, a lot of them had fences to keep people out, and most of them were built simple and hard to get into. The factories and warehouses were ideal places to pull out of the way, to roll up big bay doors where trucks had once loaded themselves down with pallets and crates of whatever the hell the place manufactured, and to pull their little convoy in and disappear for a while.

So when they saw the familiar buildings – most of them corrugated steel, white or tan in color – the convoy seemed to yank itself off the road and into that little out-of-the-way business park. The Marines got out and posted coverage while Harper, Charlie, Dylan, and the other remaining few found the quickest way into the safest compound and got their vehicles out of sight.

Julia didn't remember much of any of this. She remembered looking out the window of the Humvee and seeing scraggly, leafless trees flying by, and beyond that just dark night sky, clear and cold and brittle and brutal.

And Kensey.

He stayed with her. She held on to him with abandon and he took the pain of her fingers digging into his arm and shoulder without a single wince or hiss of pain. He just kept telling her she was going to be okay, to hold on, and that they were finding a safe place. At first she told him to shut the fuck up and quit trying to soothe her, but he ignored her and continued on.

'It's okay. You're all good.' He went on and on.

And eventually it worked.

But when the panic left, the pain came on stronger.

They had moved her into the building and by the cold, halogen light of a few flashlights and lanterns, Sergeant Kensey pulled up his medical pack beside her and began giving her broken and torn-up leg a closer looking over. He took out his medical shears and cut quickly and expertly through two layers of pants that she wore, exposing her leg. Julia had refused to look. She didn't want to see that bone sticking out again. Even the thought of it made her stomach weak and her bladder and bowels fluttery.

Even through pain, weird thoughts found their way in.

Embarrassment because her legs hadn't been shaved in months.

Really, Jules? That's what you're worried about?

She had clenched her eyes shut and refused to look at anyone or anything. She kept her teeth clenched down so hard that her jaw ached, but it barely registered over the throbbing in her leg. The ache in her jaw had a soothing quality to it, though. Like her screaming jaw muscles and teeth were little relief valves, letting off the pain like a boiler lets off steam. But not enough. There was still too much for her to get out.

After a moment, she felt a hand touch her head. It was ice cold, but in that moment, it felt nice. She realized she was drenched in sweat. Simultaneously hot and shivering. She heard Kensey say her name, so she opened her eyes. Kensey was crouched there at her head, looking down at her. Harper and Charlie were crowded in close. All their faces were half shadow and half harsh light. From the halves she could see, there was pity and concern.

'Julia,' Kensey said again. 'Your fibula is broken. It's

sticking out of your skin. I have to set it, okay? I have to set it and sew up your leg or it's going to get infected. It's going to hurt a lot. Worse than it hurts now.'

'No,' Julia groaned. 'That's not possible.'

Kensey smiled wanly. 'I can give you some morphine. I've got plenty.'

Julia bit her lip and shook her head, opting to close her eyes again. She didn't like looking at them right at that moment. She wanted the blackness. The blackness helped her focus on other things. Like every other place in the world that she would rather be in that moment than lying on her back on the cold cement of some anonymous warehouse, getting ready to experience pain she could not comprehend.

But she wasn't going to get knocked out.

'No, I don't want the morphine,' she said.

'What?'

Her eyes shot open, suddenly angry. 'I don't want the motherfucking morphine! Fuck!'

'Julia.' Harper tried to step in.

Julia shot her hand out and seized someone by the ankle – she wasn't quite sure who it was. 'No! No! I don't want to be out of it! I don't want to be loopy on some fucking drug when the infected come for us! Fuck! Just get that shit over with! Jesus Christ, please stop talking about it and get it the fuck over with!'

She imagined in her head that the three guys exchanged a look – like doctors over a patient on a stretcher, trying to figure out how best to proceed with surgery. But whatever they communicated in those looks that she imagined, they never said shit to her. There was just a long, eerie silence. Like everyone was holding their breath. And she started holding her breath, too, because she could feel Kensey's hands questing on down her leg, sending little lightning bolts of pain everywhere he touched. Eventually her lungs started to burn, so she started breathing in short, shallow little bursts through pursed lips.

Like Lamaze, for the baby you never had.

The baby that you're never going to have ...

What the fuck are you even thinking about right now?

Then she felt someone holding her arms down and she knew that it was about to happen.

No no no no no.

And then the worst thing she had ever felt happened to her. Her eyes shot open to blinding whiteness and the glare of hellfire with devils' pitchforks in her leg and there was bone grinding on bone, and bone rending on flesh, and she was positive that she was in hell because this feeling was never going to end, it just kept on going and going and going and *Jesus Christ just give me the morph—*

Then she passed out.

She didn't stay out, though. She kept coming to. It felt like floating up from the depths of a lake and breaching the surface, only to find the surface on fire, and then diving back under. When she was under she dreamt of things with mouths tearing at her and red beasts with horns and claws delving their talons into her legs and trying to burrow, burrow, burrow. In and out of these nightmares, she had no concept of time. She thought to herself that it couldn't possibly take so long to set a broken bone, that there must have been complications, because she was so sure that hours had passed, but every time her eyes opened and she felt the fire engulfing her again, Kensey was still there, huddled over her leg. She tried to tell him to give her the morphine, but then she would be under with the red beasts and the biting mouths. Finally, she started trying to tell him to stop completely, but she had no more success forming those words than she'd had before.

When she came up from unconsciousness once, Kensey was done. He was seated by her side and it was quiet in the warehouse and dark save for one source of light – she couldn't tell whether it was lantern or flashlight. The pain had faded, but it was still heavy and all-encompassing.

'Am I okay?' She slurred the words together, picking her head up off the ground with some effort, the tendons in her neck standing out and her muscles shaking badly. She still refused to look down at her leg for fear that he had not set the leg and she would see that bone sticking out again.

Kensey looked at her with eyes that seemed tired and red. She realized that he'd been dozing off before she had spoken. He reached up and put a hand to her shoulder. 'Yeah. I got it set. And your legs stitched up and bandaged.'

She realized that she was crying again. Her face already felt stiff and crusty from the tears that had dried, but being awake even for this short time had them coming again. She laid her head back again and stared at the ceiling, baring her teeth. She reached out and grabbed something – his jacket, she thought.

'Fuck it. Gimme the morphine,' she groaned.

She heard his voice very calmly tell her that she'd done good. She heard some rustling in his bag. Out of the corner of her vision she could see him lifting something into the light. A small bottle, upended onto a syringe. She turned her head and watched him draw a small dose out. She was surprised at how little there was in the syringe, but she didn't ask for more. She felt like it was bad enough that she'd given in, and if he gave her a small dose, that would be best anyway.

She felt the pin prick on her leg – like hearing a raindrop in a storm.

'Will it knock me out or just numb . . . my . . . ' Her leg felt incredibly warm. Not uncomfortably so, but like she was dipping herself into a bath. And it spread across her body quickly until she could feel it in her face, a warm, smooth sensation. After feeling the worst pain she'd ever felt in her life, this was the most blessed relief she had ever felt. The contrast was mind-boggling. 'Holy fuck, that is strong stuff,' she wanted to say, but the words smothered out on her tongue and she slept.

Dawn found the Followers of the Rapture on the run. Deacon Chalmers's camp had taken whatever could be carried in their hands and slung on their backs or thrown into the cars that they took. LaRouche stayed with Deacon Chalmers, as he had commanded, and they had left the camp mere moments after LaRouche had issued his dire warning.

LaRouche had quickly rooted around for a better rifle. He found a dead man with an M14 and an old GI belt with three spare magazines in a pouch. He dropped the crummy rifle in his hands and appropriated the superior rifle – a little weathered, but otherwise in good shape – and pulled the belt off the other man. It was a little loose around his waist and the pouch sagged it farther off his hip, but he didn't have time to adjust it. Chalmers was yelling at him.

When he looked up, Chalmers was standing up in the passenger side of a 1980s model Z71 pickup, teal green in color. The man with the bushy gray goatee waved at him. 'Let's go, LaRouche! You're driving us outta here!'

LaRouche left the dead body that he'd just plundered and ran for the pickup. The bed had some odds and ends in it. Food, and water in big, dirty-looking jugs, piles of damp-looking clothing, and a few rifles. He got in the driver seat and saw a four-speed on the floor.

Chalmers slammed his door shut. 'You know how to drive a stick?'

LaRouche cranked the car and slipped it into gear. 'Yeah, I got it.'

'Then drive. Don't stop until I tell you to.'

And then they had driven out of camp and when LaRouche looked into his rearview mirror he saw a trail of cars and trucks and campers coming after them, clouds of dust kicking up in their headlights as they went. But there were also plenty of other people that were milling about in a panic, yelling to each other that they needed to get out of there, but not seeming to be able to find a ride. One of the men caught Chalmers's pickup truck as it slowed to take a curve and vaulted into the bed. But all the rest were left behind.

By the time the camp passed out of sight, LaRouche could still see people there, and many vehicles still sitting, unstarted and abandoned, and he wondered how many people had simply run off into the woods. And he wondered about the women in the cages, and the pregnant ones in the tents, living in comparative luxury. Had anyone gathered them? Had anyone bothered to save them?

And what about Claire? Had anyone grabbed her before they all just fled the scene like criminals?

You did this, LaRouche thought. *You told them what was coming. You told them that they had to leave immediately.*

And if he hadn't told them he was almost positive that things bigger and badder than a recon patrol of Marines were going to come after them. Artillery was going to start flattening the earth around them, tanks were going to roll, helicopters were going to start buzzing overhead, spitting flame and rockets and destruction. Once he had called it a beautiful sight, but now he was terrified of it.

He was right about that, wasn't he?

They hadn't abandoned those people for nothing, had they?

Because no matter what, bad things were coming for whoever stayed in that camp. Whether it was the Marines or the infected. They might have a chance against the infected, if it wasn't a large horde. But fighting against the Marines was a losing proposition.

They drove for a time. LaRouche kept seeing pale shapes in the woods, just out of the range of the pickup's dim headlights. But when he looked at them, there was only darkness, and he did not stop. Could not stop. They needed to get away from the camp and they needed to get far enough away that whatever came for them wouldn't be able to find them again.

Shortly before dawn, LaRouche thought he heard the faint booming of explosions and when he looked in the rearview again, though it was difficult to see past the headlights of the vehicles behind him, he thought he saw a glow in the sky where their camp had been.

Maybe Chalmers saw it, too, because he told LaRouche to stop.

'Take a quick break, let the others catch up,' he said.

LaRouche put on the brakes. Behind them the convoy jumbled together as it rolled to a stop. An accordion collapsing in on itself. Chalmers opened his door, and LaRouche decided to do the same. The night had been frigidly cold, and it was still chilly, but a strong wind was blowing and it carried with it the smells of warmer, stormier weather.

No sooner had they opened their doors than people began to shout and yell back and forth. Questions were being asked, LaRouche thought, mostly of Chalmers. But though the organization was loose, even the Followers had ranks and divisions and a chain of command, and the leaders of squads that had survived were getting out of their vehicles and trying to make contact with their underlings, trying to get head counts and see what their strength was.

But Chalmers was not concerned with them, and he did not answer even the few questions that were directed at him. Eventually the panicked askers ducked out of sight, realizing that Chalmers was not paying them any attention. He was standing up on the running board of the pickup truck and looking out in the direction where they had come from, eyes on the sky.

LaRouche looked in the same direction. Still not quite sure whether that was the glow of fire he was seeing. He had the itch to continue on. His stomach was in knots, and it was burning again. He wanted to get moving again, though he kept scanning the crowd and looking for Claire.

'LaRouche,' Chalmers called. When LaRouche turned to look, the other man had a faint smile on his lips. His eyes shimmered in the glow of headlights and he looked zealous and full of righteous anger. 'You were right. The Lord delivered us from the evildoers. And you were the mouthpiece that he spoke through.'

LaRouche stood there, hand on the cold roof of the pickup, speechless.

Chalmers reached a hand out and grasped LaRouche's. His fingers were hard and calloused and oddly hot. The grip was ferocious and trembling, but the man that held him was still smiling madly. 'The Lord rewards his true servants.'

LaRouche could only nod, his hand crushed in Chalmers's vise of a grip.

He looked out again at the convoy, overflowing with

people trying to find where they belonged, jostling and bumping shoulders, and he thought, *Where's Claire?*

Clyde drove the flatbed truck with the wooden cage on the back. The cab of the truck was meant for a maximum of six people, but there were eight crammed in. He drove fast, hauling over bumps and curves, always on the ragged edge of the sensation that the truck was going to tip over. Especially with all that jostling weight in the back. The thing was top-heavy. When he took curves hard, he could hear the women in the wooden cages, crying out in alarm. It grated at his nerves. He hadn't wanted to take this truck. He'd wanted to leave them behind. But he rescued them and they were repaying him by squealing and complaining.

Ahead of him the roads were empty and the sky was gray turning to pale blue. The barren trees writhed in their rooted places along the side of the road and trash and debris and leaves skittered recklessly in front of the van, caught in the wind. To the southwest the sky was still dark as night, a column of black clouds coming in, its vanguard tinted pink by the rising sun. Pink and turning to orangey red.

Red sky in morning, sailor take warning.

Clyde looked to his right and saw his passenger, a thickly built, bearded man that Clyde recognized but whose name he could not seem to remember. Craig? Or Clegg, maybe? Whoever he was, he held a battered Soviet bloc AK with the buttstock on the seat between his legs and both hands clutching the foregrip. He leaned on it like an ancient sentry on a spear. Behind his grizzled, threatening appearance, his eyes were worried. The man kept checking the side-view mirror on his side of the vehicle. Perhaps looking for pursuers.

Would the Marines come after them like that? They seemed

to hound and harass, but they'd never really chased them down before. The new guy, LaRouche, seemed convinced that the Marines were going to wipe them out indiscriminately, not caring whether they were chewing through men or women, innocents or combatants. But in Clyde's experience, the Marines seemed to press, to prod, to poke, and every once in a while they gave a solid attack.

Except for the bridge, Clyde thought, feeling sick to his stomach.

Yes, the bridge over the Roanoke River. The one he'd been stationed at with his crew, trying to stay a step ahead of reports about a convoy of military vehicles heading in their direction. A convoy of supplies, according to the man they had captured. *Nick was his name*, Clyde recalled. Chalmers had tortured him until he told them everything, and to be honest it hadn't taken long. Chalmers never took very long to get people to tell him the truth. He didn't waste time getting down to brutality. His was instantaneous and unrelenting. Clyde had stood outside Chalmers's little farmhouse where he had the man captive and all he'd heard were the man's screams and not once did he hear Chalmers ask a question. Not until the man named Nick was begging him to let him talk.

He'd told them about the convoy, and how they were heading to that bridge, though he seemed to not want to say why they were going to that bridge specifically, and Chalmers didn't appear interested enough to pursue that line of questioning. Chalmers had only wanted to know how many men, and how many guns, and how much supplies, and what kind of supplies.

Food. Water. Medicine. Fuel. Guns. Ammunition. Ordnance.

The man named Nick had never answered the question as to *why* that convoy full of supplies was heading toward the Roanoke River, but Chalmers's eyes had been alight with a panicked sort of greed. He didn't care about the reasons, even if Clyde did. Chalmers only wanted to take the convoy. They rarely had the chance to take a target so rich, even if it was more heavily guarded than they were used to.

Then Chalmers had carved words into the man's chest and given them instructions to set up on the bridge and send him out on the road to meet his old friends. Chalmers didn't actually want to scare them away. He wanted to goad them into a reckless fight.

And for a moment it seemed to have worked. Clyde was standing there in the woods with two of his squad mates, watching the road when they saw the Humvee come hurtling around the corner, heading for the bridge. But there had been no convoy behind it. The Humvee made a screeching U-turn, all its windows open, bristling with rifles, the turret on top chattering heavily away at them. Clyde had hit the dirt and watched the earth around him become speckled with bark and wood particles as the heavy machine gun tore up the trees over his head.

He'd found LaRouche that night as he patrolled the woods that bordered their encampment at the bridge. He'd captured the man, a sodden wreck who seemed on the verge of taking his life and being done with it, reeking of booze and madness. He'd taken his prisoner back to the main camp.

Later, he'd heard about the helicopters.

They came in fast and wiped out the bridge, and everybody in the encampment. Marine helicopters, he'd been told. Two men had been on a ranging patrol, trying to see if they could catch sight of the convoy with all the supplies again, and they had returned to Chalmers with this report, and ever since it had reached Clyde's ears, he had unconsciously listened for the beat of rotors in the air.

Now, as he kept catching his bearded comrade glancing in the mirror, he wondered if he, too, was looking for those helicopters. Looking for dark specks in the sky to suddenly raise up over the tree line and come after them, rockets and chain guns blazing.

When LaRouche had made his warning, and Chalmers had ordered their immediate withdrawal, Clyde had taken off running, disturbed by how readily Chalmers seemed to trust LaRouche. Clyde himself wondered about the man's loyalties and could not decipher where the man stood. Wherever it was, he was holding something back from them.

But Clyde had done as he was told and had run through the camp, shouting, 'Grab what you can! We're hitting the road in five minutes! Five minutes! Everyone get the fuck out of here!'

The call had been taken up by others and soon Clyde could hear the command, made in a hundred different voices, echoing around the camp. And when he heard that, he stopped shouting and started trying to find a vehicle to take out of the compound.

In the truck, with dawn taking the sky and storms coming, and no fucking clue where the rest of their people had gotten off to, he looked into his rearview mirror and locked eyes with the girl in the middle of the backseat, directly behind him. The girl with the green eyes that called herself Claire. She stared right back at him, her green eyes mournful in a way that he did not expect. She, of all people, he thought would have looked at him with a sort of pleasure in this moment, as though silently acknowledging that they had gotten what they deserved.

She had not said a word since he'd found her standing outside the cages with the other women. She'd begged him to take them, and he had been conflicted for a moment. Here was a truck that was just as easy to take as any other vehicle. But in this truck were only the women. And when Chalmers judged him on how he had performed, how would he view Clyde for taking the women as opposed to a truck with supplies or weapons?

The truckload of women was essentially a truckload of mouths to feed.

In the end, expediency had won out. The truck was there, the keys were there, and he was ready to go. As he had cranked the truck, the sound of the engine had called others to him. Claire had jumped into the backseat, and he had allowed that only because he didn't have the time to shove her in the back with the others. Then the cab of the flatbed truck was suddenly filled with men clambering to get in. Filling it up with their bodies and their packs full of food and water and weapons so that there was barely room to move.

They were not the last to leave the camp, but they were still far behind the main column that had left with Chalmers. They had driven at dangerous speeds through the back roads in the last direction that Clyde had seen the main column headed, but he had yet to even see the hint of tail-lights ahead of him.

Are we lost? Are we by ourselves now?

He looked into the rearview mirror again and saw Claire still staring right back at him. He couldn't tell what she was thinking, but he wanted to know. For reasons that he could not explain she gave rise to old feelings. She resurrected something in him that he thought he had killed a long time ago. And he resented it. Bitterly.

Who the fuck does she think she is?

How dare she look at me like that!

For the very briefest of moments, his thoughts flashed back and it was like they were dreams rather than memories and even the few months that had gone by since they had been his reality seemed like geological ages. He remembered *her*.

Haley . . .

The one that he did not want to remember. The one that he refused to think about as if his mind were a castle and his shame a wall and she the siege force. Every night in the darkness she tried to creep over his walls, tried to sneak in on the backs of others.

Was it *her* that Claire reminded him of?

I don't wanna think about it. I don't wanna think about.

Please just leave it alone . . .

He remembered *her* face in colors and textures and concepts, but not in its totality. He could see blood, though. So much blood. And a box cutter in his hands. And he could hear his own voice, weak and tremulous, saying he was sorry. And he felt the cold floor of a convenience store. And the hot air of a summer night. And the thing, the *thing* cradled in his arms . . .

LEAVE IT ALONE!

'Where the hell are you taking us?' the bearded man said suddenly.

Clyde snapped out of the memory like a man startled from sleepwalking. He slammed on the brakes. The ABS kicked in, the tires chirping across the roadway as everyone in the back cried out in alarm, a chorus of yelps and screams and tumbling bodies and hands slapping for purchase on the windows and seats. The van lurched to a stop in the middle of the road.

In an instant Clyde saw all of the things he had done, the good and the bad, the truly evil, the inhumane. And he saw the things that others had done in front of him. The things that Chalmers had done. And LaRouche. He saw an old man on his back, spitting blood and snot and whiskey and drowning in his own vice.

Shock and disgust become rage over time.

Clyde was shaking, but not from fear or adrenaline. He shook because he could barely control himself. He stared at the man with the beard and imagined the man's throat opening and the life spilling out of him. He saw himself doing it. With a box cutter.

'Get out,' he said, his voice almost a whisper.

'What?'

I gave him a chance. He didn't take me seriously.

He shoved the shifter into park and in one swift motion reached across the center of the van, swiped the man's rifle away from his clutching fingers, and drove a fist into his throat. The man gagged and choked. Clyde felt his anger rise, like an animal tasting blood. The weakness of this other man only spurred him on. He shoved the man into the door and unlatched it so the door sprang open with the man's weight against it. He tumbled out of the van onto the pavement. Clyde leveled the rifle at him and pulled the trigger.

The trigger would not depress.

'No!' the man croaked, one palm held out to stay his execution. 'Please!'

Clyde realized the safety was on. He saw the man on the ground in front of him, but he was visualizing the old man with the whiskey bottle in his throat. LaRouche had shown no mercy. LaRouche had been brutal, and it seemed that he had been shown favor for it. Perhaps what goes around didn't come around. Maybe might made right. Maybe the meek didn't inherit shit and everything went to the strong and the malevolent.

He flicked the safety off and shot the man four times.

The voices behind him cried out in surprise, but then were deathly silent even as the last shot echoed. He reached over the seat and closed the door. The man was still alive, screaming, kicking his legs, but Clyde was through with him. He sat back in his seat. His hands were shaking when he pushed his glasses back up onto his nose. Then he pulled off and left him there. And it wasn't until a mile down the road that he felt the faintest notion of regret.

TWENTY-ONE

LATE

JERIAH WILSON AWOKE TO Dorian's face, staring down at him with concern scribbled all over his features. He was standing over Wilson and shaking him by the shoulder. Wilson came out of sleep like a drunkard. The previous day and night had been long and strenuous, both physically and mentally. Wilson and almost every man in his crew were delirious with exhaustion. And like a drunken man he reeled for a moment, swiping Dorian's hand from his shoulder as his brain slowly reasserted itself.

The very next thing that he noticed was that it was light out.

Yesterday, they'd bought their time by rushing through a bridge demolition that was so quick and haphazard it made Wilson clench his sphincter as he activated the detonator. But it went off without a hitch and then they had made a sprint for the next bridge, as the sun was slinking off toward the western horizon. They made it there while it was still light, skirting the edge of a small town called Weldon and hoping to God that whatever was in there – if there was anything – would not hear them, or at least choose to leave them be. They didn't hear a peep from the town as they worked, and it seemed that their luck would hold. They had hoped to get the bridge rigged and blown, earning themselves a two-bridge lead. But darkness had fallen after rigging only the first two I-beams, and the dark made it treacherous to continue. Wilson had not wanted to use light for fear of attracting attention from anything in the town that lay at their backs. They'd made camp a half mile from where they'd rigged the explosives. The bridge was a longer one, so even at that distance they were still sitting at the base of the bridge. It wasn't technically necessary – 'C4 is completely stable,' Lance Corporal Gilmore kept repeating – but everyone felt a little better not sleeping right on top of it.

Wilson had slept in the bed of the LMTV. He usually slept in the Humvee, but he'd been developing a crick in his back and thought it would be good to sleep with his legs stretched out and his back straight, rather than slumped in the tight seat of the Humvee. It wasn't as warm, though, and the cold metal bed of the LMTV soaked through his clothes and blankets alike and chilled him all night long.

Now he could see the sky was clear and cobalt. Not just the gray of dawn approaching, but the brilliant blue of dawn *already passed*. All around him, he could hear everyone else coming out of their sleep and uttering swears as they kicked off blankets and unzipped sleeping bags, everyone in a sudden rush to be upright and moving.

Wilson came upright out of the pile of blankets he'd slept under. 'What the fuck?'

Dorian looked pained. He had taken last watch. No one set alarms to wake them at dawn. It was the last watchman's job to go around and wake the camp up to another cold dawn. But here they were waking up at least an hour past, with bright morning sunshine hitting them from the east and dark, ominous clouds encroaching from the southwest. There was only one explanation for this.

'I fell asleep,' Dorian said lamely. 'But listen . . . '

'Fuck!' Wilson threw his blankets off and grabbed his rifle. 'We're already behind the fucking wire and then you go and pull some dumb shit like this!'

'Listen!' Dorian almost shouted.

That stopped Wilson. Dorian rarely raised his voice for any reason. Clutching his ice-cold rifle, Wilson looked at the other man with a furrowed brow. Around him, the others must have heard Dorian's raised voice because they too had fallen quiet for a brief moment. Wilson was about to tell him to spit it out, but then realized that Dorian had nothing to say.

He had only wanted Wilson to listen.

To listen to that sound.

Like the sound of a rolling river.

'I woke up as soon as I heard it,' Dorian said, a miserable look coming over his face, his hand flying up to clutch his head. 'I'm sorry, man. I fucked up. But we need to get the fuck out of here. Or . . . or . . . '

'Or what?' Wilson didn't want to sound angry, but the words came out like the snap of a whip. He swore again and walked to the end of the LMTV's bed, where he looked over the side at their small encampment and started searching for the sight of Gilmore's desert camouflage.

He saw the man rolling, still bound up in his bivy sack, out from under the HEMTT tanker. He thrashed for a moment like he was caught by his own bedding and then finally extracted his legs. Then he looked right up at Wilson with a hard look in his eyes. He raised his hands, his mouth asking the same question Wilson had asked.

Wilson swung down out of the LMTV, Dorian's screwup forgotten for the moment. Wilson ran to the Marine, cursing the whole way until he was close enough to speak without shouting. Gilmore was kicking his feet into a pair of boots glistening with hoarfrost. His rifle lay on the bivy sack next to him.

'Don't fucking tell me,' he said. 'Just don't fucking tell me.'

'They're coming.' Wilson looked out at the bridge. He could see slim sections of the opposite bank to either side, but he could not see any movement. 'Maybe we have time . . .'

'We don't have time for shit.' Gilmore came to his feet. 'They're gonna be on us before we can get anything accomplished.'

'What about the charges from last night? How much of the bridge will that blow?'

Gilmore snatched his rifle up into his thick hands and slung into it. 'No idea. I've never half-assed a demo before. P is for Plenty – you're supposed to give it more than you think it needs. I dunno. It might just make a hole on the side of the bridge.'

For the first moment, Wilson felt the chill of the morning – not quite as cold as the previous night – and the stiffness of sleep still clinging to his face. He rubbed it vigorously, groaning. 'Fuck me. Fuck *me*. We've gotta blow what we got.'

Gilmore grimaced, also staring out at the bridge now.

'Otherwise it's just a waste of fucking ordnance. We're not getting the shit down. It's already there and rigged. We might as well hook up a detonator and see how much of the bridge it will take down. Maybe we can take some of them with us.'

'You mean wait until they're on the bridge?'

'If it's not gonna blow the whole bridge anyway, we might as well get something out of it,' Wilson argued.

'If you wait for them to come on the bridge, then you have to be watching it.'

'So?'

Gilmore looked around. 'There's really not a safe location to watch the bridge from.'

'You mean safe from the blast?'

'Yes,' the Marine said, a little exasperated.

Wilson shook his head. 'It's the best of a bad situation, man. I gotta take some of those fuckers out with the blast or this will be for nothing. And from where I'm standing, it might not be the textbook distance, but I should be okay.'

Gilmore squinted, calculating the distance between them and the blast. Calculating how many pounds of explosives were going to go off, and how many yards per pound they would need. He wobbled his head back and forth, but there wasn't time for a calculator and a pencil and measuring tape. Wilson had already made the decision, and time was slipping quickly away from them.

'Okay, okay,' Gilmore finally said, nodding. 'It'll be close, but you should be okay. We just got to get the detonator wired up.'

The previous day, before turning in, they had made sure that the I-beams they had rigged with explosives had also been fully wired with det-cord. All that was necessary now was to splice in a new line of det-cord, run it back to the *relatively* safe location, and then hook up a detonator. It was a five-minute job at most.

Do we have five minutes? Wilson wondered, but even as he thought it, he was running for the back of the LMTV that held all of their ordnance. Gilmore was beside him, his mind made up, and Dorian was running to catch up.

Wilson clambered up into the back of the big vehicle and grabbed a roller of blue det-cord, tossing it behind him to Gilmore, who snatched it out of the air like it didn't weigh thirty pounds. Wilson turned to Dorian as he ran up and pointed away to the rest of the convoy.

'Dorian!' he shouted. 'Me and Gilmore got this!'

Dorian looked crestfallen. It was Wilson's understanding that Dorian and Gilmore had come to some words the previous day when they had taken Wilson for dead, and that it had come close to blows. Now it seemed that Wilson was taking Gilmore over Dorian, which he wasn't, of course, but he didn't have the time to explain or spare people's feelings. Dorian would just have to get the fuck over it.

'Get the convoy packed up,' Wilson instructed him. 'And get everybody the fuck out of here. Leave me and Gilmore one Humvee. We're gonna blow this shit and then rally with you down the road. But there's no reason for all you guys to be here.'

Dorian put a hand up on the tailgate of the LMTV. 'Man, there's no way ...'

Wilson's father had been a soft-spoken man, but when he had meant business his voice carried effortlessly and the timbre of it deepened like his chest had become a deep chamber for the sound of his voice to resonate. Wilson had always called it the 'Voice of Authority,' and it brokered no arguments. What was said with the Voice of Authority was to be done immediately and without question or else the belt was coming out.

Like his father before him, Wilson did not often shout. But there was no time for argument.

'Dorian! Do what I told you to do!'

Jeriah! You get down from there or I'll whoop that hide!

Dorian took his hand off the LMTV. He frowned for a half a second, but then turned without another word and took off to do what Wilson had instructed. There was no reason for any of them to be there. This was a quick, two-man op. Anyone else standing around was just inviting unnecessary injury, and probably just going to add to the confusion. He would explain all of this to Dorian later. Dorian would understand. He was a little hotheaded at times – he claimed it was the Italian in him. But he was a reasonable man – he claimed that was the southerner in him.

Wilson turned back to his business in a rush. He yanked open a wooden crate and delved in, removing a detonator from the dozens packed snugly inside.

'You got it?' Gilmore called, already making for the bridge.

'Go,' was Wilson's only response. He slid down off the tailgate and ran after Gilmore.

The bridge over the Roanoke River was a long one, and wide for its two lanes. Instead of the typical, narrow bridge for two lanes of traffic, this one also had a breakdown lane, or maybe it was a bike and pedestrian lane. Wilson wasn't quite sure. All he knew is that it added three more I-beams to the usual five and so had increased their job by more than half. But no matter all of that now. They had two I-beams rigged, and that was all they were going to get off.

Beneath them, the river was wide and flat. A little rocky to the right and southern side of the bridge where it forked off and rejoined about a half mile down, creating a little island in the middle of it. To his left he could look out and see the steel monstrosity that made everything he was doing an exercise in futility.

A railroad bridge, about a quarter mile upstream.

The thing was raised for nearly a mile even after it was over land. They would have had to make their way into Weldon to be able to access the bridge, or they would have had to do some serious climbing. It would have been a bitch and taken a long time, but even now Wilson was staring at it, wishing that he had that time, no matter how hard it would have been. Because there was no way he was going to be able to blow it now. Even if a miracle happened, and the charges they laid out for the two I-beams managed to somehow blow a hole in the bridge big enough so that the infected could not cross, there was no way they would have been able to scale, rig, and demo the railway bridge before the infected found it and started making their way across.

Couple of helos from Colonel Staley would make pretty fucking quick work of that . . .

But he put the thought out of his mind. It wasn't going to happen. Why dwell on impossibilities? It was a great way to become resentful and bitter.

Like LaRouche . . .

Gilmore reached the jumble of blue cordage that came up and over the side of the bridge. He began rolling out a length of det-cord. Wilson reached him and shoved the detonator in one of his pockets and took the end of the det-cord that Gilmore had unspooled. Then he took the leading piece of det-cord from under the bridge and began to marry the two together.

Behind him, the sound of diesel engines hiccupping, coughing, then whirling to life.

In front of him, the sound of millions of feet.

Gilmore started running with the spool of det-cord. Wilson was still trying to tie the two ends together properly, but his hands were shaking and his fingers unwieldy. He felt abruptly naked and exposed standing in the middle of the bridge with no vehicles, no cover, no friends to back him up. He dropped one of the ends of det-cord and stooped to snatch it off the ground.

The bridge trembled.

He had felt this same feeling before. It was the feeling when you were walking across a bridge and an overloaded semi hit it going ten miles over the speed limit, sending tremors through it and up his feet. The uneasy feeling that the bridge was not as sturdy as you thought it was.

But Wilson knew there was no semi going across this bridge.

He raised his head, his fingers still working furiously to tie the knot.

Almost there . . .

At the foot of the bridge on the far bank, a mass of pale grayness, like rushing, filthy water, flowing onto the bridge, filling it from guardrail to guardrail. A thousand screams suddenly filled the air and it was like the water was suddenly being tilted into a downhill run. The center of the thick, shoulder-to-shoulder column broke into a run, spearing out from the main body.

'Shit,' was the only thing that Wilson could get out of his mouth.

Finally, the knot was tied. He cinched it down with a quick yank and then ran. Ahead of him, the other vehicles in the convoy were rolling away and it was just his Humvee there at the base of the bridge. Gilmore was almost there, hobbling backward on tired legs as he let the spool roll out behind him. When he reached the Humvee, he threw the spool into the truck and cut the cord with a swift move of his knife.

Wilson stumbled to a stop behind him, his booted feet slapping concrete. He grabbed the end of the det-cord and fished the detonator out of his pocket. Neither of the two men said anything to each other. Gilmore just stared at Wilson's shaking hands while they worked, both of them breathing hard, the air in front of them turning to a loose cloud with the chill of their breath. Gilmore seemed to want to put his fingers in to help Wilson, but it would only cost valuable seconds. He dared not even to speak.

Wilson got the cord into the detonator. He pulled the plunger up, arming the explosives.

'We should get behind something,' Gilmore said.

Wilson looked over his shoulder. He saw the infected reaching the halfway point of the bridge where he and Gilmore had been standing just moments ago. Wilson couldn't wait to press that plunger. He couldn't do it, because each second that he wasted, another hundred of them would cross out of the kill zone, and if even fifty of them got across unharmed, then Wilson and Gilmore were going to die. They would not be able to fight that many of them off.

Maybe we'll be able to drive away...

BLOW THAT SHIT!

Wilson saw and understood and made his decision in less than a second. Gilmore was still working his way to the other side of the car. Wilson just dropped into a crouch, shoulders shrugging up to his ears, teeth bared, eyes squinting almost shut. One great cringe. Then he pressed the plunger.

The center of the bridge was suddenly just a rapidly expanding cloud of dust. Like the entire cement and steel structure had suddenly gone supernova. Wilson watched in awe as the shock wave advanced toward him across the bridge, all in a microsecond, dust and gravel and debris that Wilson had not even been aware of stirred in its perfectly circular path and then it slapped him full in the face and punched him hard in the chest. He saw the infected that had been running toward him and they broke apart almost instantly and their bodies were engulfed in a cloud of dust and out of it the limbs and pieces of them came flying, a hundred different broken bits and parts. The lower part of a leg tumbled into the guardrail just a few yards in front of him, the meat so suddenly ripped that it had barely even begun to bleed yet.

Wilson stared at the leg.

We got 'em. We got 'em. Maybe the whole bridge blew …

He heard something whistling through the air and then things were black.

When he opened his eyes everything was red and gray. He could tell he was staring at the underside of the Humvee. The detonator was still in his hands. There was an unspecified pain that seemed too big for his nerves to comprehend and it seemed to engulf his entire upper body. It was one of those pains that doesn't hurt very bad at first, but which you know is going to grow to be monstrous in only seconds. He was choking. He couldn't breathe. He tasted blood. Something was wrong with his face. He tried to call out to Gilmore, but only made a rasping, gurgling sound that at first confused him because he did not think the sound was coming from him. All his perceptions seemed to have been shattered.

He rolled onto his stomach. He felt thick liquid pouring out of his mouth. The gravity of facing the ground made something on his face *dangle*. It felt strange and it terrified him. He stared down at the liquid he was spilling and found that it was red and dotted with the little white bits of his broken teeth. He coughed and more blood came out. Panic struck him. Sick panic. He tried to call out again but his mouth would not form words. He only made a strange, animal moan.

'Wilson? Wilson!'

He tried to look to where Gilmore was calling him. He felt the dangling thing on his face shift again, and this time it hurt.

The pain seemed to be radiating inward now, finding its center. It was his face. His face was broken.

Wilson curled onto his side and saw many things at once.

The world around him was a shifting, shimmering unreality. It seemed like everything was engulfed in a roiling mirage, but he knew it was too cold for that. He felt the thing on his face dangling and realized that it was his jaw. That was why his teeth were missing and why he couldn't seem to move his mouth. His jaw was hanging off him, ripped out of place. And the culprit sat on the cement beside him, a chunk of concrete the size of his fist that had not been there a moment ago. Then he felt hands grab him up and he feared that they were the hands of the infected, but when he looked out at the bridge, he could see them. They were pouring through the smoke, seemingly undeterred. Many of them were on the ground, dead and dismembered, though many of them were only injured or stunned, crawling along.

But there were still hundreds of them. So close, and getting closer. The bridge had not blown all the way and they had made it across and were still coming, they were still coming, so fucking many of them that for a moment Wilson was just positive that this was not real. It could not be real. He had horrible luck, but not *this* bad.

Gotta run . . .

Run run run!

He tried to rise to his feet, but his legs were like pillars of stone – useless and immovable and numb. He turned his head, the pain in his face spiking around his jaw. He could see Gilmore there, trying to get him to his feet while he simultaneously looked over his own shoulder and his eyes widened in terror. Wilson looked out and saw that the infected had closed to within a hundred yards of them.

Too close. They're too close.

Where's my rifle?

Gilmore struggled with the door, but he could not hold Wilson upright and get the door open all at once. Wilson kept jagging his eyes this way and that, his mind scrambling in growing fear as he tried to find himself a way out, some path that would show itself to him.

Dear God, please, don't let me die out here! I don't wanna die like this!

Wilson scrambled at the door with Gilmore and managed to unlatch it and pull it open.

They were so close now that Wilson could hear their shivering shrieks on his skin.

Gilmore shoved him into the open door. Wilson's top half hit the first seat, his face brushing up against the seat back and nearly blinding him in pain. His legs still dangled out and he tried to scramble up inside, but nothing seemed to be working right. Except for his hands. His hands could feel everything in oddly exquisite detail. And his eyes. They were crisp and clear and strangely overfocused in a way that he had never experienced before.

'Get in the fucking truck!' Gilmore bellowed.

Wilson tried to tell him that he was trying, but only that weird moan came out again. He tried to pull himself with his arms and had little success. It seemed like his arms were weak. He looked over his shoulder again and saw Gilmore, turning away. The Marine was standing in the open doorway now, with his back to Wilson, and he was bringing his rifle up and around from where he had slung it onto his back. Beyond the Marine, sunlight was shooting through the thick cloud of smoke in dazzling rays and the screeching creatures were pouring out of it like some hell-mist and they were within fifty yards now.

As Gilmore's rifle began to *crack-crack-crack*, Wilson kept struggling to get himself into the seat, even though he knew it wasn't going to happen. But his eyes traveled up and they stared into the sky, brown with the pulverized concrete that high explosive had plumed into the air, shot through with beams of light from a yellow dawning sun. He looked to the sky, perhaps waiting for helicopters that he knew would never come, or perhaps waiting for some divine intervention.

Anytime a door closes, look for an open window.

But this time Wilson found himself in a room with no windows and no doors.

A dead end, so to speak.

He felt Gilmore pressing backward into his shocked legs. They were beginning to recover some feeling, but he still didn't seem to be able to command them. Gilmore was yelling. Wilson thought maybe he was yelling, too, but it was all swallowed up and lost in the great screaming horde that rushed at them. Gilmore's shots were well placed, but he only had so many of them, and there were always more infected.

Not like this! Not like this!

The daylight around Gilmore was suddenly dark. The Marine struck out with the buttstock of his rifle and reached for the knife he kept strapped to his belt but then he was swallowed into darkness and he went kicking and shouting curses and stabbing and slashing at everything within reach of his blade. They consumed him like some collective mouth and then Wilson could feel their hands on him, cold and hard as iron.

The bridge the bridge the bridge.

They're crossing the bridge and there's no one to stop them.

They didn't pull him out of the truck, but rather went in after him. He fought them with fumbling hands and fingers and they bit at him, yapping like dogs. If he could have reached his rifle, he would have fired twenty-nine rounds and then swallowed the thirtieth, but it was strapped to his back and he was pinned down on top of it.

He was full of hatred. He hated God for not rescuing him, and he hated his father for being dead when he needed him, and he hated Dorian for falling asleep on watch, and he hated Colonel Staley for not helping. But he also hated himself for not seeking cover, for not being faster, for fumbling with the cord and the detonator and *they're crossing now, they've made a breach and nothing is going to stop them, you're not here to stop them, you didn't stop them, you failed, you failed, you failed, you failed*, and that was the thought that his mind decided to circle like a murder of crows until one of the infected mounted him, its whole body shuddering with excitement as it clamped its jaws over his face, covering his mouth and nose so that he could not breathe.

And then he just thought, *not like this, not like this . . .*

TWENTY-TWO

TECHNIQUES

ABE WAS HALF AWAKE when the door to the cell opened. Fully awake when the cold water hit him. He thrashed in the cold wetness, like it was something trying to smother him. But he knew that would come later. He knew the drill just like his captors knew it.

They kept him wet and cold. He had only just managed to stop shivering long enough to fall asleep when the door to the cell had opened to another rude awakening. Was it even a cell? It could have been a damn broom closet for all he knew. Whatever it was, it had a cement floor with a drain in the center. A small room. A door with no handle on the inside. It was cell enough for him to call it one.

He blinked and swiped water out of his eyes, air sucking into his lungs with the shock of the cold water seeping through his shirt – they'd taken his vest and his jacket and left him only his undershirt. Outside of his dark cell there was bright light, but he could tell that it was artificial. It had all been artificial. They were someplace without windows. In here there was no concept of time. He could have been there for hours or days. There was no way to tell.

Captain Lucas Wright and Major Abe Darabie had been taken in the dead of night. Lucas had been on watch at the time, while Abe caught a few hours of sleep before they moved on again. Abe had no idea how Lucas had been taken, or whether he was even still alive. His eyes had come open at the sound of something thrashing – he believed now that it had been Lucas – but when he had tried to look up, a black burlap sack that smelled of piss and shit had been wrapped around his face so tight that the soiled fabric had pressed into his mouth and cinched down on his neck, choking off anything he might have said. He had groped for a weapon and gotten a hard kick in the ribs and what felt like the buttstock of a rifle into his face, which had stunned him long enough for his arms to be yanked behind his back. Through his own ringing ears and the taste of blood in his mouth he felt the heavy plastic straps and heard the *zzzzzzip* sound of flex cuffs tightening.

He heard a single voice, strained and tight and on the verge of panic: '*Abe?*'

And that was the last thing he had heard from Lucas.

Is he dead?

Why would they kill him and keep me?

He had no concept of how to answer these questions. He had been carried for a long time – at least two men carrying him, he thought. After maybe an hour's hiking without a break, they threw him into something that rumbled and rolled and sounded like a diesel pickup truck to Abe, but there was no way to be sure. Once he was laid down against cold metal, someone sat on his chest and never said a word to him. He thought about speaking or shouting, but he knew it would do him no good. Probably earn a rifle butt upside his head again, this time probably taking some teeth with it.

Instead, he listened. He listened to everything he could possibly register. His entire world became whatever sounds he could pick up, past the rasping brush of the coarse burlap fabric as it rubbed against the side of his head. There was the rolling engine for a while, and nothing else. Then he could feel the vehicle pulling to a stop and then there was a very brief, quiet exchange.

The creaking of metal on metal.

The rattle of chain link and barbed wire.

A familiar sound. A gate being opened.

In the momentary quiet, Abe tried to listen to how many people were in the truck with him. He could hear someone breathing, and it was out of rhythm with the breathing of whoever was sitting on his chest, but too close to be the driver, he thought. So three people at least?

Then he thought that maybe this was all useless information anyway.

But it kept him from despairing, and when you're in enemy hands, keeping a sharp mind is half the battle. It gave him something to do. Something besides giving in and waiting for them to do something to him. He would not simply be a lamb to the slaughter. He would keep listening and he would wait for that opportunity to present itself. Because the only way to know when they fucked up and when your one opportunity to get out came along was to pay very close attention.

It had been very cold. Then they'd come through a door. He had seen the glimmering of artificial light glowing when they entered the building, and it was marginally warmer inside, though not by much. But now he knew something important: *They have electricity.*

Random bands of thugs didn't have electricity.

Then he'd come to the cell, or the broom closet, or whatever it was. They had set him on his knees on the floor, pulled off his burlap sack, and then slammed the door behind him.

He was in complete darkness. There was some shuffling outside the door and then there had been death metal playing at an ear-shattering volume that made him wince at first. The same song on repeat. Over and over.

He tried to count the number of times the song played, just to give himself something to do. Some way to tell the time, but somewhere around thirty times he lost count. The door had opened again, though he hadn't heard it over the clash of music. Someone had rushed in, thrown a bucket of water on him, kicked him in his belly, and then quickly removed the flex cuffs from around his wrists. Then they were gone, the door slammed, and the music went silent.

In the cold, wet silence, Abe began to shiver. He realized he was chewing the cuticles of his thumb again when it smarted and his lips tasted like blood. He spat and hugged his arms around his body. He worked through the cold, tightening his core until it threatened to cramp, just to keep his body temperature up. Cold would make him compliant, make his thinking and his focus fuzzy. But after a while, the water had dried enough that he wasn't shivering anymore and then he fell asleep.

He had no idea how long he'd been asleep, but the door had opened and more water had come in to wake him up. No daylight. No sense of time. No one said anything to him. Just splashed the water on him and then slammed the door again. He would fall asleep and then be woken up the same way. This had happened four times so far, not including the latest.

He was confused, disoriented, and his abdominal muscles ached and cramped. The water running over his head and soaking his clothes wasn't enough to quench his thirst, and the bit that he did get into his mouth tasted bitter and fouled and he feared trying to drink more of it.

He knew all of these techniques, and he knew them well. He had been through Survival Evasion Resistance and Escape. In fact, he'd attended it in the swamps of Fort Bragg, very near where they were, by his reckoning and by the last check of the map he'd done before curling up in his bivy sack the night they had been taken. In SERE school you learned about all the wonderful ways to make people crack. And you endured most of them yourself. The only rule for the instructors was that they couldn't break your bones. Other than that, it was open season.

Having been through the training did not make the knot in his gut go away.

He suspected the worst was still to come.

He peered into the blazing light of the open doorway, and then it was shadowed by a figure. It was a very large form, the light coming from behind the figure catching in wild hair and bushy beard and creating an odd, red-gold halo. The figure moved quick for its massive size, and the voice that came from it was a rumble like a bear growling.

'Don't fucking look at me.'

A huge hand reached out and grabbed the top of Abe's head, pushing it down so his eyes were averted to the ground, and then the black, shit-smelling sack was over his head again, pulled tight against his face and his throat. He felt the man move quickly behind him. There were more people in the room, he could hear their quiet footsteps, but aside from the big man's single command, no one spoke. The big man hauled him to his feet while another person to the front of him bound his wrists again. This time it felt like tape. Packing tape, or maybe duct tape. All the while the big man that he'd caught that momentary glimpse of was behind him, holding that hood tight over Abe's head, and Abe could hear the man breathing – slow and steady.

Silently, they pushed him out of the room. All of their movements felt rough and designed to either hurt him or intimidate him. There was a certain aspect to it that got his heart beating faster – *Where the fuck are they taking me? What are they going to do to me when we get there? God, this is gonna hurt, isn't it? You can handle pain. You just need to buckle down and be ready for it* – but Abe forced himself to focus on the sounds, on listening. He tried to sense which way he was being turned, this way and that, how many doors they were going through. Did they open freely? Did they have to be unlocked? Was there a passcode given? How big did the door sound? Did it sound like wood or metal? Were they going up? Down? Were there other people? Did he get the sense that he was in an enclosed space, or a bigger, more open one?

So far he was having a hard time answering these questions, but he tried. And that was important. It was important to always be thinking about how you were going to get away. It was important to never start thinking about giving up. The instructors at SERE would tell you that everyone cracks given enough time and pressure and pain. It's just a matter of how long you can keep it together. Can you keep it together long enough to be rescued?

But that was back in the day when Abe Darabie had been a person worth rescuing. Now the people that he had fled from probably wished him dead, and the people he was fleeing to didn't even know he was coming – and probably wanted him dead, too.

So now he just had to focus on . . . rescuing himself?

Why not? What else do I have?

And that made him think about Lucas again. About whether he was even alive. And he felt something worming its way through him and it felt like worry and dread and nausea, all in one. He had coerced Lucas into coming on this journey. Coerced him at the muzzle of a rifle. Abe was not in the habit of pointing guns at his close friends, but the circumstances had been ... complicated. In the end, Abe believed whole-heartedly that Lucas had not begrudged him those actions. And he believed that Lucas wanted to be there with his commanding officer and friend.

Abe had convinced him to come along, and now this had happened. Now Abe was being marched to a place where there would be pain and terror, and he had no idea of whether his best and only friend in the world was still alive, or whether he was enduring pain and terror of his own.

What are they going to do to me?

No. How many doors have you passed through?

Three. Three doors. Heavy doors. Metal, I think. Not locked.

He wished he could *smell* something besides the fecal smell on the inside of the burlap sack. Maybe he could figure out what type of place he was in, though he wasn't sure what data he could extrapolate from that.

As long as you're making wishes, why not wish to see?

Why not wish to be free?

Why not wish to turn the clock back and pick another place to camp?

Abe closed his eyes – black on black.

Where are you?

Someplace cold. Someplace with cement floors. Someplace with electricity. Someplace with doors, and small rooms that seem like cells. And a place where they take people to interrogate them. Surely they have some facility? Or do they just strap you to a chair and beat the fuck out of you? Or maybe stand you on a metal table with a car battery hooked up to it?

Someplace ... someplace ...

The last door they entered sounded different from the others. This one clanked heavily, like solid metal. While the others had sounded like your average industrial doors, this one sounded as close to a jail door as you could get. Iron hinges creaked as they shoved him through and closed it behind them with a loud bang, and then a single, sharp *clack*, like a dead bolt being thrown.

They sat him in a chair. It was cold. Metal. A folding chair, Abe thought.

The tape came out again. Abe could hear the unique sound of the tape being pulled from its spool in large amounts. Then it went around his stomach and chest a few times, keeping his torso locked into the chair. And finally, around both of his feet, so that they were secured to the legs of the chair.

Abe's heart pounded, but he forced his breathing to stay level.

Prepare yourself for pain.

The burlap sack was suddenly released and ripped off his head.

He took in as much as he could of the room, but there wasn't much there. It was a small square, only slightly larger than the cell they had thrown him in. Same cement floors, same drain in the center. There was no light in the ceiling – the bright light in the room came from a pair of hot-burning halogen lamps that stood mounted on a yellow stand in the corner. He could feel the heat of them on his face and in any other circumstance it might have been nice after so long in the cold, but here and now the heat seemed aggressive and stinging.

He had the sense that there were one or two men standing behind him, but the only person he could see was in front of him. This was a man of about average height. He had close-cropped hair on the sides, but the top of his head was going slick and bald. He wore a full beard, but unlike the one on Abe's face or the huge man that had come to fetch him, this man's beard was neatly trimmed. Dark brown, almost black, with some streaks of gray. He was not fat, nor skinny, nor well muscled. He appeared decently fed, but not overly so. But by far, the oddest aspect of the man standing in front of Abe were his clothes. He wore pressed khaki pants and a tweed sport coat. He seemed to belong in front of a chalkboard in a college classroom, rather than in an interrogation room.

The man was holding a bottle of water.

He smiled as Abe stared at him, a congenial expression, and held up the bottle. 'Hello. Are you thirsty? Would you like some water?'

Despite the cold wetness, Abe's thirst was becoming desperate. He considered the possibility of poison, but that made no sense. Why capture him in the middle of the night and go through all this trouble, just to slip him some poison when they could just as easily have slit his throat? Then he thought about drugs. There was a strong possibility that the water in the bottle was laced with something . . .

The oddly dressed man seemed to read Abe's thoughts. He stepped forward, uncapping the bottle, and he took a long swig from it. He swallowed and smacked his lips. 'See? Just water. Would you like some now?'

Abe stared at the bottle for another moment, the clear, cold liquid undulating inside it, catching the light of the halogen lamps. The desire for the water was intense at that moment. He must have been more dehydrated than he had realized. He nodded.

The man brought the water bottle to Abe's lips and tilted it back. He did it gently at first, until Abe was greedily sucking the bottle dry. The plastic bottle crinkled and wrinkled and collapsed in on itself as Abe got every drop of water out of it. Then the man in the tweed sport coat capped the water bottle and set it down a few feet away.

When he stood straight again, facing Abe, he folded his hands in front of him. A very formal gesture. The kind smile was still on his lips. 'I'm Carl Gilliard. You can call me Carl. I'm going to start off cordially, and we'll go from there, okay?'

Abe absorbed the information. 'Okay.'

Carl put his hands into the pockets of his pants. 'What's your name?'

'Abe Darabie.'

An eyebrow went up. 'What about your title, Mr. Darabie? Your rank?'

Abe considered this. Were there any benefits to telling this man the truth? For that matter, were there any benefits to lying? One thing was becoming clear to Abe: he didn't think these were thugs or bandits. Only one type of person gave a shit about rank, and that was people who were a part of a ranking structure.

Or people that will hold you for ransom ...

Another thing that Abe did not like was that neither he nor Lucas had borne anything that would have identified them as military personnel. Their clothes had not been any type of uniform, nor did either of them bear any rank. Their weapons were military, but there were a lot of military weapons floating around in the hands of civilians since the collapse. They had driven the tan Humvee they'd taken from Eddie Ramirez, but military vehicles were no different from military weapons – they were sprouting up everywhere, seized by whoever found them abandoned, or sometimes taken by force.

There was no reason for the man that called himself Carl to

believe Abe Darabie was military, unless it was just a hunch he was pursuing.

In the end, Abe went for the plain, ungilded truth, because it seemed the safest thing to say: 'I don't have any rank anymore.'

Carl frowned. 'No rank. Okay. Then tell me what your rank was before?'

And we're back to square one. Abe coughed, cleared his throat. 'What's *your* rank, Carl?'

Abe had feared this would break the tense strings of civility that had so far governed this exchange, but Carl just shook his head, unconcerned. 'My rank isn't important. Let's stay on task, Mr. Darabie, and remember what I said in the beginning.' He tapped one of his feet and when Abe glanced down he saw that Carl was wearing suede Dockers. 'What was your rank before?'

'Major,' Abe said quietly, then added, 'But not anymore.'

'Major, but not anymore,' Carl repeated slowly, as though he were divining the truth of the words by speaking them out of his own mouth. 'Why not anymore? What happened?'

Are these guys from Briggs? Is that why they're asking these questions? This was not the first time the thought had occurred to Abe. In fact, the second that the shit-smelling burlap had covered his face, he had thought, *Briggs tracked me down. Briggs and Colonel Lineberger, those sons of bitches!*

But if they'd tracked him down, then wouldn't they already know what was going on? Did they just want him to admit to it? And if so, then why? There was no rule of law anymore. No due process that needed to be followed. Briggs had sent men to assassinate Lee Harden without any questioning, so why would he treat Abe differently? No, if these men were from Briggs, then they would not be asking questions. They would have killed him and Lucas right at their campsite and left them there for the infected to find and clean up.

Unless there was something here that he wasn't putting together.

Where is the GPS? he thought for the millionth time since he'd been taken captive. It was less a thought now than a permanent background in his brain. A blinking billboard that lit up the darkness in his mind at a constant and steady pace: *Where is the GPS? Where is the GPS? Where is the GPS?*

There is something here that I'm missing. I have no idea who I'm talking to, so it would be best if I said nothing at all. At least until I figure out who these people are, and who Carl is working for.

Abe took a deep breath and blew it out slowly through pursed lips. Cooperation was easy. It was comfortable. It required no conflict. But digging your heels in had the tendency to get you hurt, especially when you were taped to a metal folding chair in a dark room with a smiling man that you knew did not have your best interests at heart. But Abe would not show his hand when he had no idea who he was showing it to.

'Mr. Darabie?' Carl had a cringing look on his face. 'You look like you're struggling with whether or not to tell me the truth. I encourage you to speak truthfully to me. Lies have a tendency to sour any relationship.'

Abe shook his head. 'Who are you?'

The kind features of Carl's face were simply gone, like they had never existed. Now he was carved out of stone and his well-trimmed beard was made out of wire bristles and his eyes were just cold orbs of ice. He looked at something behind Abe and gave a slight nod.

Abe clenched his teeth. *Here we go . . .*

The chair flew backward and crashed to the floor. Abe felt the back of his head bounce off cement and his sinuses tingled. For a microsecond he was staring up at the ceiling – acoustic ceiling tiles with water spots on them. Then there were two faces – one clean-shaven, and the other was the big wild man that had taken Abe from his cell. Then there was the sound of something being ripped out of water and a thick, wet cloth covered his nose and eyes. They were holding it down hard to keep his head locked in place and it pressed against his eyes, causing a cold ache.

Abe's first instinct was to start thrashing, but he forced himself to remain still. Thrashing would only burn up the oxygen in his body, and he would need it. He knew what came next, but knowing didn't make it any better.

Carl's voice was an emotionless monotone. 'We used to do this with jugs or buckets of water, but I've found it's a lot more effective when you have running water. A little more likelihood of drowning, but that's kind of the point.'

Ice-cold water hit Abe's face in a steady flow, like it was coming out of a hose. It soaked the wet cloth already over his face and he could feel water seeping through and leaking down in to his nostrils, burning in his sinuses. He coughed violently, unable to keep himself. The men holding him down only pressed down harder. The water tasted muddy and foul, like it had come from a drainage pond.

The stream of water left his face.

Warmth from the halogen lights.

Abe couldn't breathe through his nose so he was forced to spit water out of his mouth and suck in air that way. He coughed a few more times, then gritted his teeth and tried to force himself to relax, even though it felt like every muscle in his body remained taut.

Carl's voice and breath on his cheek. 'There is nothing you can say or do that is going to make this stop. The things you say in this room have consequences. You will deal with those consequences, but while you do, consider answering my questions: Where did you come from? Why are you here? Who sent you here? What happened to your rank?'

Then the water came again.

TWENTY-THREE

Newcomers

THE RAIN STARTED POURING around eight o'clock. It seemed that the sun had no sooner managed to lift itself up over the trees and shine down on Camp Ryder, than black clouds roared in from the southwest and covered it all up in shadow again.

And isn't that appropriate? Angela thought as she stood at the front door of the Camp Ryder building and looked out over Shantytown and the glistening roofs made of tarpaulin and sheet metal and in a few instances, just plain old rotting plywood. *As soon as we get our feet under us, another haymaker cleans our clock. When is it okay just to lie down and let the ref count you out?*

Is it ever okay?

She thought she knew how Lee would answer that question. Despite how different he was these days, he was still Lee Harden. And it seemed that Lee Harden never knew when to quit. He would be that proverbial boxer that just continued to stand up until the stuff between his ears had been punched to a bloody pulp. He was the type of person to die before giving up. And it wasn't hubris, she didn't think. More like . . .

Well, she really didn't have a word for it.

Lee just *was* what he *was*.

And what about you, Angie-Girl? Her own mind using the name her father had called her when she was in pigtails and jumpers. A name she hadn't heard in decades and which came back unexpectedly and somewhat disconcertingly to her mind. *How's your clockwork? Can you take a licking and keep on ticking? Are you built for the long haul?*

The words had the flavor of something her father would have said. If she'd been a superstitious person, she might have claimed it was his ghost. But no matter how long a father has been in the ground, he always speaks to his children. A person forever remembers their mother's arms and their father's words.

She wondered about her father. She wondered whether Abby would have loved him and hated him as much as she had. Because she'd loved him until thirteen, and then hated him until he died when she was sixteen. And then she'd loved him again, but a little too late. Because, while he'd been a loving man, and a good father, he had been frank, and his rules had been iron. And when you're a teenage girl the last thing you want is honesty and strict rules.

She regretted it, of course. But dead is dead and cannot be changed.

Perhaps she should thank him for the sometimes cold practicality that she had. A strength, she thought, though her late, philandering husband had disagreed. To him, it had been a lack of heart, a lack of warmth. But his quest for the warmth he so desired had eventually killed him. Or at least it had set forward a chain of events that led to him being killed.

By Lee.

Angela shivered. She remembered Jenny's words and they skittered up her spine and back down again and made her entire body feel nervous and uncomfortable. *Things aren't what they seem,* Jenny had said. *When you stop lying to yourself.*

About Lee, of course.

Whatever she felt for Lee – and to be honest, she wasn't sure what that was – she had to remember that Lee had his own brand of practicality, which had always been harsher than her own. He had done and would continue to do things that Angela would never do. She wondered what dark places he'd already been, and what Jenny had meant when she had said that things were not what they seemed.

And it was not just Lee that concerned Angela now.

It was Jenny as well. The woman seemed ... dark. Detached.

And then there was Abby to think about. And Sam, of course. She couldn't forget about him. The two were close, and growing closer. They were with each other almost every minute of the day now, and in some aspects Angela thought it was good. Sam being there for Abby not only gave Sam something to do, but it gave Abby someone to talk to that was a little more accessible than her mother – which she felt guilty for, of course.

But on the other hand, their closeness bothered Angela in certain ways. They conversed with each other and grew silent when others came around. They didn't play with the other kids. Instead, Sam clung to his rifle and Abby clung to him. Sam had been teaching Abby the basics of shooting, though he had not actually let her shoot the rifle yet.

At least to her knowledge.

She wasn't comfortable with Abby learning to shoot, though she couldn't figure out why. Sometimes maternal instinct overrode even the most practical personalities. She didn't want her baby playing with guns, even though, when she closed her eyes and thought about it logically, she knew very well that Abby knowing how to use a gun was more likely to save her life than hurt it at this juncture.

Conflicted, she had said nothing. She watched when Sam put the rifle in Abby's hands and taught her how to hold it. Even that small, .22-caliber rifle seemed enormous in Abby's hands, but Abby never seemed intimidated by it. When Sam was 'teaching' her, Abby's expression became dogged, and Angela saw herself in ways that twisted her up inside.

Abby and Sam. And Jenny. And Lee. And elections.

Worries, worries, worries.

They wore her down.

Now the rain was coming in sheets, and the wind was picking up again. It had gusted the dark storm clouds in and then calmed as the rain started falling, but now it was coming down harder than before and the wind was pushing it this way and that. A swirl of wind shoved the falling rain toward Angela and she took a step back to keep dry. Misted droplets clung to her hair, making it seem like a layer of frost had settled on it.

Out of the gray-wash of rain a figure came running. It wore a dark green parka, Angela could see as it drew closer, the hood pulled up and kept there by a hand. A small-statured person, small boots pounding through puddles that were steadily gathering in the gravel lot between Shantytown and the Camp Ryder building.

Marie took the steps two at a time. When she was out of the rain, she threw the hood of her parka back. Her curly brown hair was in tangles. Despite the hood, she had not been able to keep the rain off her face and she swiped a palm across it to clear the water.

'Hey,' Angela said with a smile, reaching out and touching the other woman's shoulder with one hand as she opened the door to the building. 'Let's get inside. Kitchen fire's heating the place up pretty good.'

Marie shuffled inside, shaking the water off. 'Yeah, wood's

runnin' low, though.' Before Jerry had mucked everything up, Marie had taken care of the kitchen and preparing community meals for the entire camp, usually just breakfast and dinner – sometimes just dinner, if supplies were getting low. Since Jerry had been ... dispatched ... she'd taken over her previous duties. She lit the fires in the morning and stoked them back to life in the evening and the building was one of the only places in the camp that stayed somewhat warm.

Wood running low. Yet another thing to worry about.

Harvesting wood meant people going outside camp, which meant a whole big operation just to keep them safe while they cut up downed trees and hauled the wood back into the camp. They'd stocked up mountains of wood in the late summer, but burned through it quicker than most had imagined.

Marie had called it, though. Angela distinctly remembered standing next to the woman sometime in late September, and watching Marie's face screw up as she eyed the piles of wood. It had seemed like too much to Angela, but Marie just shook her head. 'That'll get us into winter, but not through it.'

For now, the interior of the Camp Ryder building was somewhat warmer than outside, though for once the weather seemed to be warming, rather than cooling. More people than usual had gathered inside today. Some were holdovers from breakfast, simply not wanting to brave the rain just yet. Others were trickling in to escape it. The shanties were good for privacy and to give everyone a living space, but they weren't very watertight and once you were wet, there seemed to be no way to get dry and warm except to come inside the building.

'How's the food looking?' Angela asked as they began making their way to a table – the same quiet corner table where Angela and Jenny had spoken. The office was quieter, but it was beginning to be a negative place for Angela. She preferred to be away from it when she could. There was too much blood and violence and bad news that had been spilled and committed and given in that little upstairs room.

'Same as the wood. Don't think we've had a hunting party since Lee came back. And scavenging has dropped off significantly since Greg died.' Marie snorted. 'I guess he was good for *something*.'

'Marie . . . ' Angela looked around to see who might be listening. No one seemed to be.

Marie looked down, almost ashamed but not quite. 'Yeah. Shouldn't speak ill of the dead and all. But, to answer your questions, with those infected . . . hunter . . . things out in those woods . . . ' She made a face. 'Nobody wants to go out past the wire.'

'Well.' Angela sat at the table. 'I'm sure they don't want to starve, either.'

Marie took a seat with a sigh. 'I'm sure they don't.'

'We'll set up a party for wood and some hunting and some scavenging.' Angela tucked stray blond hair behind her ears. 'Or should we just do the election? Let whoever gets elected handle it? Maybe there's some good ideas out there that we're just not thinking about yet.'

Marie looked amused. Like she knew something Angela didn't. But she just shrugged. 'We've only got wood and food for a few days, so we better hold the election quick.'

Angela nodded. She just wanted this to be over. While she was glad to contribute, somehow she had fallen into a spot where everyone thought that because she was close to Lee, she was in charge. It made her feel almost physically heavy. The weight on her shoulders felt very real. She couldn't wait to shove this off to someone else and get back to things she needed to focus on.

Like Abby and Sam . . .

'Angela!'

The voice snapped at her like a whip, almost making her jump. It was not Marie – it was a man's voice, and coming from across the room right along with the sound of the front doors slamming against the back wall. Everyone in the Camp Ryder building twisted to look that way.

Immediately, Angela's thoughts went to the worst things: *Abby's hurt. Sam's hurt. Lee's hurt . . . or dead.* She stood up sharply from the table, staring at whoever was calling her name.

'Angela! Marie!' A man was running toward them, waving his hand. He wore a yellow poncho, but he seemed a larger man than it was intended for and the sleeves of the jacket he wore underneath looked soaked through. His boots squeaked and squished as he jogged toward them, leaving a trail of water behind him. His face and hands were flushed from the cold.

'This doesn't look good,' Marie muttered as the man ran up to them.

Angela thought that she recognized him. He was one of the men from the group that had escaped the Followers, and then found Smithfield and Jacob. Brett was his name, she thought.

'What's wrong?' she said, voice already tight. 'What happened?'

Brett pointed back behind him, water dripping from his nose. 'People at the front gate. A bunch of them.'

Angela came out of the front doors of the building, trailing Marie and Brett. Her hand was on her belt line, checking for her pistol and making sure she could get to it under the parka.

Her mind seemed in the habit of jumping to the worst possible conclusions, but maybe that wasn't such a bad habit. Maybe that was the type of thing that kept you alive.

Are they friendly?

She kept straining to hear the sound of fighting, but there was nothing but rainfall, heavy and insistent. Angela was so focused on listening, her hand still grasping the pistol at her side, she didn't even think to flip the hood up until the rain had already soaked her head. She released the wet but comforting grip of her pistol and flipped the hood up as she came down the steps to the building, peering through the rain at the front gate.

Muddy rainwater and wet gravel splashed and crunched under her boots. She wasn't quite running, but she wasn't walking, either. She was already on the balls of her feet, like someone ready to start fighting. Through the downpour of rain she could see the gates were still closed, and that took some of the tension out of her belly.

There were two Camp Ryder guards standing at the gate, rifles in hand, but they weren't brandished – just held at port, across their chests, or pointed at the ground. The gate itself had once been regular chain link, but had since been reinforced with a mishmash of random hard objects – some of them ballistically safe, and others not. But across the gate, about eye level, they had left a gap of about six inches that went across the entire gate. Beyond that gap, Angela could see the shapes of many people, though they stood as still as trees, even in the rain. Probably too soaked to really care.

She peered around different pieces of stuff that had been used to reinforce the gate, trying to get a better idea of who was standing beyond it. She couldn't see a vehicle. These folks had been walking, and the closer Angela got, the rougher they looked, and more tired, and more wet and cold. There was a lot of potential cases of pneumonia brewing in that group, she thought.

Don't take pity on them yet, she thought. *You have no idea who they are.*

As she drew up to the gate, her pace slowed. She was counting heads, scanning the crowd at the gates. There had to be thirty of them, at least. And then came the equation of practicality, the math of survival: *If I let thirty in, will we be able to push them out again?*

Simple numbers game. Thirty of them. Against how many in Camp Ryder?

The parka's hood did little to stop the often sideways rain. The water ran down her face and trickled onto her lips and into her mouth and it tasted salty by the time it got there. She spit it out and glanced over her shoulder at her companions. Marie would know how many people were inside those gates, down to a man. Angela could take an educated guess, though.

Forty. Maybe fifty?

That's a big difference, Angela told herself. *Thirty versus forty is almost a toss-up. Thirty versus fifty makes me more comfortable.*

'Marie, how many people are in Camp Ryder right now?'

'Originals, or everybody?'

Angela gave her a pinched look. 'What's originals?'

'You and me.' Marie smirked. 'Hell, there's only eleven of us left. But if you count all of Old Man Hughes's group and Brett's folks that came in with Jacob, and all the others' – she looked skyward, thinking – 'minus the ones that left with Lee ... we got ... fifty-two.'

As the two women spoke, Brett remained silent, watching the gate and the people beyond. Angela was now about ten feet from the gate and there she stopped, assessing the people on the other side. If they meant to rape and pillage, they hid it well. They were a depressing lot. Several children huddled by mothers and fathers and a few old people that Angela didn't think would last the winter. Young and old, weak and strong, they were soaked to the bone and looked it. They had the same limpness as waterlogged plants, like a stand of wheat beaten down by storms.

'I don't see guns,' Brett mumbled.

'Guns can be hidden,' Marie answered.

Angela nodded in agreement. Then she raised her hand to the people outside the gate. 'Who is in charge of your group here?' She had to raise her voice to be heard over the all-encompassing sound of rain.

One of the men that was already standing at the front raised his hand back to her and took another cautious step toward the gate so that he was within arm's reach of it. For some reason, Angela didn't like him being so close, but when she looked at him, he seemed as nervous as she was.

When the world is full of wolves in sheep's clothing, how do you decide who to let in the gate?

Angela stepped up to the gate, looking through the gap at the man on the other side. 'What's your name?'

'Mac,' he said. The single word had every bit of exhaustion to it that Angela had expected. It was like he knew the drill, knew not to ask for shit, just to answer the questions. Maybe he'd been through this before. Maybe he'd found himself hat-in-hand at some other folks' doorstep.

And maybe those folks are dead now.

Maybe the whole pathetic act took them off guard, too.

Angela swiped some rain away and narrowed her eyes. 'What do you want?'

'Same thing as everybody else that comes knocking, I guess.' He wore a hat, and a hooded sweatshirt underneath a thick leather jacket. He had the hood pulled up, though it was cotton and didn't seem to be doing him much good anymore. Water gathered at the brim of his cap and came off in streams. He looked up at her from underneath the brim and behind his miniature waterfall. 'Whatever you can offer us, really. Safe place to sleep. Get warm and dry, maybe. I know food and water is hard enough to come by, but we can work for it. If you got things that need gettin' done.'

Angela looked behind him. Her eyes fell on a young girl. She looked nothing like Abby, and yet she looked *everything* like Abby. Something in the eyes. Something that shouldn't be in children's eyes, and it broke Angela's heart looking at that little girl, just like it broke her heart when she saw the look in her own daughter's eyes.

Cold practicality.

'How many people are in your group?' she asked, keeping all emotion out of her face and her voice flat. Disinterested. The suffering of children could not drag charity from her. Not when the survival of her family, as well as every other family inside that gate, depended on her making a good decision.

'Thirty . . . two.' Some hesitation in his answer.

Angela looked at him distrustfully.

'Was thirty-three,' he explained, almost inaudible over the rain. 'We lost one. During the night.'

'Infected?' Angela asked, almost like she was trying to change the subject.

'No. Sickness, I guess.'

'Any of you been bit?'

'No.'

'Then lemme ask you this.' Angela hung a hand on the

chain-link fencing, one finger sticking through and wagging at the crowd that huddled behind the man who called himself Mac. 'Why's a group of thirty-two people wandering around in the middle of a rainstorm? With winter coming on? Shouldn't you guys be holed up somewhere? You're telling me that four months after everything goes to shit, you folks are still wandering around?'

'No, ma'am,' he said. 'Not wandering. Running.'

'Running?'

'Things are a little dicey up north,' he said. 'There are hordes. Thousands. Maybe more. Coming out of the cities. Filling up the roads. They all seem to be moving south. So being out there ain't safe. We're trying to stay ahead of them, but it's tough. We have to rest, but it sure as hell doesn't seem like they do.' The man's lips pressed together for a moment. Then he tilted his head and looked up at the sky, as though wondering if it was going to stop raining anytime soon. Angela got the sense that he was holding back a bit, but what he was holding back and why was a mystery. When he looked back down at her, he sighed, clouding the air in front of him. 'Listen ... we can earn our keep. For a place to stay warm and dry, and maybe even a little bit of food? I got twelve strong men and ten strong women, and we can do all kinds of things. And if bringing you news from up north is one of those things, then I'd say we'd be happy to exchange that, too.'

'Weapons?'

'Yeah, we got 'em.' He nodded. 'Not a lot, though. Might be able to spare one, but we don't have much ammo.'

It actually brought a wry smile to Angela's face. 'We don't want your weapons. I ask for our protection.'

Mac glanced at the guards, to either side of Angela and Brett and Marie standing behind her. He might've been able to see the gun on Angela's hip, but he definitely saw that each of the others was armed. 'Ma'am, you got more guns in your little crew right there than all of us combined. And I suspect there's more inside.'

Angela didn't respond. She looked at the crowd again. 'Who would you consider your second in command?'

'Well,' Mac said with a shrug. 'We don't have much of a ranking system or nothin', but I suppose it would be Georgia here.' He turned and nodded to a middle-aged woman. A hand came out of his pocket and made a short, introductory gesture.

Georgia stepped forward and stood beside Mac. She was in her late forties or early fifties by Angela's estimation. She had graying hair that showed signs of having once been a brilliant red color. She had unfortunate square features and a hawk nose that gave her a more masculine appearance. Grayish green eyes looked at Angela, giving almost as much suspicion as she got.

'So you two run this group?' Angela said.

Georgia and Mac both nodded.

'Can you vouch for your people?'

'Yes,' Georgia said.

Mac remained silent.

'Good,' Angela said. 'Because you two are going to stay with me at all times, and if any of your people do anything to hurt any of my people, me and my friend Marie here are going to immediately kill both of you, no questions asked.'

Silence, except for the rain.

Angela glanced behind her. Marie was there, thumb tucked into her rifle strap. She just nodded once. Angela turned back to Mac and Georgia. 'Now that you know how things are going to be, do you still want to come inside?'

Mac and Georgia exchanged a glance. There was some silent give-and-take there, but they seemed to come to an agreement. They turned back to Angela. This time it was Mac who spoke. 'Yeah,' he said. 'We still want to come inside.'

TWENTY-FOUR

INTROSPECTION

THEIR CONVOY MEANDERED OVER long stretches of back roads, windshields white with driving rain. They went slow, especially in the low points of the road where the water sheeted across and threatened to flood the roads.

Lee sat with the window closed, the wind and the rain more than he was willing to deal with. He looked in the side-view mirror and saw the headlights of the vehicles that were following him and his small crew. He sighed, heavy and slow, and leaned until his forehead rested on the cool glass of his window. He wanted to close his eyes, but a closed window was as lax as he was willing to be.

Some haggling with Colonel Staley had occurred. Eventually, with the storm threatening, the decision was reached that Colonel Staley would follow Lee back to Camp Ryder. It was a risk for both of them. Neither wanted to follow the other back to their home crowd, but they both knew that Staley could do more damage than Lee, even on Lee's home turf. Neither seemed happy about it when they went to their respective vehicles. But Lee had been told that was the sign of a good compromise.

Or a great way to sour a relationship.

To Lee, Colonel Staley and his Marines were a dangerous

animal. A *friendly* dangerous animal? Perhaps. But dangerous nonetheless. And which is worse – letting the dangerous animal into your home, or going to the den where the dangerous animal lives?

Lee didn't think that Staley was out to get them – he kept returning to the argument that if Staley wanted them, he would have already taken them. But the decision demanded caution anyway, so Lee had consulted with Old Man Hughes. They had agreed that both options were shit, but that the less horrendous of the two was to play host for the Marines.

Let them see Camp Ryder. Let them see the people they were going to be dealing with – good and bad. Let them understand the severity of the situation beyond the gates of Camp Lejeune, because after a few moments of speaking with Staley, Lee got the sense that living with a bunch of Marines on a military preserve had sheltered Staley from the worst of it.

The meeting had been tense, neither man truly knowing the thoughts of the other. But now, sitting in the pickup truck with the heat blasting and the rain driving and the rhythmic beating of the windshield wipers, Lee felt ... melted. Fatigued.

Depressed seemed too strong a word, but not by much.

He was thinking about things that he didn't want to think about. His mind went on its own, and like a child lost in the forest, it tried to find its way out but just kept wandering deeper and deeper. And the trees in that dark forest were hung with the bodies of the dead – the lost, the killed, and the murdered. And he knew every face in that multitude, and they were friends and foes alike. He thought about the way he had killed some of them, and the way others had been mercilessly snatched from him. And it all bored down into him and poisoned his blood.

God, there's been so many.

And it had not just been after the collapse. It had been before, when the world had been relatively normal, if not tumultuous. It seemed like all the deaths before were just previews of what was to come. Tests to see how he would handle it. As though the man behind the curtain, making the world go round, was seeing how much death Lee could handle and still be able to shrug it off and function.

He'd learned about his parents' death from his unit commander. This was after returning from one of the worst patrols in his deployment. A roadside bomb took two of his buddies out in the Humvee directly ahead of him, and a third lost both legs. He'd suffered a concussion, as well as his driver, and after he had returned to the FOB and been checked out for brain injury, his unit commander had simply asked him if he was going to be okay. Lee told him he was. And then his superior laid the truth on him without any effort to soften the words. Although, to be fair, Lee would have resented it if he had.

'Look. We got a call from the Red Cross. Your parents were in a bad accident. They're, uh ... neither of them made it.'

And that was that.

His memory of that day and the three days that followed were blurry at best. He couldn't really even remember what he did before he was on patrol that day. There had been dusty streets and shitty villages, as usual, and talk with village elders and smiling kids that might grab a rifle and take potshots at them as soon as they left. And then there had been an earth-shattering explosion and the Humvee in front of him had disappeared into dust and come out the other side just twisted steel. Two friends gone, another wounded for life that Lee would have infrequent and depressing telephone conversations with for the following years. Then he was in a hospital bed and his commanding officer was telling him his parents were dead. Eighteen-wheeler lost control, took them out along with two other cars, though his parents had been the only ones to die. He was granted emergency leave and then there had been a flight home.

He didn't really remember any of that. He remembered touching down at some airport or another and walking numbly to his next terminal and catching the connecting flight to Raleigh, and then driving home in rain very similar to this, on highways where eighteen-wheelers roared by, oblivious, and Lee wondered detachedly if he would even make it to the funeral.

No one had been there that he cared for. Aunts and uncles, and grandparents. He'd never been close to any of them. A few friends of the family showed up, people Lee remembered from church. He didn't really recall their condolences, though he was sure that they gave them. He didn't even really recall looking at his parents and to this day wondered if it had been open or closed casket. It seemed odd to him in retrospect that he drifted through these few days of his life in such a stupor. He had been through plenty before that, and since then, and yet that week seemed to be something his brain did not want to think about. He was not in denial – his parents were dead, that was just a fact – but he didn't seem to be able to comprehend it fully, or to feel anything about it. And so he figured that it didn't bother him much, though the more years went by, the more he realized how hard it had affected him, the one-two punch of the friends he'd lost on patrol, and the lone family members that waited for him back home.

He didn't think that he cried during the wake, or the funeral, or the burial. After they put his parents in the ground, he left and went back to a hotel room, rather than his parents' house. He purchased a bottle of whiskey on the way. He broke down in the quiet solitude of his hotel room and never opened the bottle. He woke in the morning, still dressed in his black suit and tie. He took it off and replaced it with his uniform. He stopped at his parents' house just long enough to drop his suit in the empty living room. Then he drove to the airport and caught his flight out, back to Iraq.

Then there had been tours, where other friends had been made, and other friends had been lost. The memory of his parents and their death was something he kept away from the rest of him. Then there had come the day when he had received an odd letter that had led him down a slippery slope to Project Hometown. And now he was here, still kicking, while everyone around him continued to die.

He despised thinking back on these things because they left him feeling open and bare. He was not the person he had been when his parents had died. He had changed in cataclysmic ways, and yet he was very much the same. Still stubborn. Still always pushing the envelope. Still always trying to make things right when they seemed out of whack to him. But different all the same.

Project Hometown and the months of training that followed the signing of that little piece of paper had been a sort of escape for him. A way to run from the man he had been before and to become something different. In Project Hometown, he did not need a family; in fact, it was best that he had none. In Project Hometown you prepared and prepared and prepared and you trained until you were sick and it girded you up and made you think that you were so ready for anything that might happen.

And he was different still from the man who had signed that paper, and even from the man who had come out of that training. His life seemed a never-ending series of changes, pressing him, pushing him toward ... what?

What was he now?

A soldier? A protector? A diplomat? An advisor?

All of those things, perhaps. And none of them, truly.

What was the endgame? What was he being pushed toward?

He knew what he *wanted* his ending to be. He wanted to finish this mission, this life, this calling. He wanted to be able to look back and say that he did what he had been called on to do, and he had done it well. He wanted to be able to say that he had fought long and hard, that he had accomplished his purpose, and in completing his work, he wanted simply to rest.

He wanted to be done.

Something nudged Lee in the arm and when he looked he found Deuce there, eyeing him. The dog had his forepaws up on the center console of the pickup truck. He grumbled, but it was not the sound of him alerting to the presence of infected, but more of a friendly verbal acknowledgment. With the rain threatening, they'd decided to pull the dog into the cab of the truck, rather than have him soaked and shivering in the back bed. He didn't seem to like being sandwiched between Jared and Noah, two people with whom he was unfamiliar, but he was at least not aggressive with them.

Lee reached over and touched the muzzle of the dog. If they could converse, Deuce would understand where Lee was at. Deuce would understand because he was a working dog, whether he'd been bred for it or not. Deuce would understand, because even though it meant he was in danger when he could be curled around a fire, entertaining children, this dog had a purpose, and he seemed to know it. His purpose was to smell the infected, and to alert his human pack when they came close. And he never stopped. Never stopped sniffing, never stopped circling the perimeter, never stopped searching for the threat. Deuce would never shirk his duties, never shy away from his purpose. His instinct demanded that he protect his pack, at least until there came a day when the threat was gone or he was too old to do it.

One day, buddy, Lee thought. *One day we will both be done. And when we're done, both these dogs can have their moment in the sun and be left alone. But until that day, you have to sniff, and I have to fight, and we both have to keep watch.*

He nodded to himself and looked straight ahead again. The wipers slapped water out of the way, but were futile in their efforts. The pickup truck and the MATVs following it had slowed to thirty miles an hour and the vehicle was consumed with the sound of the rain. A cleansing sound, but a threatening sound as well. An angry sound.

Maybe that's what I am. Maybe that's what I do.

I am not a soldier or a politician or an advisor. I'm a watchman.

Maybe it was the rain, or the cold, or perhaps just plain old luck, but the roads to Camp Ryder were deserted. Lee's little convoy made good time on the roads, without running into trouble. As the scenery began to be familiar, Lee leaned forward in his seat and held his rifle a little tighter. It was hard to see through the rain-dappled side windows, but he was trying to keep an eye on the woods. He knew what kind of infected were lurking out there. Some of the other people in Camp Ryder might be tricking themselves into a false sense of security, telling themselves that the hunters had moved on, but Lee knew better.

They just hadn't attacked because Lee had been *feeding* them.

344   D. J. MOLLES

What would they do now that Lee wasn't dropping bodies on their doorstep? Would they come back to the source of food? Would they move on?

It wasn't just the infected that concerned Lee. It was the Marines as well. Miles away from Camp Ryder, it had been an easier decision to allow them to follow Lee home. He put his doubts away and focused on what needed to be done – they needed allies, and allies had to have some sort of trust. But now, as he saw the unpaved inlet approaching them – the very same gravel drive that led to Camp Ryder – he felt the doubts reemerging.

The Marines possessed helicopters, artillery, and armored vehicles.

Basically, enough firepower to reduce Camp Ryder to rubble.

But Lee's options were limited. He did not have intelligence or background to rely on, so he had to go with his gut. And his gut told him that Staley wasn't there to hurt them, but to work alongside them for the mutual interest of cutting off the massive hordes in the North. He'd already made the decision to hold this meeting at Camp Ryder, and Staley was taking his own risk of sorts by following Lee.

Best to trust yourself.

Camp Ryder wasn't meant to be a hidden fortress. It was well-known to everyone in the area. They had expanded across several towns to establish security in the region, and though it had been threatened by Jerry's isolationism, it was still safer here than in many other parts of the state. Now was not the time to back down and go into hiding. Now was the time to make powerful allies and expand influence, and anytime you did those things it bore its own set of risks.

But they are necessary risks.

Old Man Hughes looked at him from the driver's seat. 'You good with this?'

Lee nodded. 'It's gotta be done.'

Hughes cranked the wheel to the left and then they were pulling onto the gravel drive. Muddy, potholed dirt, with giant ruts and splashing puddles. Lee eyed his side-view mirror again, watched the MATVs trundle onto the road behind him.

Through the trees you could see the outline of the Camp Ryder building. Lee felt simultaneously relieved and nervous. It felt like coming home. And with the MATVs behind him, it also felt like being exposed.

The gates of Camp Ryder stood, reinforced and nasty look-ing with barbed wire and sharpened poles. They'd looped the tops of the fences almost excessively with concertina wire, but Lee was still hesitant to call it safe from the hunters that lurked in the woods. There were weak points that could be exploited. And the hunters seemed smarter than the other infected.

The gates had been so heavily fortified that they'd had to reinforce the hinges. Two gallons of gas into a big Honda generator, and some creative welding yielded a clumsy but workable sliding gate. It took some effort and made all kinds of noise to get the gate open, but at least it held. He saw two yellow ponchos at the front gate, looking in his direction with rifles raised. They'd also mounted a scavenged M2 .50-caliber machine gun into the bed of a defunct pickup truck that was parked by the gate, but they only had a spare one hundred rounds for it.

At first, the guards seemed comfortable with the pickup truck, recognizing Hughes and Lee, but when they saw the MATVs following, they exchanged a quick glance, shouted some things, and one of the guards jumped into the broken pickup and manned the mounted M2. Up on the Camp

Ryder building, Lee saw a flicker of movement. The guard up there settled onto the abutment of the wall, his scoped rifle clearly aimed in the direction of the incoming convoy.

Hughes pulled to a stop directly in front of the gate. Lee opened his own window and leaned out. The rain pelted him, hard and heavy. He squinted at the narrow slot across the gate where one of the guards in the yellow ponchos looked out at him with suspicion.

'We're good,' Lee called loudly, then threw a thumb over his shoulder. 'They're with us.'

Lee watched the guard – he hadn't yet seen enough of his face to recognize him – as the man leaned, peering past Lee at the bulky military vehicles. Probably wondering to himself what the hell they were. Civilians knew about Humvees, but the MATV wasn't so ubiquitous as to be readily recognizable just yet. After another few plumes of hot breath into cold air, the guard nodded and began hauling the heavy gate open. The sniper on the roof and the guard on the M2 continued to track the small convoy as they slowly began moving forward into the camp.

Lee was okay with the caution. It was what they had trained to do.

When the gate was wide enough for the pickup to clear, Hughes rolled. The expanse of gravel parking lot had turned into a river delta in miniature, with dozens of tiny streams carving out pathways through the dirt and rock and gathering into giant puddles that trickled off into other streams. The tires of the pickup obliterated them and created its own wide swath through the mud, pulling off the right, partially in front of the Camp Ryder building.

On the front steps, Lee could see someone at the doors. Another guard perhaps. It was difficult to tell, because almost everyone walked around with a rifle. Whoever it was looked hard at Lee and the two MATVs as they pulled in next to the pickup. Then the person turned, opened the front door, and looked like he was yelling something inside.

Lee opened the door and stepped out, flipping the hood of his parka up. Deuce came down after him, a little hesitant as the first few heavy drops hit him, but then getting his gumption up and jumping down into the mud and water. He stepped lightly for a few paces, and then trotted over to the fence. He stuck his nose through a small gap and huffed the air a few times, testing it for the smells of danger.

When Deuce seemed satisfied, he lifted his leg and pissed on the fence.

Lee walked to the front of the pickup truck and looked to his left, where the two military vehicles were parked. Marines were sliding out of the two trucks. At first Lee had an insane thought that they were about to start assaulting the Camp Ryder building, but once the men were free of the vehicles, they simply stretched their legs and shrugged their shoulders against the rain, their rifles hanging loosely in their arms. They spread out, creating some containment. Two of them stayed close to the MATV that had been directly behind Lee's pickup, and from this Colonel Staley emerged.

He had donned an olive drab slicker. The older man stepped out of the MATV and looked skyward with an accusing glance, his teeth bared as though he might bark an order at the clouds and they would listen if they knew what was good for them. But he remained silent, and instead brought his gaze back down to Lee. When they had eye contact, Lee knew something was wrong.

Staley approached, hands on his hips. 'Captain Harden, I just got a call from my command. They've been updated by my man Sergeant Kensey, who is with one of your groups. The one up near Eden, I believe. Harper's group?'

Lee nodded, stiffly.

Staley pointed to the building. 'Can we talk out of the rain?'

Lee felt the weight of the words on his chest. He turned without comment and started walking toward the building, motioning Staley to follow. The two Marines walked with their commanding officer, and Old Man Hughes stayed with Lee while the others jogged ahead to get out of the downpour.

Ahead of them, Lee watched the doors to the building come open and Angela emerged. She was followed closely by Marie, and two people that Lee did not recognize – a man and a woman. The fact that they were strangers to him hovered around the periphery of his thoughts. Mainly they were focused on Harper, and he kept thinking, *What happened? What happened?*

Lee, Hughes, and the colonel with his two Marines jogged up the couple of steps to the recessed door. Angela stood there, out of the rain.

'Is that . . . ?' Angela trailed off.

'Colonel Staley,' Lee said, eyeing the two people he didn't know. He put a light hand on her shoulder and nodded toward the open doors. The group filed into the entryway. It was dimly lit by a couple of kerosene lanterns. The linoleum tile floor squeaked loudly underneath their feet and Lee could see the muddy, watery prints of the dozens of others that had come into the building recently.

Once inside, Lee shook the rain from his parka and looked out of the entryway into the Camp Ryder building and the main floor where the tables had been erected. It was crowded inside. In fact, much more crowded than it should have been. And there were more faces there that Lee didn't recognize, and they all belonged to wet, miserable-looking people.

He looked to his right where Angela and Marie were standing, along with the two strangers. They had the same gaunt, waterlogged look as the rest of the strangers. He gave Angela a look that said, *I sure would like to know who these people are.* But instead he turned and gestured to Staley, who was standing close by.

'Angela, this is Colonel Staley. Colonel, this is Angela. She kind of runs things around here.'

Staley patted his hand dry on the inside of his jacket and then extended it. 'Good to meet you, ma'am. You're the one in charge?'

Angela shook her head and accepted his hand. 'For now, anyway. Pleased to meet you.'

Lee had a very blank-looking smile on his face, but his eyes still showed some edge. 'Hughes, would you mind taking the colonel and his men up to the office? I'll be up in just a second.'

Hughes nodded and motioned for them to follow. Jared and Noah did so. Lee wasn't sure if he really wanted the two younger men to be standing around in the office while Lee and Staley talked about sensitive matters, but he let it slide for now. He had too many things going on in his head, and his worry for the news about Harper was tweaking at him.

'Angela, have you heard anything at all from Harper's group?'

'No, but ...'

Lee raised an eyebrow.

Angela seemed to be judging how Lee would take it, then decided to push on. 'I haven't really been in the office.'

Lee wanted to swear, but honestly, there wasn't much he could be mad about. He'd been gone for several hours, not days at a time, and if he wanted the radios monitored during the short time he was gone, he should have assigned someone to sit and listen, rather than assuming Angela was going to kick her heels up in the office until he was back.

'Sorry, I didn't even think about it.'

Lee shook his head. 'Not your fault. Who are these people?'

'Just a group that came knocking about an hour ago.' Angela gestured to the man and woman that stood beside Marie.

As she gestured, the man stepped forward and introduced himself. 'Mac. You are ...?'

'Lee.'

The woman introduced herself as Georgia.

Her name didn't mean anything to Lee, but the name 'Mac' rattled around in the back of his head and set off a muted little warning bell. But he had nothing to put it to. No facts or memories to connect with it. Nothing concrete to substantiate the feeling with.

'We'll earn our keep,' Mac said. 'For however long it takes.'

'How long is that?' Lee asked.

Mac pursed his lips. 'Until the rain clears out. Maybe sooner.'

Lee's eyebrows went up. 'That's not real long. Why the rush?'

Mac's face stretched into something that could have been a smile, or could have been a grimace. Lee wasn't sure. 'Bad things coming this way.'

Lee stared at the other man for a few beats. 'Yeah. It sure seems that way.'

Then Lee made for the stairs, motioning for Angela to

follow him. They stepped up to about the halfway point, and then Lee stopped, looking behind him. Mac and Georgia and Marie were involved in some conversation. None of them were paying attention.

'Is everything okay?' Angela asked.

Lee just shrugged. 'I don't know. Just keep an eye on those guys, okay?'

Angela nodded. 'Oh, I've had a detailed conversation with them. I'm already on it.'

'Okay. Good.' He pointed upstairs. 'Are you going to join us?'

She looked at the door upstairs, then gave a negative look – something that looked like distaste. 'No, I'm going to pay attention to our guests down here. You can fill me in later.' She pointed a finger up at him. 'Don't introduce me as the leader, by the way. I'm not.'

Lee just sighed and nodded. Heavy with decisions and the sickness of anticipation and worry. He didn't really feel like squabbling about titles just now. 'Well, you're the closest thing we have until everyone votes, but ... '

'No.' Angela started down the stairs. 'That's you.'

TWENTY-FIVE

CAT'S OUT

SAM SAT WITH ABBY in the back corner of the Camp Ryder building. No one had ever taught Sam that the corner was the best place to watch everyone in the room at the same time – it was just something he had learned on his own. The world was a good teacher, if you were smart enough to pay attention to the lessons.

Sam was seated on top of the table, with his feet on the bench and his rifle in his lap. Abby was seated similarly next to him, but instead of a rifle, she had a bowl of food – rice and some canned vegetables and maybe a little meat mixed in, he couldn't quite tell. He thought the meat was canned as well.

Abby didn't seem terribly interested in it.

Sam tapped the edge of her bowl with his finger. 'You need to eat more than that, Abby.'

She just huffed. Then brought an oversized spoonful to her mouth and chewed loudly while staring at him.

He smiled back at her and then turned to the crowd. Across the room, Angela was near the metal stairs, talking with the man and woman who led these newcomers. Ms. Marie was over there as well. The way that the four of them stood with each other and spoke awkwardly, Sam could tell that they were edgy with each other.

Months ago, Sam would not have understood.

But now it made perfect sense. Angela and Marie would never have let these strangers into their camp had certain things not been made clear. And if Sam had an ounce of common sense in him, and he liked to believe he was fairly sharp for his age, there had been very explicit threats made so that the newcomers knew exactly where they stood as guests.

Come in and eat our food, but don't look at me sidewise or I'll kill you.

'I'm full,' Abby announced.

Sam eyed the bowl. She had polished off a good third of it, but it had been a small portion. She hadn't seemed very hungry lately. But that was fine. Her appetite seemed to come and go every couple of weeks. He reached over and took the bowl from her.

'You're good. I'll finish it for you.'

'Garbage Can,' she dubbed him.

'I could eat everybody's food,' he said, shoveling some into his mouth.

'Why don't you go back for seconds? I'm sure they'd give you some. Everybody likes you.'

Sam nodded toward the line. There was still a dozen people waiting for food. 'Not everyone has gotten food yet. Going back for seconds would be selfish. Besides, not everybody likes me.'

'Well ...' She rolled her eyes. 'The *adults* do. Screw the stupid kids.'

Sam shot her a look. 'Don't say that word.'

'Screw?' She grinned. 'But you say it all the time.'

'Yeah, but Angela would kill me if she found out you learned it from me.'

'What's another bad word?' Abby looked at him slyly. She was in a mood. She liked to press him like this sometimes, try to get under his skin. It never really worked. Sam was patient with her, where he was short-tempered with some of the other kids. In fact, that was part of the reason why they sat alone on the table and no one dared join them.

Shortly after the assault on Camp Ryder, Sam had still been trying to wrap his head around the man he had killed with his rifle. It still bothered him, made him sick when he thought about it. And then Caleb, the kid with the freckles and the annoying buck teeth, started talking about it. Honestly, Sam couldn't even remember what Caleb had said that made him angry. One minute he was sitting there thinking about how he shouldn't beat the hell out of that kid, and the next he was on top of him, trying to knock one of those buck teeth out of Caleb's mouth.

Now Sam and Abby ate alone, played alone, and generally were ostracized. Caleb, the little prick that he was, made dirty eyes at them from across the yard outside and whispered things about them to his friends. Sam had learned just to stare back with his hands draped over his rifle. Best to act like he didn't care.

The kids were annoying, and the adults weren't much better. They kept treating him weirdly. Like they thought he was going to be all broken up about the guy that he'd shot. He wondered if he should have been. And sometimes when he thought about it, his heart would start racing. But he didn't want the adults to think that he was incapable of taking care of himself.

Resented it, in fact.

'I bet I know a bad word,' Abby said, testingly.

'Don't.'

She looked around to make sure no adults were in earshot. '*Fuck.*'

Sam sighed.

'I heard someone say that the other day,' she said, matter-of-factly. 'What's it mean?'

Sam shook his head. 'I'm not telling you what it means.'

'Come on.'

'No.'

'Why not?'

'Because.'

'Because what?'

'Abby,' he said, irritation growing in his voice.

She gave him an elaborate sigh and hung her shoulders, but she knew that she had pushed as far as Sam was willing to go. 'Fine,' she said, under her breath. 'I'll just ask one of the other kids.'

'Fine. You do that.' Sam finished what was left in the bowl and set it down.

A boy that Sam didn't recognize walked up and stood in front of them awkwardly, his own bowl of steaming food in his hand. He held it to his chest like a poor man held gold and Sam guessed from his thin face and his manner that the boy didn't get a chance to eat a hot meal very often. Sam felt bad for him. Felt bad about every time he had complained about the food here at Camp Ryder – it was more than most had, he knew.

'Can I sit with you?' The boy was looking at Sam. He had an extreme southern accent, and a clipped rhythm of speech. Something that Sam's father used to call 'white trash.'

But the boy standing before him just looked like another half-starved boy, maybe a year or two younger than Sam, and his face was open and honest. He seemed like a straightforward person, and Sam typically got along with straightforward people.

The boy spoke again: 'You like a guard or somethin'?'

'No,' Sam said.

'Well, you got a rifle.' He said it like *raffle*.

Sam shifted his feet. 'You gonna stand there and ask a buncha questions or you gonna sit down and eat before your food gets cold?'

The boy shrugged, then took a seat on the other side of Abby. 'Name's Bo.'

'Bow?' Abby tapped her feet on the bench. 'Like a bow and arrow?'

'No, just Bo. Bee-Oh.' He took a bite of food and spoke around a full mouth of food, a little bit dribbling out onto the table. 'What's y'all's names?'

'I'm Sam, this is Abby.'

Abby leaned forward, her hands buried in her coat pockets. 'Hey, Bo.'

'Hey,' he replied with a half smile.

'Fuck,' she said, testingly.

Bo looked at her and then Sam with a question in his eyes.

'Abby.' Sam took one of her shoulders and pushed her back out of Bo's face. 'Quit it.'

'What's that mean, Bo?' she demanded. 'You know what it means?'

'Well, I think it has somethin' to do with sex.'

Abby laughed uproariously, clearly with no idea what Bo was talking about.

Sam just gave an exasperated sound and shook his head at Bo. 'Don't tell her anything else. She's gonna start using it and then I'm gonna get in trouble.'

Bo smiled. 'I had a brother like that.' His smile faltered and he went back to his food.

'Where are you guys from?' Sam questioned.

'Up north.' More speaking around a full mouth. 'My mom and I came from outta Chatham up in Virginia. Then we met the rest a'these people in Danville. We stayed there for a while, and then we had to run because there was a bunch of infected comin' after us. Like, thousands and thousands of 'em.'

'Yeah, we sent some people up to check that out,' Sam said.

'It was Mr. Harper and Ms. Julia and a bunch of others,' Abby said loudly. 'I liked her. They left in a bunch of big green army trucks. I miss Ms. Julia – she was nice. But I don't really miss Mr. Harper. I think he was kinda mean.'

'Abby, stop talking,' Sam said, tiredly. 'You talk too much.'

Bo had stopped eating for a brief moment as Abby spoke. Now he glanced up at them for the barest of moments, but said nothing. Then it seemed he didn't want to look at them anymore. He faced his bowl of food and began eating more rapidly. His mood had clearly made an abrupt change.

Sam's eyes narrowed. 'You all right, Bo?'

Bo just nodded, but refused to look up. He seemed suddenly unable to finish his bowl of food. The plastic spoon simply slipped out of his hands and plopped onto the table. Still avoiding eye contact, Bo excused himself from the table. Oddly polite. He turned and walked away, not looking back at them.

Abby waved. 'Bye, Bo!'

Sam watched the boy go and wondered what the heck that was all about. He kept his eyes on Bo as he weaved in between all the picnic tables and the people who stood up while they ate, or sat Indian-style on the floor. He walked with his shoulders slumped and his arms hanging at his side.

He came to a woman, one of the newcomers that Sam didn't recognize. The woman bent down and put an arm on Bo's shoulder. She was listening, and Sam could tell that Bo was talking, though Sam guessed he was talking quietly because the woman had to lean in to hear him.

'What's wrong with him?' Abby said.

'No idea.'

'Bo was weird.'

'Yeah. Kinda.'

Sam watched a brown and tan form move around through the crowd, dodging strangers and working its way along the far wall. When it saw an opening it darted, like you might cross a busy street with fast-moving cars. Deuce padded up to them, then hopped up onto the table and sat next to Sam as though that was exactly where he belonged. He pushed his cold, wet nose right into Sam's face, smelling his breath.

Sam pulled his head back. 'Hey, buddy. You must be hungry.'

Deuce wagged once, licked his lips, and managed to wet the side of Sam's face in the process.

'All right, geez ...' Sam used his elbow to push the dog away a bit. Deuce continued to watch him with his usual intense gaze. Sam felt somewhat special that the dog liked to be around him and Abby, where it disliked most others. And it wasn't just because the dog liked kids, either, because it didn't. Much like Sam, Deuce didn't seem very fond of many of the other children in Camp Ryder. Had nipped at a few of them, actually. Which only made Sam like him more.

Sam reached over for Bo's unfinished plate. He regarded what was left of the food. 'You think Bo's gonna finish this?'

Abby leaned over Sam's shoulder, then looked out into the people crowded into the building. 'I dunno,' she said. 'I don't even see him. Give it to Deuce. Deuce is hungry. Hey, Deucy-Boy! You hungry? You a hungry boy?'

Deuce was not to be distracted from his focus on the bowl.

Sam sat the bowl down on the table and Deuce cleaned it in record time.

The crudely constructed picnic table shifted underneath them. Sam looked to his right and found Jenny there, leaning partially against it, one hand planted on the rough-hewn tabletop. Sam was surprised to find her there. Not because he was surprised that she would be in the Camp Ryder building, but because she had not spoken to him or Abby since the assault.

'Ms. Jenny,' Sam said somewhat cautiously.

Jenny looked at him and Abby and smiled, but it looked pained. Her face was a little paler than usual, her eyes a bit sunken. 'Hey, guys. Are you doin' okay?'

'Yeah,' Sam said.

Abby remained silent, watching Jenny with uncertain eyes.

'How about you?' Sam offered, trying to sound conversational.

'Well . . .' She swung her leg around one of the benches and sat herself down, regarding her hands. She picked at a bandage that was on her right hand. 'I've been better, Sam. I think . . . I think I might be getting that flu that's been going around. But I didn't come over here to complain to you.' She looked at him. The smile was gone. Her eyes were bloodshot and sad. She was closer to him now, and he could see little details that he hadn't seen before.

'It's okay,' he said, quietly. Beside him, Abby was squirming uncomfortably.

Sam noticed that Deuce had gone very still next to him. He was fixated on Jenny, head lowered just slightly, and something in his canine body language told Sam that the dog did not like the woman that had sat down at the table with them. But that was strange, because Deuce had never had a bad reaction to Jenny in the past. He avoided her, as he avoided most strangers, but what Sam was seeing in Deuce was ... aggression? Fear?

Deuce didn't growl, but Sam could see his lips tense and quiver as though he were considering growling, or barking.

Jenny reached out her right hand – the one with the bandage on it – but then thought better and retracted it. She put her other hand over the bandage, like she was trying to hide it. 'I never apologized to you or Abby. For what happened.'

'It's not your fault.'

'It was my fault.' Jenny nodded. 'I made some bad choices. I did some things that put everyone else at risk. I was selfish.'

Sam didn't really know how to respond. So he just sat there.

She was staring off at the blank wall behind them now. Her mouth was still moving, like she was still talking, but no sound came out. Then suddenly her eyelids fluttered for just a second, and her mouth closed. She looked at Sam, her expression confused. 'I don't really know where I'm going. I'm sorry.'

Sam felt himself involuntarily leaning away from her. 'You don't need to say you're sorry.'

'No. I do,' she insisted. 'I'm sorry for everything I've done. And everything I'm going to do. Just remember that.' Jenny turned so she could reach out with her left hand – her unbandaged hand – and touch Sam's knee. 'Can you do that for me? Can you remember to tell everyone that I'm sorry?'

Sam felt his voice tighten. 'About what?'

Jenny just smiled. 'Just remember.'

'Okay.'

She stood up from the bench without another word. When

she moved, Deuce twitched and let out a small growl that Jenny didn't seem to even notice. But Sam did.

Jenny thrust her hands into the pockets of her jacket and walked away, head down. She headed for the door, and no one stopped her or reached out to her. It seemed no one knew her. And perhaps half the people in that building did not, because they were strangers. And the other half *chose* not, because she was a traitor.

Sam watched her all the way to the entryway of the building, where she stopped at the metal staircase and looked up for a moment, and then continued on to the heavy double doors and pushed through into the night and the cold.

The first mistake she'd made was trying to touch the infected when she was out of her mind on prescription medications. The second mistake had been not trying to hack her hand off as soon as she saw the bloody cut. The third mistake had been refusing to tell anyone about it.

Her mistakes seemed to compound on her like |no one else's did. It seemed unfair. All the other people could make mistakes left and right and all fate had in store for their stupidity was minor injuries or maybe some hurt feelings that were easily apologized for and moved on from.

Every mistake she made seemed destined for disaster. Like fate had put her on the narrowest path it could find, and one step to the left or right meant she was tumbling down the mountain. It was all very unfair.

She was capable of thinking about this somewhat detachedly because she'd been on a steady diet of antidepressants. She decided not to mix and match from the mystery bottle she'd found – that had been a dangerous proposition and had led to another bad decision. But the antidepressants,

along with some pain medication, seemed to do the trick.
They kept her floating above the situation, they kept her panic
and her pain at bay, but they didn't muddle her thoughts.

At least, not much. Not as much as the mystery stack she'd
taken.

She walked out of the Camp Ryder building on warm,
unfeeling clouds. Far down below her were the worries about
what would happen to her in the next few days, but here and
now, those things could not reach her. Besides, there was
always the chance that she really was getting sick with the flu
that was going around. She'd been taking care of so many
people that had caught it, it wouldn't be surprising at all if she
finally came down with it. The knife cut had been deep, but
she had wiped the tainted blood off quickly, and if enough of
her own blood had been pooling out, none of the infected
blood could get in the wound, right? It seemed plausible.
Besides, like Jacob had said long ago, there is no method of
infection that *guarantees* you'll catch it.

*But he did say that blood-to-blood was the most likely method
of infection.*

Maybe, maybe not, her Paxilated brain told her. *You'll just
have to cross that bridge when you come to it. No point in worrying about it now.*

TWENTY-SIX

WELCOME

THE RAIN WAS A double-edged sword. It hid Tomlin's movements, but it soaked him to the bone. And though the rainstorm had brought warmer temperatures, that didn't stop the constant wetness from making him cold. Now he stood silently among never-ending rows of dark-skinned sentinels, and he watched the forest before him from his position behind one of them.

The underbrush was thin among the pines, so visibility was good. He could see a solid two hundred yards all around him. But that was two-sided as well – if he could see them, they could see him. Whoever 'they' were. He still hadn't figured that out.

Fort Bragg – or at least the roads heading into it – was exactly how Tomlin had remembered it. Military bases had the habit of being stuck in desolate places such as this, where the government could feel free to invest in a million-plus acres of land so shitty that no one else wanted them. Because of this, Fort Bragg had two things: sand and pine trees. As far as the eye could see, there was sand, and there was pine trees, all in even ranks and even heights, like soldiers standing in some vast formation.

Bragg was a massive base, famous for being the home of the

82nd Airborne, and US Army Special Operations Command, and infamous for being one of the older and more spartanly constructed bases. A large portion of the US Army had been through the base at some point or another, Tomlin included. These sandy marshes and rows of pine trees were where he had taken his SERE course, and that was something he would not soon forget.

Tomlin slowly turned his head to look behind him. About fifty yards back and to his right, he knew Nate was there, though he couldn't see him. The man was well hidden – at least until he leaned out from the pine tree he was behind and made eye contact with Tomlin. A quick glance in the other direction and Tomlin could see Devon, crouched very still among the sand and pine needles, behind him and to his left.

Wet sand and wet pine needles, Tomlin thought, thanking whatever force was responsible for this turn of good luck. The rain might be cold and soaking, but even an inexperienced woodsman like Devon could be silent on a bed of wet pine needles.

The distance between Camp Ryder and the northern tip of Fort Bragg was about the same distance as Camp Ryder was from Sanford. However, they could make the drive to Sanford straight across Highway 421, which had been cleared and patrolled and was mostly secure. To the south, which was a direction they had yet to expand in, it was all new territory. The going was especially slow.

They'd driven a small SUV out of Camp Ryder with just enough gas to get here and return, accounting for a trip that would be far from a straight line. Nate had driven, with Devon in the shotgun seat and Tomlin in the back center, directing them with a map laid across his lap and his rifle in his arms. They'd avoided main highways, skirted around towns, and doubled back if the road looked too much like an ambush, or if it was blocked by a snarl of derelict vehicles. What would have been a forty-minute drive in better times had turned into a five-hour ordeal.

But it had given the rain time to come and soak everything into silence, and to provide a steady sound cover for their movements.

They'd parked the SUV a ways back on Johnson Farm Road, just a mile or so north of where government property began. They'd pulled it into another cluster of abandoned cars and it fit in nicely with the others with its four-month layer of dirt. Then they'd made the rest of their way on foot.

Slowly.

Tomlin was out front of the others, forming the point of a triangle. He would move forward perhaps five yards at a time, in unhurried, stalking steps, his eyes shooting from his footing to the woods around him, simultaneously making sure he didn't step on fallen branches, and that there was nothing ahead that might give him problems.

Nate and Devon hung back. Tomlin would stop and survey the scene for a second, and then wave them forward. Then they would wait, and Tomlin would continue on another five yards when he felt it was secure. Stealth could not be rushed, especially in this situation. Time was on their side. Trying to hurry would only get them caught, and they benefited nothing from getting there today or tomorrow or the day after.

It took them nearly two hours to reach this point.

Up ahead, Tomlin could see the signs: POSTED NO TRESPASSING and GOVERNMENT PROPERTY. They were hung on an old, rusty-looking section of chain-link fencing with barbed wire on top. Even when shit had been going tip-top, he was sure that sections of the fence were always rusty, though fence maintenance was probably a year-round job. It was simply impossible to fence in millions of acres and have it perfectly secure at all times.

He wondered how secure they had managed to keep it now.

He knew the fence that he was looking at would be the very same one that would encompass the entire base. And it would cross Johnston Road, a couple hundred yards to their left, and there would be a gate over that road. Whether that gate was locked, guarded, or flung open on its hinges remained to be seen. Tomlin had yet to see a single person, or a single noise that might tell him that there was anything in Fort Bragg besides dead bodies and insane people.

The stillness of the woods was absolute. Even the rain fell perfectly steady, with not a single gust of wind to push it to either side. Water ran in rivulets through his hair, which had grown irritatingly long, and he could feel the wet clumps of strands clinging to the side of his forehead and feeding the water down onto his eyebrows and from there, into his eyes, down around his nose, and into his mouth, salty and sweet all at the same time.

The stillness seemed inviting on the one hand, threatening on the other.

Sometimes it was difficult to determine whether something was good, or a little too good.

Paranoia, maybe.

Or caution. But it's all the same to me.

Tomlin stepped out from his tree. Every time he did it he expected his chest to meet with a copper-jacketed bullet and for the life to be snatched out of him. But the woods remained still and silent and no bullet came for him. He pushed forward another five yards. Got a little greedy and took a couple more. He felt instantly foolish for it.

Behind the next big tree he waited, cringing.

He looked upward, wishing to hear or see some form of nature – a squirrel dancing across tree limbs or a bird ruffling its feathers – but even the wildlife was silent. They had more sense than he did. They weren't about to get themselves soaked in the rain. Intelligently, they were hiding.

Another thing he had yet to see: a single infected.

Not one.

Most everyone that left the confines of whatever secure location they'd holed themselves into had become accustomed to the sight of the infected. Not so accustomed that it didn't peak their fear when they saw them, but it was common enough to see a pack of them chasing something through a field, or a horde standing at an intersection, still and dumb, like they couldn't decide which way to go. Sometimes they charged, but often enough they just stood and watched, their hands always clenching and unclenching manically.

But all the way here they had been conspicuously absent.

Isn't that a good thing?

Sure. Definitely. Maybe.

Tomlin decided to move forward again. He looked behind him and very slowly motioned the others to stay put. With the fence in front of them, and knowing that the road was only just out of sight, he needed to see what they were facing before he had Nate and Devon come up.

He had a small spotting scope that he kept stuffed in the pocket of his jacket. He brought this out and scanned the horizon in front of him, and then moved forward ten yards. He stopped and scanned again. He waited a few minutes. Scanned again. Moved forward another ten yards.

Thirty yards up and he could see the blacktop of the road, shimmering with rain. He followed the road until he could see where it crossed paths with the fence. There was a gate. Nothing too robust, but a simple double-hinged affair of eight-foot fencing topped with barbed wire. All around the gate, fresh, shiny concertina wire had been jumbled, creating a glittering field of steel points and razors for the unwelcome.

On the other side of the gate, the two-lane blacktop continued on. However, one of the lanes was obstructed by a Jersey barrier, and behind that and all around it were piled a wall of sandbags with the muzzle of an M240 protruding from it. Behind the machine gun, two helmeted heads alternately looked out at the woods and the road leading to the gate, and then down to however they were amusing themselves. A green tarp or maybe a poncho liner was draped over the top to keep the interior of the nest relatively dry.

Tomlin watched them for a while. He slowly lowered himself down onto his haunches, only half his face peering around the side of the pine tree, with his small spotting scope held to his eyes. He locked his core to keep himself from shivering. It sure would be nice to get out of the rain, though how and when he would be able to do that was anybody's guess.

One of the men peered out and up at the sky, as though to see if there would be a break in the rain anytime soon. But the clouds were a solid sheet of slate across the sky and the rain was steady. There was a brief conversation that Tomlin couldn't hear and then the one man squirmed out of the machine gun nest and jogged to the edge of the road, braving the rain to take a quick piss.

Tomlin studied him for the moment as he was out in the open. The man wore ACUs, but didn't appear to be wearing any body armor except for his helmet. He had an M4 slung to

his side, but this was a longer-barreled version than the car-
bines that were issued to most soldiers, and it had a scope on
it. From this distance, Tomlin could make out no patches on
the man's uniform, nor any other equipment he might have
had on him.

Designated marksman, Tomlin guessed.

The other man inside the nest Tomlin really couldn't see,
aside from his helmet moving around every so often.

Tomlin waited for the marksman to return to the nest,
shaking the rain off himself and cursing loud enough to hear
even from Tomlin's position. Then he waited some more,
waited to make sure the other man wasn't going to take a
break as well. When it seemed both had resumed their dis-
tractions, Tomlin quietly rose and melted back into the
woods.

It took him almost twenty minutes to get back within sight
of Nate and Devon. Moving unseen *toward* an objective was
always easier than moving *away* from it. When it was in front
of you, it was easier to use the angles to your advantage, keeping concealment and cover between you and them and using
the micro-terrain to your advantage. Moving away, you had to
stop more frequently to look back and see if you were hidden.

Nate and Devon saw him coming back toward them and
they both leaned out of their cover. Per his instructions, they
had stayed separate from each other. Tomlin sidled into a position behind the root structure of a fallen tree and then waved
the other two over. They slid with surprising grace from their
places of concealment and crouched down in front of him, eyes
still scanning the woods around them. He was glad he had
chosen them to come along. They seemed fairly squared away.

'All right.' Tomlin spoke in low tones. Human voices carried farther than you might believe. 'I got a gate across the

road, closed and chained, it looked like. Machine gun nest on the other side. Well defended. They've got a medium machine gun in the nest, and two guards. One's a marksman, I think. Couldn't tell on the other one.'

'Military?' Nate asked.

One of the concerns they had spoken about on the way was whether or not the base would still be held at all, and if it was held, would it be held by US military or by bandits? A third, more difficult option to address was the possibility that it could be people *posing* as US military. Which would be a great way to lure people in and then take them unawares.

Tomlin shrugged. 'They're wearing the uniforms.'

'But they could be fakes.'

'Could be,' Tomlin admitted.

'And there's also the possibility that they are US military, but aren't friendly.'

'Yeah.' Tomlin wiped rain out of his eyes. 'Those are all possibilities.'

'But ...' Nate prompted.

'But we came here to make contact.'

Devon spoke up. 'Is there any way we can be sure?'

Tomlin considered it. 'The only way I can think that we can be sure is if we camp here and watch and wait. If another party comes along, we'll see how they handle it and get a better idea of the people we're dealing with.'

Nate grimaced. 'That could take days. Weeks even.'

'Right.' Tomlin nodded. 'And we have no shelter. And only enough food and water for today and tomorrow. And we need to consider if things go bad somehow and it takes us more time to get back to Camp Ryder than we expected.'

'You seem very calm about this,' Nate observed.

'Well.' Tomlin leaned back against the root system, wiping

the corners of his mouth. 'The way I see it, Lee sent me to find help. Time and supplies are against us. And there's no reasonable, efficient way to figure out whether the people inside that gate are friendly or no. Even if we did wait for another group to happen along, there's no telling that what we see at the gate is indicative of what happens inside.'

Devon narrowed his eyes. 'Meaning?'

'Meaning they could greet them nicely at the front gate, lead them into the heart of the base where we can't see, and then rob and murder and rape. On the flip side of that, they could greet them by detaining them all, dragging them into the base, and then determining that they are not a threat and letting them go with food, water, and well-wishes.'

Nate and Devon exchanged a glance.

'So we're going to make contact.'

'*I'm* going to make contact,' Tomlin specified. 'It's a gamble, and it sucks, but I knew it was gonna be like this as soon as Lee asked me to do it. There's just no way to know until I get in there.'

Nate seemed irritated. 'Well, what the fuck are we here for?'

'You're here to carry word back if they shoot me dead on the road. You'll go back to Camp Ryder and tell Lee that Fort Bragg is a no-go.'

'And if they let you in?'

'Well, if they have half a brain, they'll throw me on the ground, frisk me, blindfold me, and then take me into the base to question me and figure out who I am and whether I'm a threat. And then you guys will sit and wait and hopefully I will send someone to come get you guys before dark, if everything turns out well.'

'And what if that doesn't happen?' Nate said, stress coming out in his voice. 'What if we don't hear from you?'

Tomlin shrugged. 'Give it twenty-four hours. Then head back to Camp Ryder.'

'You could die,' Devon said, as though it was the first time he had considered it.

Tomlin nodded. 'Trust me, I don't like it any more than you do. And if you have a better way to handle it, then please, tell me now. But I think we've all considered the angles here, and given our time and resource constraints, this is pretty much the only way to find out.'

Nate leaned back on his haunches. 'Fuck me.'

'You could have talked to us about this earlier,' Devon said, sounding slightly dejected.

'It would have been a pointless argument,' Tomlin said. 'I figured we were gonna get here and the base was gonna be in ruins, to be honest. I figured if there was a military presence here, then we would have heard about them or made contact with them by now.'

The three men sat in silence for a moment. Tomlin looked at them, and they looked at the ground. He figured they were trying to come up with a reasonable alternative, but he didn't think they would. Tomlin had already weighed the risks in his own mind. You could either be an island unto yourself and be safe, at least until you starved or got overthrown, or you could take a chance and try to make some allies. And allies were always a risk.

'We're burnin' daylight here, gents,' Tomlin said gently.

Nate and Devon looked at each other again. This time Nate nodded begrudgingly.

'Okay,' he said to Tomlin. 'I guess we gotta do it.'

Tomlin backed up a few hundred yards and then curved over to the two-lane blacktop. He watched it and listened for a while to make sure there were no vehicles coming, and then he stepped out onto it and began to walk. He figured it would be best to stay on the road, where he would be spotted a longer ways off. He feared that if he popped out of the woods too close to the nest, the guards might give him a burst from the machine gun just out of surprise.

He walked at a brisk pace, his rifle slung onto his back and his hands visible. He was as unthreatening as he dared to be. He had considered leaving the rifle with Nate and Devon, but then figured that a weaponless man might raise more questions than an armed one.

Up ahead, as he came out of a slight curve, he could see the gate coming into view.

The similarities between this and another time he had offered himself up to the mercy of others was not lost on him. The day he had stepped out in front of Lee's convoy with his hands up, he'd figured the reception would not be warm. What he hadn't figured was how pissed Lee would be, or that Lee would blindfold him and lock him in a Conex container full of scrap metal.

Here again, Tomlin knew the reception would be rough, but what came after was a mystery.

And also, how rough the reception would be remained unknown.

Bullet in the chest rough? Or blindfold and flex cuffs rough?

His eyes were locked on the closed gate ahead of him, the hedge of looping razor wire surrounding it and piled atop the fence. He could barely see the machine gun nest beyond the silvery mess of wire and fencing. But they would be able to see him.

Anytime now.

A bird burst out of a bush just inside the woods to his right, making him jerk. It streaked overhead so low that he could hear the beating of its wings. And that was all it took to kick-start his heart into overdrive. Now he was walking on a road and up ahead there was a machine gun and two guys of questionable alliance and probably what amounted to very loose rules of engagement, if they had any at all.

I'm running. If they fire a single shot, I'm fucking out of here, no ifs, ands, or buts. I don't give a shit if it was a warning shot, I'm not sticking around to find out ...

It was an amplified voice that shouted at him: 'Stop where you are!'

He halted, raising his hands up, the fingers splayed wide to show they were empty.

Don't fucking shoot me.

'I'm friendly ...' he tried to call out, but was cut off.

'Face away from the gate!' The voice was coming through a megaphone, Tomlin realized. 'Face away from the gate and keep your hands up high!'

Tomlin swore under his breath and complied immediately. He wasn't going to stand there blank-faced and give them a reason to think he was infected. By complying, he was at least demonstrating that he was sane. Sure, they might gun him down anyway, but he wasn't going to give them any extra incentives. He reached his hands up as high as they would go. A televangelist praising God. He was staring down the road he had just walked and he could feel the muzzle of the machine gun on his back like a tingling ghost presence. Just a few pounds of pressure from an itchy trigger finger and all of the sudden he would be looking at the remains of his spleen, scattered across the road in front of him.

Be cool. Stay calm.

His eyes jagged to the left, furtively, in the direction where he figured Nate and Devon would be watching. But if they were there, he could not see them. And then he got the unnerving feeling that perhaps they had decided to leave him. Maybe they figured this was a fool's errand to begin with and wanted nothing more to do with it.

It wouldn't matter anyway. They couldn't do anything for me now.

'Put your hands on the top of your head. Interlace your fingers.'

He did it, baring his teeth. He knew this was going to happen, but it didn't stop it from jangling his nerves. No one wanted to have guns pointed at their back, their life placed on the trust that the men pointing the guns had the self-restraint necessary not to gun him down for no other reason than they were bored.

'I see that rifle,' the amplified voice called. 'Do not make a move for the rifle. If you try to reach for it, we will kill you. Give me a thumbs-up if you understand what I'm saying.'

Tomlin gave a thumbs-up and felt a little ray of hope shooting through the adrenaline dump. People didn't go through all this bullshit just to gun somebody down, so there was a good chance they weren't just going to arbitrarily murder him on the road. That was good. That was great. That was step number one.

After that? Hell, only God knew what they would do after that.

One thing at a time.

'Get down on your knees. Cross your ankles. Sit back on your ankles.'

Tomlin settled into the prescribed position. He searched the woods again, but again could see nothing of his two companions. *They're there*, he assured himself. *They're just hidden. That's a good thing. It's good that they're hidden.*

'Do not move from that position. Do not attempt to turn around and look at us. Do not attempt to speak to us. If you move, we will open fire.'

As the amplified voice clicked off, Tomlin could hear the growing sound of an engine. Something was hauling very fast and for a brief moment, Tomlin couldn't tell where it was coming from. Was it Nate and Devon? Please, dear God, don't be Nate and Devon, roaring up in the little SUV trying to save him . . .

But no. This vehicle sounded much bigger than the little SUV they'd driven.

And it was coming from behind him.

The engine shifted out of overdrive for a moment and Tomlin thought he could hear the clatter and clank of the gate opening up. Then the cylinders started roaring again and now Tomlin was thinking about a big diesel truck, just running him down in the middle of the road. Slamming him flat and backing up over his head to make sure the job was done. Why waste valuable ammunition when you can just have a jackass sit down in the middle of the road and run him over?

He wanted to look behind him, but he sensed that the man that had spoken from the megaphone had been quite serious, and Tomlin believed him that if he tried to turn or to look at what was going on, he would get a full auto burst all the way up his spine.

He heard the squeal of brakes.

Doors opening and boots slamming concrete.

Tomlin gritted his teeth.

They hit him hard, plowing him into the concrete. His chin

struck the asphalt and he could feel the burn of skin being stripped off as his teeth clacked together. His arms were seized and the rifle was ripped from his sling. Then his hands were yanked behind his back, zip-tied tight enough to cut off the circulation, and a black cloth bag pulled over his head. Another set of flex cuffs to secure his feet together. Rough hands frisking him, ripping through his pockets.

'I don't have anything,' Tomlin said, his voice straining.

'Shut the fuck up. Do not speak to us.'

Then he was lifted off the ground. He could feel his body being lifted up into something – the vehicle, he assumed – and then someone was standing over him. They planted a knee into his lower back, and a hand on the back of his head, keeping his face pressed against what felt like the metal floor of a truck bed. Then the engine was roaring again, making a wide circle, and then accelerating back into Fort Bragg.

Yes, this all feels very familiar.

Nate watched from where he was lying prone, peering underneath some low-growing shrub. Devon was beside him, swearing quietly. They watched the men in uniforms – all tans and greens, some of the patterns mismatched – and they watched them slam Captain Tomlin on the ground and bind his wrists and his ankles and pull a black bag over his head. Then they threw him in the bed of a big black pickup truck and then they were gone in a cloud of diesel fumes.

The two guards slammed the gate closed again as soon as the pickup truck was through, and then they were back into their machine gun nest, watching the road, probably more alert now than they'd been in days. The sound of the truck faded behind them, obscured by the tail of mist the tires were kicking up from the wet road.

Then the truck was gone, and all was silent again, save for the falling rain.

Nate took two, long, slow breaths, then looked at his partner.

Devon stared back at him, wide-eyed. His pale skin was flushed around the nose and cheeks from the cold. He looked miserable, but now he looked scared as well. His voice was a thready whisper, straining to get out of the tightness of his throat: 'What the fuck do we do now?'

Nate shook his head. 'Ain't shit we can do but wait.'

TWENTY-SEVEN

HALF-TRUTHS

ABE DARABIE HAD TALKED, but not all the way. Talking was inevitable. And Carl seemed an effective interrogator. He'd allowed Abe to come very close to drowning to death, twice having to stop so that they could roll Abe on his side and purge out the little bit of water that had gotten into his lungs. In the moment, it was terrifying, and Abe just kept thinking, *He did it, he fucking drowned me, I'm dying . . .*

Afterward, sitting in the cold darkness of his cell, shivering and as miserable as was possible, he kept wondering if the water slipping into his lungs had been intentional, or accidental. Frankly, Abe was more frightened that it had been accidental. Waterboarding had to be done carefully so you didn't drown your prisoner to death, and if the man that called himself Carl didn't know what the fuck he was doing, Abe was likely to be killed by overzealousness.

Or maybe Carl just didn't care.

In his cell, misery made him furious and frustrated, with no way out, and no end in sight. He was in the hands of a man whose intentions and loyalties remained a mystery. Telling lies carried the promise of more pain and terror. Telling the truth carried the strong possibility of death.

Still, bits and pieces came out.

You couldn't help yourself. When you were strapped to a chair for the third time, shivering with cold, when you couldn't feel your fingers because they were numb. Until they began to hurt, of course. *Everyone talks. It's not a matter of IF, but a matter of WHEN.* And all the training that he'd received, where SERE instructors had made him miserable and scared, it was all just to help him hold out a little longer. But no one held illusions that it was going to make you torture-proof.

And Carl Gilliard was smart. He never overused one method of interrogation. It wasn't just waterboarding 24/7. It was standing outside in the cold. It was having electrodes strapped to your testicles. It was getting hit all over the body with a knotted rope. And between them all, plenty of down-time, to sit in the cold, cold dark, and to think about how fucking miserable you were.

Very, very effective.

Abe had lost all track of time. When he was in the blackness of his cell, it was difficult to even tell when he was asleep and when he was awake. His thoughts were muddled and dream-like either way, and filled with regrets. He kept thinking about Eddie Ramirez, and the way the man's head had snapped back when the bullet had hit it. And he had begun to tell himself, *That was badly done, Abe.*

'Was there another way?' he would shout into the darkness.

'No!' he would shout back. 'There was no other way!'

He had been dragged from his cell a total of six times. Twice he had been waterboarded. Once he'd been beaten and made to stand outside in the cold. Three times they had hooked the electrodes to his testicles, because he seemed to cave a little more on that one.

The last time, as the electrodes spiked pain into him

through his groin, he remembered thinking that the pain was so bad and that it was never going to stop and that he had to say something, just had to say something, just make it stop . . .

And when the current gave out, Abe found his breath and shouted at Carl. 'I left President Briggs! I fucking left him. I couldn't do it anymore. I couldn't do the shit he was asking me to do so I left. I was a major, and now I'm fucking nothing!'

Carl tilted his head, his gaze impassive. 'And where are you going?'

'To a friend.'

'Who is your friend?'

'Another soldier. Not loyal to Briggs.'

'What's his name?'

Abe stared at the ground, eyes beginning to well up.

'Where is he?'

Abe shook his head.

'What is the little black electronic device you had?'

'Something that belongs to him,' Abe answered, his voice a bare wisp.

'What does it do?'

Again, Abe chose to remain silent.

Carl regarded a yellow legal pad that was across his lap and scrawled down some notes.

Abe could not help himself. He felt stripped and empty. Cracking around the substructure of his humanity, of everything he thought he was. It was disheartening and infuriating all at once. If he could have he would have ripped himself from his bindings, and he would have thrown himself at Carl and ripped the man's throat out with his teeth. He hated the man desperately in that moment.

Carl had eventually nodded to the men that Abe knew were standing behind him. 'Get him out of here.'

Then came the black sack again. They ripped off the tape that bound him to the chair for his electrocution session. They pulled his underwear back up. Bound his wrists behind his back again. Abe wanted to struggle, but his energy ebbed and flowed, carried now only by panic and rage. And now he felt nothing, so he let his body become limp.

They threw him in his cell and he fumbled around in the dark for the clothing they had stripped from him. That was how he always knew whether they were going to use the electrodes or not – they would strip him down to his filthy skivvies. He found his pants and his shirt, still damp, and he slid into them. At first they were icy cold, but eventually his body heat warmed them.

He felt marginally warmer. But still shivered.

He tried to sleep. Woke up, coughing wetly. He was beginning to feel feverish. He touched his forehead and found it hot, while cold chills racked him. He was curled into a ball on the floor, trying to be warm, trying to be as comfortable as his body would allow. But no matter how he was positioned, the cold cement floor was pressing against a bruise or a sore muscle.

He squirmed to a corner of the room, finding his way there by touch.

I'm going to have to escape. I don't think it matters what I say to these people, I think they won't ever let me out of here alive. I think I have no more options left. It's either stay here miserable, tell them what they want, and die, or keep feeding them half-truths long enough to find a weakness and get the hell out.

What about Lucas?

In the darkness, Abe bared his teeth and set his burning forehead against the cold wall.

Lucas, Lucas, Lucas . . .

Is he even still alive? I don't know if he's even alive. And if I knew that he was, there would be no telling where he was. I could always try to pry, try to get the truth out of them, but right now they think that I'm under their power. They think they have me completely broken. If I start asking too many questions, will it raise suspicions? Will they start guarding me closer? Will I lose my opportunity to escape?

Abe found the corner he'd been looking for. The one to the left of the door. He rummaged through the darkness and felt the little bundle stuffed there. He felt elation like a fire in his chest. The fatigue and the pain were making his emotions raw and they barely hid themselves under the surface of his face. Just finding this small victory almost brought him to tears.

'Yes. *Yes*,' he said fiercely.

Here was a weakness that he might exploit.

Though they were rough with him, they still fed him. The door would open suddenly when he was slipping through strange nightmares, and a plate of food would be thrust in at him. It was always cold and it was always some starch or carbohydrate – never meat. They certainly didn't feed him a lot, but it was better than nothing. And it was enough that he could have some, and sock a small portion away.

He pulled the little cloth bundle from the corner. The interior of the pants he wore had a pocket to hold integrated knee pads, if the wearer chose. Abe had ripped these out to provide himself with some cloth to wrap things in. He pulled one of the pieces of cloth up. He couldn't see in the dark, but his fingers lightly touched a chunk of stale bread and some crackers. There were a lot of crackers – saltine-type crackers – because that was a large portion of whatever they served him. It was ideal for him because they kept well and didn't really molder. They just went stale. And stale didn't matter.

Energy mattered. Calories mattered.

And here were two victories in one: First, the bundle in the corner full of squirreled-away food proved that the guards did not toss his cell when he was being questioned. Second, it meant that he would have a good meal when the time came to give himself some extra strength.

As much as he would have liked to stuff everything into his mouth right then and there – even with the fever and sickness coming on, he was starving – he covered the bundle again and shoved it into the corner, where he hoped it would remain hidden. What else could be hidden there? A weapon perhaps?

Abe scuttled to the other side of the room. He put his ragged thumb to his lips, feeling the sharp edges where little bits of his cuticle had been nibbled away. He tried to think about what he came into contact throughout the day. Was there anything that he could possibly use as a weapon? Anything that he might be able to steal from them without them knowing it? Something that could be turned into a shiv? He racked his brain, but his thoughts were constantly interrupted by the fact that he felt horrible.

I'm getting sick. It's pneumonia. I fucking know it is.

He'd never had it before, but with the waterboarding getting fluids into his lungs, the wet cough, and the constant cold and damp that he was subjected to, it seemed the most likely culprit. He sat his back against the wall of the cell and brought his knees up close to his chest, trying to capitalize on his own body heat.

He stewed for a time. He thought his days through. Thought of anything he might use to give himself an advantage. Eventually, despite the cold and the pain, exhaustion took its toll and he nodded off into more half dreams and waking nightmares. He couldn't remember any of it, except that his heart kept pounding, startling himself awake only to drift off moments later.

He might've been asleep for a day or twenty minutes when the door came bursting open again. Abe heard it, recognized it, but didn't move. He sat across from the open doorway and stared at it. Usually they came in quick and pulled the burlap sack over his head, but it seemed that the last few times their reaction had been slower. He had never told them his background. They didn't know enough to be afraid of him, and perhaps they were beginning to view him as some already-beaten armchair commando. Maybe they thought that he was too broke to fight.

Whatever their reasoning, they didn't rush in this time. They stood at the door. Beyond, it was bright. For the first time, they stood there long enough for Abe's eyes to adjust to the light pouring in and for him to see their faces. He'd had impressions before – big men, square faces, thick beards – but they were usually behind him and then the shit-smelling sack was over his head, blinding him.

Even through the grogginess of his own fatigue, some part of him was still pulling the strings, still cataloging the information that his eyes were receiving and filing it where it needed to go. The first man was older and somewhat burlier than the other. His beard looked reddish blond and he had a fierce aspect about him that spoke of a wild Norseman. The second man was younger, darker-skinned, with curly black hair and a patchy beard that hung low on his jawline. He looked strong, but in a more wiry way than his counterpart.

They stood there, looking down at Abe for a moment and for the first time, Abe thought he saw something in their faces besides a desire to hurt him. Perhaps pity? Maybe some remorse? Had the things he had said in his previous interrogation led them to believe that Abe Darabie was on their side?

Or perhaps they knew what Carl had in store for him.

Abe didn't move. He kept his arms wrapped around his knees. His voice came out ragged and weak. 'What the fuck does he want now? It's only been ... what? An hour?'

The big Norseman just shook his head marginally, but he didn't respond to Abe's subtle attempt to try to figure the time. The lack of sunlight, not having any concept of how long you'd been held captive or what time of day it was ... it was very disorienting.

'Come with us,' the Norseman said. His voice was cold and hard, just like Abe had thought it would be.

Abe waited for some further explanation, or for the violence that he was sure was just around the corner. But after a moment had passed and the two men still stood in the doorway, not making a move to him, Abe slowly leaned himself forward and struggled to his feet.

They did bind him, which was no surprise. But this time they bound his wrists in the front and the sack they put over his head didn't smell like shit. They held him by the arms, but their grips were not rough like they'd been every other time. And all of this only began to make Abe suspicious.

I know this trick, he thought.

He'd learned this along with every other trick in the book. Beat your captive down and then act nice. It puts the prisoner off their game. Softens them up. And then you smack them down again, harder than before. It makes it even worse and has a more damaging psychological aspect.

What's worse than waterboarding and electrodes on my testicles?

Abe felt his stomach flip-flopping.

I'm sure they can think of something. Things that cause permanent damage.

In Siberian gulags, the Soviets would beat the prisoners' feet with rubber hoses, disfiguring them for life. They'd shove glass thermometers up their penises and break them with a rubber mallet. There was no end to the cruelty that the human brain can think up. Cruelty was a sickness that just compounded on itself.

He had the feeling Carl was military, or some sort of government. He handled these interrogations with a practiced hand and a coldness that could only come from years of experience. People didn't like to believe that the United States government had employed people like him, but not believing in something didn't make it untrue. During his tours Abe remembered several incidents where the jihadist they had just captured was scooped up by some anonymous men – men very similar to Carl – and whisked away to be 'debriefed.' Hours or days later, those men would come back with valuable intel and no explanation of how they'd gotten it.

Not by asking nicely, that's for damn sure.

Blind, he was led through halls that felt marginally familiar. He had been down them six times so far and had done his best to memorize the pattern: left out of his cell, through a locked door, down a long hall that felt colder than the rest of the rooms, through another locked door, and finally a right turn into the room where the black sack would be removed from his head and Carl would be waiting for him.

This time, though, things went a little differently.

They went through the last door, where they usually turned him right into the room where his interrogation would take place, but then they kept going straight. He could hear a slight echo. He could also hear voices. Other men being interrogated? Maybe. He couldn't be sure. They were muffled.

There was another door, one that he had never been through, and then he was being guided up a flight of stairs. The stairs turned to his left at a landing, and then continued up to another floor. At the top, another door. A right-hand turn down what seemed like a hallway. Then they stopped. Someone knocked on a wooden door.

'Come in,' said a voice from beyond the door.

Carl's voice.

What is this? Where have they taken me? What are they going to do to me?

His mind buzzed, but he knew better than to speak. To speak would likely only get him a violent response, and it would communicate that he felt fear. And he did not want them to know that he was afraid. It was fine to make them think that he was *compliant*, but if he showed fear . . .

The door opened and they stepped through.

It was warm inside.

They sat him in a chair that had a cushion on it. Not what he was accustomed to.

They left him bound, but they did not duct-tape him to the chair like they'd done in the previous interrogations. Then the hood came off.

He was in a small room. Something like an office. A space heater sat to one side and glowed, spilling warmth onto Abe's legs. He could feel it on his face like sunshine and for a moment he thought it was the most wonderful thing he had ever felt, until that other part of his mind spoke up: *It's all a trick. Don't relax.*

Carl was sitting on the other side of a table.

There was food. Hot food. What looked like Salisbury steak and mashed potatoes.

The two men that had come to get Abe from his cell stood silently behind him. Carl regarded him from across the table, looking impassive as usual. If he had meant to set Abe at ease, he wasn't making any attempt at acting any differently. Abe wasn't sure what that meant or how it made him feel. Confused, mostly.

Carl pointed to the plate of food. 'Eat,' he said.

Abe regarded the food with some suspicion, though his mouth was watering.

Carl observed his hesitation. 'I promise you the food isn't tainted.'

'Or drugged?' Abe said, his voice raw. He coughed.

Carl smiled without humor. He pulled a pill bottle from his pocket, then unscrewed the cap and tapped out four pink oval pills. He leaned across the table and dropped them near the plate of food. 'You seem to be developing a little bit of a respiratory infection, Mr. Darabie. Those are antibiotics. You should take them with food.'

Abe didn't move. Just stared at the food. At the pills. He swallowed.

Carl scratched his beard. 'If I wanted to drug you, I'd strap you to a chair like every other time and I'd inject you. It's a lot quicker and requires no trickery on my part.'

'Why are you doing this?' Abe asked.

Carl clasped his hands together and sighed. 'This is not easy for me, Mr. Darabie. Treating every person that comes to us like a goddamned terrorist. Like traitors. Spies. But unfortunately these are very dangerous times that we're living in. Caution is required if I intend to keep me and my people safe.

I did what I did to you because I wanted to know where you stood. It's harsh, but it's the only way.'

Abe almost laughed. 'So, what? Are we friends now?'

'Hardly.' Carl's face was blank. 'But there is a possibility that we're not enemies. When you talk to me, when you give me the truth – or at least the bits of it that you see fit to give me – then I can begin to give you some truth back. And that is how trust is established.'

'Trust?'

'You claim that you *were* a major. I suspect you still consider yourself one, but also wish to devalue yourself as a captive. That's smart. I get it.' Carl paused for a breath. 'You tell me that you left the acting president, implying that the two of you are no longer allies. I still don't know whether this is true or not, so now I'm left with some considerations of my own.'

Carl rapped the pill bottle on the tabletop, causing it to rattle. 'If you were sent by the acting president, either as a spy, or as an assassin, then I suspect you already know where my allegiance lies. In which case there's no reason for me to keep it secret. However, considering how long it took to get that information from you, I suspect you were leery about whose side I was on. So either you already know what I'm about, or you don't but are on the same side regardless. In either case, there's no point in me keeping it a secret any longer, is there?'

Abe's mind bounced around everything that Carl had just said, trying to find the weak point, trying to spot the lie, trying to see what Carl's endgame was in this. But if this was some new form of manipulation, he couldn't see it just yet. 'You're saying that you're opposed to President Briggs?'

Carl's eyes narrowed. '*Acting* president, I prefer.'

Abe shifted in his seat. His bindings were cutting into his

wrists, but at least they were in the front so he wasn't sitting on them. 'Who are you?'

Carl's face looked briefly angry and he rose from his seat. 'We're what's left of the 82nd Airborne and Special Operations Command after Briggs bled us dry with his little coup.' He walked around the table and for a moment, Abe thought that the man was going to strike him for some reason, but Carl was looking at the two men that were standing behind him. 'When he's finished, take him to a better room.'

Then he looked at Abe. 'I'm sure you won't mind if we get rid of your little sack of saltines. Take your pills and eat your food before it gets cold. I've got some other things that need to be taken care of.'

Tomlin waited, bound and blindfolded and on his knees. The drive had not been as long as he had expected, but it had still been wet and cold and uncomfortable with his captor's knee in his back and a hand smashing his face into the bed of the pickup truck.

They had kept up a quick pace. Tomlin could tell from the way his body threatened to roll and the man keeping him pinned almost lost his balance when they went into a turn. He thought about trying to jump up when the man's balance was off and just throwing himself off the pickup bed, but then he thought that he had no idea where he was or where he was going and for all he knew they could be driving through streets that were crowded with hostile forces. And then the man pinned him again with his knee before Tomlin could give it another thought.

When they stopped, they stopped hard. The crew that had captured him didn't talk much, save for a few mumbled commands that Tomlin couldn't make out. They had clearly done this before, and had enough practice that they were fluid without having to communicate each move. They took him up and hauled him out of the pickup truck. Tomlin stayed limp. There was truly no point in resisting them at this point. He couldn't run, he couldn't fight, and he couldn't see.

You're not here to fight anyway, he told himself. *You're here to try to make an ally. And this is normal. This is exactly how you would do it if some guy came waltzing into your compound.*

Well, maybe not quite like this.

He thought about how Lee had conducted Camp Ryder. Kind of an open-door policy, with a little bit of vetting mixed in. But Lee was a little kinder about it than Tomlin might have been. However, to give Lee his dues, Camp Ryder had grown a lot more rapidly and successfully than his own budding group of survivors, before he had left them down in South Carolina.

And Camp Ryder betrayed him, Tomlin thought grimly.

But that was always the catch. You could do it safe and slow, or you could do it hard and fast. Either way was a risk. And it was clear to Tomlin that whoever was in control of Fort Bragg preferred to play it safe and slow. Or they were just going to rob and murder him like everyone else that wandered into their trap, looking for help. But that remained to be seen.

Once out of the truck, they brought him into some place. He wasn't sure where, but he was sure he was inside, which brought him a momentary burst of relief. It was warm and it was dry. A little warmer than it really should have been, and Tomlin couldn't smell or hear a fire.

Electricity?

They had electricity at Camp Ryder, but it was only enough

to run the radio in the office, and certainly wasn't for such frivolous things as heat. At Johnston Memorial Hospital in Smithfield, they had big diesel generators that could be turned on to power the entire hospital, but Lee had told him that they rarely did it, due to how much fuel it used up. The last time they turned on the generators was when Jacob was there, running his tests on the infected female that he'd captured. And now Jacob was gone, as well as Doc Hamilton, and anybody else that knew what the fuck to do with a hospital.

So in the shocking warmth and dryness, Tomlin was shoved to his knees and there he stayed until he heard a heavy door swing open roughly. For the moment that the door was open, he could hear the rain driving outside.

Wet rubber-soled shoes squeaked as they crossed the floor, halting just in front of Tomlin.

'This is the new guy, huh?'

'Yes, sir.'

'Well, they're poppin' outta the woodwork now, aren't they?' There was a momentary sigh. 'Take off the hood.'

The black hood came off.

Tomlin blinked. A medium-sized man with a balding head and a trimmed beard was looking down at him. At first the man's eyes were bored and cold but then suddenly they sparked and narrowed and the man pulled his head back, as though he was trying to get a different perspective of Tomlin.

'What's your name?' the man asked, warily.

Tomlin found his own eyes narrowing. 'Brian Tomlin.'

Both Tomlin and the man's eyes went wide at the same time, but it was Tomlin who voiced the recognition first: 'Holy shit. What the hell are you doing here?'

TWENTY-EIGHT

STOPGAP

THE BAD NEWS CAME in heavy hammer blows, and it didn't stop until Lee felt almost breathless. Wilson was dead. One of the northern hordes had made it over the Roanoke River and into North Carolina. Eden was lost and Harper had been forced to retreat. Julia was badly injured and needed to be shipped back to Camp Ryder. A second northern horde was leaking out of Eden and it wouldn't be long until they were moving south as well. For all intents and purposes, the plan to keep the hordes out of North Carolina had failed.

For all the bitter pills to swallow, one kept lodging in his throat.

Wilson died. And LaRouche is gone, probably dead. That was the group I was supposed to meet up with. Before everything fell apart and Eddie Ramirez stole my GPS. I should've been there. I could have helped them.

In the office, it was Lee sitting in a chair behind the desk with the radio receiver clutched in white knuckles. Colonel Staley sat in front of the desk. Between them, the desk was laid with the map of North Carolina that Lee had appropriated from the wall. The points where the Roanoke River plan had failed were marked on the map with little black X's. Behind Staley, Brinly hadn't spoken much, but he absorbed

everything in his silence and kept watching Lee, always evalu-
ating, it seemed.

Deuce had found his way back to the office. He looked perturbed when he came through the door, and then even more
so when he looked around the room and saw how many
people were crammed into that small area. Strangers that he
didn't know. He grumbled, his head and tail hanging low, and
slunk around to the desk, hugging the wall. Then he curled
up at Lee's feet, underneath the desk.

Lee leaned over and hung the radio receiver back onto its
cradle. Staley had had the information before Lee, and had
relayed it to him once they were behind closed doors. A quick
hail from Lee's radio setup received the same information
from Harper, and after a few calls, Dorian responded from
Wilson's group and confirmed the bad news on their end as
well. Both elements had attempted to contact Camp Ryder
when things had gone bad, but Lee had been out of Camp
Ryder, and Angela had been avoiding the office. Lee was
pissed about that at first – pissed and feeling a little guilty –
until he realized there was absolutely nothing he could have
done for either group just by hearing the bad news. Wilson's
group was on the run, back toward Camp Ryder, trying to
pick their way south through prickly unknown territory they
believed might have recently been covered by the Followers.
Harper's group was holed up with a squad of Staley's Marines
in a small town several miles southeast of Eden, waiting for
further instructions.

Staley spoke softly, as he was in the habit of doing. The very
opposite of the leather-lunged Marine that people somehow
expected. 'Far be it from me to tell you what to do with your
people, Captain Harden. However, having them in the north
is not doing us any good anymore.' He leaned forward and

pointed to the map. 'I understand that you wanted to use Eden as the pinch point. That was a good plan, I'll admit, but I don't think it's manageable right now. Without the bridge east of Eden being demo'd, the area they can spread through would be too large for us to hold them to.'

Lee felt a small measure of indignation rising up in him. But that was just prideful feelings. Everything Staley said was correct. And at the end of the day, Staley was a colonel, and Lee was just a captain. Lee was not holding himself to military decorum – he would do what he saw fit – but he was smart enough to recognize that Staley had years of experience on him and his advice was likely sound.

Besides, Lee had already come to the same bitter conclusion.

Staley continued, gesturing to the Highway 421 corridor. 'You say this is your supply route that has been cleared, correct? The route to Eden?'

Lee nodded. 'Yeah. It should be clear. Harper's group can probably make the trip within a day, as long as something doesn't slow them down. We haven't been seeing roadblocks much, but there's always the chance of infected.'

'Of course.' Staley considered the map.

Lee rubbed his chin. His beard was getting a bit long. 'I was honest with you about both our strengths and our weaknesses here at Camp Ryder. I know it's uncomfortable for you, but in order for us to come up with a plan, I need to know what you're capable of.'

Staley leaned back. He looked over his shoulder at First Sergeant Brinly. 'I think First Sergeant Brinly would likely have more up-to-date information on that than I do. He is the one in charge of keeping the day-to-day operations out of Camp Lejeune running smoothly.'

Brinly stepped up and leaned a single fist on the desk,

looking down at the map with a slow, thoughtful sigh. He was likely doing the same thing as Staley and Lee: trying to come up with another plan. And for a moment, Lee found it nice to not be completely alone in his impossible deliberations. Misery loved company.

'Our strengths.' Brinly seemed to consider the words. When he spoke, he rounded his consonants and shortened his vowels. Some mixture of rural Midwest with a dash of Chicago. Despite his somewhat stony demeanor, he spoke with plenty of inflection. 'Our strengths are in numbers and equipment. We've got plenty of fighting men, and a whole shitload of civilians that have volunteered and gone through an abbreviated boot camp. I wouldn't call them Marines, but they're more than just cannon fodder. As far as equipment goes, we've got helos. Mostly SuperCobras, but we have a few Chinooks, as well. And some arty. I think we have fourteen M198s, and plenty of trucks to tow them with, and men to drive the trucks.'

Brinly rubbed his face. He kept himself clean-shaven but had a five o'clock shadow now, and his fingers made a raspy, sandpapery sound as he drew them across his cheeks. 'Our weakness is aviation fuel and small arms and ammunition. We've got plenty of ordnance for the helos and arty, but I've got Marines that don't have weapons and not enough ammunition to go around to the ones that do. We can pound shit into dust, but we can't hold territory.'

It was not what Lee wanted to hear. His group was much the same, though on a smaller scale. Without access to his bunkers, Lee was not able to keep the people inside Camp Ryder armed. He had hoped that Camp Lejeune would have been able to throw some small arms and ammunition their way, as well as the help from air support and artillery pieces.

At the same time that he felt himself cringing at the news, he supposed it made sense. Camp Lejeune was a large military base, and the city around it would have had a lot of citizens trying to get inside the gates of the base. The Marines had probably spent a good amount of their resources not only protecting themselves, but, with a larger population to care for, they would have had to invest more small arms and ammunition in scavenging parties.

Plus there were the Followers. *That* was clearly taking up some resources.

What came as an unpleasant surprise to Lee was the issue of aviation fuel. He glanced between Staley and Brinly. 'How much longer do you think you can keep running your birds?'

The first sergeant grimaced. 'We started out with plenty. Unfortunately, with our small arms becoming depleted, we had to figure out other ways of keeping pressure on the Followers.' Here Brinly paused and exchanged a quick look with Staley. If Lee hadn't been paying attention, he might have missed it. But there was something there. Something between the two men that smelled to Lee like an unresolved issue.

With a quick breath, Brinly continued. 'We were consistently mounting ground assaults on the Followers, mostly hitting their raiding parties and supply chains, but about two weeks ago we started to realize that the cost of ammunition for these raids was getting too high to sustain. So keeping pressure on them has now fallen to our air wings. Prior to that, we'd burned through maybe a thousand gallons of fuel. In the last two weeks alone we've gone through almost thirty percent of our reserves. We're running nine birds – seven SuperCobras and two Chinooks – depending on what's down for repairs at the time. We can reliably have one of the

Chinooks available for transport, like today, or four of the attack helicopters on the ready at any one point in time.'

Lee leaned forward and looked at the map. There was really no skirting around the issue. He knew that he didn't like playing word games with people, and he wanted to assume that two military men that had survived the collapse of the nation they were sworn to serve would also have no time for blowing sunshine in each other's asses.

'I think we both know that we're playing a stop-loss game here,' Lee said. 'I'd meant to cut off the threat completely, but obviously that ain't gonna happen now. So we know that the infected have busted through at two points, and maybe some points between that we don't even know about. But I think we both know that what has managed to get across the Roanoke River so far is just the tip of the iceberg. And neither of us is prepared to deal with the whole iceberg.'

Staley smiled humorlessly. 'You make me feel like the *Titanic*.'

Lee shook his head. 'I've no intention of drowning, but we need to plug up the leaks while we're still afloat.' He dragged his finger along the thin blue line that skirted the top of North Carolina. Along it the points where bridges crossed the Roanoke River were circled in red. 'I've still got more than a dozen possible crossing points sitting intact over the river and no way to get to them at this point. It's clear that the teams I sent were too little, too late.'

Staley leaned forward and tapped the map with one, long index finger. 'You want to know if we have the fuel to run demo sorties with our birds and take out the rest of the crossings before more of them get across.'

Lee shrugged. 'It's either that or we go ahead and call it a day. Pack up and head for Middle America and hope that

President Briggs is a forgiving man. And I can personally attest that he is not.' Lee splayed his hands out in front of him. 'It's a foregone conclusion for me, gentlemen. I'm not sure how you feel about the issue, but for me there's only one way out of this shit storm, and I think everyone in this room knows what it is.'

Staley glanced up at Lee, then back down at the map. Lee shifted his gaze to Brinly and found the man's gray eyes settled on him, not communicating much of his thoughts except that he was deep within them.

Staley dragged his fingers off the map. 'This is by no means a commitment on my part. But if we are even capable of carrying out the number of sorties necessary to demo every bridge that crosses the Roanoke, we still have the two hordes that have already broken through. Based on the reports I'm getting from my men, they're quite sizable. Even one of them has the potential to wipe us out or put us on the run.'

Brinly leaned over the map to take a look. 'From everything that we've seen – and, Captain Harden, feel free to correct me if I'm wrong – these larger groups, or hordes, tend to follow lines of drift. The most popular being highways. They go along the path of least resistance. So isn't there a chance they just follow whatever road they're on south and eventually right out of the state? Hell, we just lie low for a few months, they could be gone.'

Lee gave him an uncertain look. '*If* you guys blow those bridges, and *if* it's only those two hordes we have to deal with ... yes. There is a possibility that they will just pass us right by. There's also a possibility that they won't – there's a whole lot of roads that crisscross this country, and there's no telling where they might randomly decide to hang a right or left. Just because they're heading due south now doesn't mean that's what they'll continue to do. As it was put to me when I found out about this whole thing, it seems like they're moving where the food is. In general, they're moving south, but it's only because there's no food left up north. They could just as easily come south, spread out and rip everything bare, and then move on to South Carolina.'

Lee turned to Staley. 'Which brings me to my second point. Call me a hopeless idealist if you want, but I can't just let a half million infected roll by me and wish the next fuckers in line best of luck. That's not how it works for me, and I hope to God that's not how it works for you.' Lee shook his head, finding himself getting angry with no real reason. 'The buck needs to stop with us. We can't just shirk this off on somebody else. We're not talking about *maybe* some people die. We're talking about a fucking massacre.'

He took a breath to chill his indignation. He didn't want to get too fired up and appear like a hothead on the issue. 'If the moral obligation isn't enough for you, I can give you a good practical reason. Have you had any opportunity to observe these ... things?'

'What?' Staley frowned. 'Hordes? Or infected in general?'

'Either, but mainly the hordes is where we've seen it.'

'Seen what?'

'They're people, Colonel. They're not fucking mindless. They think, though it's stunted. And they still have every bit of instinct coursing through them that we do. That's what leads them to group together, to hunt, to feed.'

Brinly seemed to catch on before the words were said. His face twisted up. 'No ...'

Lee explained what they had learned. From the dark, smoky back room of the den in Sanford where they'd first discovered them, to the information that Jacob had recorded in his journal, he spilled it all out and held nothing back. There was no point in keeping any of it a secret. It would only benefit them to understand the gravity of the situation.

Afterward, Lee allowed them their moment of silence as they absorbed the information. He'd needed that moment himself, when he'd found all of this out. When it seemed that they had managed to wrap their brains around it, he raised his brow. 'Do you guys see why this needs to be handled now and not later?'

Staley nodded grimly. 'I understand the need. However, I need to understand your plan for doing it. It's one thing to recognize that you need to exterminate a population numbering in the millions. It's another thing to actually carry it out. And with resources the way they are ...'

'Tell me about your field artillery,' Lee said.

'Hundred-fifty-five millimeter howitzers,' Brinly replied. 'We've got fourteen pieces operational and crewed. I've got three more pieces that are good to go, but I got no crews to serve them.' Brinly took a seat with an exhausted huff. 'But ... problem is, and always has been, the Followers. We've managed to push them away from Camp Lejeune and give ourselves some breathing room. But it's a fucking game of Whac-A-Mole and it seems like they don't intend to leave. We hit one compound, but it just moves and sets up someplace else. And with our infantry running out of ammunition and small arms, it's becoming impossible to hold the ground we take with our attack helicopters. So the Followers have essentially created a moat around us. Pretty much everything between Wilmington and here is their territory. If we try to move fourteen field artillery pieces out of Camp Lejeune without a proper infantry escort, we won't own that artillery very long.'

Staley nodded in agreement. 'Though we've pretty much cleared Wilmington and the smaller surrounding towns, we can't secure them, so the Followers keep small scouting elements posted all around us. We can't send out a scavenging party without the Followers finding out about it. Sometimes they hit us, sometimes they don't. Most of the time we back them off without too many casualties, but at a monumental cost to our ammunition stores.'

Lee looked thoughtful. 'Sounds like a fucking insurgency.'

'Not too different,' Brinly said.

'How'd you manage to punch out to meet us?' Lee asked.

Staley smiled. 'We parked our truck in the back of a Chinook and had them fly us over.'

Lee considered all of this in silence for a moment, looking at the map. 'What's the effective range of the howitzers, First Sergeant?'

'Eighteen kilometers is tops for regular munitions,' Brinly answered. 'We can jack that up to thirty if we use Rocket-Assisted Projectiles. We had some of the newer M777s, but the GPS has been out of whack on them for some reason. Targeting is ... unreliable. So we're using the M198s. But, on the plus side, we have a whole shit-ton of the RAPs.'

'Fuck ...' Lee tapped his fingers on the map. 'Only eighteen kilometers.'

Staley frowned at him. 'If we agree to all of this, and we somehow manage to get you our artillery pieces, how were you thinking about using them? On a moving target like the hordes, spread out over miles, the artillery won't be very effective.'

'No, they won't,' Lee said, his feet now tapping on the ground beneath him, rapid to the rhythm of his thoughts. 'But if we can get them all in one place ...' He stopped long enough to take a glance and see a pair of incredulous looks aimed at him. He held up his hands. 'I know. It sounds ridiculous, but we've done it before. When we had a larger city area to handle that we knew would hold a horde of a couple hundred or so, we would sneak in at night and rig up a bunch of claymores. We found out that they're attracted to the smell of cooking food, so we dumped deer guts into a hot pan. Then we'd go up to the top of a building and we'd wait for them. They'd always come en masse and when we had them in the killbox, we'd blow the claymores and pick off the rest with rifle fire.'

Staley and Brinly both nodded, appreciating the ingenuity, but staying reserved.

'That's feasible for a horde of hundreds,' Brinly said. 'But hundreds of *thousands*? Even millions? There's no way.' He leaned forward in his seat. 'I understand what you're getting at here, Captain. If you had the artillery within range, you could call down a fire mission on them. And maybe that would be effective. But first of all, how are you gonna get them there? And second of all, how are you gonna keep them there? Because I don't think a pan full of burning deer guts is gonna cut it.'

'No.' Lee stood up, thinking out loud more than explaining an already-formed plan of action. 'But we both have seen these hordes. They're like cattle. They can be herded.'

'Cattle don't try to eat you,' Brinly said flatly.

Lee pointed at him. 'You're right. And to herd cattle, you have to push them in the right direction and it takes a lot of manpower over a lot of area. But with these infected hordes ... they'll just give chase. And when one is chasing, the whole group follows. You don't need to prod these guys along. You need a carrot on a stick.'

'*Meat* on a stick,' Brinly mumbled.

'Meat on a truck, actually.' Lee smiled, hesitantly. 'A pickup truck with a couple of guys and a clear path to lead the horde where we want them.'

Staley rubbed his face. 'We've still got the issue of the Followers to deal with, Captain. I've got limited small arms capabilities here. Not enough to keep my base safe, continue scavenging, *and* get a convoy of artillery through hostile territory. And if I rely on the helicopters to clear the way for the arty, then I don't have enough fuel to demo the bridges. It's one or the other.'

Lee's lips compressed. 'The bridges. The bridges need to be blown.'

'Yeah.' Staley nodded, but before he was able to say anything else there was a rapid knock on the door to the office and then it flew open.

Outside the door, the sounds of Camp Ryder were spilling in and it was the sound of hostility brewing. Marie stood in the doorway, her face flushed, her brown kinks of hair hanging in her eyes. She looked at Lee and spoke with urgency. 'We got a bit of a problem.'

TWENTY-NINE

FRICTION

LEE CAME DOWN THE stairwell in a clatter of boots. The noise in the room was escalating quickly. People were spreading away from the center of the room like oil separating from water. Lee paused halfway down the stairs, trying to determine what the hell was happening.

Two men were the center of attention, both of them strangers to Lee. One of the men – the taller man – was holding the shorter man by the lapels of his coat, and nearly lifting him off his feet. The tall man's face was close to the other man's, but the shorter man wasn't paying attention. His eyes were wild with rage and they were fixed on Angela.

Angela, who stood very close with a pistol leveled at him.

About five steps up, Lee had a good vantage point and noticed other things. He noticed the knife on the ground at the feet of the two men. He noticed that not everybody had retreated from the conflict. Some of them were crowding close in again. Some of them looked like they might jump in to start a fight.

'These sons of bitches!' the shorter man spat, his greasy, wet hair flying about madly. 'These murdering sons of bitches!'

Lee realized the taller man wasn't just holding the shorter

man's lapels, but he had yanked one of the man's arms behind his back as well, trying to restrain him. He could take one look at the shorter man and tell that he wanted to cut Angela, and the taller man was holding him back.

'Mac,' Angela said, her voice harsh and loud in the confined space, cutting through the loudness of the crowd. 'You better get your man on the ground before I put him there!'

Angela was so intent on the two men struggling that she hadn't really noticed the fact that it was her and about five Camp Ryder people, surrounded by the entire group of strangers. And the crowd all around them was not watching like a crowd watches. It was stirring, like people that were about to be involved. One side or the other, a collective decision was about to be made, and the dam was very close to breaking.

'You *cunt!*' the man spat.

The taller man reared back and gave the other man a short right hook that took him in the side of his face.

Immediately the crowd jerked, like they'd been slapped into motion. The volume of voices went up sharply, and the tone became undeniably aggressive.

The shorter man hit the ground. He sprawled, reached out, and managed to get his hand on the knife. Mac jumped onto the shorter man's back, growling like an angry dog. Both men rolled and squirmed around in each other's grips. Lee saw the blade of the knife flashing between them.

A few of the bystanders lurched forward.

Lee wasn't sure who they were planning to help. He wasn't going to wait to find out.

He pointed his rifle at the ceiling and let off three quick rounds.

Everyone cried out at once. The rounds were deafening in

the enclosed area and took them all by surprise. The collective note that they issued was high and frightened. Dust and small chunks of concrete from the ceiling dropped and peppered the people underneath. Everyone ducked their head and there was a moment where the crowd was paralyzed. Shocked into submission. Their eyes looked around, then up at Lee. They saw him standing on the stairs with the rifle pointed up. He even had the attention of Mac, and the man with the knife still clutched in his hand.

Lee realized his own hands were trembling with anger, white-knuckled on the grip of his rifle, like it was a neck that needed strangling. He didn't see people or survivors staring back at him. He just saw a bunch of mindless animals. No better than the infected. A horde. Staring up at him with their hollow eyes. Not understanding the calamity that he could bring down on them.

Do they know me? Lee's mind spat flames and burning coals. *Do they know what I'm capable of?*

There was the briefest instant where Lee just thought about opening up. Solving a whole lot of problems. Putting some people in their fucking places. Lee wanted to show them how the world was. It wasn't a world where you could just come into another man's camp, eat his food, and then try to knife his people. It was a world where thieves were executed and traitors were left outside the gates, to be devoured by things that lurked in the woods.

'What the fuck is this?' Lee bellowed. He pointed an accusing finger at the short man, lying on his back. Lee looked right into his eyes as he pointed. 'You. You piece of shit. I should shoot you dead right now.'

'Lee ...' someone said, but Lee wasn't listening.

Lee turned his face to the rest of the strangers gathered and he thought about killing, and dying, and none of it mattered. Sometimes things needed to be done. Sometimes points needed to be made. And the consequences were often cloudy, or insignificant no matter how bad.

'Any one of you put a finger on me or my people and I'll kill you.' Lee started down the stairs, his pace clipped, his footsteps sharp in the silence. His words came out sharper, to the same beat as his boots. 'I swear to God, I'll fucking kill you. I got twenty-eight rounds left in this thing. Are there twenty-eight people here that want to die tonight?'

At the bottom of the stairs, the crowd parted.

Lee walked through them without looking. Any one of them could have leapt forward and taken him out with something as stupid as a homemade knife. But he knew just as much as they did that they weren't going to make a move on him. He could feel it in the room, the shift in the mood. The manic violence of moments ago was no longer the crowd's. It was his.

'Lee!' Angela's voice.

He was locked on to the man on the ground. Mac was climbing off of him, putting a hand out to Lee, trying to ward him off, all of a sudden trying to protect the man that had only a moment ago been intent on putting a knife into Angela. And that ... that ...

'Listen ...' Mac said, palms out.

Lee kicked the knife out of the grip of the man on the ground, then put the rifle in Mac's face. 'Shut up. Don't say another goddamn word.'

Lee registered the front doors of the building flying open. In the back of his mind, he figured that the guards and the Marines standing watch in the rain had probably heard the gunshots and come running to investigate. There was a brief exchange of shouts – the Marines checking on Staley, and Staley telling them to stand down – and then silence again.

Lee looked down at the man on the ground, the muzzle of his M4 tracing over the man's face and chest. He thought about pulling the trigger. That was what he wanted to do with the man, though he knew he should do it outside. The man needed to die. He needed to die because ... because ...

Because there was no other solution. What else did you do with people like him?

What else do you do? Lee suddenly wanted to scream. *WHAT THE FUCK AM I SUPPOSED TO DO?*

You couldn't just let people do this kind of thing to you. You couldn't leave this type of thing unanswered. It wasn't the goddamn civilized life anymore. There weren't police to help anyone handle an idiot with a knife. It was up to him. It all came down to him ...

He felt a hand on his shoulder.

'Lee,' Angela's voice said. It was calm, but there was very little warmth to it, and that alone was enough to make his head turn. He looked at her. Her blue eyes could be cold sometimes, like ice under water. They were that way now. Her lips set hard. Her face no longer kind. 'If I wanted him dead, I would've shot him myself.'

Lee matched her tone and expression. 'He had a knife. He was getting ready to cut you.' As though that was all the explanation necessary. And perhaps it was.

Angela's hand on his shoulder was squeezing him now. She leaned into him and her words were very quiet in his ear, so that Lee wasn't sure if anyone else heard her. 'We should think long and hard about something like this before we do it.'

There's nothing to think about.

But he kept silent.

Her grip on his shoulder eased and her voice softened. 'I know,' she said. 'I know.'

For a second, his stomach flip-flopped. He thought about Kyle and Arnie and the others that he'd shot dead on the road out of Camp Ryder. The men that he had ... murdered? Yes, murdered. There wasn't another word for it. Perhaps ... executed. Did she know about them? Was that what she was talking about?

I did it for the camp. I did it because I had to. Because the bad guys always come back to bite me in the ass, and I'll be damned if I'm letting it happen again. Like this motherfucker ... this motherfucker needs to die before he causes more problems down the road. Surely she understands ...

But when Lee looked back into her eyes, he saw some of the kindness had returned to them and he knew without truly knowing that she'd only been speaking in generalities. She had only been telling him that she understood where he was coming from. Understood his anger.

Angela turned away from Lee. She ignored the man on the ground and directed herself at the man she'd called Mac. 'Who the hell is this guy and what is his problem?'

Mac looked around quickly. 'He didn't hurt anybody. I stopped him. That was what you said. You said if any of your people got hurt. And no one got hurt.'

Angela holstered her own pistol to show that violence was off the table.

Lee was thinking, *Speak for yourself.* But she reached a hand out to his rifle and lowered it so the muzzle was pointed at the floor, rather than the short man cowering on it.

'Look ... ' she began.

But the woman named Georgia stepped up and stood over the man on the ground, stooping down to help him to his feet but keeping her suspicious eyes locked on Angela and Lee. 'Your group hurt ours, Ms. Angela.'

The expression of congeniality melted from Angela's face. 'What are you talking about?'

Mac looked rapidly back and forth between Georgia and Angela, gauging his loyalties against his desire for a place to rest in relative safety. If Lee were to take a guess, he thought that the group of strangers was likely split in half. There would be some who would probably do anything to make peace and stay safe. And there would be others who would never be able to function here without resentment.

'Maybe we should talk about this privately,' Mac suggested, but his voice was small.

Georgia's face twisted into anger. 'Fuck privacy. Everyone in this room knows the truth. Ain't no point in hiding it.'

Lee had some choice words to say, but he bit his tongue. He had the presence of mind to know that he should stay silent. Nothing peaceful was going to come out of his mouth. His thoughts were muddled with violence, and compromise was barely comprehensible.

Angela fielded it calmly. 'Georgia, no one here except for your own people knows what you're talking about. To my knowledge, all that any of my people have done is take you out of the rain and give you half of what's left in our food stores, and trusted you to treat this place with respect. I don't think one little scuffle is the end of the world, but if there are bigger problems going on, then I'd like to hear them.'

Her characterization of a man trying to gut her as a 'little scuffle' seemed to deflate Georgia. The tension ebbed. And for a moment, Georgia – and quite a few others, Lee noticed – glanced at the ground in something that might have been shame.

Do beggars and thieves have shame?

Lee's jaw clenched. *You need to take a deep breath and settle yourself, buddy. No one in this room needs you pissed-off right now. Cooler heads prevail. The moment for anger is gone. Let it go.*

He deliberately breathed in through his nose and let it out slow. He had never considered himself an angry person, nor ever had trouble controlling his temper. But there were deeper things at work. He knew himself enough to recognize that. Things were forming inside him like mineral deposits and they were sharp and jagged and drew blood. For a moment there, he'd felt as out of control as he'd felt when he had been on the roof of that building in some small town west of here, surrounded by infected, with Shumate and his men across the street, waiting to kill him.

In some ways he hated it. In others, he loved it.

He hated it because it was not who he was, or who he had been – *You cannot be who you were* – and it reminded him of how much had changed, and how much he was being forced to change with the world. He hated it because for his whole life he had disliked the men that *reacted* and respected the men that thought things through.

And he loved it because there was no thought of consequences. Things were much simpler from that viewpoint. Things were easier to accept, to deal with. Violence begot violence. Might made right. The ends justified the means. The Machiavellian methods that made sense to the baser instincts of his mind felt satisfied.

But, love or hate, the moment had passed, and the wisdom to see that trumped all.

'We met one of your people on the road,' Georgia said suddenly. 'Harper. Julia. I don't remember the rest of their names. Except for the guy ...' Her face sneered. 'Mike was his name, and he was a murdering bastard. Killed one of our men in cold blood. Claimed our man was trying to steal from them. But your guy just got scared. I saw the whole thing happen. Then Harper threatened to shoot us all because we wanted Mike to pay for what he did.'

At the mention of Harper's name, Angela immediately turned to Lee. She knew some of what had happened, but not all. Lee had not kept it from her intentionally. But he'd given her a brief summary of what Harper had told him, and only glossed over the fact that they'd had a run-in with another group of survivors, never going into any details about what had gone down.

But Lee knew the details.

And he knew the aftermath of that night.

Lee stared at Georgia for a while, at the angry man that she'd gathered off the floor that stood behind her now, like a kid might stand behind his mother's legs. Finally, she realized that Angela was diverting the question to Lee and she made eye contact with him. She must not have liked what she saw in his eyes, because she only attempted to hold his gaze for a second or two before breaking and looking away.

'Mike,' Lee said, distantly. 'Yeah. Mike Reagan. And his wife. Torri Reagan. I heard about what happened.'

'Oh, you did?' Georgia said with some contempt. 'What was your man Harper's version?'

Lee took another breath. *In and out.* 'He said that he heard a gunshot. Went running over. Saw your man on the ground, bleeding out. Saw Mike standing over him with a rifle. He said he didn't know what had happened. He said that Mike claimed that your guy pulled a gun on him, but then later admitted that he'd shot without justification because he was scared. Just like you claim.'

The crowd around them murmured. It was a sound of displeasure.

'I bet you want Mike dead, don't you?' Lee said slowly. 'Blood for blood, right? That's the way the world works now. Georgia? Mac? You want Mike dead?'

Mac and Georgia exchanged an uncertain glance.

'My man's life for your man's life. And what about Mike's wife?' Lee asked. 'What about Torri? You want her dead, too?'

'No . . .' Georgia said quietly.

'Nonsense,' Lee said. 'Both of them. Mike's life to pay you back, and Torri's as interest for your troubles. Blood for blood. That's how it works. That's the currency of lives when we swap and trade them like fucking canned goods, isn't it? The old two-for-one deal?'

Silence.

Lee raised his voice to a demand: 'Would that satisfy you?'

Georgia's face pinched down. Angry at being called out. 'Yes. Both of them dead.'

'Well, it's fucking done,' Lee said, and then spat on the ground. 'You got your wish. Mike was so fucked in the head because of what he did that he told everyone he couldn't live in this world anymore, and he said he couldn't *let his wife* live in this world, either. So he shot her dead and then swallowed his own goddamn rifle. How's that for justice? Does that satisfy your fucking needs?'

The silence continued. No one had the nerve to speak.

Lee's stomach was roiling and he wanted to tell these people that they made him sick, but in truth, it wasn't them that made him sick. It was the fact that they were just alike. The anger of the man with the knife and the woman named Georgia had been the same anger that he'd felt when he'd seen Angela about to be hurt. The same anger that made him think of executing the man right there on the floor, made Georgia want Mike's life.

Lee's rifle sagged, then slid out of his left hand, so it was just dangling at his side, held loosely by his right. He was suddenly very aware of himself, and after the anger went away there was always the feeling of exhaustion. Not physical, necessarily, but mental. Sick to his soul, as well as his stomach.

This is the way of things now. If you want to be angry at anyone, be angry at yourself.

Or better yet, be angry at no one and recognize the necessity of things.

What were they now but tribes? Stone Age tribes. And tribes feuded, and they fought, and it was blood for blood. If a son of one tribe killed the son of another, it was either war or, if they sought to maintain peace, the murdering son's life was forfeit. That was the way of things long ago, and its time had come again. Due process and trials by jury were kind concepts to ease the sensibilities of a populace that was basically gentle and harmless as sheep.

But there weren't too many sheep left in the world now. Most of them had been killed during the collapse. What was left was mostly wolves and coyotes, Lee thought. And packs of domestic dogs turned feral again.

Lee felt the energy draining out of him, and what replaced it was the tingling sensation behind his eyes that heralded a bad headache coming. He shook his head at Georgia and Mac both. 'I think both our groups have lost enough. Don't you?'

He turned away before they could answer.

THIRTY

GATHERING

THEY WENT UNDISTURBED ALL DAY. In the little warehouse behind a small storefront in a cluster of businesses, they had waited. Sergeant Kensey had sent Marines to the front of the shop to keep watch out the windows for sign of the infected. They took two-hour shifts while the others slept. None of them had raised an alarm. It seemed that the pursuing horde had either lost interest or passed them in another direction.

Harper stood over where Julia lay as she clenched her eyes shut and tears came out of the corners to stream down her temples and wet her hair. She was half in, half out, her brain still groggy with medication but with enough pain coming through that she could feel Kensey's fingers as he spread open the ragged wound where her leg bones had split her skin, and began to irrigate it with a syringe.

'Does it smell?' Julia croaked.

'No, I think you're gonna be okay,' Kensey replied. He'd been brusque with Harper and clearly wasn't on the same page as them, but Harper appreciated the kindness he'd shown to Julia, and the care he'd given her.

Through the single door to the warehouse from the shop front, Harper could see that the day was failing, the light dimming, and along with it, the rain. The gales that he could hear hitting the metal roof above them had stopped about an hour ago and given way to a long, steady drizzle, and now it seemed to only be spitting. Soon it would clear up and move on, he guessed.

Inside the warehouse, they had turned on two battery-powered lanterns, but they seemed to be losing some of their juice, and Harper had only enough spare batteries to replace one of them. He'd scrounged around the interior of the warehouse but not come up with anything useful besides an old Sara Lee Zebra Cake, still in its package. He saved it for a special occasion. Maybe when they got back to Camp Ryder.

The Marines cracked some chem-lights and tossed them on the ground. There were four of them total, framing the area where the group had laid their gear and bedrolls. As the one lantern faded, Harper stooped to replace the batteries on the other, leaving them momentarily with nothing but the ghostly green light of the chem-lights.

Kensey paused in his work as he waited for the light to return. It was chilly in the warehouse, but he wiped his brow on his sleeve as though he were sweating. He seemed calm, though. Always calm, Harper had to give him that.

Harper tossed the dead batteries and heard them clatter into a dark corner. He slapped the fresh ones in and turned the light back on. It was much brighter this time, and would last for several nights. He set it back down near Julia's broken leg and Kensey returned to his work.

When he was finished irrigating the open wound, he bandaged it again, then looked at the splint they'd constructed for the broken leg. It was shoddy, but it worked, and Kensey said that it felt like he'd set the bone pretty good. Just the fact that he'd said that he'd *felt* it had made Harper a little queasy. But her leg looked normal, at least, rather than the odd angle it had taken when they'd dragged her out from under the water tower where her stubborn ass had gone.

The thought of it still pissed Harper off. But how mad could you be at someone who broke their own leg trying to prove a point? A little mad, it seemed. But not much. And not enough to bring it up to her. Maybe she realized she should have listened to him, or maybe she still felt she was in the right. Now wasn't the time to get on her case, though. Harper was well aware how bullheaded she could be and knew that the conversation should wait until she was a little more whole.

Julia seemed to realize that Kensey's operations were finished. She opened her eyes and blew out a long-held breath. 'You done?'

'Yeah, I'm done.' Kensey reached into his bag and rummaged through a few items. 'How's your leg feeling?'

'Horrible.'

Kensey smiled wanly and pulled out a syringe from his bag. 'You want some more?'

She stared at him for a moment, and then at the syringe. She bit her lip and Harper could tell that she wanted it, and the pure *hunger* for the relief from pain that the morphine would bring inspired both fear and pity in Harper.

'There's no shame in it,' Kensey said with a slight shake of his head. 'I've seen big, tough men wail like little bitches when their bones are broken. You're handling yourself well. It's my gift to you for being an easy patient.'

She nodded and he stuck her.

A few moments later she was passing dreamily into La-La Land. Not enough to knock her out, though she looked like she might fall asleep soon, but she definitely wasn't *with them*. Her brain was elsewhere, and for a moment Harper envied her, because she sighed a sound that was something like contentedness and the barest smile touched her lips. It was honest and true and something he had not seen, or worn, in months.

Kensey watched her for a minute, then took her pulse, timing it on his wristwatch. Satisfied, he left her alone and packed his bag of tricks. 'I've been informed that we'll be accompanying you back to Camp Ryder,' he said without looking up.

Harper regarded him with a pinched expression. 'Informed by who?'

'Colonel Staley.'

The fucking colonel, Harper thought. *The author of my woes.* 'You know, if it wasn't for that motherfucker dragging his goddamned feet, we wouldn't be in this position.' Harper kept his voice low as Julia's eyes closed sleepily. 'We'd have the fucking bridges blown to bits and all those infected that chased us into this hole would be on the other side of the river.'

Kensey zipped his pack up and stood. 'Yeah, you're probably right.' He looked at Harper. 'If it wasn't for us, you would have gone in there, guns blazing, and taken that shit over, right? I mean, we really held y'all back. Shit. You woulda just nuked the damn place it if hadn't been for us. You'd'a done it with all those helicopters . . .' He looked elaborately confused. 'Wait a second. Those are *our* helicopters.'

Harper wanted to knock the man's teeth out, and might have tried if the words hadn't hit their mark. As bitter as they were, they were the truth. If it had just been Harper and his group up in Eden, they would have found the same damn situation – infected continuing to come across the bridge, and no real way to keep them from doing it because they didn't have the manpower. Shit, they didn't have the manpower to hold them off long enough to place the charges and blow the bridges. Essentially, they would have sat there, doing exactly what they did, but they would have done it alone.

'That's fair,' Harper said begrudgingly. Then he pointed a finger at Kensey. 'But you need to admit we were right. Your colonel waited too long because he wasn't sure about us. And I get it. I do. Believe it or not. But that doesn't change the fact that *we were right*. He should've helped us blow the bridges and then the original plan would still be intact. Now we're running with our tail between our legs.' Harper threw his hands up and growled with exasperation. 'Shitfire, maybe it's nobody's fault, but that don't stop it from being hard to swallow.'

Kensey's sarcastic and argumentative expression softened and he nodded. 'Nobody wants to retreat. But sometimes you have to. Sometimes even *Marines* have to, even though we claim that we don't know the word.' He shook his head. 'Colonel Staley made decisions because he has thousands of people looking to him to keep them alive. I'm sure you can respect that. It might not have been the right decision, but hindsight is always twenty-twenty.'

Harper clenched his jaw and swallowed any other biting words he might have. He waited for kinder ones to crop up in his mind. 'You really have a great amount of respect for this Colonel Staley.'

Kensey nodded. 'I do. He's given everything he had for the Marines and their families at Camp Lejeune, not to mention the thousand or so civilians we've taken in from the surrounding cities. I mean, the man lost his daughter, for chrissake. But he's still out there, trying to make the best decisions. I haven't agreed with every single one that he's made, but I hold my tongue, because for the most part the things he does are with good reason. At the end of the day, none of us knows how this shit is gonna turn out.' Kensey looked angry for a second. 'Our entire future has just been completely blacked out. And now we're just all placing our bets on how shit's gonna turn out. And when the dust settles, some of us will be traitors, and some of us will be murderers, and some of us will be heroes, and it's pretty much just a flip of the coin which one you're gonna land with. But you make your bets and you deal with the consequences of your choices.'

Harper had nothing to say to that. Kensey was communicating something to him, but he wasn't sure what it was. Maybe he was just venting. Kensey didn't seem like the type of man that needed to vent very often, but maybe Harper had caught him at a bad time.

A bad time? Harper almost laughed at himself. *That's pretty fucking hilarious. Bad time. What a comedian I am. It's all bad times, isn't it?*

Harper chewed his lip for a moment. 'With y'all with us, we should be able to hit the trip in, oh, maybe four or five.'

Kensey nodded. 'You told me you have the path back to Camp Ryder clear, right?'

'Right. We did it on the way up.'

'So, no traffic snags or roadblocks?'

'Not since we came through about a week ago.'

Kensey looked down at Julia, slipping quietly into sleep. 'We'll wait until morning comes. Then we'll hit the road.'

It was in another small town where the Followers stopped and regrouped. It had been a rural town that had tried to upstart itself with a new-built business center full of columns and banks and sandstone walls, and maybe they would have made it had things not gone south for the entire country.

Figuratively and literally, LaRouche thought.

That had been burning in his mind again lately – to tell or not to tell about the hordes coming south. But here and now he had little to gain by holding back, and his life and the lives of many others to keep by speaking up. The prospect of telling was becoming increasingly attractive.

The town had been selected by Deacon Chalmers based upon what sounded to LaRouche like a previously agreed-upon rally point. He also made veiled comments concerning having scouted out the safety of the town. And true to the reports that Chalmers had cited, LaRouche had not seen a single infected in the area. Nor bandits. Nor civilians. It seemed to be one of those areas that had been abandoned by everyone and for no real reason that LaRouche could see.

While LaRouche had driven, Chalmers had been staring at a map, and directing LaRouche where to go and on what streets to turn. During the longer stretches of road, when directions were not necessary, Chalmers remained pensive and kept saying, 'We knew this was going to happen. We knew it from the beginning.'

Eventually they had come to the town and parked there amid the newly constructed buildings. A few had been occupied before the collapse – a restaurant, a hardware store, a salon. But the majority were vacant, still with signs in the windows that advertised them for lease.

The small convoy that had gathered with them on the side of the road hours earlier pulled in behind them. Men began to get out, some of them looking confused. All of them murmuring among themselves. Chalmers put them to work, directing them where to go. Onto rooftops and into abandoned businesses. The larger vehicles blocked the roadways in and out of the town center. The way the buildings were organized created a sort of wall around them, so that when the roads were sealed, there was the disarming illusion that they were secure.

LaRouche paced about the confines of the business park, gripping his rifle and never taking his eyes off the skyline or the trees, when he could see them past the buildings. That was where they would come from, if they came for them at all. They would come in and rocket the shit out of them with helicopters, or they would send in a strike team through the woods.

Or maybe they'd do both.

Why am I doing this? he kept asking himself.

Because I have to do something.

Because I'm completely fucking lost.

It was like his forebrain, which thought about consequences and morals and how to differentiate between right and wrong, had simply shut down when he'd killed Father Jim, and ever since then the choices had been invisible to him.

Eventually he worked some of the nervous energy out of himself. And then the lack of sleep from the previous night began to toll on him. He found a shop windowsill to sit on. His muscles and bones ached when he sat. He leaned on the M14 rifle he'd found, and he closed his eyes against the world. His ulcer was churning, insisting that it not be forgotten.

He never slept, though. Just dabbled at the edges of it.

As the day crept on, people continued to murmur about what they were doing there, and Chalmers continued to remain aloof. LaRouche saw him atop a roof several times, pacing and praying, and often looking out toward the east. LaRouche watched him and wondered when he was going to send up the call that the Marines were coming down on them again and they would have to run.

Around midday, the sound of engines reached LaRouche and his fatigue was snuffed out in a wave of adrenaline. He snatched his rifle up and ran for the easternmost barricade of vehicles with two other men. Chalmers was atop the roof and LaRouche saw him out of the corner of his eye as the man raised his hands far above his head, a look of relief on his face.

That gave LaRouche pause and he stopped running, though he still had his rifle shouldered, his body still gearing itself into battle. The other two men that had made for the barricade continued on, but LaRouche stayed there in the middle of the street, looking up at the man who had become his . . . what?

Master.

No . . .

Chalmers looked down at him and shouted out. 'Open that barricade, LaRouche.'

The barricade was opened and vehicles began to pour in, filling up the town center with exhaust and noise. Chalmers remained atop his roof, but when he caught LaRouche's eye again, he summoned him with a wave of his hand. LaRouche looked up at him and felt the urge to disobey, but then he started moving. He made his way around the vehicles and the men that were pouring out of them, shouting and yelling when they recognized others that they knew. Slapping hands. Grinning like apes.

LaRouche made it inside the building and found his way up to the top of the roof where Chalmers was standing, over-looking the scene below. From a bird's-eye view, LaRouche could make out the segregation of squads and units, though none were dressed alike. They simply bunched together in groups of ten or fifteen, and one of them would appear to have control. They were packing the vehicles in tight to make room for more. The interior of the town center was big, but it seemed that they would need every bit of the room if the Followers continued to trickle in.

'What is this?' LaRouche asked.

Behind them, the door to the roof opened and closed again. LaRouche turned and saw that Clyde had joined them. LaRouche greeted the other man with a nod and received the same greeting back, though Clyde eyed him suspiciously. LaRouche couldn't help but wonder what that was about.

'Ah, Clyde.' Chalmers smiled wearily. 'I'm glad you're here. I'm glad we all made it out.'

Clyde shoved his hands in the pockets of his coat. 'From everything I'm hearing down below, it sounds like LaRouche called it. The last few stragglers that left the camp said they heard helicopters incoming and explosions shortly after they left.'

'How many have we lost?' Chalmers asked, his tone guarded.

Clyde shook his head. 'Too early to tell. Once we get everybody here and all the squad commanders do head counts, we'll have a better idea. I know most of our squad commanders are reporting some men missing right now, but we don't know if they're going to show up soon or not.'

'Will they know where to find us?' LaRouche looked down again at the people below. 'And where did all these people come from? These aren't all from our camp.'

'No.' Clyde took up answering the question for Chalmers. 'Some of the men will know to come here, and others will not. This location is not known to everyone. It's our ... backup plan.'

LaRouche looked between the two men with the question in his eyes.

Chalmers had his hands on his hips, his face compressed into that unsteady anger of his. Something that might simmer or might explode at a moment's notice. 'Our means of communication are old, LaRouche. We don't have radios like the Marines. Most communication comes and goes by couriers on motorcycle, or it comes with supply convoys. Or we have a prearranged plan.' He spread his hands out to encompass the town center. 'This is one of those prearranged plans.'

Chalmers spoke sourly. 'For the past month we've had good containment on Camp Lejeune, with assault teams at the ready to press the Marines anytime they tried to leave their gates. Our very own Pastor Wiscoe was overseeing this himself. This was to keep them contained. We knew that we couldn't necessarily overpower them, but we hoped that we could keep them from pressing us west.'

'But they *have* been pressing you west,' LaRouche said, not meaning to make it sound like an accusation, but that's how it came out anyway.

Chalmers looked at him sharply. 'Yes. After a fashion. But we've kept the damage contained by making their forays costly to them. And we've been gaining strength while they've been hiding, trying to figure out whether to let their birds fly or not. We didn't really know the strength of their airpower – still don't. They've been holding it back, I anticipate because they have limited fuel to put them into the air.'

Chalmers looked out at the barricades, his face fallen to hard lines and bitterness. 'I knew this day was going to come. I knew it from the start. Pastor Wiscoe . . . ' Chalmers looked pained. 'He's a good man, but he's lost the faith. He's been losing his faith for months now. Each time we're struck down by the remnant military, he loses a bit more faith.'

Chalmers folded his arms across his chest and faced

LaRouche. 'I just received word the other day that Wiscoe is giving up his containment of Camp Lejeune. He believes we should head west. For the mountains. Where the presence of a military force is not as prevalent, and where we can regroup and restrengthen ourselves. But these are the thoughts of a man whose only faith lies in practicalities. I'm a practical man as well, but I also have faith. I believe these challenges only build our faith. And I believe that the time has come to prove it. The time has come for a small force to take a large one, like Gideon took the Canaanites. So all the men under my command, most of the eastern front, we're going to gather our forces. And we're going to strike back, rather than run.'

Some little part of his national pride was pricked down deep inside him, but he kept his face impassive. He shouldn't even care anyway. The vestiges of the US Army had abandoned him in Smithfield with a group of sick and injured. Their last-ditch effort in the form of a man called Lee Harden and a plan called Project Hometown had not gone well, and LaRouche was not even sure if Lee was still alive. What government there was left seemed determined to leave everyone east of the Appalachian Mountains to be wiped out by the massive hordes coming out of the northeastern cities. On all counts, the US government had failed him.

But Chalmers didn't know these things.

LaRouche felt the acid rising in his stomach. The sting of it in his throat.

He turned suddenly to Chalmers. 'We need to talk. Inside.'

THIRTY-ONE

WHOLE TRUTHS

THE INTERIOR OF THE building that Chalmers had chosen as their temporary headquarters was empty. It was one of those spaces that had never been leased or rented and still sat there with anonymous white paint on the walls and bare, tile floors. There was nothing to it but a wide-open space where you could have put anything – cubicles, tables for a restaurant, a small warehouse – and then a few doors in the back that led to restrooms and a small office.

LaRouche imagined that it had once smelled of new dry-wall and plaster and industrial paint. That fresh smell of progress that went along with newly minted houses and businesses. But now it smelled dingy, heavy with the stink of men.

There were only six men, including LaRouche and Clyde. Chalmers was there with three of his men, who seemed more like bodyguards than high-ranking members, because they had not said a word the entire time and they stood to either side of the room and glared at LaRouche. LaRouche found himself staring back at them, wondering what their expressions would be if he got a knife in their throat . . .

Chalmers, however, stared at nothingness.

A protracted, internal conversation that was carried out in silence.

Clyde stood beside and slightly behind LaRouche. There, but not there.

LaRouche waited for his verdict. He did not feel nervous, though he probably should have. Several days had passed since they'd taken him, and he was sure that Chalmers had expected him to come clean about something like this long before now. Chalmers had put trust in him. If he did not like the scent of what LaRouche was telling him, it would be Chalmers that put a bullet into LaRouche's head.

Or maybe he would have Clyde do it.

LaRouche felt an odd peace about the whole thing. Perhaps *peace* was too gentle a word. But whatever you called it, LaRouche was not concerned. His life had been forfeit when he'd knelt before Chalmers, and Chalmers had given it back to him. Some might call LaRouche a traitor to Camp Ryder, a murderer, or an evil man. But LaRouche was a man of violence. He was capable of violence, and he showed a skill for it. Over the course of the last week he'd been settling into that realization like you put on an old pair of boots.

In the grand scheme of things, how else was he useful but as an instrument to inflict violence? The cause didn't seem to matter. One was just as bad as the next. If it wasn't the United States government trying to cling to power through people like Lee Harden, then it was people like the Followers, determined to raise a new thing from the ashes.

In the end, it was all dirty. No matter what the crime, no matter the brutality, it was the winning team that got to tell the story, and such inconvenient facts like massacres and rapes were typically left out. But the men that brought a cause from inception to fruition remained the same across the globe, from cause to cause, and throughout history. They were all men of violence. And in the end they would all be damned for the things that they had done, whether the winner hung medals on their chest, or the world scoffed at them and held them on trial for war crimes. It was all the same in the end.

Live by the sword and die by the sword.

That's what Father Jim would have told me.

LaRouche was just another one of these violent men. And his particular skills were of no more use to Camp Ryder. So they went to the next person in line that would take him. And that was the Followers. They had taken him in. They had given him a place to sleep. A safe place, and now that he was in their good graces, they had fed him, and given him responsibilities.

Like the responsibility to make sure that people die.

But that is what I do. That is what I'm good at. I have no other skill.

Chalmers stood up, his intentions unknown to LaRouche. He looked at LaRouche with a bit of suspicion, perhaps some hesitation. A man choosing his words carefully. He took a single step and was standing in front of LaRouche, and he reached out a hand and placed it on LaRouche's shoulder. His touch was iron. He had a lean musculature that was tacked on his frame, stiff and tense. And yet he still managed to look and talk like a relaxed man.

'LaRouche,' he said, in a voice like a grandfather speaking to his grandson. 'Why are you here?'

LaRouche looked at Clyde, then back to Chalmers. But Clyde would not make eye contact, and Chalmers was waiting for LaRouche's answer, and his other hand was hanging close to the big nickel-plated revolver that hung on his side. LaRouche simply had to say one wrong thing and Chalmers would hollow out his head.

'Honestly?' LaRouche asked.

Chalmers smiled a ghostly smile. 'God is always our witness. And a righteous man is honest, even to his own undoing.'

'I have nowhere else to go.'

'Nor do the rest of us.' Chalmers nodded, his face becoming serious again. 'I believe you, LaRouche. And I believe that you mean the best for us, because you understand the situation that we are in, like many others do not.' Chalmers tilted his head down, looking at LaRouche from under graying eyebrows. 'You understand that we are facing long odds. You understand the difficulty of the task that has been set before us. But do you know why?'

LaRouche did not respond. He wasn't sure whether it was a rhetorical question or not.

Chalmers pointed a finger at him. 'Because if everything came easy to us, there would be no faith. There would be no need for God. That's what happened to this country in the first place, LaRouche. God blessed us so much that our lives were so easy and we forgot that he was there. That's what people do. They never remember God until their lives are difficult again. And that is why God has visited this plague upon us, and that is why he has called upon his faithful followers to rebuild this great nation, and not in the secular, twisted mindset of modern morals and ethics, but to rebuild it as *one nation under God*, the way it was meant to be from the start.

'You know Gideon was sent against the hordes of Canaan with a great army, but by the time it came down to fighting, God had made Gideon give away most of his force. First, he made Gideon tell his men that if they didn't have the stomach to fight, they could go home, and more than half the army left. Then God made Gideon's army drink from a brook and all the men that lapped the water up like dogs were sent home, and only the ones that stood and brought the water to their lips with their hands were allowed to remain. And from Gideon's army of thousands and thousands, there remained only three hundred, and these lonely three hundred were the men that took Canaan. And God made it this way so that Gideon would have faith. So that he would have to *believe* in God.'

Chalmers wagged a finger in the air, smiling. 'Do you think that's what God has done here? Do you think that there are many comparisons between this time and that?'

LaRouche bowed his head. 'I think the odds are stacked.'

Chalmers shook his head. 'You are here because this is the only place for you, just like so many others. But God has brought you here for a reason, LaRouche. Just like he brought Clyde. Just like he brought me. And I think that your reason for being here has yet to be revealed. I think you're holding back just a little bit more.' Chalmers spread his arms. 'Tell us, LaRouche. We are the Lord's Army, and we are your only friends left in the world. What is it that you aren't telling us?'

LaRouche opened his mouth, but hesitated. What was he feeling at that moment? He wasn't sure himself. He should have felt shame. He should have felt like a traitor. But he didn't. He was just a slave. And these were his masters. His new masters. That was what he did. He obeyed.

Chalmers spoke the first words for him: 'Camp Ryder, yes? The Camp Ryder Hub, as they call it?'

LaRouche looked at his boots, but he couldn't find the shame there, either. He picked up his gaze and gave it directly to Chalmers. 'Yes. Camp Ryder. I think ... I think that in order for us to survive this, we need to hit some richer targets. Guns and ammunition. Some medical supplies. Food and water as well. And the Camp Ryder Hub is where these things are. If not Camp Ryder itself, then some outlying areas that they've given arms and ordnance to, as well as food and medicine. They're still hurting, but they're better off than most of the rest of the state, and faith or no faith, I think it would behoove us to get our hands on a lot more hardware before we return to the Marines.'

Chalmers regarded LaRouche with a very serious expression. It was obvious that he did not like the sound of LaRouche clearly not seeing him as Gideon conquering the Canaanites; however, the thought of a set of rich targets could not be completely dismissed offhand. Even Chalmers knew that.

If he had any serious reservations about what LaRouche had stated, he kept them to himself. It could have been that he'd considered this very thing himself. Whatever his stance on it was, he remained silent and he walked back to his seat. Then he sat, leaned back, and crossed one leg over the other.

When he was seated, Chalmers motioned at LaRouche with a sweep of his hand.

'Tell me about the targets,' he said.

THIRTY-TWO

THE WATCH

BRETT STOOD ON TOP of the Camp Ryder building, cold and angry. Cold because the day was wet and soggy, and as night crept in and stole darkness over the camp, it brought a harsh chill with it and Brett could have sworn it was dipping into the teens, or at least was going to before the night was over.

Angry in part because of the cold and how he was stuck up on the roof, where the wind howled and no warmth was to be found. But also angry over what had happened earlier. He had no right to be angry, he figured. He was not a card-carrying member of the Camp Ryder club. Hell, he had barely been around them for more than a week. But he knew some bullshit when he saw it, and the outsiders taking to their weapons like that over some slight committed out beyond the wire . . . that was unconscionable in his book.

The world had become a shitty place. Sure, everybody knew that. Brett knew that, right along with them. Not that he had a dismal outlook on things, though. On the contrary – he was a very positive guy. But there comes a point when you have to realize that things are not going to go the way that you think they should. And you have to be able to work around that. He was very disappointed in the man they called

Mac, and whoever the fuck his dumbass compatriot was that pulled the knife. They should know that things out beyond the wire are unstable and volatile. If one of their people tried to take anything – hell, even if he just *looked* like he was trying to take something – then Brett thought it was perfectly justified that he be gunned down where he stood. There was no room for error out there. No room for civility. They were lucky enough that the superior force from Camp Ryder had let them go without ripping them to shreds in the roadway. They certainly shouldn't be complaining about one shitbag friend that they'd lost.

Of course, there were other concerns that abounded.

Camp Ryder had been a sort of legend in the minds of people out east. Folks traveling through that had come into contact with Camp Ryder, or had passed through the Hub in one capacity or another, brought with them stories of how wonderful life was in the Hub. Of course, Brett was not a rube and he had not bought all of this hook, line, and sinker. He had chalked some of it up to hyperbole – and rightly so. Camp Ryder was not a haven of stability in the region, they didn't have electricity, they weren't in contact with a new federal government, nor were they receiving foreign aid, or any of the other bullshit stories that Brett had heard.

Instead, he had found Camp Ryder much as he had expected to find it. Troubled and unstable, but doing better than most.

What he'd seen earlier in the night ... shook him. All along, through all the stories that he'd heard, and even through meeting Captain Harden, the man had seemed very calm. So calm, in fact, that Brett sometimes wondered if he was capable of doing the hard, nasty things that needed to be done.

But seeing him come off those steps and call the stupid fucks out for trying to pull a knife on Angela? That had been an interesting thing to see. Not a completely positive experience, mind you, because it was shocking to see someone that had previously been so even-keel erupt into such anger. But in the same breath that Brett took in shock, he breathed out, hoping that Captain Harden would have pulled the trigger on that fucker lying on the ground.

In the end, Captain Harden had refrained, either based on his own choices or from the urging of Angela. In either case, Brett was half disappointed and half relieved. Disappointed because he thought the man that had pulled the knife had deserved it. Relieved because all hell would have broken loose inside that building if Captain Harden had pulled the trigger.

He supposed they had made the wisest choice.

Which led him to this point now. Because of the tension and the double occupancy, the guard shifts had been doubled, and so it had fallen to Brett to fill in where it was needed. Two of his compatriots patrolled the wall. Another stood by the front gate. And he stood atop the building, keeping a bird's-eye view of things. The worst duty, and the most important, rolled into one.

He'd been a smoker, when you could still get cigarettes, and he wanted nothing more than to have that cheerful little cherry dancing in front of his lips while heat filled his lungs and made him feel a little better about life. But he could not have that. So he stood atop his watchtower, hunched down into his jacket, his rifle slung onto his back. And he paced. And he sat on the cold cement abutments of the roof. And he paced some more. It was difficult to see when the sun first went down, but as the evening deepened and his night vision sharpened, he could see past the fence and the ramshackle fortifications that had been erected. He could see into the woods, where the leafless trees swayed in the cold, cold winds.

You could see small animals back there, trotting the fence line. Deer, of course – there were tons of them, though he suspected their numbers would begin to dwindle again as everyone was forced to hunt them for food. But during the four or five times he had pulled roof duty, he'd also seen a fox, and a coyote, and one time something that might have been a large feral cat, or perhaps a bobcat.

He scanned the woods for these creatures, wondering if they were out and about that night. Wondering if they had any concept of what was going on with the dumbass humans all around them, and if they could think, whether they would truly give a shit or not.

Probably not.

Hey, we noticed that a bunch of y'all have gone crazy and are trying to kill and eat each other. That's pretty fucked-up. Well ... good luck with that!

Brett turned toward Shantytown and looked down at it. He was entering the last hour of his watch, and by now, almost everyone in the camp was asleep in their shacks, the campfires dwindling, but smoke still rose off them in four ghostly pillars, evenly spaced through the camp. The camp was quiet. Somewhere in the back section, someone coughed.

The situation with the newcomers had mostly been squashed. There were still some grumblings, but they were camped inside the building below him, with another guard posted at the top of the stairs, keeping an eye on things. Whatever they resented about a single man dying, they were able to put it aside to stay warm for a night.

A lot of the Camp Ryder folk had started sleeping inside

the building during cold nights, though they still kept their shanty outside. Those folks had given up their spaces on the floor to make room for the newcomers to sleep there. Brett hoped that the act of kindness shamed them.

He turned back to the woods.

Something big slipped between trees – there one second and gone the next.

Brett drew a sharp breath and stood frozen for a moment, his eyes wide, while his heart kick-started into overdrive. His first thought was *animal*, but he knew that wasn't right. It had been too big. Maybe it was a large deer or a small black bear. There were bears around here, though they were pretty few and far between. But he didn't think that was it, either.

Bandits.

He crouched down low, so that whoever was out there could not sight him through a rifle scope. He crept up closer to the abutment of the roof so he could peek over with his own scoped rifle and maybe get a better idea of what was out there. He thought about sounding the alarm ... but what if it turned out to be just an animal?

It's not an animal.

But then he thought, *If it is, everyone is going to think you're a fucking coward.*

'Just wait,' he breathed to himself. 'Verify the threat before you go hollering out like a goob.'

But his hard-beating chest was telling him differently.

He scooted up to the edge of the wall and hunched over his legs. They were cold, pressed against the roof. He shouldered his rifle and got his cheek weld about where it should be and then slowly rose himself up so that he could see over the ledge and into the woods where the shape had disappeared into the trees.

He pictured some wild-eyed bandit with a long gun taking a lucky potshot from two hundred yards away, offhanded, and clipping the top of his skull off. *Like a cigar cutter.* Not quite enough to kill him instantly, but enough to make him flop around for a few moments, his jangled brain sending mix-and-match messages to his body. He'd seen it happen.

Through the scope, the image of the woods was stark, but it wavered with his own unsteady hands. He thought he saw something else again, but when he tried to focus on it and still his hands to get a better image, it was gone. If it had ever been there in the first place.

Something rattled the fence, far off to his left.

He whipped the rifle in that direction and his thought was panicked, but true: *Deer never rattle the fence! Deer never rattle the fence!*

He focused on the fence out to his left – there were serious fortifications there, in the form of tall spikes and loops over loops of barbed wire and razor wire. But when he was able to hold the rifle still enough to see through the scope, he saw the big, pale shape on the other side, and the iron fingers stuck through the chain link, and the wide, insane eyes that were staring at him.

Then the thing thrust itself off the fence and hurtled back into the woods, but at an angle almost parallel with the fence. Brett cranked off a single round from his rifle, more out of reaction than anything else, and when he had found his voice through his own fumbling fear, he shouted at the top of his lungs.

'Hunters! Hunters on the fence!'

Lee had lain down for a while, but not slept. In the abandoned office, he waited in the dark for the pain to go away, but though he felt exhausted, his body kept twitching to keep him awake and his eyes did not want to close. Besides that, the pain wouldn't let him rest. He endured it for perhaps two hours before it slowly began to abate. By then most of the murmur of voices from inside the Camp Ryder building had died away.

He rose around ten o'clock to stare at the map that was still laid out across the metal desk. He did this by the light of a single lantern. It was cold enough in the room to see his breath in the glow. He looked at the map intensely for a while, and then began to feel the weariness in his bones. The Marines had bunked in their trucks, including Colonel Staley. All the strangers were inside the Camp Ryder building, under guard. Occasionally Lee could hear the thump of the roof guard's footsteps. Other than that, it was dreamily quiet.

Lee went to his chair and sat down. He was staring at the map, but no new revelations were really coming to him, nor was he trying to hash them out of his scrambled brain. The same strategies he had told Staley were playing over and over, and mixed in was an occasional sense of irritation and gloom that went with feeling his body fail. It made him feel weak, and he was not a man accustomed to that feeling.

Eventually his eyes did close, though his legs and arms kept twitching just as he began to doze, so he never fully slept. He just kind of meandered around in the shallows of sleep, never quite committing to the plunge. He woke up to the sound of Deuce growling from underneath the desk. He thought for a moment that Deuce was dreaming, but when he opened his eyes, he saw Deuce, wide awake and alert.

Then the rifle shot.

Lee was out of his chair, his head spinning with loss of blood pressure, his eyes darkling. His face felt flushed with sudden adrenaline, and the first thing he thought of was the man that had tried to kill Angela earlier, and whether he had just been successful.

He was sprinting around the desk for the rifle that lay next to his bedroll when he heard the cry.

'Hunters! Hunters on the fence!'

Better or worse than he had imagined?

Worse, he thought. But at least Angela was not dead.

She's not dead, is she?

Then Lee thought of the thirty-some-odd people that would come stirring awake in the Camp Ryder building. And he pictured a mass panic and people trying to run out the doors, when in fact they were sleeping in not only the warmest and most sheltered place that Camp Ryder had to offer, but the safest.

He grabbed his rifle off the floor, feeling his ankle and his side yelp out in unison. He swore and then hobbled to the door with two hitching strides and threw it open. Down on the ground floor, he could see people rising, and their voices were beginning to grow, two whispering, then four demanding, then ten of them yelling.

'Hey!' Lee bellowed as he raced down the steps. 'No one moves from inside this building! This is the safest place! We need to get everyone else inside of here, so everyone start scooting your shit against the back wall! Move!'

He didn't wait to see if they complied. The guard they had posted on the stairs – a younger guy from Old Man Hughes's group – took up the call without hesitation, pointing to the back wall and hollering at everyone inside the building to back it up and make some room.

From outside, three more gunshots.

At the bottom of the stairs, Lee shot down the hall, the

stiffness either working itself out of his ankle and side, or becoming lost in the adrenaline dump. He pushed through the double doors of the Camp Ryder building and surged out into night air that was harsh and stinging in its chill. It smelled like ice and snow.

More gunshots, this time a smattering of them coming from the far side of the camp, where the empty shipping containers were stacked. Lights were winking on – both flashlights and lanterns – and they were emerging from all the hovels of Shantytown.

'Back side!' someone shouted. 'They're moving toward the back side!'

That was a relative term, but Lee knew it was generally used to describe the section of camp out past Shantytown, where all the empty shipping containers were stacked. It was also the one section of fence that they had not been able to build up against the hunters with pikes and concertina wire.

People were already pouring from their shanties, heading for the Camp Ryder building, but Lee cupped his hand around his mouth and yelled anyways. 'Everyone inside! Now! Get everyone inside the building!' Then he stood off to the side, holding one of the double doors open with a foot while he held his rifle tight to his chest and scanned what he could see of the perimeter.

He didn't have that good a view.

The first few people reached the doors to the building and started filing in. Their faces looked haggard and worried. They were right to be worried. The last time the hunters had hit them they'd carried away four people. That was what they did. They jumped the fence and they raided the camp, and Lee still remembered thinking, *foxes in a henhouse*.

Lee grabbed the first man with a gun and posted him at the

door to keep it open for the others. Then he pushed out of the recessed doorway to give himself a better view of the camp. The guard at the gate was still holding his position, though his feet were prancing, unsurely. He looked at Lee as though seeking his permission.

Lee waved him on. 'Get the fuck in here, man!'

The guard sprinted for them, leaving the gate unattended.

The gate was solid, though. It was topped with tangled loops of barbed wire, which seemed to be the best defense against the hunters. They seemed to have learned from previous experiences and they avoided the tangles of barbed wire now, though they could scale a fence, or even the walls of a building, in the blink of an eye.

Lee stepped to the side, letting the guard pass him and get into the building. Lee tried to see through all the fortifications. The fence was more like a wall now with all the shit they'd strapped to it, but it was mostly effective. The only downside was the visibility.

Still, he didn't see anything by the gate.

Deuce had made his way down from the office and stood at the doors to the building, barking loudly, nonstop.

The Marine truck was parked to the right of the gate, and its doors were open, the Marines standing around it defensively, their rifles shouldered and sighting in all around them. Colonel Staley stood by the back passenger-side door, scowling.

'Colonel!' Lee called out. 'Bring your men in the building!'

Staley broke free of his men's containment and stalked to Lee with a rifle in hand. 'What's going on?'

'Infected.'

'They won't come over the fence,' Staley said, as though it were fact.

Lee shook his head. 'These ones will. I need your men on the roof. I need a fire team up there now to cover the people running for the building. Can you do that?'

'Absolutely.' Staley turned to his small group of Marines. 'Y'all heard him. Let's get on the roof. We gotta earn our keep tonight.'

The Marines shouldered rifles and two of them ripped open the back of the MATV and started pulling boxes of ammunition out. Heavy-laden, the Marines took off for the Camp Ryder building, the ammo cans and gear rattling as their boots pounded gravel.

Lee heard his name shouted. He turned back toward Shantytown. Angela was jogging up, Sam beside her, dragging Abby along with him. He felt a sense of relief seeing them, knowing that they would be inside, where it was safe. Or safe*er*. Abby still hesitated to loosen up around him, but they were the closest thing to family that he had. Thoughts of their safety were something that plagued him against his will.

'You guys okay?' he demanded as they got closer. 'Did you see anything?'

Angela shook her head, pushing Sam for the building. 'Take Abby inside and wait for me there.'

Sam nodded quickly and pulled Abby toward the building. He stopped long enough to put a knee gently against Deuce's side and push the barking dog back. 'Come on, Deuce!' he called. 'We know! We hear you! Let's go inside!' After a few more barks, Deuce began to concede.

Angela drew her pistol in one hand and held it down by her side. She looked at Lee. 'Have you seen Jenny? Has she come in?'

Lee shook his head. 'I have no idea. I didn't notice.'

'She seemed out of sorts.'

Lee had his eyes back on Shantytown. The last of the tiny exodus was filtering out now, the rear taken up by the two guards that had been on perimeter duty. They were pointing behind them at the back side of the fence.

'Captain! There's at least three of them!' one of the guards shouted. 'I saw them in the woods, moving that way!'

'Fine,' Lee said. 'Get inside and get upstairs. You know the drill.'

They nodded and ran.

Lee turned his attention back to Angela. 'Jenny . . . what's the problem?'

Angela seemed irritated. 'I think she's sick. I think she caught that pneumonia thing.'

'Okay.' Lee nodded rapidly, realizing what Angela was getting at. 'You think she didn't make it out of her tent?'

'We should check.'

'I'll check, you go inside.'

'No, I'll come with you.'

'Fine.' Lee didn't argue. He took off for Shantytown at a run, his feet crunching in the gravel and Angela keeping pace beside him.

THIRTY-THREE

WEAK POINTS

SAM PULLED ABBY OUT of the way just before the front steps of the Camp Ryder building. The door was clogged with people trying to mill in, and those that were inside were not making room as quickly as they should have been. Sam watched it with a growing sense of fear. He wanted to be inside with the others. He wanted to be inside, but he wasn't going to get caught up in the smash of bodies.

You'll make it inside. It's okay. You have time.

The Marines were shoving through the bodies now, urgency carrying them. They started with 'S'cuse me, s'cuse me,' which quickly became 'Move! Everyone get outta the fuckin' way!'

Inside the Camp Ryder building was a roar of voices, like nearing a waterfall. Sam could hear it through the open doors. It sounded like panic. Inside the building was the safest place, but when people were all jammed in together like that, they tended to start acting strange. Sam had seen it before. He'd seen it during the collapse, and when he and his father were trying to make it to a FEMA camp.

That's what this felt like. That's why his gut was in knots. Running, helpless sheep. Cattle being circled by wolves.

Sam looked out into the darkness of Camp Ryder.

Flashlights were playing across the tops and fronts of the shanties. Faces were illuminated in stark, fearful paleness. Small bands of people running for the Camp Ryder building, the rear being taken up by a few of the guards that had been on perimeter duty. And beyond them, Lee and Angela, running the other way, running *back into* Shantytown.

'What are they doing?' Sam said aloud, his voice clenched and tight.

'What?' Abby's own words were shaky and uncertain. 'What's going on?'

'Nothing,' he responded. Telling Abby that her mother was running back into danger was only going to set the little girl off worse. She was on the edge as it was. 'It's nothing to worry about.'

Sam took her by the shoulders and was about to turn her back for the door, to try to push into the mess of bodies milling to get through the front doors, but something flashed in the periphery of his vision and made him stop. He wasn't sure why he stopped, wasn't sure what about that particular thing in the corner of his eye had caught his attention like that. Perhaps something in his subconscious.

He turned and looked, eyes wide, brow furrowed.

Another face staring back at him.

The face was familiar, but for some reason, in the darkness, in the hectic battling of people to get into the door, it took Sam a moment to place that face. He couldn't see the freckles in the darkness, but the annoying buck teeth stood out, the white bone seeming almost to glow.

Caleb.

Standing there with his mouth open. Staring at the doors to the Camp Ryder building, but not moving toward them. He was standing there at the very first row of shanties, at the very corner that was closest to the fence. Maybe a hundred feet from the Camp Ryder building.

What the hell is he doing? Sam thought, immediately full of anger, though he couldn't quite put his finger on why. Caleb stood there, his arms hanging limply at his sides, his hands kind of fluttering in the air, his feet prancing.

But he wasn't coming.

'Let's go!' Sam heard Old Man Hughes bellow from inside the Camp Ryder building. 'Make room! Let everyone inside! Get as close as you can to the back wall!'

Sam glanced behind him. The backlog at the doors was smaller now, maybe just a dozen people shuffling their way inside. They would be in and the doors would be locked and barred in less than a minute.

'Come on, Sam!' Abby urged him.

Sam held steady and turned back to Caleb, who still stood there in the shadows. 'Caleb!' Sam waved him on. 'Come on! What are you waiting for? Come on!'

But rather than come running, Caleb seemed to snap out of whatever trance the overload of fear hormones had put him into, and he turned abruptly and ran back into Shantytown.

Sam had taken two steps to run after him before realizing that Abby was still attached, and screaming her head off for Sam to go inside with her. He spun around and grabbed the girl by the shoulders. 'Abby, I need to help someone get inside ...'

This is stupid, he was thinking, even as his mouth spilled other words.

'Go inside and find Marie ...'

Don't go out there by yourself, Sam, don't do it, you're being stupid, and you don't even like that kid, you don't even like him, who cares what happens to him?

'Tell Marie that I had to help Caleb get inside, okay? Can you do that?'

Abby's eyes were wide and gushing tears. 'What? No! Don't go out there! It's dangerous! You have to get inside! You have to come inside with me so we can be safe!'

Sam extracted his arm from her and pushed her for the doors. Now that he was in the shadow of the building, the light splashing out from the open doors was an inviting square of illumination on the gravel, but he was no longer in it. 'Abby! Do what I tell you to do!'

Sobbing, she turned and ran in the headlong manner of terrified children, as though her feet could hardly keep up with her and she might topple forward in mid-stride.

Sam turned and ran for Shantytown, thinking, *I don't even like Caleb. I don't even like him. But he'd scream. He would scream if they got a hold of him, and I would hear it from inside. And I don't think I could hear that. I don't think I would ever sleep after that. I need to get him inside before the hunters get him and make him scream …*

They made it halfway into Shantytown before Lee realized he had no idea where Jenny's shack was. He forced himself to hold back a few paces and let Angela take the lead. She moved ahead of him without question or comment. He ran after her, following her down a row of blue tarpaulin hovels. They were close to the fence, and Lee kept looking up at it, trying to see if something was climbing over. But it was empty, and the woods beyond were still.

Angela pushed her way into the shanty, Lee directly behind her. The interior was small and cluttered. There was a series of large blankets spread out on the floor, on a layer of cardboard. This was a makeshift bed. Curled in the corner of this thing was a lump of blankets. Steam came from the top in billows, along with the sound of rattling breath.

'Shit.' Angela moved to the lump of blankets. 'Jenny?'

The blankets stirred. Jenny looked at them, but her eyes seemed glazed and feverish. 'Angela . . .' Jenny's voice was a croak. 'I feel horrible. I can't . . . can't even walk.'

Angela bent down over where Jenny was lying and pulled the blankets away. In the dimness, Lee could see crusted and frozen vomit on the blankets and on the side of Jenny's face. 'Oh my God.' Angela's nose wrinkled. She touched the other woman's forehead. 'You're burning up.'

Jenny's eyes flickered open and closed. Her head lolled. 'I need some help . . .'

'I know, hon.' Angela waved Lee forward. 'Help me with her.'

Lee stooped, not relishing the idea of taking his hands off his rifle. But he told himself the Marines were on the roof. They would cover their run. They were professionals. He could trust them. So he slung his rifle onto his back and slipped his fingers under Jenny's armpits.

'Ready?' he said, his voice breathy.

'Uh-huh,' Angela replied and then lifted.

Jenny grunted and moaned as they pulled her up off the ground. 'Where you guys takin' me? Where we goin'? You takin' me home?'

'Yes, Jenny,' Angela said as they struggled to get her through the cluttered shanty and to the door. 'We're taking you home.'

Lee moved backward through the door, stopping to poke his head out of the flap. Jenny's shanty was close to the fence and the woods beyond. He could not see the hunters, but he could hear them, the snuffling, shuffling, growling sounds of them working through the woods, rattling the fences, looking for the weak points that they could exploit.

Sweat, cold and clammy, on his neck and chest.

Please, Marines, have my back . . .

He headed through the door. The tarp brushed past him, like weak hands trying to grasp him, desperate ghosts begging for his attention. He ground his teeth together, baring them, feeling the cold, bracing air hit them, drying them, and making them ache.

'I'm so sorry,' Jenny was mumbling. 'I'm so sorry about this.'

Something hit the fences hard, perhaps a few rows of shanties away. The sound of metal rattling and creaking and tearing loose. Then Lee heard it, right along with the sound of the defenses being mounted and torn away – the sound of feet hitting the ground. Multiple sets. Hitting, and then running.

Somewhere in Shantytown, a hunter screeched.

Jenny twisted violently in their arms, eyes going wide and fearful almost to the point of panic. 'Are there infected? Where are they?' She tried to look around and almost ripped herself out of their grip.

Angela struggled and then clamped down on Jenny's arm. 'Chill out, Jenny,' Angela said sternly. 'We got you. We're getting you inside the building. It'll be warm and safe.'

'Don't . . . don't let 'em get me,' Jenny said.

Lee was hauling backward, his leg muscles burning and his ankle screaming. He was moving so fast that he was pulling Angela along as he moved, the pain a peripheral reality to the concept of being carried away and fed on while his heart was still beating in his chest. He kept glancing behind him to see how close the Camp Ryder building was. He kept thinking they'd gained more ground than they had, but when he looked, it seemed that they were no closer.

Go, go, go! Gotta go! Gotta get inside!

He was breathing hard. He looked back around. Angela was straining to keep the pace and still hold on to Jenny, who was still writhing in their grip, falling into some sort of delirium. Her fever must have been cooking her brains. She seemed more out of sorts than anyone else Lee had seen come down with the pneumonia bug.

'Almost there,' Lee said breathily, though his own heart was sinking, thinking, *Are we gonna make it?*

The sound of bare feet slapping across the hard-packed dirt and gravel of Shantytown. A throaty roar. A shadow among the shadows, just over Angela's shoulder.

'Fuck . . .' Lee tried not to drop Jenny, but her head hit the ground anyway and she mewled out a pathetic sound of pain.

'What are you doing?' Angela demanded, though she barely had the breath in her lungs to speak.

'Grab an arm!' Lee barked, then whipped his rifle around and tucked the buttstock under his armpit, holding the rifle in tight as he stooped to grab Jenny's other arm. Now Jenny was strung between Lee and Angela as they lifted her and started moving again, her heels dragging across the gravel, bouncing along loosely, uselessly.

Lee was facing forward now, running for the Camp Ryder building.

They were within fifty yards.

'They're behind us,' Jenny croaked. 'Behind us!'

Lee twisted as he ran, a clumsy version of the 'karaoke' drill he'd learned in high school football. A dark shape loomed toward them, close on them. Lee pulled the trigger, firing his weapon single-handedly from the hip.

He had no idea where the rounds went, but a louder sound than the report of his 5.56 mm cartridges boomed over Camp

Ryder and the thing that was so close on their heels suddenly face-planted in a tumble of arms and legs, spraying black blood across the gravel.

Lee turned forward again, pushing, pulling, trying to get to the building. They were so close. He looked up and could see the shape of one of the Marines on the roof, shouldering a large rifle. When he looked back down, three Marines were pouring out of the doors to the Camp Ryder building, running for them with their rifles up.

'They're behind us!' Lee shouted hoarsely. 'Behind us!'

The Marines bolted past them, already firing as they formed a thin line directly behind Lee and Angela and Jenny, giving them cover for their retreat. Between the gunfire Lee could hear his breath rushing in his throat, harsh and cold and raw, and he could hear the crunch of gravel underneath his feet, and he could hear them inside Camp Ryder now, more than before, their barking and roaring filling up the blackness. But every time Lee turned there was nothing to see but shadows, jilting at odd angles from the muzzle flashes of the Marines' rifles. Streaks of pale, bare skin that moved through Shantytown with incredible quickness and agility.

The Marines were backing up as they laid down suppressive fire.

The night around them screeched at them like one giant, angered beast.

It moved, and crawled.

Lee was about to turn around, when a shape leapt out of the darkness between two shanties, slamming one of the Marines to the ground. In a single second, Lee saw it. What had once been a man, now a creature with flailing dreadlocked hair and a mangy beard clinging to his impossibly wide mouth. Long, iron-corded arms wrapped the Marine up as the two of them hit the ground, the greedy, gaping jaws clamping over the Marine's face, stifling his scream before it could even come out. The hunter ripped its head back and forth, snapping the Marine's neck.

The two other Marines pivoted with their rifles, shouting out for their downed comrade. Lee was still sidestepping, his rifle pointing in the direction, still deciding whether or not to pull the trigger – the Marine's neck was broken, but did that justify firing indiscriminately into the tangle of limbs?

And then the hunter did something that Lee had not seen them do.

It bounded away into the darkness, leaving the crumpled body of the Marine there on the ground, bloody, twisted, and twitching.

Lee turned and ran for the doors.

The hunters weren't just killing for food. They were eliminating threats.

It was on the second row of Shantytown that Sam heard the gunshots and stopped dead in his tracks, his left side pasted up against the tarpaulin wall of some construction, feeling the cold of it come through the shoulders of his jacket.

Out beyond his little circle of reality, the sounds of screaming and screeching battled, echoing back and forth inside Camp Ryder, ringing around his head like a ricochet. He felt the terror in him, heavy and black and immovable. Like rusted hinges, it made his limbs difficult to move.

They're here. They're here, right inside of Camp Ryder.

What are you doing, Sam? Just go back inside the building . . .

Somewhere close to him he heard the sound of whimpering.

Dammit . . . he's somewhere close. Just get him and go. Grab him and take him back, it's just that simple. You have to do it.

You have to do it so that you don't have to hear him scream when the hunters get him ...

But they'll get you.

They'll get you, Sam, and then you'll both be screaming.

He leaned around the corner of the shanty that he hid behind. He could see all the way down the row and into the Square. He saw a flash of bodies in the darkness, the shape of them lit by one side from the light that was pouring out of the open doors of the Camp Ryder building. The rest of the figures lay in shadows. He saw rifles, spitting yellow and white, and the figures didn't stop running. There was something chasing them.

Sam leaned back into cover, trying to catch his breath. The air around him seemed like it was short on oxygen. He kept sucking it in, but it didn't seem to be doing him much good. He felt his knuckles aching because of how hard he was gripping the little rifle.

Twenty-two caliber.

Not big enough to stop a hunter.

You're screwed. You're so screwed.

You can't find that guy that you don't even like, and if you ran for the building now, the hunters would see you, and they would chase you down and tackle you before you got there. You'd be exposed out in the open.

You're so screwed.

You tried to be a hero, and now you're screwed.

Sam closed his eyes, but that lasted only for a fraction of a second. The complete darkness terrified him. He wanted to shut out the horror around him, but he didn't want to be blind to it. He didn't want to let it hurt him. He had to keep moving.

'Keep moving,' he said, his voice a thready whisper.

It seemed like good advice. Like something Captain Harden would say.

Almost laboriously, he turned back in the direction he had been heading. Back in the direction of the whimpering noises. Back in the direction that he had last seen Caleb. He moved slowly, his feet feeling heavy and burdensome. His shoulder slid along the tarpaulin wall, a steady, quiet *zzzzzz* sound.

Gunshots to his left.

The sound of heavy, animal breathing.

Footsteps speeding through the woods on the other side of the fence, so very close to where he was.

A voice in the darkness, thin and childish: 'Go away. Please, go away.'

Sam peeled himself off the tarpaulin wall as he came to the beginning of the next row of shanties. He stood there at the corner and listened, but for a long moment, all he could hear was the sound of fighting. People were shouting back and forth, and all around them, the infected hunters were growling and screeching.

Don't let them get me, please, God, don't let them get me.

A brief lull in the sound of gunshots and screaming, and this time Sam heard it, very close: 'Go away, go away, go away. Make them go away.'

'Caleb!' Sam hissed through the darkness.

He thought the sound of the other boy's voice was coming from the next row of shanties. Sam was staring straight across at it, a simple wooden construct with some plastic siding to keep water out of the cracks. The door was made of canvas, but it was pulled aside and slightly inward, as though someone had run haphazardly through.

Someone like Caleb, trying to hide.

But now the voice was silent.

'Caleb!' Sam said, just slightly louder.

Somewhere very close, an infected barked.

Sam ducked down, almost flat to the ground.

He felt cold dirt on his hands and knees. The rifle in his grip, reassuring and not, all at once. It was something, but it was so small, and the dangers were so big. The creatures in the blackness were strong and powerful and he knew all in an instant that he was woefully undermatched. He had made a mistake. He had made a Big Fucking Mistake.

Frozen to the ground for a time. Like frost was making him stick to it. And then finally he forced one hand in front of the other, his knees shuffling across the ground. Jib and jabs of sharp gravel rock stabbed him in the palms of his hands, but he could not convince himself to stand on his own two feet. He wanted to be low. He wanted to be invisible.

He made his way to the shanty that was sitting half open in front of him, and he slipped inside.

It smelled of foul breath and dirty socks.

He could hear his own breath huffing in the air.

Something moved just outside.

The air caught in his lungs. He listened, staring at the blackness inside the shanty, waiting for his eyes to perceive something in the sludgy darkness. There were cracks in the wall of the shanty, and dim light shone through, the source of which Sam had no idea. Perhaps the lights of the Camp Ryder building, or perhaps ambient starlight, perhaps neither. But he could see those glowing cracks blotted out as something moved stealthily on the other side. Just a shadow laid against the wall. And the sound of breathing.

Nasally. Heavy.

Sniffing the air.

Don't smell me. Don't smell me.

Sam lay frozen on the ground, his heart beating out of his chest.

The shadows kept creeping across the siding, the cracks, all the way to the corner, where the door was situated.

Sam wanted to move away from the door. His feet were there, just inches from it, and the door was only cloth, hung to provide privacy. The thing on the other side was there. Sam couldn't see it, but he knew that it was there, listening, sniffing for prey, sniffing for *him*. Waiting for him to move, to make just the slightest sound, and then it would burst through the flimsy curtains and rip him to shreds with its teeth and its claws.

He felt the urge to pee. His bladder spasmed.

He wasn't sure why he gave a shit, except that maybe the infected would smell his urine. So he gritted his teeth and tried to hold it in. Felt a little bit dribble out. Just barely wetting his underwear. He didn't want to block out the world, but that's what he had to do. He had to close his eyes and hunker down inside himself, like he'd done before. Go to that place inside him where nothing could get him. That was the only place left for him now.

He wasn't sure how long he lay there in silence. The world outside that shanty was chaos, but it was lost on him. People were still yelling, the infected were still growling and barking and screeching in the background of it all, but he refused to hear them. After a time, he regained control of himself.

He fidgeted slightly, felt the slight wetness in his underwear getting cold.

He opened his eyes.

Still dark, but now he could make out some forms and shapes inside the shanty. Shapes that made his heart beat fast until he was able to interpret them and figure out what they were. The shape near the door that loomed over him was only a jacket, hanging from a peg. Some boxes in the corner, though he didn't know what they contained. A tiny table with some unlit candles on it.

He realized that he had been holding his breath, the air burning stale and hot in his lungs. He let it out with a sudden huff and sucked in cold, parched air.

'Who's there?'

The small voice hit him with all the force of a bullhorn.

Sam shot into an upright position on his knees, his rifle held level at his hip, sweeping the darkness back and forth. He searched for the source of the voice, even as his mind told him through his fears, *It's Caleb, it's just Caleb. Calm down. You have to be calm. You have to be the one in control.*

'Caleb?' his voice was shaky.

'Sam?' the voice responded.

'Yes!' he whispered back.

In the corner of his vision, the darkness moved.

Pale, white eyes, staring at him through the gloom. So close that Sam could feel and smell his breath. 'Did they see you come in here? Oh my God, Sam, why the hell did you come over here?'

Sam was taken aback. He forced his voice down to a whisper, though he wanted to scream. 'I came over here to get you back into the Camp Ryder building, you dumb shit! What the heck are you doing running off into Shantytown like that?'

Caleb – or the white, glistening eyes that were all Sam could see of him – just stared back blankly. 'Everyone was jammed up in the door. Don't you remember what happened last time? Don't you remember? They were ... they were carrying people off, still screaming, still alive ...'

Sam reached out with his left hand and groped for Caleb. He found the other boy's arm and gripped it tight, intentionally hard, and he shook it back and forth. 'Shut up! Just shut up!' Sam breathed harshly. 'Everyone's inside the building now. It'll be fine . . .'

Somewhere outside, there was the sound of metal on metal, hard, distant. Final. Like a cell door slamming home.

Caleb's face turned in the direction of the Camp Ryder building. 'That was the doors,' he moaned. 'They just closed and locked the doors!'

Abby tried to swim through a violent sea of people. She felt like her heart wasn't beating anymore. Like the blood was dying in her veins. She kept trying to breathe but it was only ragged sobs, like someone had knocked the wind out of her. She pressed through legs and hips, and the people looked down at her as she moved, and perhaps they looked at her with pity, but none of them tried to help her. She was in a state of panic, and so were they; everyone was just cramming themselves into the Camp Ryder building, trying to get as far away from those open doors as possible, as far away from the bad things outside as they could get. But Abby wasn't trying to get away, as terrified as she was, and that was not what was putting her into a panic. She was trying to find Marie. She had to find Marie, in all these people, these strangers, this crush of bodies; she had to find Marie, that friendly face, and she had to tell her that Sam had run off into Shantytown. Oh my God, Sam had run off into Shantytown and if they didn't help him get back then he was going to get eaten by the infected, and then he wouldn't be here anymore, he would be gone like all those other people that Abby had once known. Sam couldn't be gone like all of those people, he just couldn't. He was *Sam*.

He was the big brother she had always wanted. He was supposed to be there to take care of her. To make sure that she was safe. What would she do if he was gone?

She couldn't breathe. Could barely keep moving her feet.

She stopped in the middle of the building and let the panic out of her chest and it came out in a scream, and it burned her like fire, but afterward, she was able to take a deep breath to cool her lungs.

She had been loud, but so was everyone else in the Camp Ryder building. Only the ten or twelve people that immediately surrounded her looked down at her, their faces surprised, concerned, even a little irritated.

'Honey,' said a woman that Abby didn't recognize. 'Are you okay?'

Abby's chest hitched, she blinked tears out of her eyes, and then she pushed the woman out of the way and delved into the crowd again, this time yelling as she did. 'Marie! Marie! Muh-REEEEEE!!'

She made it another ten struggling steps before hands shot out of the tangle of bodies and seized her by the shoulders in mid-scream, twisting her around, and then she was face-to-face with Marie, her dark brown, almost black curls framing her slightly astringent features, which were currently screwed up into a look of fear and concern.

Abby felt relief unlike anything she had felt before. She almost melted to the floor.

'Abby, what's wrong? Why are you screaming?' In the same breath that the questions fell out of Marie's mouth, Marie looked around and seemed to realize that Abby was alone. And Abby was never alone. Abby felt Marie's grip on her shoulders tighten. 'Where's Sam? Is he inside? Did he get inside?'

The words were like an avalanche.

'He's outside!' Abby sobbed. 'He's outside and he's gonna get eaten! The bad guys are gonna eat him, you can't let them eat him, don't let it happen, don't let it, don't let it! He ran off into Shantytown! He ran off and he told me to find you! Please! You have to get Sam!'

Abby had gotten a little turned around as she'd been pushed back and forth in the throng of people. And when you're only four feet high, and can't see past most people's midsections, it's easy to be disoriented in a crowd. But she realized that she was standing in the middle of the Camp Ryder building, facing the back, when she heard the front doors slamming closed and the sound of people yelling.

'Bar the doors!' a voice shouted.

'Someone get me some water.' That one was her mother's voice.

'Strip her down,' the original voice ordered, and Abby realized it was Captain Harden.

Marie was standing on her tiptoes to see what was happening at the front of the building, but her face was still screwed up with the concern of what Abby had told her. She looked back down at the girl, very serious, trying to gauge how much of what Abby had said was true and how much of it was the hysteria of a young girl in a panic.

Finally, she grabbed Abby's hand and started pulling her through the crowd. 'Come with me,' she said. 'And come quick.'

Lee almost dropped Jenny as they hauled her into the main area of the Camp Ryder building. The metal steps up to the office were immediately to his right, and he could see people standing on them, peering down, trying to get a better look at what was going on.

Lee was heaving air. His legs and arms were burning.

He heard the heavy metal doors of the building slamming closed behind him and he looked, going down to one knee. Then he pointed at the two guards that were locking the doors. 'Bar the doors!'

No sooner had he said it than something slammed into the doors on the other side. A howl rose up, muffled by the concrete walls and thick doors. But the two guards took a hesitant step back as the doors rattled and shook. Then they dove forward and barred the doors with a two-by-four.

'Get me some water!' Angela shouted out.

Lee turned back to her and saw that she was hovering over Jenny, shouting out to the crowd. Jenny was on the ground and looked horrible. Her face had turned ashen, but it was dotted with sweat, despite the cold temperatures. Her eyes looked hollow and miserable. Lee had seen several others come down with this flu, but this was by far the worst he'd seen someone react to it.

Lee pointed to her and spoke loudly for Angela's benefit. 'Get her out of those clothes. She's burning up. She needs to be cooled down. Even if she fights you about it. She's gonna get brain damage if we don't lower her core temperature.'

Angela began fumbling with Jenny's zippers and buttons, but the other woman was not being cooperative. Lee was about to stoop to help when Marie emerged out of the crowd, towing Abby behind her. The look on Marie's face made Lee immediately stop and stare, waiting for the other shoe to drop.

'Lee! Angela!' Marie pulled Abby up next to her. The little girl was sobbing.

Lee reached out and touched Marie's shoulder, then Abby's. 'What? What's wrong?'

Angela did the same with her daughter. 'Baby, what's wrong? What's wrong? Where's Sam?'

Marie spoke for the hysterical girl. 'Abby says that he ran off into Shantytown. He didn't make it inside.'

'He ran off because of Caleb!' Abby sobbed. 'He went to help Caleb, because he wasn't coming inside.'

'That kid he got in a fight with?' Angela balked. Then her hand went to her head as she realized the full implications of the situation. 'Oh my God. Oh my God.'

Lee knelt, looking Abby square in the face. 'Abby, did you actually see Sam go into Shantytown? Are you sure he didn't make it inside?'

'I'm positive!' she yelled in his face. She tried to take breaths that were escaping her for a second, and then yelled again, this time tilting her face to the ceiling. 'He went out there to help Caleb and he told me to come inside and to find Marie so I could be safe. But he's out there! He's out there and he's gonna get eaten! You gotta help him! You gotta help him right now!'

Lee stood again and turned away, swearing.

Old Man Hughes was standing there, shaking his head. 'Cap, we can't open those doors.'

As if to reiterate, the thing outside the doors slammed them again and screeched. The people inside the Camp Ryder building jumped, everyone at the same time, and a gasp worked through the crowd.

Mac and Georgia pushed through the crowd and appeared to Old Man Hughes's left. Mac spoke for both of them. 'Don't open those doors! You can't open those doors again!'

Angela was suddenly beside Lee, fists clenched at her sides. 'What the fuck are you talking about?' she demanded. 'We've got kids out there, by themselves. And one of them is my kid.'

'Your adopted kid,' Georgia said bluntly.

Angela's eyes went wide and she took a step in Georgia's direction, raising her fists, but Lee put a hand out and pulled her back. Angela pointed in Georgia's face. 'You stupid bitch! You think that makes a fucking difference? All of you were about to have a fucking heart attack because one of your people got capped trying to steal some shit! And he was a grown man! Blood or not, those are our children out there, and we can't just leave them there! They're a part of our group. How do you not fucking understand this?'

'All right!' Lee shouted over the turmoil. 'Everyone shut the fuck up.' Mac opened his mouth to speak again, but Lee raised a finger and put it in his face, staring into his eyes, deadly serious. 'Shut up.'

Abby couldn't hold back her tears. 'Please. Please go get Sam!'

Lee turned to the girl and he saw her red, blurry eyes, the tears staining her cheeks, and the misery scribbled all over her young features. Angela had been right. Abby was losing little bits of herself. It had started at the beginning of all of this, and Lee had not made it any better when he'd gunned her father down in front of her. He hadn't known it at the time, but it didn't change the facts as they were.

And now she was looking at him. Asking him to save one of the only people she had left in the world beside her own mother. She was looking at him desperately, and whether she meant to or not, the look on her face made him cringe and want to look away. He had fought the feelings of guilt for some of the things that he had done, but this was one that bothered him, not because of what he had done, but more out of empathy for the girl who seemed secretly terrified of him, no matter what he did – good or bad.

'Please,' she moaned. 'You can get him. Please go get him. You're the only one that can do it.'

Lee gave her his full attention, sinking to his knees in front of the girl. 'Abby, you have to be quiet.' He held a finger to his lips, then he looked up at the crowd of people surrounding him, watching him. 'The more noise we make in here, the more the hunters are going to try to get in.'

'But . . .' Abby whispered. 'But what about Sam?'

Lee put a hand on Abby's head, gently, and for the first time, she didn't flinch away from him, or seem uncomfortable. Her desperation was beyond what feeling of reproach she had for this man who had killed her father.

'I'm gonna get Sam, okay? Don't you worry about that.'

'Captain,' Old Man Hughes said.

Lee stood, shrugging into his rifle strap again. 'Not a discussion, Hughes.'

'I'm going . . .' Angela started.

'No you're fucking not,' Lee said sharply. 'No one is going with me. The more people go, the more chance someone else is going to be left behind. For God's sake, just let me handle this. No more talking.' For the benefit of the crowd around him, he raised his voice just slightly. 'Everyone stay quiet. Get your weapons ready. Get on the doors.'

Then Lee bounded up the metal staircase and onto the catwalk that led to the roof access.

In the silence, in the dark, Sam crouched, facing the barely visible outline of Caleb. A kid he wanted to hurt with his bare hands, but couldn't bear the thought of him being ripped apart by the hunters. Someone he was willing to risk his life for, though he didn't know it before the instant that he did it.

The gunfire had stopped. It seemed oddly quiet in the camp.

There were rustling noises through the trees. The sound of gravel shifting, sometimes from this direction, sometimes from that. In the distance, shouts from the men on top of the Camp Ryder building, but again, no shots were being fired.

They're still here, Sam told himself. *Still inside the camp. Just prowling quietly through Shantytown. Looking for stragglers. Easy prey. An easy meal. Like me and Caleb here.*

Sam's voice was barely audible even to himself. 'Caleb. We need to go.'

Caleb just stared for a while. The sound of light footsteps in gravel to the right of their shanty drew his attention. He watched the right side of the shanty for a time. Perhaps an entire minute passed in silence. Sam was having a hard time keeping track of the time that was passing.

Finally Caleb shook his head, still staring at the opposite wall. 'I'm not going out there. Not until it's light out again.'

Sam felt his stomach drop. 'It's not gonna be light for hours!'

Slowly, Caleb pulled his legs up to his chest and hugged them there. The human body's method of trying to become a stone. Motionless. Senseless. Dead to the world. If I can't see you, you can't see me. If I play dead, maybe you'll go away.

Sam was beginning to feel panic again. The darkness and the closeness of the shanty had a calming effect. Like a good hiding place. But it was just an illusion. The walls were thin. They offered no protection. And now Sam's heart was beginning to slam in his chest again, and he could feel the adrenaline tingling in his fingers, muddling his thoughts, playing with his perceptions of things.

I need to get out of here. I can't stay in this shanty.
I want to go. I want to go now.

Lee pushed the hatch of the roof access open and stuck his head out. The night air on the roof was cold, and oddly still. The first thing he saw was Staley, Brinly, and their half dozen Marines, crouched against the roof abutments. The creaking hinges on the access hatch caused Brinly's head to snap around. He saw Lee and then motioned sharply.

Lee hauled himself up onto the roof and ran, low to the ground like he was taking enemy fire. He went to his knees beside Brinly, who was hovering over a Marine that appeared to be their designated marksman, or DM. The Marine was hunched over an AR-platform rifle, but the barrel was much longer, and it looked like it might be a larger-caliber rifle. It had a large, electronic-looking scope attached to it.

'What's happening?' Lee whispered. 'What'd you see?'

Brinly pointed outward. 'They hit that door right after you guys, but then they backed off after a minute or so. They all ran in separate directions. But they're still inside the camp.' Brinly gestured to his DM. 'We're watching them on thermal.'

'Good heat signatures,' the DM put it quietly, squinting one eye as he looked through his scope. 'Those fuckers burn hot. And they ain't got no clothes on.' He stiffened as he spoke. 'Okay. Got two more. Moving in the back of all those shacks. Over by the shipping containers.'

Something crashed through the woods, near the gates.

The DM snapped his rifle in that direction and scanned the darkness. 'Two ... three more signatures on that side. Moving parallel to the fence. Looks like they're circling around back.'

Lee reached out and grabbed Brinly's shoulder. 'I've got no time to argue. I'm going out the front door. I need your guns tracking with me. Shoot any of those fuckers that start chasing me.'

Brinly turned and met Lee's gaze, a little disbelieving. 'You goin' back out there?'

Lee nodded. 'Just keep them off my back. Please.'

Brinly nodded in return. 'Well, now's your chance.'

The DM intoned, 'Got three more. Other side of those shacks. Five total. Two on one side, three on the other. Looks like they're moving this direction again.'

Lee had already risen to leave, and he didn't let the words stop him. They only spurred him on. The hunters would be coming back. They had regrouped and were approaching the Camp Ryder building to figure out how to crack that nut and get to the meat inside. And if they had enough time, Lee thought that they would do it. But no matter what, he couldn't sit inside and look at Abby and tell her that he was just going to let Sam stay outside those doors. He had to go. And if he was going to go, then he needed to go *now*.

Sam couldn't take it any longer. In the stillness of the shanty, staring at Caleb and waiting for him to snap out of it, Sam could hear the faint rustlings out in the camp, drawing closer it seemed, closer and closer.

His blood felt like battery acid. He needed to move.

Sam lurched forward and seized hold of Caleb's arm, pulling him toward the door. 'Come on,' he whispered. 'Caleb, we need to get out of here.'

'No,' Caleb jerked back. 'It's safe in here.'

'It's not fucking safe in here, you idiot!' Sam kept pulling, and succeeded in dragging Caleb to his feet so that he stutter-stepped toward the door. 'It's safe in the building! You're gonna get us both killed if we stay here.'

'No . . .' Caleb's voice suddenly spiked into a shriek and he flailed backward. 'No! No! No! I'm not goin' out there!'

Sam stood frozen like a pillar of salt, staring wide-eyed at Caleb. 'Okay! Just shut the fuck up! Please . . .'

Caleb was backpedaling. 'Not gonna go! Not gonna go!' he kept shouting.

Sam was waving his free hand in a calming gesture, though it belied the sudden terror in his eyes. His other hand gripped his rifle hard, his palms going damp and sweaty. 'Caleb! Shut. UP!'

Caleb put his back against the shanty wall, sinking down into a squat and shaking his head. He was no longer the young man that Sam knew. The buck-toothed, freckle-faced fuck that Sam had given a straight jab right to the mouth, trying to knock that stupid front tooth out because the other kid talked too much. He had become something else. Childish and weak. Unable to comprehend or to cope with what was happening.

'Leave me alone, Sam!' Caleb was half-shouting, half-whimpering.

The cracks in the wall behind Caleb. The ambient light through them.

How they darkened so suddenly, blotted out.

Sam reached a hand out, though too much space lay between them. 'Caleb,' he whispered one more time, but it was not this time or any other time that the other kid would listen to. His eyes were locked shut to the darkness, to the violence, to the danger. His head was shaking back and forth, his hands up next to his face, like they were trying to shield off imaginary blows.

Mentally, Caleb seemed gone.

He could not hear Sam. He could not see what was happening.

The walls of the shanty stopped a good three or four inches from the gravel ground. The rest was hung in some places by tarpaulin, and in others by blankets – just some sort of barrier to keep the chill out. And this was where Caleb was crouched down, whimpering and yelping to himself.

Run, Sam told himself as he watched the darkness that framed Caleb, the shadow of something on the other side of that wall. *Run while you still have a chance* ...

'Caleb, they're behind you,' Sam said.

Caleb didn't open his eyes.

And then there was the sound of something bursting through plastic tarp, and this time Caleb's eyes went wide, as a hand seized his ankle from underneath the wall, clamping onto him like an iron shackle.

Caleb tried to stand up, tried to jump away, but he was suddenly sprawled on the floor, his caught right foot being pulled underneath the wall, and the creature on the other side grunting and barking and not letting go.

Both of Sam's hands were on his rifle now, bringing it up to his shoulder.

Caleb reached out to him. 'Sam!'

One leg under the wall.

Caleb struggled against it. His hands clawing for purchase in the gravel. Then it seemed he was ripped back and forth, his small, wiry body suddenly limp as he was thrashed like a rag doll. Caleb looked right into Sam's eyes as this happened, and the whole time his body was being yanked back and forth, his eyes remained locked with Sam's, and Sam watched them change from terror into agony.

Don't scream, Sam was thinking. *Please don't scream.*

The thing on the other side – or maybe it was another one entirely – reached under the wall again and seized hold of Caleb's other leg, pulling it under the wall so quickly that it seemed that parts of Caleb were simply disappearing.

'Sam, please!' Caleb cried out, and those were the last words he said. More of him was sucked under the wall, so that his hips were underneath it now, just his torso and his flailing, grasping hands still inside the shanty where he had thought he was so safe. He started to scream, wordless, panicky pain.

Sam wanted to run to help, but he was rooted where he stood. He didn't even pull the trigger on his rifle, because he knew it would do no good. It seemed like he held a flimsy stick in his hand now.

The thrashing of Caleb's limbs grew abruptly weak as shock blanketed him. More of him disappeared under the wall, just the chest and head and arms now, jerking around not of their own volition, but following the movements on the other side of the wall as the rest of him was ripped to shreds. Caleb's cries suddenly ran out, like a bellowing teakettle removed from the heat source. Now his breath just came out in ragged gasps.

Eyes still locked on Sam. Still holding on.

Sam realized he was backing up. He felt the tarpaulin door on his back, the cold air beyond shocking the sweat-dampened back of his neck.

He heard gunfire, but he couldn't look away.

Hands grabbed him.

He felt his knees go out.

'Help,' he managed, but it barely came out.

Bullets were ripping into the shanties all around him, Sam could see them like he was watching them in slow motion,

watching them splinter the scrap wood and punch holes
cleanly through the metal siding of people's small hovels.

The hands that had a hold of him were rough, and they
bore him up, and he felt his feet leaving the ground, and the
ground was moving quickly underneath him, and then the tarpaulin door of the shanty where Caleb had hid and died was
flapping back into place, and the rows of shanties were flying
by.

He heard the words, 'It's me, Sam, it's me.'

He watched the rows of shanties suddenly disappear as he
was carried forcefully out into the open, and it took what
seemed like long, unending moments for the words to per-
meate the layer of fear in his chest, and to actually embed
themselves in his consciousness and make sense.

He was being carried through the Square now. Open space
all around them.

From the shadows behind a row of shanties, dark shapes
loped around the corner, long and muscular and low to the
ground, pursuing like wolves.

'We're almost there,' the voice said, straining.

Sam managed to turn his head just enough to see the side
of a face, to see the jagged, ugly scar that ranged from the top
of his temple, all the way back through his hair, and he knew
that it was Captain Harden that had ahold of him, so he clung
to the man with his left hand, and he clung to his rifle with his
right, and he felt as weak and as devastated as he had the day
that his father had been murdered, and Captain Harden had
scooped him up and carried him to safety, just as he was doing
now.

*But I'm not that kid anymore. Four months ago, I was a
child.*

Now I'm a man. I should be fighting like one.

Captain Harden was strong, but he was carrying Sam's full weight on an injured body and a not-quite-healed ankle, and the hunters were fast, too fast for them to hope to get away.

'I can run!' Sam suddenly shouted, his legs kicking. 'Put me down!'

Captain Harden didn't hesitate, but instead almost slung Sam over his hips and onto the ground, as though to give him a head start. Sam's kicking legs hit the ground. He turned as he did, looking at the captain's eyes, hard as diamonds. They seemed fearless, though Sam knew that no man was without fear.

'Then run!' Captain Harden bellowed at him, and then turned to face their pursuers.

Lee planted his feet, squared his shoulders, and brought his rifle up. He could see the hunters in the darkness, could see them by their movement, and by the ambient light that shone off their pale, naked skin. They raced toward him, and around him, long limbs reaching for ground, eyes and gaping mouths like black holes in their faces. He could see the ones in front of him, and he knew that there were others moving to his right and left, too many for him to be able to take out. But he stood his ground and he hoped.

He fired, forcing accuracy out of himself. Not conscious thought, but just old habits, good habits, repeated and practiced time and time again. He watched their faces in the strobe of his muzzle flashes. He watched the bullets rip into them, but not stop them. They kept moving forward.

BOOM!

The rifle from Brinly's marksman sounded out and Lee watched one of the creatures spill backward like it had run its neck into a clothesline. Lee kept firing at his own target, five rounds, eight rounds, twelve rounds, center mass and tracking up into its chest cavity and finally splashing through its cranium and spilling the thing limply to the ground.

He turned, found another target, started shooting at it, knowing he would have to change his magazine in the next few rounds, knowing that there was zero room for error, and that even if he was perfect, even if he did everything right, his chances were slim.

He pulled his trigger, and he listened in the briefest respite between gun blasts, listened for the sound of those big metal doors opening up and letting Sam in, getting him to safety, because that was what had become important. But he could not hear the door opening. All he could hear was a strange, thrumming, buzzing noise that seemed like it was growing out of his chest.

This time the hunter fell at his feet, one gnarled hand clutching its chest wounds as blood spewed out of them, and the other still grasping for Lee's feet, forcing him to take a few steps back.

Did Sam already get inside? Did he get in?

New target. Shoot it. Shoot it. SHOOT IT!

The hollow, stunted feeling of the bolt locking back. No more rounds. Empty magazine.

Shapes around him. Darkness. Darker shadows.

BOOM, the DM taking another down, but still too many.

Listening for the sound of Sam, for the sound of the doors, but hearing only the buzzing, which was no longer a buzzing, but a roaring sound, something mechanical, and he could definitely feel it in his chest now, all the way down into his gut, into his feet. He could feel wind kicking, could see it stirring everything around him, flinging dust from the gravel up into his eyes, but all of this was peripheral.

His only thought was: *New mag . . . new mag . . . quick quick quick!*

Lee ripped the empty magazine out of his rifle. Slammed a new one in.

Pale arms reaching for him, impossibly close, making every nerve in his body scream. Lee sent his bolt forward and pulled the trigger the microsecond after he felt it slam home. Then twice more. Each time he watched his sight picture fall down back onto the creature's chest as the rounds split it open, three and then four holes in its chest, and then it was pitching backward.

All at once the thundering, mechanical noise became so obvious that Lee felt like an idiot for not knowing what it was, and at the same moment, the rotor wash beat him down and the sound of high-pitched turbines filled his ears. There was a roar and Lee looked up and got only the barest impression of something big and black going over the top of the Camp Ryder building, maybe a mere twenty feet above the roof, if that.

A yellow bloom erupted from the side of the hovering black shape, and in its explosive glow, Lee could see the relief of a UH-60 Black Hawk. Streaks of red tracers lanced out and Lee had time enough to fear that they were aimed at him, before he realized that the rounds were directed at the creatures that surrounded him.

Lee fell to a crouch, hands up over his head, knowing that those rounds were 7.62 mm projectiles, and they would smash his arms in two on their way through his body, but the reaction was instinctive as the bullets slapped the ground around him, so close that he could feel the impact through his boots. He squinted his eyes to protect them from the debris flying from the impacts, and he could feel the sting as chips of rock pelted his face, his bared teeth. But he didn't dare close his eyes. He couldn't bring himself to do it.

The big black bird was rolling in a slow circle, displaying its broadside to give the gunner a clear shot down at the targets. The gunner was unloading, not stopping, giving it everything he had. Lee could see the outline of someone behind that angry muzzle. They worked the M240 back and forth in raking sweeps. Then they would concentrate ten or fifteen rounds in one spot. Then go back to raking.

Lee was staring straight across at one of the hunters, just six feet from him. And all he could see was stark, animal eyes, and jaws that were open wide enough to latch on to his jugular . . .

Then the fire from the M240 concentrated again, and the thing was pummeled to bits and pieces.

Lee's heart felt like it was hammering in his chest to the same speedy rhythm of the rotors. Or maybe it was just the sensation of them beating the air, and the air beating his chest, and the gunfire chattering away. And then it ceased for a second. Lee's eyes had been dazzled by the strobe effect of the machine gun and he couldn't see the helicopter anymore. Then the machine gun lit up again, then paused, then lit up again, as the bird finished a slow sweep of the Camp Ryder compound.

'What the fuck?' someone shouted from the roof. Their voice was neither happy nor angry. Just bewildered.

Lee looked around him, saw nothing but devastation. The hunters were sprawled around him, some close enough to touch. A few were still alive, though their death throes were weakening even as Lee watched them. Others twitched, but in the way that Lee knew there was no real life left in them.

He put a hand to steady himself, felt the blessed gravel hit his palm, felt glad that he was alive to feel it, though shocked.

He looked behind him to the front door of the Camp Ryder building and he could see the light coming from inside, the doors hanging open. He could see Sam standing there, still holding his rifle, and Abby beside him, holding to him with the same tenacity.

They're alive. They're alive. That's all that matters.

Helicopter . . . who the fuck sent the helicopter?

Lee watched the bird do another quick pass of the grounds, looking like it was sweeping the area for any more targets, and then it drew up into a hover and started sinking down. Lee watched the dark shape becoming clearer and more defined as it lowered past the tree line, straight into the center of the Square.

'You wanna tell me who the hell this is?' Staley demanded, appearing next to Lee's side. He must have been at the door, waiting for Lee, when the bird showed up. His voice showed a rare strain of anger. Whoever had been manning the gun on that helicopter had just saved their lives – Lee's in particular. But they could just as easily have taken them out. And Staley clearly didn't like that.

Lee looked at the colonel, confused. 'It's not yours?'

'No, it's not fucking mine!'

Lee looked back out toward The Square. The Black Hawk was settling onto its wheels, the whine of the rotors changing in pitch. Men poured out. Lee raised his rifle but didn't call out to the men because he knew that he wouldn't be heard over the helicopter's massive engines.

The men moved swiftly and expertly. There were five or six of them. They all had rifles, but they weren't assaulting. They were clearing. Addressing the fallen infected to make sure they were dead. And two of the men were running straight for the Camp Ryder building. Lee could see that they both had rifles, but they were holding their hands up, waving in an obvious nonthreatening manner.

Lee lowered the muzzle of his rifle, feeling suddenly loose and limp with relief. One of the men grinned broadly at him and held a thumbs-up for him to see. Lee shook his head, managing to grin back. Then he returned the gesture.

'You sonofabitch,' was all Lee could think to say, and it came out breathy and tired. Tomlin met him just a few yards from the front doors of the Camp Ryder building as people began to push out and speak to each other in low, excited tones. Tomlin's grin was still there, though it had more of a worried look to it now. When he saw Lee he shook his head, his eyes going wide. 'Jesus, Lee . . . how's that for timing? Is anyone hurt?'

Lee grabbed Tomlin's hand, pulling him in for a slap on the back. 'I'd say that's good fucking timing. It was about to get real nasty, though.' Lee looked over Tomlin's shoulder. 'With all of that said . . . what the fuck is this?'

Tomlin turned and pointed to the man that had come out of the helicopter with him. He was of medium build, with a balding head and a manicured beard and eyes that were sharp to the point of being unpleasant. He wore nondescript clothing: a black parka, tan pants, and tan boots. The weapon strapped to his chest was a stubby MP5 that was almost lost in his parka.

The man stepped forward and smiled a smile that didn't reach his eyes. 'Master Sergeant Gilliard. Delta. You must be Captain Harden.'

'That's me,' Lee replied. 'You must be from Fort Bragg.'

'Yes, we are.'

Lee gestured to Staley. 'Colonel Staley with the Marines out of Camp Lejeune.'

The two men shook.

Master Sergeant Gilliard seemed amused. 'Shit. You got the joint chiefs inside?'

Lee shook his head. 'No, but we got a lot of civilians.'

Gilliard shrugged. 'What's the difference, right?'

Tomlin touched Lee on the shoulder. His face had grown serious. 'C'mon, Lee. We gotta talk.'

extras

www.orbitbooks.net

about the author

D. J. Molles is the bestselling author of The Remaining series. He published his first short story, 'Darkness', while still in high school. Soon after, he won a prize for his short story 'Survive'. *The Remaining* was originally self-published in 2012 and quickly became an internet bestseller. He lives in the southeast with his wife and children.

Find out more about D. J. Molles and other Orbit authors by registering for the free monthly newsletter at www.orbitbooks.net.

if you enjoyed

THE REMAINING: AFTERMATH

look out for

FORTUNE'S PAWN

by

Rachel Bach

CHAPTER 1

'You're quitting the Blackbirds?' The shock in Anthony's voice was at odds with the finger he was languidly sliding over my naked back. '*Why*? You just made squad leader last year.'

'That's why,' I said, swatting his finger away as I pulled on my shirt. 'Nowhere left to go. Squad leader's the last promotion before they stick you in a desk job.'

I stood up, grabbing my pants from the chair. Still naked, Anthony rolled over to watch me dress with growing displeasure. 'I don't get you, Devi,' he grumbled. 'The Blackbirds are the top private armored company on Paradox. It takes most mercs ten years in a lesser outfit before they can even apply. The fact they let you in straight out of the army should be the miracle of your career. Why the hell are you leaving?'

'Some of us have ambition, Anthony,' I said, sitting back down to put on my shoes. 'I had five good years with the Blackbirds, made a lot of money, got my name out there. But you don't get noticed if you sit around on your laurels, do you?'

'If you got any more noticed, I think they'd have you arrested,' Anthony said. 'They were talking about that stunt you pulled on Tizas in the office just yesterday. The duke of Maraday's apparently thinking of offering you a fat contract with his Home Guard.'

I rolled my eyes and combed my fingers through my hair, wrestling the dark brown mess into a ponytail as best I could. My hair never could take mornings. 'I am *not* joining the Home Guard. I don't care how good the money is. Can you imagine me sitting around on some noble's pleasure yacht playing bouncer for his cocktail parties? No thanks.'

'Home Guard *is* dull,' Anthony agreed, his boyish face suddenly serious. 'But it's safe.' He reached out, catching my hand as it dropped from my hair. 'I worry about you, Devi. You've done eight full fire tours in five years. I know you want to make a name for yourself, but that kind of work will kill you, and I'm not talking about taking a bullet. If you got a job with the Home Guard, you could take it easier. Hell, if the Maraday thing actually came through, the duke never leaves the capital. You could live here, with me. I'd even let you redecorate, and we could be together every night.'

I didn't like the way this conversation was going, but I knew better than to let that show on my face. Instead, I smiled and gently pried his fingers off mine. 'It's a sweet offer, Anthony, but I'm not looking to settle down. Here or anywhere else.'

Anthony heaved a huge sigh and collapsed on the bed. He lay there facedown for a moment, then rolled onto the floor and started pulling on his boxers. 'Can't blame me for trying.'

When he was dressed, we took the plush elevator down to the building café. I didn't regret turning down his offer, but I had to admit Anthony had a nice setup. His apartment was in one of the new sky towers that dominated Kingston's shoreline. Through the enormous windows, the royal capital lay spread out as far as I could see. Enormous skyscrapers rose like silver and glass trees from the dense underbrush of the older, smaller buildings. The sky was hazy with the usual smog and the clouds of commuter aircraft darting between the official sky lanes. The café was on one of the sky tower's middle floors, but we were still high enough to see the starport and the towering shadow of the Castle behind it from our booth.

I might just be sentimental, but seeing the Castle's shielded battlements and the shadows of the building-sized batteries of plasma guns behind it always filled me with pride. It wasn't the tallest building in the city anymore, but the Castle was still the largest, dwarfing even the deep-space trawlers that were waiting their turn to dock in the starport below. It was a good, strong fortress, feared by all on planet and off, and a worthy guard for the Sainted Kings of Paradox.

As always, I bowed my head before my king's sacred fortress. Anthony followed suit a second later. He'd never been as much of a believer in the power of the king as I was, but then, he hadn't taken as many bullets as I had.

Once we'd paid our respects, Anthony called the waiter over. He ordered large and well, and the spread of food that arrived at our table was a mini-heaven all in itself. Thanking my king again, I fell to with a mercenary's efficiency. Anthony watched me eat with amusement, drinking something red out of a tall, frosted glass that looked like a cocktail. I really hoped it wasn't. Even I didn't drink this early in the morning.

'So,' he said, spinning his now nearly empty glass between his fingers. 'Why are you really here, Devi?'

'Last night wasn't enough?' I said, popping a tiny coffee cake into my mouth.

'Last night was marvelous,' Anthony admitted. 'But since we've established you aren't exactly pining for my company, I thought we might as well get to the point before you crush my ego again.'

He was still smarting from the rejection, so I let the

comment slide. I'd known Anthony a long time; we'd been in the army together before he got his captaincy and his cushy desk job with the Home Guard. We had good chemistry, and he was always the first person I called when I came home. We'd been friends with benefits for nearly seven years now, and I'd thought we had a good understanding. Obviously, things had changed. Still, this was Anthony. An apology would only make him feel worse, so I honored his request and got to the point. 'I need you to tell me the qualifiers to become a Devastator.'

I had his full attention now.

'Are you out of your goddamn mind?' he cried. '*That's* why you quit your job?' He flopped back against the booth's deep cushions. 'Devi, you can't be serious. The Devastators are the king's own armored unit. They're *above* the best.'

'Why do you think I want to be one?' I said. 'I'm sick of wasting my time on the edge of civilized space crashing pirate camps for corporate money. Devastators serve the Sacred King directly. They get the best armor, the best guns, they go on the most dangerous and important missions. They have power you can't buy; even the nobility listens to them. I was the best in the Blackbirds—'

'This isn't like the Blackbirds,' Anthony snapped. 'I can't even tell you the qualifiers, because there are none. You can't apply to become a Devastator. They ask *you*, not the other way around, and they don't ask anyone who hasn't spent a minimum of twenty years in active field service.'

'Twenty *years*?' I cried. 'That's ridiculous!'

'They want experience—' Anthony started.

'What do you think I spent the last nine years getting?' My shouting was attracting weird looks from the other diners, but I didn't care. 'I got twelve commendations in four years when

I was in the army. You know, you were there. *And* I've gotten five promotions in five years in the Blackbirds. I'm not exactly fresh meat.'

'Devi, you're not even thirty.' Anthony's voice was calm and reasonable, the sort of voice you'd use with a child who was throwing a tantrum. It made me want to punch him. 'You've already proven that you're exactly the sort of suicidally brave, workaholic lifetime soldier the Devastators look for. They'll come calling, I'd bet money on it, but not yet. Not until you've got at least ten more years on your record.'

'In ten more years, I'll be dead.' I said it plainly because it was a goddamn fact. The average life span of an armored mercenary was just shy of twenty-five. I was two years past that. After thirty, survival rates fell to almost nothing. Shooting for cash was a game for the young. You either got a desk job, applied to the Home Guard, or went back to your parents in a body bag. A desk wouldn't impress the Devastators any more than it impressed me, but I couldn't do crash jobs and pirate clearing forever.

'I'm good enough to serve the king right now,' I said, lowering my voice. 'I've seen Devastators in their thirties, so I know they make exceptions to the experience requirement. I want to know what and how, and I'm not letting you out of here until you tell me.' And just in case he didn't believe me, I kicked out my leg and slammed my boot onto the booth beside him, blocking him in.

Anthony glanced at my foot with a deep sigh. 'You're impossible. You know that, right?'

I didn't answer, just leaned back, crossed my arms, and waited for him to cave.

It didn't take long. Less than a minute later, Anthony shook his head and pulled out his ledger. 'It just so happens you picked a good time to have your crazy idea,' he said, tapping the screen with his thumb. 'Here.'

I took the ledger he offered, squinting to read the glowing screen in the bright sunlight. It took me a few moments to recognize the short paragraph for what it was, a job listing from the general employment boards. A tiny one, too, barely three sentences long, but what I saw was enough to make me think Anthony was seriously trying to jerk me around.

'This is for a security position on a trade freighter.'

'Not just any trade freighter,' Anthony said, smiling for the first time since we'd gotten out of bed. 'That's Brian Caldswell's ship.'

'I don't care whose ship it is,' I said. 'I am *not* doing guard work.' Guard work was just above deep-space mine clearing for crap armor jobs. No Blackbird would be caught dead on a freighter, even an ex-Blackbird like me.

'I wouldn't have shown it to you if it wasn't something you'd be interested in,' Anthony said. 'Have a little faith, darling.'

When I finally relaxed my scowl, Anthony went on. 'Caldswell's a bit of a legend in trading circles. They say his ship is cursed. He gets into more trouble on one route than an entire fleet could find in ten years, and he goes through security teams like tissue paper. That's where you come in.' He leaned closer. 'Don't spread this around, but the Royal Army considers one year with Caldswell to be worth five anywhere else. If you can survive a full tour on that ship, I'm pretty sure even the Devastators would sit up and take notice.'

I glanced down at the ad again. It looked perfectly normal, the sort of short-notice grunt job that kept army dropouts in beer money, nothing like the deadly golden ticket Anthony was painting it to be. 'You're not putting me on, are you?'

'I wish I was,' Anthony said. 'Maybe you missed the part about how quickly Caldswell uses up his people? I like you as you are, all in one piece.'

It was mean to laugh at his concern, but I couldn't help it. 'And maybe you've forgotten who you're talking to.'

'I haven't forgotten,' Anthony said, his voice deadly serious. 'I've seen you fight, remember? That's not something you forget. But this is the fast and dangerous route, Devi. I know you're ambitious enough for any five normal mercs, but there's nothing wrong with a life of being safe, prosperous, and happy.'

'I am happy,' I said, pulling out a pen and writing the dock number from the ad on the back of my hand. 'And the faster I get to be a Devastator, the happier I'll be.' I handed his ledger back. 'You'll tell them, right?' The Devastators did whatever the king told them to, but they were technically part of the Home Guard. Anthony worked for them sometimes, which was why we were having this conversation.

'If Caldswell takes you, yes,' he said. 'Don't know if they'll listen, they mostly don't, but I'll be sure to tell everyone what a reckless glory hog you are.'

I grinned and dropped the leg that had been fencing him in. 'You're a prince as always, Anthony,' I said, sliding out of the booth. 'Thanks for the breakfast, and the job tip.'

'I'll put them on your tab,' he said. 'You can settle up next time you're in town.'

I kissed him on the cheek one last time and walked away. The last thing I heard before I squeezed into the crowded elevator was Anthony calling the waiter for another drink. I worried about that as the elevator whipped me down, but twenty seconds and seventy floors later, I had more immediate concerns.

The crowd on the street level was brutal, and I had to throw my weight around to break through the rush to the cab stand, something I enjoyed more than I should have. I'm five six on a good day, and between that, my bird bones, poofy brown hair, and the fact my face looks closer to thirteen than thirty, normal people tend to underestimate me. It used to piss me off to no end, but that was before I cultivated an appreciation for watching the patronizing look fall off a businessman's face when the little girl he was trying to push aside elbows him in the stomach hard enough to knock his wind out.

After a few minutes of unnecessary roughness, I'd made my way to the front of the taxi line and flagged down a ground cab. Air would have been quicker, but I wasn't in enough of a hurry to justify the cost. Fortunately, my cabbie was a stereotypical Kingston driver, utterly insane. Despite it being rush hour on a workday morning, we made it to the starport in less than twenty minutes.

He offered to take me into the departures plaza, but one look at the traffic and I told him to drop me on the street. I tipped him well for not getting us both killed and ran up the pedestrian ramp, ducking through the enormous mirrored doors with the rest of the morning crowd before taking a sharp left toward the lockers where I'd bunked my gear when Anthony had picked me up late last night.

I found my locker and opened it with a thumbscan, pulling out my duffel. My handset was on top, right where I'd left it. I flipped it open, working fast. I trusted Anthony, but only an idiot applies for a job without doing her research first. A quick search for Brian Caldswell turned up surprisingly little, but Anthony hadn't been kidding about the prestige of serving on his ship. After five minutes of searching, I'd found no fewer than seven of his former security grunts who were now enjoying fantastic positions, including one who'd gone on to be a Devastator.

But my digging also showed that Anthony hadn't been exaggerating how dangerous Caldswell's ship was, either. The number of crew deaths and disappearances he had on file with the Trans-Galactic Trade Union was staggering for any vessel, but it was especially bad when you considered that Caldswell captained a ten-man freighter on a fairly safe route through the major systems. From his numbers, you'd have thought he was helming a battleship on a bloody front. All of this should have made me think twice, but I'd made my career by beating impossible odds. As soon as I'd verified Anthony's tip to my satisfaction, I got to work hauling my armor case out of the locker.

In addition to my fast elbow, I'm a lot stronger than most people think, a product of spending all day in armor with my resistance turned way up. Some mercs let their suit do all the work. Why bother with flesh-and-blood muscles if you're in powered armor all the time? But I don't like being weak in any way if I can help it, and real muscles come in handy when the most precious thing in your life folds up into a hundred sixty-pound case and all you can get is a top locker.

Bracing my knees, I heaved my armor case down and set it on its wheels. When it was balanced, I slung my duffel over my shoulder and started walking toward the dock number I'd written on my hand.

Considering its black reputation, I expected Caldswell's ship to look sinister, but the freighter sitting at dock C23503 was disappointingly shabby. Its belly sat directly on the ground, while its hull rose in an old-fashioned, ungraceful beige block six stories into the air. The whole ship was spotty with patches, but thanks to a fresh paint job I couldn't tell if the repairs were from cannon fire or just the usual wear and tear you saw on older vessels.

Old or not, though, Caldswell's ship was still an impressive hundred and fifty feet long from nose to thrusters, with the vast majority of that in its cargo hold. The ship's nose was boxy as the rest of it, a squat thrust of metal with its windows covered by steel shutters coated in high-burn plastic against the heat of entering the atmosphere. The tail of the ship was all engine, a pair of long-haulers and a hyperdrive coil that looked pretty new.

That gave me hope. Hyperdrive coils weren't cheap. If this Caldswell could afford a new model, he could certainly afford a top line Paradoxian armored mercenary with an exceptional record.

Like all the noncommuter ships, Caldswell's was docked in the overflow landing. But, despite being in a good spot relatively close to the main port, no other ships were docked around him. That didn't surprise me. Spacers were a superstitious bunch. Docks would have to be pretty scarce for a captain to risk leaving his ship where Caldswell's curse could reach it.

I believed the Sacred King could do miracles just like any good Paradoxian, but I didn't believe in curses. Neither did a lot of people, apparently, or maybe most mercs just didn't bother to do their research, because as I rounded the nose of the ship, I saw that the ramp in was packed with people hauling armor cases not so different from my own.

Never one to let a little competition scare me off, I walked right up and got in line. There were fifteen people ahead of me, but the crowd was dwarfed by the enormous and strangely empty cargo bay. Other than a few dusty crates lashed down in the back, the only thing inside was a suit of armor.

Unlike my armor, which could be broken down to fit in a case, this was a serious heavy combat suit, Count class, the kind the army used to rip up Terran tanks. Even powered down, it was seven feet tall and obviously someone's baby, judging from how nicely the bright yellow paint job sparkled. I scowled. Armor like that belonged to a serious professional who'd spent a lot of time in the armored corps. Clearly, some-one had already gotten a job today. The ad hadn't said how many openings were available, but the ship wasn't that big. It couldn't take more than two security guards to cover it all, and if one of those spots was already taken, then this wasn't the sure thing I'd been counting on.

I eyed the line with new rancor. None of them looked like serious competition, but then, standing around in the tight pants and flowy shirt I'd worn to meet Anthony with my hair tangled in a post-sex ponytail, I probably didn't either. Nothing for it but to wait and see. I used the time to fix my appearance, brushing and braiding my hair as discreetly as I could. The line moved quickly, and by the time I was decent, I was next.

There was a stair leading up from the cargo bay to the rest of the ship where the interviews were being held. People had been going up and coming down again with only a few min-utes between the whole time I'd been waiting. Some looked dejected, but most looked relieved, and I bet they were the ones who hadn't actually wanted a job on a ship that had a reputation for being a flying coffin, no matter how scarce armor work had gotten now that the king had wrapped up all our wars.

The man ahead of me was certainly one of these. He was

almost grinning as he walked back down the steps and stabbed his thumb over his shoulder, letting me know it was my turn. Grabbing my bag and lifting my armor case so it wouldn't bang, I started up the stairs to tempt my fate.

The interviews were being held in what looked like a combination lounge and ship's mess. There was a tiny galley kitchen with a bar, a table for meals, and a small sitting area, all empty. My interviewer sat at a folding table with a small desk fan pointed at his face. He was older, maybe early fifties, and wearing an old-fashioned white button-up shirt and brown flight vest. His short, red-brown hair was frosted with silver, but his stocky body was still fit and solid when he stood to shake my hand and wave me to the chair.

'Name?'

I flinched. He was speaking Universal. I spoke it, of course. Everyone did. It was the standard language of civilized space. But the Blackbirds were solid Paradoxian, and we spoke our own King's Tongue exclusively in everything we did. I'd been all over the universe, but because I'd always been with my unit, I hadn't spoken Universal other than to ask where the bathroom was for almost three years.

Looking back, I don't know why I was surprised. Traders, even Paradoxians, always spoke Universal. It was, after all, the language of trade. But the man at the desk didn't look Paradoxian, he looked Terran, and that could be a problem. After so long not speaking Universal, my accent was pretty thick, which put most Terrans off. Usually, I wouldn't care. Paradoxians don't like Terrans any more than they like us. We might both be from Old Earth, but a century of border wars carries a lot more weight than a shared ancestry from some dead rock a thousand years ago. Still, if the Terran was the one with the job, then that was all water under the bridge so far as

I was concerned. I'd just have to trust that he was willing to overlook a few dropped consonants in return for a stellar record.

The man glared at me, still waiting for his answer, and I snapped into business mode. 'Deviana Morris,' I said, pronouncing each syllable as crisply as I could. 'I go by Devi.'

I set my handset on the table and tapped the button for the projected screen. It flickered to life, throwing my record, commendations, and references into the air right in front of his face. The man flicked through my history with a finger, his expression neutral, though I saw his lip quirk when he got to my last tour with the Blackbirds. A glorious time, even for a glory hog like me.

'That's quite an impressive record, Miss Morris,' he said at last. He spoke the words grudgingly, like he didn't like being impressed. 'It's my understanding that most Paradoxian mercenaries spend their careers trying to get into the Blackbirds. Why did you leave?'

'I'd reached the top of the active duty promotions, sir.'

The man smiled. 'Your ambitions don't run to desk jobs, I take it?'

I smiled back. 'No sir.'

'Fair enough,' the man said, glancing at my armor case. 'What equipment are you bringing?'

My smile turned into a full-on grin. This was my favorite part of any interview. I reached down and turned my case so he could see the insignia on the front. 'Custom Verdemont master craft knight's armor.'

My opinion of the man rose significantly when his eyes widened in an appropriate expression of shock. 'And this is your suit?' he said. 'Not leased from the Blackbirds?'

'No sir,' I said proudly. 'I own all my own gear.' It had

taken me two years' wages plus some pretty extreme hazard pay to buy my armor, and it was worth every cent. 'I also have my own guns and ammunition as well, and an automated repair case for my suit.'

'We'll supply your ammo,' the man said, leaning back in his rickety folding chair. 'This is a security position. Your job will be to work with your fellow security officer to protect this ship, its crew, and its cargo at all times. We usually run a wide circuit spanning Paradoxian space, the Terran Republic, and the Aeon Sevalis, but that can change without notice. The contract is for one galactic standard year with fifteen hundred Republic Script paid monthly. Shifts are twelve hours during flight with overtime for planetary landings and time off when we're in hyperspace, plus one day paid shore leave per month. So long as you are an employee of this ship, we'll provide food, lodging, and ammunition, as I said earlier, plus a stipend for maintenance and repair of your equipment.'

I considered this for a moment. It was a pretty standard contract, but the pay, while high for ship guards, was pretty low compared to what I'd earned in the Blackbirds. I might not be doing this for the money, but a merc had to protect her worth. 'Is there hazard pay?'

'Thousand RS for every incident,' the man said.

I bit back a smug smile. That was where the money was hiding. Considering this ship's reputation for trouble, that hazard bonus might well end up making me more than I'd earned as a squad leader.

'Sounds good to me, sir,' I said, reaching for my armor case. This next bit would be pure fun. I loved showing off my armor. 'What would you like me to do for my demonstration? I can do any accuracy challenge you can think of, maneuvers, a strength test, whatever you want.'

'I don't think we'll need any of that,' the man said, turning off my handset and handing it back. 'You've got the job.'

I blinked. 'That's it?' I blurted before I could stop myself.

The man shrugged. 'Unless another decorated ex-Blackbird with her own suit of custom, high-end armor is waiting in my cargo bay, then yes. That's it.' He held out his hand. 'I'm Brian Caldswell, welcome to the *Glorious Fool*.'

I took his hand, head spinning. That was the fastest interview I'd ever had. 'Fool?'

'The *Glorious Fool*,' Caldswell repeated, smiling like this was an old joke. 'My ship.'

Weird name for a ship, but I didn't give it much thought. I was too busy absorbing the fact that the short, stocky man in front of me was the cursed captain, Brian Caldswell. The man who went through security like tissue paper, and I was now in his hands.

'Thank you, sir,' I said before I found some way to ruin things.

The captain nodded. 'We'll get you a bunk when we're ready to go. In the meanwhile, you can store your stuff behind the bar. No one will touch it.'

No one but me could touch my armor without getting ten thousand volts, but I kept my mouth shut about that and stowed my bags as directed. Honestly, I was still reeling. My brain couldn't quite get around the idea that after years of fighting like a dog for every step up the ladder, I'd gotten what could well be the make or break job of my career with an interview that had taken less than five minutes.

While I was putting my things up, the captain walked over to the cargo bay door and shoved his head out. 'Position's filled!' he yelled, and then he shut the door.

I thought that was a bit harsh, but the captain seemed to

have forgotten the other applicants entirely the moment he turned away. 'I have to go take care of some business,' he said, walking past me toward the hall on the opposite side of the lounge. 'Basil will get you settled. He's my second, and you'll obey him as you would me.'